"The Camp Grant Massacre has been written about from many points of view, yet Venetia Hobson Lewis brings a different perspective to the forefront by featuring women from diverse backgrounds and how they may have experienced this historic event. Her expertise of the massacre and her knowledge of Arizona history explode across the pages of this spellbinding novel."

—Jan Cleere, author of *Military Wives in Arizona Territory: A History of Women Who Shaped the Frontier*

"A bright new voice in Southwest fiction, spinning compelling tales of the women who peopled the Old West."

—J. A. Jance, author of *Nothing to Lose: A J.P. Beaumont Novel*

"In riveting scenes narrated by a culturally diverse suite of unforgettable characters (Aravaipa Apache, Mexicano, and Anglo), Venetia Hobson Lewis transports me back to Tucson, Arizona Territory, where simmering tensions between frontier parties build inexorably to the Camp Grant Massacre of 1871. Just as that event forever alters the lives of the Apache survivors and the morally conflicted perpetrators and their family members, the story of Changing Woman continues to resonate. A must-read."

—Susan Cummins Miller, author of *A Sweet, Separate Intimacy: Women Writers of the American Frontier, 1800–1922*

"Imagine if Jane Austen had lived in Tucson, Arizona Territory, throughout the year of 1871. She would have journaled about the tumultuous clash of cultures she witnessed between the Anglos, Aravaipa Apaches, and Mexicanos until its tragic culmination, the Camp Grant Massacre. *Changing Woman* is a historical novel of great anthropological value akin to Austen's impeccably recorded manners, told largely from the perspectives of women intimately and peripherally affected by the death and capture of nearly two hundred Apache women and children. The remarkable achievement of this novel is Venetia Hobson Lewis's skillful handling of these disparate and desperate female voices and how they merge into a united spiritual appeal for mutual empathy and respect. These voices went ignored in the nineteenth century, and it would be our own spiritual loss to ignore them now."

—Sidney Thompson, author of *Follow the Angels, Follow the Doves*

CHANGING WOMAN

*A Novel of the
Camp Grant Massacre*

VENETIA HOBSON LEWIS

UNIVERSITY OF NEBRASKA PRESS   *LINCOLN*

The University of Nebraska Press is part of a land-grant institution with campuses and programs on the past, present, and future homelands of the Pawnee, Ponca, Otoe-Missouria, Omaha, Dakota, Lakota, Kaw, Cheyenne, and Arapaho Peoples, as well as those of the relocated Ho-Chunk, Sac and Fox, and Iowa Peoples.

Library of Congress Cataloging-in-Publication Data
Names: Lewis, Venetia Hobson, author.
Title: Changing woman: a novel of the Camp Grant Massacre / Venetia Hobson Lewis.
Description: Lincoln: University of Nebraska Press, [2023] | Includes bibliographical references.
Identifiers: LCCN 2022044597
ISBN 9781496235138 (paperback)
ISBN 9781496236449 (epub)
ISBN 9781496236456 (pdf)
Subjects: LCSH: Camp Grant Massacre, Ariz., 1871—Fiction. | Western Apache Indians—Fiction. | San Pedro River Valley (Mexico and Ariz.)—Fiction. | BISAC: FICTION / Historical / Civil War Era | FICTION / Westerns
Classification: LCC PS3612.E9875 C47 2023 | DDC 813.6—dc23/eng/20221012
LC record available at https://lccn.loc.gov/2022044597

Map courtesy of Sharon K. Miller, Buckskin Books.

Set and designed in New Baskerville ITC Pro by Mikala R. Kolander.

For those who perished . . .

CHANGING WOMAN

Winkelman

177

Santa Teresa
Mountains

Camp Grant

Arivaipa
Canyon

Charles McKinney
Ranch

Apache
Ranchería

Arivaipa Creek

Camp Grant Wash

Hammon

Sierra Calitro
(Galiuro Mountains)

79

Oracle

Main Road to Camp Grant

San Pedro River

La Iglesia/Santa
Catarinas
(Santa Catalina
Mountains)

Cebadilla Pass
(Redington Pass)

77

Rillito River

Tucson

Santa Cruz River

Pantano Wash

Rincon
Mountains

N

San Xavier
del Bac

Map Not to Scale

THURSDAY, JANUARY 5, 1871

"Injuns! Injuns! Injuns!"

Valeria Obregón bolted upright on the bench seat. *¿Qué fue eso? What was that?* Now fully alert, the tedium and ennui into which she had fallen during her three-hundred-twenty-mile stagecoach journey vanished. But apparently the constant threat of Indian raids and certain death she and her husband, Raúl, had endured along the way from their hometown of El Paso to Tucson remained. Crushed between Raúl and a meaty prospector, Valeria had, for three days, politely tolerated the men's jostled elbows nudging and jabbing into her sides, along with the discomfort of her corset constantly poking her ribs and her slight pregnant swelling. Every jolt of the stagecoach over vast stretches of flat, desolate desert had been bone jarring.

Rat-a-tat-tat. Rat-a-tat-tat. Boom. Boom.

At the commotion in the street, all seven people inside the cramped coach pushed toward the window, the others blocking Valeria's clear view. She peeked under someone's arm and over another's belly.

A boy of about fourteen or fifteen, wearing a battered Union Army hat and beating on a big drum strapped over his shoulder, marched through the dusty town of Tucson alongside a man carrying a large banner painted with bold lettering and a cartoon of flaming rifles and arrows. The man shouted the sign's message, "Big meeting at the courthouse—come, everybody. Time for action has arrived!"

Valeria saw the troubled interest on the faces of Tucsonans hurrying out of saloons, opium dens, and blacksmiths' workshops to gather on the streets.

"Where?"

"When?"

"Anyone killed?"

She grasped Raúl, whose dark brown eyes mirrored the same concern she must have in hers. *Have we arrived at our destination only to find more immediate danger here?*

"Come tonight! Meeting at the courthouse." Time after time, the boy and man repeated their drumbeat and announcement as they marched down the street and turned onto another.

"Injuns. What else?" the prospector grumbled.

What kind of town have we come to? I wouldn't even call it a town. It's a village of squat adobe buildings, most of them saloons. Through the window, Valeria saw a large pack of gaunt dogs overtake the narrow street, scavenging for something, anything, to eat, like the dead horse left out to rot, around which the coach navigated. *This surely can't be the largest and most important city in Arizona. Home? ¿Mi casa?*

Her shoulders scrunched up to her ears, her wealth of brown hair slipping from its pins, and her porkpie hat riding lower and lower over the side of her face, Valeria sighed as she sat back on the bench. *Is this coach ever going to stop? I have never been so miserable.*

As they neared a large stable, the strong stench of horse manure rose.

Unexpectedly the stage hit a bump. The meaty prospector fell against Valeria, and her hat tumbled to the floor. With apologies, the prospector grabbed it and handed it to her.

Broken. The small straw brim of her only hat was cracked beyond repair. Poking a broken twig into the brim's battered weave, Valeria tried not to care. *But I do care. I love how the black netting ties around the hatband. How its brim angles down my forehead from high atop my hair. I love everything about it.*

Catching Raúl's discerning eye, she gaily laughed instead of showing disappointment and tossed the hat out the window. "Let the horses eat it."

Valeria and the other passengers rocked from side to side as the stagecoach pulled to a halt in front of the Overland Stage Station on Calle de la Alegría, or Congress Street as one traveler called it. Her knees and elbows knocked by everyone in the coach edging forward on the bench seats, Valeria folded them tightly to herself when, finally, the shotgun flung open the coach door and said, "Time to git." Valeria sighed gratefully.

First out, Raúl stepped down quickly on the coach's tiny metal steps. He eagerly looked about at the flat-roofed buildings.

Valeria stooped in the door opening, concerned she would be hit by one of the three men clambering down from the top of the stagecoach. They had spent their cross-country ride hanging onto the small rail and sitting atop luggage that was now being thrown to the ground. Prodded from behind by passengers wanting to get the hell out of the coach as much as she did, Valeria said, "Raúl." A small, beseeching call for help.

He reached inside for her hand, but her voluminous skirt hid the small step from view. Missing it, Valeria fell with a startled "¡oh!" into Raúl's arms.

"¿Estás bien?"

"Uh . . . sí." Her face flamed at her misstep.

They cleared the doorway for the other weary passengers, several of whom paused to say goodbye to the winsome little lady who'd cheered them with humorous comments along the way.

"We made it without a scare." Valeria swayed and swished the hem of her skirt in a small celebratory dance that brought a chuckle to some fellow passengers. Stepping aside while Raúl collected their valises, Valeria swallowed several times, her stomach upset now from all the swaying and jolting of the coach. She placed her hand protectively over her expanding waist and looked from building to building, each one more shabby and filthy than the other.

Raúl promised somewhere better than El Paso. He has aspirations. Money, lots of money for our baby, will line the streets, he'd said. No, not these streets.

"Mira." Raúl pointed at a large building one block north.

"Is that the store?"

"Yes, that is where I'll work. Zeckendorf's."

Valeria smiled wearily at her husband, whose uncontained and unbounded enthusiasm had remained the same since they were small children in El Paso. *He will want to go to the store immediately.* Hearing the jangle of unbuckling chains, straps, and reins, Valeria glanced at the horses being unhitched and led to the stables for a rest. She longed for a soft mattress and a nap herself.

Valeria wrapped her serape tighter about her, the chill in the air an abrupt change from the closeness of the coach. Summoning what energy remained in her nearly empty well, she said, "That is a substantial establishment. You should get there early tomorrow, for you will be busy. Ahora, could we find the rooms? ¿Por favor?"

Raúl's eyes dulled with disappointment. Regretting she was the cause of his sullenness, Valeria joined Raúl already walking south on Calle Real. When they passed a large, impressive house at the corner of McCormick Street, Valeria's hopes rose until they crossed three more narrow dirt lanes, along which they saw only ramshackle houses. *These casas are thrown together with wire, bent sticks, and mud.*

While Raúl spoke with the landlord about the rooms they'd reserved, she waited before the long, low adobe building on their corner. A woman swept dirt and food scraps onto the street. A rough-looking Mexicano in torn and stained clothing swaggered from the adobe's zaguan, a small covered passageway leading to the common courtyard, privy, and horse stalls.

That man looks as rough as the hombres around Raúl's brother. These neighbors didn't find money in the streets. Shop owners don't live here. Perhaps they live in the opposite direction.

Valeria turned at the sound of Raúl's voice. He waved for her to join him before the third of six entrance doors opening directly onto the street. Standing before the splintering door painted a weather-beaten turquoise, Valeria chuckled despite everything. *A new home. It is exciting. Raúl's dream of a new life here for our baby begins.* The door opened easily.

How small it is, our new home.

Valeria took in the entirety of her casa: a long, rectangular space divided by a door into two rooms with hard-packed dirt floors. *It is not what I hoped for. Why do I always hope for too much?* She entered and slowly circled the cramped main area. *The walls! Splattered grease from the grill. At least smoke escapes through the window. And the wobbly chairs . . . they're as bad as at home. Accept it.*

Raúl stood in the bedroom doorway, having thrown their valises at the foot of the bed. "Está bueno. ¿Te gusta?"

Is the casa "good" like Raúl believes? Can I come to like it? Valeria eyed the iron bedstead and moved past Raúl into the compact bedroom. *A narrow bed. Boards can bolster the sagging mattress, but the chipped washstand bowl I can't fix.* Valeria turned toward Raúl and with conviction said, "This will do."

Then . . . the room turned dark.

Her vision of Raúl faded. Clammy sweat beaded Valeria's forehead. Queasy, her stomach in upheaval, she leaned on the washstand. *Something is not right.* Severe stomach cramps jolted her. Pains stabbed her lower groin repeatedly with such a punch that Valeria staggered backward and grabbed the iron railing of the headboard for support. *What is happening?*

A voiding sensation swept through her. The intense pain now gone, she instead felt sticky and damp. In discomfort, she raised one foot, and then the other. Wanting to pull her undergarments away from her body, she lifted her skirt and looked down at her drawers, open between her legs. They were red. Streams of red flowed down her legs. "¡Raúl! ¡Raúl!"

Blood, tissue, and fluid streamed from her, forming a puddle beneath her feet. Running along the dirt floor to the wall, the blood was dark and clotted.

Woman's blood.

On the floor, pitifully recognizable, was a tiny mass. An insignificant, gory clot. Their baby.

Without releasing her grip on the bed railing, she slid to the floor. "¡No! ¡No! Mi bebé."

Trembling, she stretched out her hand to touch what was to have been their child.

Raúl grabbed her hand, circled it around his neck, swept her up in his arms, and placed her on the mattress. He climbed in beside his wife, and they clung to each other.

"¿Por qué? Why?" she wailed. "Why?"

"I'll find a doctor."

"Cuesta mucho." *Doctors cost too much.*

"Valeria, I . . ."

"Una partera. A midwife'll know . . ."

"Don't leave the bed."

While Raúl was gone, Valeria's sobs ebbed into exhaustion. She stared at the ceiling—rows of ocotillo latijas wedged between pine vigas. *We saw thousands of ocotillos along the way. Sticks; long, bare arms in winter. The Sonoran Desert invades even our bedroom. Why? Why did we come? Raúl thinks Zeckendorf's means more money for the baby. The baby who is no more. Can we go back home to El Paso now? Even if we're near Mateo again? We have no family, no friends in Tucson. No help. No one even cares.*

The sight of a Mexican midwife rushing through the doorway brought little comfort, only certainty. Quick, sure, commanding, la partera was all Valeria expected.

Raúl waited in the main room only minutes before la partera returned to his side. "Su esposa está bien. Puede tener muchos bebés en el futuro. Pero, por ahora, sea atento, Señor, y espere."

Relieved with the good news that Valeria was fine and could have many babies in the future, Raúl pressed a few dollars in the woman's hand and closed the street door. Hesitating at the side of the bed, he vowed to himself to be extremely attentive to Valeria's needs, as la partera had requested of him.

Valeria turned to her husband. Raúl's stricken face and trembling lips shattered her. She threw open her arms and he collapsed on the mattress. She felt the weight of his head on her breast. "Cariño." Tightly wrapped together, not letting go, they wept.

He sputtered, "We'll have babies. Many babies. We just need to wait until you feel better."

"¿Me prometes?" Her voice wavered as her chin trembled.

"I promise."

She ran her finger over his strong, imperfect nose, broken in a childhood fight with his brother. "Sólo te quiero a ti." *I only want this man.*

"And babies."

She choked out the words, "And many babies in our casa."

"Sh-sh-sh, mi vida." Raúl moved a tress of his wife's damp hair from her forehead. "Mi amor, mañana todo será mejor. Yo te prometo."

Willing herself to believe that everything would be better, Valeria found sleep.

Cautiously Raúl rose from the bed to begin the task of cleaning up.

SANTA TERESA MOUNTAINS

Her thin shoulders quivering in the early morning cold, Nest Feather knelt on the hide spread before her in the ceremonial structure and faced east, the holiest of the four sacred directions, where the sun, the primary force of the universe, resided.

She Who Sits in Quiet, a weathered elder over sixty and selected by many as the attendant for a daughter's initiation into womanhood, brought an earthenware bowl of fresh water before Nest Feather. With three fingers, the attendant scooped pulverized yucca root pulp from a small pot and swished her hand in the water, making it foamy. Gathering the slight girl's long black hair in her hands, she dipped it in the soapy water and washed Nest Feather's head.

Nest Feather suffered the hair pulling and the attendant's enlarged knuckles knocking her head. She almost smiled as she remembered past initiates speaking of this attendant's hair washings, but Nest Feather closed her eyes and regained her spiritual composure with thoughts of the solemn significance of *na'íees*. Now fertile, Nest Feather would no longer be the caretaker of others' *mé'* but of her own children. She would bring forth new life from the wellspring of her young body, ensuring the divine destiny of her *Tséjìné*, "Black Rocks People," or Arivaipa Apaches in the White Eyes' tongue.

With her eyes still closed, as the fresh water poured down the length of her hair, Nest Feather imagined the cleansing of not only her hair but of her soul that she might encounter Changing Woman completely unsoiled. The wood comb sliding through her tresses and parting it down the middle of her head straightened her mind and her will to fulfill the promise that Changing Woman bequeaths to each girl as she transforms into womanhood.

Nest Feather opened her eyes when the attendant raised her to a sitting position. The attendant then reverently cupped in her hands a hollowed-out gourd filled with pollen.

It was time.

She Who Sits in Quiet had schooled Nest Feather for many weeks about the puberty ceremony. Now they regarded each other. Without words, the attendant encouraged her to remain calm throughout the ceremony, its test stretching over four days. She tacitly instilled confidence in Nest Feather, who, during the events to transpire, would possess great spiritual powers among her People and her tribe.

Nest Feather's heart fluttered with last-minute qualms. *Will I be strong enough—mentally and especially physically—to endure four days of rigorous motion?* The constant dancing, running, providing of food and needs to the elderly, the granting of wishes to members of her band. Several girls her age had refused the expensive ceremony, knowing in their hearts that they would falter and endure the everlasting embarrassment of failure. *Onawa, being the beautiful sister, regally represented our gowah with success.* With that thought, Nest Feather vowed to herself, *Being the homely one, I cannot shame those who remain of my family. I must succeed. I wear the ceremonial dress sewn for Sister.* Nest Feather's heart slowed, regaining its steady rhythm. She inclined her head downward. Her signal of readiness.

She Who Sits in Quiet pinched pollen from the gourd between her fingertips and ran them down the line of the hair part. Pinch after pinch of the dried, golden-yellow pollen from cattails, *hoddentin*, dropped upon the girl's face, this blessing to be repeated several times over the next four days and which Nest Feather must never break. The attendant smeared pollen on her right thumb, firmly pressing it on Nest Feather's straight nose that flattened at her nostrils, drawing her thumb across its bridge, making a long mark of pollen.

The pollen tickled. Nest Feather sniffed. One glance from the attendant caused the twelve-year-old girl to resume her reserved aplomb.

Next the attendant brought before Nest Feather finely sewn moccasins made with one doeskin. On her knees, the attendant held her charge's right foot and positioned one moccasin to slip over it.

Nest Feather took in an expectant breath. The moccasin eased on, first over her toes, over the short length of her foot, until fitting snugly over her heel. *My childhood is over.* From the first moment of wearing the fine, soft skins, she became a woman, infused with the power bestowed by Changing Woman, the ancient one created at the beginning of creation by Yusn, the giver of life.

Nest Feather rose and allowed She Who Sits in Quiet to slip over her nakedness a skirt fashioned out of two full doeskins sewn flesh side out and a blouse also created out of two doeskins, flesh side in, that was greatly beaded and rubbed with pollen until yellow. Nest Feather staggered with the added weight. The attendant threw over the girl's hair and dress more pollen, which adhered to rows of beads sewn on by her mother and her father's second and third wives, all Who Were Gone. The responsibility and the importance of na'íees weighed on the slight girl as much as the heavy dress.

She Who Sits in Quiet took a small slice of cactus meat between her fingers and offered it to Nest Feather from the direction of the east. Pulling the succulent flesh away from Nest Feather's open, birdlike mouth, the attendant repeatedly offered the cactus meat from two other cardinal directions, south and west, denying her charge each time, until allowing Nest Feather to partake at the fourth attempt—from the north.

Finally the attendant placed two eagle feathers in her charge's hair at the top of her head. The moment had arrived.

Nest Feather advanced her right foot, nudging the heavy skirt that swept the ground. When Sister wore the ceremonial dress, the skirt's lower edge hovered above her ankles. Because she was so much shorter and smaller than other girls her age attaining womanhood, Nest Feather realized the dress would impact her throughout the ceremony, testing her mental and physical strength. Nest Feather endured a flutter of worry. *No, take care. I may not be among the swift, but I will proceed in my usual manner.* She dispelled notions of failure or weakness with a shake of her head. How Nest Feather proceeded through the ceremony would be indicative of how she encountered the rest of her life.

Again Nest Feather nudged the cumbersome skirt forward until she stood at the ceremonial structure's entrance. *I am ready.*

She Who Sits in Quiet presented to her charge a long, bent cane from which hung several white eagle feathers and strips of cowhide painted yellow, black, tan, and green. After quick scrutiny of Nest Feather's appearance, the attendant threw aside the deerskin that covered the entrance.

Cane in hand, Nest Feather prodded the doeskin skirt and advanced into the darkness of a cold January morning.

Every one of Nest Feather's tribal band of Arivaipa Apaches stood in a circle on a small, flat clearing in the barren, rocky Santa Teresa Mountains. Winter had been bitterly cold with low, dense clouds that spread snow, sometimes deep enough to reach Nest Feather's knees, sometimes sparingly, reaching only her ankles. The morning of na'íees dawned crisp and clear, despite an overnight dusting of more snow, frosting the area's large boulders with white. Her Black Rocks People, wearing threadbare clothes taken from the White Eyes, stolidly watched every movement made by Nest Feather.

Not looking at anyone directly, Nest Feather nevertheless was aware of the presence of her attentive sister Onawa, whose long hair fell down her back in the fashion of married women and whose toddler straddled her hip, Sister's husband, as well as his first wife and their child. *Perhaps they are as cold as I.* And like a hovering aura she sensed the spirits of her departed parents, gone long ago from injury and illness. Nest Feather's body tingled. *The power comes upon me. I will adequately perform my duties.*

Nest Feather briefly noticed the leader of their band, Hashké Bahnzin, whom the White Eyes called Eskiminzin, his pudgy face and broad, round nose distinctively different from the hawklike features of many Apaches, making him instantly identifiable. Surrounded by his wives and beloved children, perhaps the leader told his little girls that in a few short years, they, too, would experience the meeting with the spirit of Changing Woman, who changed from an old woman to a youth, rejuvenating, refreshing, and ensuring eternal life of her spirit with each young girl's passage into womanhood.

It was due to the natural maturation of her body that her band gathered that morning. Several days ago, when Nest Feather relieved herself behind a flat paddle cactus away from the gowah, her water flowed red. Her first menses had begun.

Woman's blood.

At first Nest Feather was astonished at the sight, then excited, then aware of a new, terrible aching and cramping in her lower region that worsened until she fell to the rocky earth where she vomited the poor amount of food left in her stomach. No massaging of that area relieved the cramp. Rising, she lurched back to the gowah of Sister and Sister's husband, crawling through its opening as her lower regions pulsed in waves of rage at being awakened to new responsibilities and functions.

"Sister," welcomed Onawa.

Nest Feather collapsed on her blanket near the opening. "I die."

"Attacked?" Sister clamored to Little Sister and turned her over as another spasm hit.

"Oh . . . I die."

"Show me the wound."

Hand hovering over her lower region, Nest Feather pressed her legs together and writhed to and fro.

Observing no wound and quickly guessing the reason, Onawa burst into musical giggles. "At last!"

"I die . . . the Di-yin . . ."

"You bleed for the first time. It always hurts. Wait until a baby wishes to appear."

"During this arc of the sun?"

"No, not this sun or moon. Not many moons. But now you are able."

"Ooooh. Take the ability back. I have no desire for a baby."

"You adore children."

Another spasm hit Nest Feather. "Not now."

Again Sister giggled. "We have spoken of this blessing many times. Already I have secured all loose beads on the celebration dress. It has awaited your wearing since last snowfall. And now your new journey begins."

"When?"

"Soon. I must tell Husband and Hashké Bahnzin. They will rejoice. Our leader will set the date in the coming days." Sister rose and bent over to leave the gowah, but before she left, she said, "Bless our band with many children." Apache populations dwindled rapidly due to age and losses in conflicts with the Anglos and Mexicans. Sister's husband had impressed this concern on his wife, who, like the meaning of her name, was wide awake and alert to her People's need to reproduce.

"Wait," Nest Feather implored. "Do you still hurt?"

"There are times. Yes. Birthing our boy child hurt."

"And you wish to inflict more pain upon me? You are not a good sister." But Onawa was already gone.

While she rested, Nest Feather heard Sister's tinkling laughter as she ran through the ranchería to Hashké Bahnzin's domed gowah, where he received the eagerly anticipated news of Nest Feather's capability of bearing children. He decreed festivities would occur in three suns, enough time for notification of two other Apache bands to arrive from their winter camps.

Today, the day of the festivities, when Changing Woman would appear to this maiden, Nest Feather moved into the circle of her People and stood facing east. She Who Sits in Quiet, her attendant, joined her, standing to Nest Feather's left.

Although the skies brightened, the sun still had not shown its face over the rocky crests of the mountains.

Nest Feather waited.

The Apaches waited.

The singer waited.

Finally a golden-yellow arc nudged over the far mountain rim. The rising sun.

Abruptly the elderly singer beat the water drum in a steady rhythm. His mouth a wide gash in his deeply lined face, his eyes clouded by age, he lifted his strong voice, piercing the silence held by the entire Arivaipa band, in a song about Changing Woman:

> I'm going to the Sun, going, going.
> The light, the daughter of the Sun,
> Comes from her.

Nest Feather lightly danced, bouncing from foot to foot, tapping the cane when she changed feet. All of the Apaches danced with her.

> I'm going to the Sun.
> Goh jon sinh' di yih.
> On behalf of this girl,
> Grant her Changing Woman's power.

The Arivaipa women ululated, demonstrating their approval. Each time the singer repeated the last phrase, the women brilliantly tongued their high call, sweet as honey to the ear.

As abruptly as the singer began, he stopped.

Nest Feather could sense the attendant's worry and anticipation over whether her charge remembered the next phrase. Pleased with herself and without hesitation, Nest Feather spoke her prayer in a strong voice, filled with power, "Da hązhę esh dali. Ih sta nedlęheh." Long life, no trouble, Changing Woman.

Nest Feather knelt on more buckskins covering the hard, frozen ground of the mountains. The sun now well into its heavenly sweep over the sky, she spread her knees apart and faced east, toward the sun's home. Swaying from side to side, her hands at shoulder level, Nest Feather imagined the sun impregnating her.

She Who Sits in Quiet came forward. "Lie."

When Nest Feather was prone on the skins, the attendant kneaded her charge's slender legs, barely perceptible through her skirt's doeskins.

Nest Feather knew the attendant molded her for the rest of her life, molding her into the Apache ways of womanhood and ensuring a good future for her. She endured the attendant's deep massage of her back, shoulders, arms, and hands, the sources of Nest Feather's strength to resist evil events. Nest Feather must be ready to help her band and her relatives at any time. She arose.

The older woman pulled the bent cane from the ground and, walking east, pushed the cane into the earth. Sounds of the Tséjìné women's high-pitched ululations and the singer's chants filled the crisp air. Nest Feather took a deep breath and began her run.

Striding as widely as she could under the weight of the doeskin skirt, Nest Feather ran around the cane and turned back toward the hides upon which she had lain. The attendant moved the cane farther to the east, doubling the distance. Without stopping, Nest Feather ran around the hides and headed toward the more distant, bent cane.

Nest Feather had trouble seeing the cane itself due to the glaring sun, but farther out she thought she saw a shimmering. *A shimmering of a person coming from afar off. Perhaps an Apache from a related band, late for the ceremony.* As Nest Feather progressed toward the cane, the shimmering became more distinct. *It is an old woman.*

Nest Feather rounded the cane. The ululations of the women seemed louder to her. She ran toward the skins, and when she turned back to the east, she saw that the attendant had moved the cane farther out again, once more doubling the distance. The weight of the dress tired Nest Feather, her footfalls heavier with each stride.

She wanted to lift the skirt from the ground but believed it to be an unforgivable indiscretion. Scampering faster despite her dress, Nest Feather saw the woman again from a closer distance. The woman appeared younger than at first glance—her aged, bent form more upright. With each stride Nest Feather took, the woman looked younger and happier.

Nest Feather ran about the cane. *I do not believe this is a member of another band of Apaches.* A cold frisson ran through her, but not from the winter's chill. *This person is Changing Woman.*

More and more quickly Nest Feather circled the buckskins back toward the bent cane that the attendant had—for the fourth and last time—moved, again doubling the distance. Nest Feather must see Changing Woman again. *Is she still there? Yes.* Changing Woman approached, now a youth of less than twenty. Smiling, radiant, waiting, Changing Woman did not move as Nest Feather ran toward her. Beckoning, Changing Woman motioned to Nest Feather as if saying, "Run to me. Run through me. Become Changing Woman."

The spirit apparition before Nest Feather glowed. *I want to be her.* Closer and closer she ran, breathless with joy and anticipation, until Changing Woman, radiant and beautiful, spread open her arms. Nest Feather lunged forward. She ran through the apparition, becoming one with Changing Woman. Blinded by a light and weightless in her ceremonial dress, Nest Feather ran around the bent cane and sprinted toward the ceremonial structure. She did not hear the ululations, or the singer's chants, nor did she see her Black Rocks People. Nest Feather, glowing with boundless hope, gathered speed and energy as she ran into the darkness of the ceremonial structure.

She was Woman.

THURSDAY, JANUARY 12, 1871

Sprawled over the bed, Valeria pressed her open mouth into the thin blanket and made no attempt to wipe away the salty tears coursing down her cheeks. The small of her back ached, and her throat was sore from wrenching, guttural wails.

Day after day she spent the entirety of her time either weeping on the bed or wandering through her two rooms like a somnambulist, floundering as in a dream—a dream from which she wished to wake. Raúl did the best he could. He was gentle and kind. And above all, patient. After Raúl left for Zeckendorf's before seven, Valeria succumbed to an emptiness that consumed, a guilt that had no end, and a lethargy that lingered.

Every day Valeria went over each minute detail of her short pregnancy. *What did I do wrong?* She danced at their last party in El Paso and, maybe, drank a little too much. They climbed aboard a stagecoach and traveled hundreds of miles to Tucson, where she stumbled out of the coach and into Raúl's arms. She had been tired. And then . . .

Valeria had heard other women say they were happy not to come to term. They would say that dropping babies every year or two took an enormous toll. Some might laugh and tell her she should be glad. That she was young. That this happens, sometimes often. These were mothers of as many as ten children speaking from experience, well past their temporary childlessness. She knew the risks of childbirth seemed greater in the desert.

Valeria rolled over on her back. Her head fell to the side of the blank wall—the wall where a bassinette should be placed. Shuddering, she turned her head to the other wall where their one small bureau held the entirety of their belongings: laces her mother had tatted, her fiesta outfit, one other dress change, three shirts for Raúl, two pants, his bolero jacket, and her Bible. Above the bureau hung a small mirror and a small iron cross from which she had draped the rosary she'd owned since childhood.

Her blessed mother did not know what had occurred. Valeria must write her. *Bad news travels on fleet horses when good news is expected.* No, she'd wait for a more welcome announcement to be read to her mother.

Valeria tore herself from the bed and lurched toward the bureau, where the tiny mirror reflected her swollen, red eyes; her pale cheeks and dripping nose; her normally beautiful black hair, stringy and lackluster. Appalled, she splashed water from the basin on her face. *Raúl cannot see me so deformed and ugly. He will turn to others.*

She grabbed her rosary from the cross, found her heavy shawl, and fled the tiny casa into the streets where a band of dogs scavenged near the doorway to her left. She headed in the opposite direction.

Overhead, one of the few cloudy skies she had seen in Tucson threatened either rain or light snow. She closely wrapped her shawl about her torso and leaned into the gusting wind as she walked toward the street to the east. A few houses down stood a water cart, its old mule hanging its head, eyes half closed, and front right hoof poised on edge.

Valeria advanced, hoping to pass the cart unnoticed, but once there, she stopped. Not since her early childhood had she seen a mule's eyelashes as long as these. While a young, redheaded man poured water from an olla into a neighbor's pitcher and, with thanks, accepted the coin slipped into his hand, Valeria dared stroke the mule's coarse hair and inhaled its barnyard odor.

"Top o' the mornin' to ya, missus."

What delightful accent is that? Valeria turned her attention from the mule to its owner. "Hola." She lowered her face. *He is too cheerful.*

"Ahhh, shy of Martin Touhey? Is that it?" Touhey placed the olla in the cart bed, next to a large, hide-lined wooden tank filled with water.

Sensing his inquisitive gaze, Valeria obliged him with a weak bowing of her lips and a quick glance.

"No, 'tis something else. You've troubles, missus."

He wants to talk. Not today. It is too much. She turned away, but a dry muzzle nudged her palm, wanting more rubs, like the old mule she used to ride to her infrequent lessons with a tutor.

"Up until a few months ago, I had troubles too. And you know how I lost them?"

What kind of person talks so intimately to a stranger? Valeria stroked the mule's nose.

"Well, I'll tell you. I lost my troubles when I found a purpose."

No one's ever spoken to me of having a purpose. A Mexican woman married, had children and grandchildren, and happily died to be received into Heaven. "A purpose?"

"I found a need. A simple need of people in Tucson and I fill it. Fresh water. Spring water from the natural spring above Jimmie Lee's flour mill. A fine, hardworking man, Jimmie Lee. A fellow expatriate from the old country. Ireland."

It's an Irish accent. "Spring water . . ."

"A simple need. And I fill it. But then, I'm a simple man. Find yourself a purpose, that's what I'm saying."

"¿Cómo?" *Perhaps he sells more advice than water.*

With a tip of his head Touhey said, "Come to the end of the street with me. I have another delivery, and I want to show you something." Touhey made a clicking sound, and roused from apparent napping, the mule edged forward slowly, matching Touhey and Valeria's pace to the end of the street—the end of civilization.

Before them stretched the vast Sonoran Desert. Only small cacti and an occasional low-lying creosote bush and acacia tree broke the barren and unforgiving landscape of the flat Santa Cruz Valley floor. Ringing the small village of Tucson were mountain ranges to the east, west, and south, but the most majestic of these ranges loomed to the north. Bare palisades of craggy granite broke from the upthrust of ground strewn with manzanitas and boulders; knobs and outcroppings of rock appeared like the gnarled spines of prehistoric animals; defined ridges sloped angularly to the desert floor.

"There." Pride deepened Touhey's voice. "The Santa Catarinas. Aren't they grand? The soldiers in the old presidio called them 'The Church.' La Ig . . ."

"La Iglesia."

"'I will lift up mine eyes unto the hills, from whence cometh my help.' Trouble is, these mountains swarm with Indians."

In the week since her miscarriage, Valeria had walked only once before to the end of her street, head down, crying all the way, watching the dust settle over the tips of her brown boots and tingeing her skirt hem, only to find another barrier: the mountains that kept her from escaping the filthy *calles* in the village of Tucson, where walked men who spoke only of the latest depredations and gave warnings. Never go beyond the settlement alone, only with as many escorts as possible. The land is unforgiving with no water for many miles to the east of the Santa Cruz River. Marauding Indians—the Apaches—can pop up from behind any bush or any rock to steal and kill.

Yet now to Valeria, the Santa Catarinas took on greater beauty and significance under the magic charm of Touhey's lilting voice. "Son muy bonitas. Very pretty."

"Yes." Breaking the spell, Touhey spoke with alacrity, "Well, I must leave you here, missus. I've more water deliveries. Isn't that true, Daphne?" The mule nodded as Touhey rubbed her long nose. Turning to Valeria, the Irishman grinned. "Remember me for water. 'A penny a pitcher or a little more for a bigger pour.' Top o' the morning." With a creak of the cart's wheels and the clanking of ceramic jars, the man and his mule rounded the corner to more tiny bungalows and squatter-like hovels.

Valeria brought her rosary, tight in hand, to her lips. *I must go to the church today.*

Immediately she turned, and seeing that the pack of dogs had moved on, she hurried west on her street until reaching the main thoroughfare, where she veered north, finally finding la Plaza de Mesilla, the church plaza, around which lay San Agustín Church and the new St. Joseph's Convent. Valeria placed her shawl over her head, and through a cove flanked by columns of adobe brick, entered the modest church.

Until accustomed to the dim light coming from a circular window over the entrance, Valeria waited. Hoping for a soothing place of worship, Valeria sighed at the church's dirt floors and adobe walls. *Like any other building in Tucson.* No triptychs beautifully depicting heavenly glories hung on the whitewashed walls. Votive candles on a small table flickered their dim light in an alcove painted deep reds and ochres and brilliant blues, the only spot of color in the church. Nearby, before a statue of the long, gaunt figure of crucified Christ hanging above the altar, a pair of wimpled nuns genuflected, made the sign of the cross, and disappeared through a side door into their convent.

Perhaps the Lord is teaching me acceptance. Because the church is not beautiful, my prayers must be more worthy. Valeria touched her right knee to the floor as a sign of adoration to Christ, and moving down the center aisle to a chair, she went on both knees to pray, mumbling, "My Lord, Holy Father, I need your help . . ."

SATURDAY, JANUARY 14, 1871

Surprised by the sudden appearance of William Zeckendorf's fluffy muttonchops and wireless, round eyeglasses inches from his face, Raúl tried to focus on his employer's urgent request: "Take this box of cigars to Juan Elías. He's waiting for these."

"Where is his house?"

"No, no. He's at the courthouse. He's a representative. Go. Hurry."

Raúl left Zeckendorf's with only a fair knowledge of where the courthouse was but guessed he couldn't go far wrong with Tucson as small as it was. Raúl followed the path of several men in dark suits walking north on Court Street, only two blocks away. Once at that corner, beyond a private walled yard, Raúl saw twenty or more men greeting each other, some deep in conversation, others shaking hands and moving on to another person. *That must be the courthouse. In their Sunday best, the men all look alike. How will I know which one is Juan Elías?*

Raúl wandered through the gathering, hearing phrases of conversations about "tax for public schools," the "Apache Indian crisis," and "that bastard George Stoneman." Realizing he saw only four Hispanics in this gathering, Raúl asked one, "Excuse me, are you Juan Elías?"

The man laughed. "No, you want the young, good-looking one over there."

Raúl approached a dark, attractive man in his early thirties finishing a conversation with someone. "Señor Elías, yo soy Raúl Obregón from Zeckendorf's. I am to give you these cigars."

Juan studied the wooden box topped with a colorful picture of ladies lounging about in togas. "Ah, I've been waiting for them. Good timing. Muchas gracias."

Before Elías could turn toward someone else, Raúl asked, "What is this assembly of men?"

"The Sixth Arizona Territorial Legislature. Some are members of the Council, the higher house, but I'm in the House of Representatives. I represent Pima County."

"I've heard these men talk of many interesting topics."

"Yes . . ." Both men turned as the doors to the courthouse opencd. The other legislators surged forward to take seats inside. "I'm sorry, but I must hear the governor's address."

"Por supuesto. Of course."

"If you're interested in politics, go to the town meetings. You'll see me there. And thanks again for the cigars."

Raúl watched Elías enter the courthouse. It was not a large building, merely another adobe structure with windows. *Yet inside today they hear the governor's speech. I should take the advice of this important man.*

✦✦✦

One of the last inside, Juan Elías chuckled at how the legislators sat in the intimate courtroom. *Grown men who feel the need to separate themselves according to Council or House. Governor Safford makes friends. He'll draw us together.* Like a faithful and generous Catholic should, Juan leaned over shoulders to shake hands with those he'd missed greeting that morning. *The only thing that matters is that these men are from all Arizona Territorial counties.*

Juan nudged his friend and Councilmember Hiram S. Stevens, brother-in-law to Tucson's civic leader, Samuel Hughes, and waved the box of cigars—redolent of fine tobacco even through the wood—under the man's nose. Stevens raised his eyebrows.

Near to bursting with pride, Juan took a seat among the representatives. His older brother Jesús María had been a representative to the First Arizona Territorial Legislature. *I carry on the tradition. Next maybe my nephews, or someday I'll have sons who'll serve.*

"All rise for the governor of Arizona Territory!"

Juan stood, as did all members of both the Council and the House of Representatives, and applauded warmly for A. P. K. Safford, the "little governor," who reached a height of less than five feet four inches. This small, ambitious man had big plans for Arizona Territory, never mind that the inveterate prospector and former surveyor general of Nevada mined the political arena in the territory with the same fervor he had mined mineral resources and the back rooms of hotels and brothels. Juan and those few in the know overlooked and forgave Safford for his indiscretions, given that the governor's energetic and enthusiastic promotion of Arizona's vast expanse of Sonoran Desert would bring wealth to its current residents and those willing to mine the land currently under siege by ruthless, savage tribes of Indians, primarily Apaches.

Waving his arms high, Juan encouraged the legislators to sustain the applause. *This is the governor's first Legislative Assembly too. He deserves this big welcome.*

The way he smiles and shakes his head, I think he's much taken by this and maybe even a little embarrassed.

When the applause died down, Safford placed his speech on a podium and motioned for the members of the august congress to take a seat. "Thank you. Thank you very much. That gladdens my heart. It truly does. Thank you."

Intent to capture every word, Juan leaned forward in his chair. His English sufficient for everyday events, a dignified address tested his limited fluency, requiring complete concentration on his part to gain a satisfactory understanding of what was said.

Safford began, "Gentlemen of the Legislative Assembly of the Territory of Arizona. It is the duty of the Executive to lay before you, at the commencement of your sessions, such information and make such suggestions as to the territory's affairs, interests, and wants as may aid you in your deliberations. Since the last convening of the Legislative Assembly two years ago, the improvements and population of the territory have steadily increased. Arizona has vast deposits of precious metals locked up in her rockbound mountains, and her grazing and agricultural resources are unsurpassed. The development of our resources demonstrates the necessity of amending some of our statutes and of framing new ones.

"The Indians. The question of paramount importance since the acquisition of the territory has been, and is now, the hostility of the Apache Indians."

At the word "hostility," Juan jumped to his feet. Never far from his mind was the killing of his brother, Cornelio, eight years ago. *We followed the tracks of Apaches who stole my cattle and came upon their rear guard. We fought. But Cornelio . . . They shot him in the head. Dead.* Juan's black hair brushed back, his fierce eyes shining, he urged the entire legislature to rise en masse to their feet. Applauding and whistling and cheering, he kept the thunderous reception going for as long as possible until it inevitably dwindled at the governor's repeated requests. Juan and the other legislators resumed their seats.

Safford continued, "The history of these Indians is written in blood. They have caused the bones of our people to lie bleaching along every highway and in every settlement of the territory. Their tortures, murders, and robberies hang like the dark pall of night over every enterprise. No people, in the early settlement of any of our territories, have suffered more or met with greater loss of life and property, in proportion to the population and wealth, than those of Arizona, and none have faced these dangers and endured these hardships with greater fortitude.

"The troops in the territory have been active and, in the main, commanded by brave and efficient officers, but the force is entirely inadequate to the prosecution of an energetic, aggressive war, and no other kind of war will ever reduce the Apache to submission."

Again Juan led the healthy applause. *This is the governor to help us. This is what we need to hear.* With each understandable word from Safford, Juan's breathing quickened. *I am ready for the fight. Jesús is ready for the fight. And our people, who have lost so much.*

Quickly Safford took a sip of water from a ready glass. "Several previous legislatures have petitioned Congress to give our governor authority to raise volunteers. I am of the opinion that volunteers raised among our own people, acquainted with the habits of the Indians and the country, fighting for their homes and firesides, would be found efficient and more economical for the government than regular troops.

"The Apache Indians have never manifested the least disposition to live on terms of peace until after they had been thoroughly subjugated by military power, and any attempt to compromise before they are reduced to this condition is accepted by them as an acknowledgment of weakness and cowardice. Therefore my opinion is that the war must be prosecuted with relentless vigor until the Apaches are completely humbled and subjugated. After which, the government should remove these Indians to a reservation of such circumscribed limits that constant watch could be kept over them. The reservation, instead of being held in common, should be divided into reasonable subdivisions as would give to each family a home and the necessary land to grow the food they require. Let the fact be established in their minds that in a state of peace they will be better fed and clad than in a state of war. Let this policy be, and they will be rapidly drawn toward civilized life. If the Indian Department does not offer an immediate helping hand and the Apaches are permitted to roam at will, quite invariably and certainly they will fall back into their habits in avowed hostility."

This time Juan allowed other legislators to begin the sustained applause, which eventually lessened to a point that Safford continued his speech on many issues, including the need for public schools, the importance of legally establishing towns, and obtaining titles of ownership for private property.

"In conclusion, I would say that, to you, the people have entrusted the important duty of passing such acts as will aid in protecting life and property, educating the youth, encouraging industry, and developing the resources of the territory. It will be my pleasure to render you any assistance in my power in the performance of these duties, and trust that you will be guided in your deliberations by the great ruler of the universe, who rules over all nations and peoples, and from whom all good gifts come. Thank you."

Safford stepped back from the podium to his immediate reward of a standing ovation, soon becoming engulfed with congressmen pumping his hands and offering their congratulations, questions, and requests. By the time Juan and Hiram Stevens, waiting at the end of the line, reached Safford, it was obvious to them the governor's buoyancy had flagged. So that no one other than Safford and Juan could hear, Hiram said quietly, "My wife's got a hearty lunch planned, and I'm heavy on the whiskey."

"That's grand, boys."

+++

At the Stevenses' commodious adobe home on Main Street, used as a meeting site for previous Legislative Assemblies, lunch was heavy and the whiskey hearty. After the meal ended, the men rose, giving the cue for Hiram's wife, Petra, sister to Sam Hughes's wife, Atanacia, to graciously and quickly leave the men to themselves. The niceties over, they each pulled back their chairs to stretch their legs.

Juan exerted himself to grasp the governor's disappointment that his days spent planning and soliciting prospectors to sojourn through some of the mountains in southern Arizona among formations promising significant minerals and ores had come to naught, his ambitious plans scuttled by Stoneman's inaction against the Apaches.

Safford threw his napkin on the table. "I've climbed mountains before; Stoneman is a hill and proving to be a formidable one."

Grateful for a lull in the conversation, Juan produced the impressive cigar box from under his chair and slit the paper securing the top with his dinner knife. The delicious smell of compactly rolled tobacco wafted out.

Giving due respect to this luxury, the men carefully selected a cigar, rolled it between their fingers, and ran the length of it under their noses to breathe in the quality of its Cuban tobacco before cutting off the butt end and lighting up. Juan, pleased and proud of his contribution, watched satisfaction spread across Safford and Hiram's faces as they inhaled.

Smoke rose to the vigas and encircled the Spanish iron chandelier. Sensing that this was the appropriate moment to broach their main cause, Juan admired the nonchalance Stevens displayed when he asked the governor, "Has your opinion of Colonel Stoneman changed since you first met him?"

"That insufferable son of a bitch hasn't changed one iota. I sized him up faster than a whore in heat. His opinion of himself is as high as he is tall and as big as his head."

Stevens agreed. "He certainly doesn't think too much of us here in Tucson, according to his report."

"That goddamned report! Sure as shit, Stoneman's not fully invested in our defense. Not when he advises such draconian cuts to the number of camps and supply depots."

Any calming effects from his expensive cigar ceased abruptly for Juan. Anxiety shortened his rehearsed remarks. "We invest so much in our lands. Money. Cattle. Sweat. Lives."

"Do you know what he told me one night in Washington a year ago?" Without waiting for an answer, Safford leaned forward to talk directly to Juan. "He thinks it was a mistake taking away from the Indians such a worthless country as the desert of Arizona and New Mexico. How can a man who thinks that protect Arizona's residents?" Safford held out his empty snifter.

Juan's throat as dry as an arroyo in mid-June, he also extended his glass.

Stevens poured generous brandies. "He certainly hasn't engaged the enemy."

"Stoneman finds no credit to be gained fighting Indians." The governor mulled over his drink.

Riled, Juan opened his mouth to speak, but Hiram languidly, yet with great import, spoke first, "Governor, this legislature must intercede in some way."

"I'm not done yet. I didn't get satisfaction when I asked General Sherman for a younger, more ambitious man as commander of the Department of Arizona. All Sherman said was, 'The White House supports the humanitarian efforts of the Quakers.' They think Bible readings are supposed to convert savages who eviscerate and scalp a living man." Safford jumped up and paced the dining room, Stevens following with the brandy. "I'm going back to Washington next month after the legislature adjourns. I'm determined to speak to the president himself."

"Will Grant listen?"

"I'll make him listen. We can't suffer any longer with an imperious fool who headquarters at Drum Barracks on the coast of California. By God, Stoneman hasn't fought Indians for more than fifteen years." Safford returned to sit at the table, and placing his elbows on it, held his head.

Realizing Safford's rage was spent, Juan extracted a folded sheet of paper from his breast pocket, and taking Hiram's nod as encouragement, presented it to the governor. "Nosotros preparamos una propuesta."

Safford gazed at the prepared proposition Juan extended. "The legislature still has four more weeks. Business should begin on Monday."

Removing the stogie he had rolled around in his mouth, Hiram held the wet end away from his suit. "We would like for you to review our resolution before we introduce it into the records."

"Ah." Safford took the document, placed it on the table, and read.

Juan and Hiram watched as Safford scanned the lengthy "whereas" clauses that culminated in the "therefore" clause. With each gesture Safford made—pursing his mouth and smoothing his chin whiskers with his hand—Juan imagined the thoughts going through the governor's mind. But when Safford's gaze drifted to the floor, Juan grew irritated and testy.

Safford shook his head. "Boys, you can't introduce this."

"¿Por qué?" probed Juan.

"Every word in this resolution is true, but in a few days all of you return to private life. The fight to oust Stoneman, ineffectual though he may be, would rest almost solely in my hands."

Hiram refreshed the governor's glass. "We stand behind you."

"Every last one of us would love to adopt this resolution. But I think . . . no, I know it would serve as a public notice of our intent to force Stoneman out. My going to Washington, even if it is known, does not send that signal. My business there could be for a myriad of reasons."

"We want him out."

"But even Stoneman must have some supporters, and he'd muster all of them to prevent removal. My small patronage and influence as territorial governor would not equal the patronage of a department commander and an assured office for life."

"There has to be something we can do. There has to be."

Juan's mouth filled with English words, but they came out in a heated, disorderly mess. "Stoneman go. Best for Arizona. All better."

"This doesn't mean that won't happen. I'll continue working through governmental contacts to find a replacement. But . . ." Safford again shook his head.

Hiram blew an important amount of smoke toward his ceiling. "The public needs to know that we, as congressmen, are working for them on their problems."

"Their losses," added Juan. "My losses. General Stoneman does not know how many suffer? How many lose? He does not care?"

Juan watched the governor lean wearily back in his chair. The brandies, the excitement of the speech before the legislature, the heavy meal, and a stogie all had taken their visible toll on Safford.

The governor drew in a long breath. "I have to suppose that he is updated daily as to the situation. Perhaps that does not make a sufficient impression."

Hiram placed the stopper in the brandy decanter. "Would a complete, compiled listing of losses—human and property—presented to him make the requisite impression?"

The men gazed at Safford running the idea through his mind and his obviously growing interest in the idea. "There are distinct benefits to such a memorial of losses. It could be presented to the secretary of war, to the president, to the general commander of the army, to the United States Congress, to the people themselves. And to Stoneman. But would this memorial bring about the desired result— action?" Rising from the dining room chair, Safford enthusiastically shook the men's hands. "Get right on that. Get people's oaths. Immediately. Time's a-wastin'."

SUNDAY, JANUARY 15, 1871

On the morning after the events of na'íees concluded, as the eastern horizon lightened with the promise of the rising sun, Nest Feather and She Who Sits in Quiet retired into the recesses of the Santa Teresa Mountains for the traditional four days of rest for the newly initiated woman and her attendant. They climbed over the desert formed by Yusn and into the giant boulders strewn into a maze of granite, its surrounding land heavily marked with signs of mountain lions' and bears' paw prints. In silence they traversed through and over remote canyons, deeper and higher into the mountains and their boulders—the bones of the earth.

Nest Feather closely followed She Who Sits in Quiet, whose every stride seemed more labored than the previous. *The attendant looks more and more like the frail image of Changing Woman.* Pain, like a penetrating arrow, filled Nest Feather's heart. *The attendant cannot rejuvenate like Changing Woman.* Nest Feather stopped.

She Who Sits in Quiet halted and turned around.

Having lagged behind, Nest Feather suffered the attendant's stare with a contrite heart.

With no threat to their journey, She Who Sits in Quiet continued on their true course up a steep slope until they reached a small glade among low yew trees, some growing out of seams in the boulders. Shallow, ice-covered pools of fresh water formed in rock depressions.

Folds in these sharp granite hills created small nooks or caves. Nest Feather knew that some were secretly used by the Tséjìné as food storage, which was critical to their survival in an emergency. Despite their toil, the Arivaipas reaped less and gathered far fewer wild fruits in these higher elevations. Not even cactus or agaves, the People's most sought-after staples, grew. Fleeing from intertribal struggles and the arrival of White Eyes' military troops almost ten years ago meant abandoning the lower elevations of their sacred ancestral lands of Arapa in Arivaipa Canyon. Countless hardships had fallen upon Nest Feather's family and all of the Arivaipas.

Nest Feather longed for the promised rest at their destination, and in an area sheltered from the snow, hastened toward one of the folds in a recessed granite wall. They stopped. *Something is amiss.* Strewn in front of the cave's protected opening, corncobs mildewed on the damp earth.

The enemy is near. Both Nest Feather and She Who Sits in Quiet crouched on the ground. They scanned the hillsides for movement; they read the air for any scent of the unfamiliar.

Nest Feather's sharp eyes discovered moccasin tracks. Inching forward she read the ground. "Many moccasins stepped through this area only two days ago. See the dry edges of the prints?"

Danger not imminent, Nest Feather and She Who Sits in Quiet crept into the cool dark cave. Many roasted and flattened mescal plants and ears of corn that had been stacked along one rocky wall months ago by the Arivaipas now lay hacked up, strewn about, and unusable. Bean Eaters or even the White Eyes had raided this storage cave, not for want or need of food but to make certain the Arivaipas could not eat it. *The backbreaking work of so many destroyed! The months of finding, gathering, caring, and nurturing the plants—all for nothing. And the crop is so meager its loss will drive our People closer to starvation.*

She Who Sits in Quiet cupped her aged hands over her watery eyes, her suppressed sobs shaking her entire body.

Please, don't shudder so. You are strong, Nest Feather wanted to say. *What can I do to comfort you?* Hesitantly Nest Feather placed her small hand, already accustomed to fieldwork, on the quivering back of the attendant. The loss of the food paled in comparison to the elder's wrenching cries.

Taking the small sack of provisions from the elder's shoulder, Nest Feather assisted She Who Sits in Quiet back to the quiet glade by the yew trees and helped ease her onto her knees to sit against the moist granite rocks. Worried when the older woman began to labor for breath, Nest Feather snatched up her gourd ladle, ran to the rock depression, and smashed the thin ice. She quickly scooped the fresh water, spilling only a few drops as she scampered back to hold the ladle while the old woman drank. A tired smile was her thanks. Settling against the rock next to She Who Sits in Quiet, Nest Feather drifted in and out of sleep.

In her waking moments over the next four days of recovery—four being the spiritual number of directions—Nest Feather reflected upon the solemnity of her great task ahead: the gift to Apachería of her future children. *Such a big responsibility falls upon me. I'm neither pretty nor tall like Sister. I have no particular talent. I'm brown and plain, like the molted feathers from sparrows that are tucked into nests of other birds.*

Nest Feather vigilantly looked for the animal sent by Yusn and Changing Woman that would symbolize the powers bestowed on her for the rest of her life.

In solitary strolls about the glade and the cave's area, Nest Feather scanned the skies, peered in every deep copse for recent signs of animals.

Nothing. It will appear. I am confident. Will the symbol of my power be the beautiful mountain lion or the spotted bobcat? Yet, they do not cross my path. Not even a quail struts by.

On the fourth and last day of her recovery, Nest Feather stopped hoping that a majestic and stately mammal would appear. Resigned to that fact, she joined She Who Sits in Quiet for a midday meal under the yews where they had laid blankets for warmth. Nest Feather's eyelids drooped heavily. One last nap before the return journey to the Black Rocks People.

Deep in sleep, Nest Feather dreamed she heard the rustling of an animal. In her dreams, the green eyes of the fierce mountain lion glared at her from a close distance. Inching ever closer, the big cat gracefully drew its massive paws, one by one, along a straight line to Nest Feather, whose own black eyes widened in alarm. Her feet were leaden. *I can't move. I can't run. I am rooted to the spot.* The mountain lion snarled and growled and pounced. Tossing and turning in sleep, Nest Feather awoke with a start. Sweat beaded her forehead. Chest heaving, a sensation grew upon her. *I am not alone.*

Two gleaming eyes watched her from the dark opening to the cave.

Nest Feather dared not move but lay on her side and watched.

The animal stirred. It blinked. It swiftly moved out of the cave's shadows and into the fading sunlight. A brown mouse. It twitched its nose. Raising up on its back legs, the mouse grabbed a kernel of corn from the ground, clutched it in its small, bony paws, and ate it quickly. Selecting another morsel, it chewed, eyeing Nest Feather.

A mouse. A common, brown mouse. This animal symbolizes the power the Creator has bestowed upon me? Nest Feather sighed and hung her head. *I am small and brown. Sometimes my hair sticks out on the sides despite my care, as the mouse's whiskers protrude out. A mouse.*

Consigned to this creature, Nest Feather fought her disappointment. *What good qualities are there to being small, brown, and plain?* She watched the mouse nibble on another corn kernel as she thought of the courage that the small animal used to seek food—raiding, scavenging against all odds, hiding in the darkest recesses until the time to forage was ripe, venturing out among giants, gleaning what was necessary.

Now on the path to appreciating the tiny creature, Nest Feather studied its guard hairs, almost transparent in the low light. The mouse's fast, abrupt movements registered its nervousness; peering steadily at her, it gauged her regard. For many moments they stared at each other, becoming one.

Yes, this animal is most suitable for me. Nest Feather grinned. She sat up, scaring the little mouse. A glimpse of its thin tail tip was the last she saw as it darted away.

"Thank you, Changing Woman, you have chosen wisely for me."

The return from the heights of the mountains to the camp seemed swifter than their ascent, probably due to the weight of the news Nest Feather and She Who Sits in Quiet brought of the raid on their dwindling food stores.

Hashké Bahnzin stood before his gowah, warmed by the small fire inside, to greet the returned women. When they spoke of the unfavorable happening, he scowled. Nest Feather believed the snows of sorrow entered his eyes as they moistened and chilled in deep thought.

Some of the Black Rocks People, overhearing the news, clamored all at once.

"Our food is limited."

"Game is not plentiful."

"Now the food caches destroyed."

"What will our People do?"

"How do we go on?"

Little children wailed as the cold winds blew in more misery.

Hashké Bahnzin lifted his voice that all might hear, sonorously speaking with the depth of experience, "I will call on all the leaders of the clans. We will hold council."

One of the most outspoken women, whose face bore deep, fissured crevices brought on by age and her serious nature, announced, "Our women will also hold council." Arivaipa women followed her into her gowah, which routinely was avoided. But this predicament required that the Black Rocks women raise their voices in tribal matters, as tradition dictated.

Following the other women, Nest Feather hesitated at the gowah opening where the rancorous woman lingered. Small children separated from their mothers to be tended by older children. Nest Feather turned to follow them, but she heard a low grunt. The Serious One waited, holding the entrance flap open, extending permission for Nest Feather to attend. Acceptance as Woman brought many new duties. Her initiation still in progress, Nest Feather bent and entered the gowah.

TUCSON

"No one was killed today." Since working at Zeckendorf's, Raúl brought home stories of atrocities committed by the Indians upon Anglo and Mexican citizens, or he begrudgingly commented on the lack of it that day.

Valeria wished he wouldn't, but she wanted to hear of his day over dinner and accepted it. "I am proud that you will attend the town meeting. This is important."

"Valeria, you must eat something." Her hunched shoulders concerned him. "Should I stay home with you? I don't need to go."

"I want you to go to the meeting. You're interested in politics."

"Will you eat?"

"When you've gone. I've heard others speak of Juan Elías. He is a good man. Listen to what he says."

"Yes, teacher." Raúl stood.

"You loved studying with the tutor. You did very well. Juan will now direct you." Valeria hugged him, placing her ear against his chest. "You are a great man. Going to these meetings, you can become important."

A kiss on her cool forehead, a waiting at the door, and a concern that Valeria would only grieve cast Raúl into quandary as he looked back at her.

"I'm fine. Go." Valeria shut the door and looked about the empty casa. *Raúl must wonder when his spirited wife will return to him.*

She viewed the bare bassinette wall. Sighing, she noticed that on the bedroom floor lay Raúl's socks, the heels worn through. *Where did I put my sewing kit?* From the second drawer she opened, Valeria took her kit and returned to her chair. *Let's see how this turns out.* She quickly threaded a needle and within a few minutes had repaired one sock. To her own astonishment, she realized she enjoyed doing that.

She rose and heated a tortilla, which she salted. *Hmmmm.* She couldn't remember if she had eaten all day, so she ate another tortilla and repaired the second sock. *Is there something else about the casa that needs sewing?*

✦✦✦

Raúl Obregón approached the courthouse well before half past seven and asked a handful of Tucsonenses standing in the doorway, "Any room inside?"

"You can try, amigo. Too crowded for us." They turned away.

Raúl elbowed inside, where the tumult and circulation of people in such close quarters stunned him. Their angry voices raised as high as the room's temperature, Americans and Mexicans, the wealthy and the poor, store owners and madams ranted about resolving the Indian problem. Who of their neighbors lay slain, mutilated on the trails of southern Arizona Territory? Responding again to the drummer boy's insistent drumbeat and the man's shouting out the news of a meeting that night at the courthouse, the citizens of Tucson bundled into the small courtroom.

Raúl maneuvered toward Juan Elías close by. After delivering the cigar box, Raúl had quickly learned that Juan and his brother Jesús María were the voices for the common man in Tucson. Stoked with eagerness to join in and show Valeria how he could make a good footing here, Raúl came ready to learn from one of the most prominent Mexicans in town.

Juan placed his arm around Raúl's shoulder and yelled into his ear, "Glad you've come. I'll point out a few men you'll want to know. First off, this is my older brother Jesús María. He's the Tucsonenses' hero. Jesús, Raúl Obregón, new employ of Mister Z."

Shaking hands with Jesús María, the man's intense and fiery stare captured Raúl. No one could ever question that Jesús María, at forty-one and much lighter in complexion and smaller in stature than Juan, wielded power over the Elías family and over his Mexican compadres.

"We need more people interested in politics. Someone like you." Jesús María's fixed gaze never left Raúl's face. "Tucson burst through the Presidio walls not that long ago. Now that the walls are broken, safety in the desert has become very difficult."

Raúl couldn't help but be mesmerized by the hypnotic Jesús María. "And the military . . ."

Interrupting, Jesús María explained, "All of Tucson supplies the military posts in southern Arizona Territory—cattle, foodstuffs, horses, hay, leather goods, ironworks. Working for Zeckendorf you know that already."

From Zeckendorf's thriving retail enterprise, Raúl had already sent off provisions and other supplies to quartermasters located at all of the U.S. military camps in the southern region of the territory: Camp Lowell and the military's warehouse, Tucson Depot, blocks away; Camp Bowie, a hundred miles to the east; Camp Grant, fifty-five miles to the north; Camp Crittenden, forty-five miles to the southeast; and Camp Apache, two hundred miles to the northeast.

"We need action. But this new department commander, Stoneman—George Stoneman—wants to upend everything we've put in place. And Eskiminzin and his band continue their raids. A new report out . . ." Jesús María brushed his almost shoulder-length, graying hair away from his face.

An Anglo man at the advanced age of fifty-four, whose high, receding forehead and grizzled, prominent eyebrows cast his eyes into shadows, pulled on Jesús María's elbow and spoke in very tolerable Spanish, "Sorry, I need to interrupt. Fish and Tully want to speak with you before the meeting starts."

"Los anglos encantan las juntas."

Jesús may have spoken in jest, but by the looks of the crowd, Raúl was certain that the Anglos did indeed love meetings.

Juan intervened, "Before you go, meet Raúl Obregón. This is William Oury."

Oury crushed Raúl's hand. "Welcome." Turning, he and Jesús conferred as they walked to the front of the courtroom where well-known retailers E. N. Fish and Pinckney R. Tully waited.

Juan's attention remained on Oury. "Bill's an active leader in everything. Always has been since he arrived."

"He looks ready to take anyone on."

"And has. From the Alamo to San Jacinto and, finally, to the Mier expedition where he pulled a white bean from a jar, sparing his life."

Raúl whistled. With increased interest, he watched Oury and Juan's brother approach the two Anglos at the front. While neither Oury nor Jesús María were tall men, their size belied their apparent conviction and anger: Jesús María a pugnacious Chihuahua to Oury's snarling terrier.

Juan tilted his head toward the entrance. "You know who's coming in now."

A wide swath, as wide as his personality, opened up for the arrival of a Jewish man in his late twenties with an open-mouthed smile for everyone. Recognition of his employer's mannerisms made Raúl chuckle. An eager handshake here, a wave there, William Zeckendorf—"Mister Z" as he affectionately was known in the newspapers—adjusted his small rimless spectacles and ran the backs of his hands up his cheeks, fluffing out his muttonchops. Seeing his newest clerk, Zeckendorf waved at Raúl, who returned the gesture.

"Mister Z frequently helps track down stolen horses and cattle. You know about his army service." At the shake of Raúl's head, Juan explained, "He fought Indians in Colorado and New Mexico not long after arriving from Germany."

"Union or Confederate?"

"Union. Tucson's filled with both Union men and Confederates. When the North took over Tucson, Oury spent the war years in México."

"And you?"

"As descendants of a Presidio soldier, we Tucsonenses stay."

Juan pointed out other notables to Raúl: William Fisher Scott, a narrow-faced Scot, and Irishman Jimmie Lee, business partners in mining and the Eagle Flour Mill in town.

"And now coming in, the one smoking a pipe, that's Andrew Hays Cargill, bookkeeper for Lord & Williams."

Raúl recognized that company name. "Another military supplier."

"Sí, most retailers are. Cargill's rather interesting. He's everywhere and nowhere. He's his own best friend."

"Was he in the war?"

"Confederate. Born in Mississippi and raised, from a baby, in a rich section of New York City. I told you he is interesting."

Raúl turned back to the room's front when Ed Fish bellowed, "Silence, please."

Ignored by the crowd, Fish looked for assistance from Tully and D. A. Bennett, proprietor of the Stevens House Hotel. Bennett put his fingers in his mouth and blew a high-pitched tone that carried over the people's mounting volume. Silence, as loud as an argument, filled the room.

"Now the fun begins." Juan drew Raúl toward a side wall where Jesús María and many Mexicans stood.

Fish announced loudly, "Let's get this meeting started, folks. Thank you all for coming tonight. We have important business."

Jesús María whispered to Juan, "Habla y habla. Habla hasta por los codos."

Overhearing, Raúl tried not to smile. *Everyone here talks and talks. They all talk a blue streak.*

"What about Stoneman's closing of camps?" someone shouted out.

Welshman Samuel Hughes, newly appointed adjutant general to Governor Safford, stood, although many could not see him due to his small stature. "Why is Stoneman's report so slow to circulate in the territory? It is dated October of last year. We have only recently received a synopsis. This timing benefits only him."

"That's right!" yelled another.

Another stood. "Abandon seven more camps? Is this man mad? Apaches are killing us."

Fish interposed, "We can't speak to Stoneman's state of mind, but, in the interest of our public safety, how or what can we do to better our protection through the military?"

"Get another department commander!"

"Any other suggestions?" Fish scanned the room for a more restrained voice of reason.

Juan Elías raised his arm. "Keep Tucson Depot open."

The Mexicanos whooped their agreement.

Someone else yelled, "And no reduction to Camp Bowie and the rest."

"Camp Grant don't need no movin'. It's fine jist where it is," called out another.

Fish tried again, "Gentlemen . . . and ladies, how can we make this message clear to the military?"

A man standing up front asked, "Aren't the dead bodies proof enough that we need more protection?"

At the back of the room, Cargill clenched his unlit pipe between his teeth. He'd never forget his first supply train to Camp Grant. Traveling at night, north along the Cañada del Oro wash, he and his team had come upon the burning remains of Newton Israel and Hugh Kennedy's wagon train shot through with arrows. Newton's body smoldered.

Tully said, "We need solutions. Ideas."

Bored and disconsolate, the Elías brothers changed weight on their feet, back and forth.

Juan told Raúl, "Same arguments, same people, and nothing ever done."

"There is much to decide." Raúl concluded he must contemplate. *Perhaps as a newcomer, I might see where the others have become blind.*

Oury stood. "It seems to me the Apaches are enlarging their target areas of depredations. It calls for more personnel rather than less. We have Indian fighters and trackers in our attendance tonight."

Jesús María straightened.

Sweeping his hand toward the crowd, as if indicating the Indian trackers in the courtroom, Oury spoke louder, "Can't the military employ our native trackers to better steer them in their scouting expeditions? They might have improved success."

Applause rumbled throughout the small hall.

Fish winced. "I believe many people, here and in Prescott, have been suggesting that for some time."

Tully stepped forward as a lull followed. "Now here's another issue we want you to think about. Incorporation of Tucson. Tonight we only want to put that idea forth. We'll have another meeting devoted to that in the next couple of months. But listen, folks. The railroads are coming in. We can't let the railroad take possession of the land we live on. Legally the village of Tucson must incorporate. Of course, to do that, we need to elect commissioners and city officers and address a few other issues."

Cargill smiled ruefully as most others seemed puzzled. *There are always issues with whatever topic comes up. The main issue is that a majority can't come to any decision.*

"Will incorporation make us safer from Indian attacks?" someone asked.

Cargill shouldered his way out the door. *Another raucous meeting without resolutions.*

✦✦✦

Raúl found Valeria asleep in one of the main room's chairs, sleep erasing from her face the despair and heartache of almost three weeks ago. Even as a little girl she'd experienced life's highs and lows to the greatest extent. A skinned knee in the dirt produced brimming tears and wails of such hurt and outrage that her mother wrung her hands of her, but not Raúl. His heart was so full of love for Valeria; he kissed her forehead.

She awoke and smiled in recognition. "How was your meeting?"

"Exciting. Much was discussed. Many people, many important men there." Raúl's heart danced. He slipped his arms under her and carried her to the bedroom.

"It is too soon."

"I'm only holding you and telling you how much I love you."

TUESDAY, JANUARY 31, 1871

In the church plaza, Valeria wandered near the cathedral bells hanging from rough wooden supports, where a few Apache Mansos had spread their daily vegetable yields on blankets. She had learned that these friendly Apaches had farmed the northern edges of Tucson for a very long time. Both Apache Mansos and Papagos walked Tucson's streets in complete accord, and yet the Apaches outside of town—the wild Apaches—endured as Tucson's most reviled enemies. *The Indians' skin color, their cheekbones, their hair, and features are not unlike my own. El Paso wasn't without its dangers, but in Tucson, I sense the threat of Indian attacks much more. After my prayers, I'll buy the Apache Mansos' vegetables.*

Valeria settled on her knees, first giving due adoration to her Lord. "My Lord, Holy Father . . ." She stopped at the high, chattering voices of little children entering the church. *Quiet, please.* She jerked her head to the left but glimpsed nothing. *Back to my prayer.*

"Shhh, niñas, por favor. Silencio," a young woman's voice sounded amused.

From the corner of her eye, Valeria saw two little girls, one about five or six and the other about four years old, shepherded by their mother down the aisle to chairs on the left.

I'll start my prayer over. "My Lord . . ." *The mother closely watches her children. Look how the elder child wiggles and the mother arches her eyebrows in warning. She couldn't be more than a year or two older than I. Twenty? Twenty-one? And already a mother of two. Lord, how I envy her.* Valeria ran a bead or two down her rosary's chain, but again stopped. Her attention kept straying toward the small children and their mother. Half rising, Valeria sat properly on her chair. *My Lord, forgive my fleeting concentration.*

Her prayers finished, the mother gathered her children.

Waiting until they stepped up the aisle, Valeria rose and left the church, passing two mature señoras draping their heads with black lace mantillas.

One woman whispered, "En el Congress Hall, en dos semanas. Todos los importantes asistirán."

"¿Con música?" inquired the other matron.

"Pues, por supuesto. Es la fiesta más prestigiosa del año. Y además, estarán allí los legisladores . . ."

Valeria turned back to eye the women who spoke so animatedly. Quickly they genuflected, possibly embarrassed that at the Lord's house they spoke in excited anticipation of a prestigious society party, honoring the legislators and featuring music, to be held in two weeks' time at a saloon.

The open square, where the little girls ran about while their mother watched them with a little exasperation, was—due to cloud cover—not much brighter than the interior of the church. In what light there was, Valeria could see now that the mother's coloring was much darker than that of the children. *Perhaps the young woman is instead a nursemaid. No, three gold rings worn on two different fingers are wedding bands. The materials and cut of her dress and her light coat are expensive.*

The little girls held her spellbound. Valeria feigned interest in the Apaches' vegetables, only to watch the girls play and scurry about, their hair ribbons bobbing and their long stockings falling to their ankles. Valeria placed her hand over her flat stomach. Hesitantly she picked up an onion but replaced it on its pile at the Apaches' vending blanket. *I have to get closer to those little girls. Someday, perhaps someday soon, my daughters will play like them. Until then . . .*

The elder child took a ball from her short coat pocket and threw it at her sister, who missed it. Seeing the ball roll along the ground toward her, Valeria scooped it up and tossed it underhand to the first child. The child seemed delighted with a new playmate, even one who was quite old. She threw the ball back to Valeria, who, pleased and excited, trotted several steps to catch the ball and—laughing like a small child herself—returned it. *Not so long ago, I played ball in courtyards.* Two more catches by Valeria made the younger sister cry. She had been left out.

Ball in hand, Valeria approached the tot. Squatting to the little girl's height, she placed the ball in the child's hand. "Para ti. ¿Te gusta jugar con pelota?"

Eyes wide and scared, the child bobbed her head, confirming that she did like to play with the ball, and ran to the skirts of the dark young woman, who kissed the child's head.

Smiling, Valeria rose and approached the mother and child. "Las niñas son muy preciosas."

The young woman beamed. "Muchas gracias. ¿Estuvo usted en la iglesia?"

"Sí." While watching the girls at play, Valeria nodded that she had been in the church. "¿Son sus hijas?"

"Cuando se portan bien." They chuckled at the joke that the mother only claimed the precious children as her daughters when they behaved.

A few moments more, then I'll leave. Over the girls' laughter, Valeria said, "Me llamo Valeria Obregón."

"Y yo soy Atanacia Santa Cruz Hughes." Her last name came out a bit stilted, as though it was difficult for her to pronounce.

The Anglo last name explained the lighter-skinned children. Valeria switched to her sometimes acceptable English. "My husband and I arrive in Tucson tres semanas ago. And you, Atanacia?"

Despite her engaging smile, Atanacia shook her head. "No hablo inglés."

She doesn't speak English. Her name seems to be English. "Ay, disculpa. Su nombre parece inglés."

"Mi esposo es del país de Gales. Él habla inglés y yo hablo español. No nos entendemos y estamos perfectamente felices." She laughed that she and her Welsh husband couldn't understand one another and were perfectly happy.

An older woman in a plain dress approached the children. The little girls ran and hugged her. She addressed Atanacia, "Señora, su desayuno está listo."

This is the nursemaid calling them to breakfast, Valeria quickly surmised.

"Vámanos, Lizzie, Maggie." Atanacia gathered her girls and turned to Valeria. "Hasta la vista, Señora Obregón."

"Es un gusto conocerla." *It was so good to meet her.*

WEDNESDAY, FEBRUARY 1, 1871, AND ENSUING DAYS

Pacing her steps to stay behind five old women, among them Hashké Bahnzin's mother and She Who Sits in Quiet, Nest Feather gazed about the countryside. For the first time in many years, she walked the sacred ancestral lands of Arapa. The five women and Nest Feather had shuffled westward from the arid Santa Teresa Mountains and along the rises and descents of Sierra Calitro's foothills, with each step coming closer to the heart of Arivaipa Canyon and Arivaipa Creek, known to the *nnee* as Little Running Water.

A hawk screeched overhead. Nest Feather looked up to watch its lazy loop in the sky over the mighty saguaros and ocotillos that rose on the low, undulating hills where huge jackrabbits—their long ears twitching—loped about.

Sometimes when looking at the lofty tops of the immense cacti, Nest Feather lagged too far behind the women. She Who Sits in Quiet turned to hurry her charge closer to the group of elders, tired after two days of walking. Yet they continued on, proudly wearing either their handmade camp dresses or threadbare, commercially woven clothes taken in raids upon the White Eyes. As the cold, blustery winds kicked up, the women wrapped their thin shawls closer about their chests.

Nest Feather and the five women descended into meandering Arivaipa Canyon, white with winter's patchy snow. Arapa. Nest Feather walked thoughtfully along the creek. *Listen to Little Running Water gurgling. The massive sycamores and cottonwoods, though barren now of leaves, their roots are still thirsty for the creek's cool water. In only two months' time, they will burst into bloom with the warmth of spring.*

Legendary and sacred though it was, within Arapa lurked great sorrow as well as joy for the Black Rocks People, as Nest Feather knew too well. She studied each sycamore along the banks of Little Running Water. *Did Mother choose this sycamore or the next to shade our family's gowah? I toddled about like a duck then, and later as quickly as the quail. Father would have hunted the scampering does for meat and hides.* Only her father could not scamper away quickly enough from the rifles of the U.S. Army's California Column in a raid led by Captain Tidball. And within twelve moons of those killings in 1863, her mother and her father's second and third wives succumbed to the lingering death. *These past happenings will not color my future, which, I hope, includes a return to this sacred land.*

The women continued westward, following the length of Little Running Water as it fled the canyon's sanctuary and wandered through a wide flat plain where in spring, grama grasses—waving their flags of seeds—would soon stand as tall as Nest Feather's waist. For nearly five miles, the women walked farther west, passing fissured cliffs on either side. They found an easy slope, climbed it, and soon stopped atop a hill covered with brush.

Nest Feather edged forward to see why the women had stopped. Directly ahead, Arivaipa Creek poured into the northward-flowing San Pedro River.

One of the women whispered the name of this confluence of rivers, "Túdotł'ish sikạn." Blue Water Pool. And to the north, on their right, lay Camp Grant.

Several small adobe buildings stretched out in a straight line along a flat area cleared of all grass, cacti, and rocks; perpendicular to them some distance away stood another adobe shack from which pinging sounds of metal on metal rang. In the middle of the open ground stood a flagpole; nearby three cannons poised in silence.

From the hillside, the women saw little activity at the camp. Winds kicked up dust, spraying three uniformed soldiers who halfheartedly repaired slanted roofs made of cut ocotillo branches that gave the adobes their only shade. Two soldiers, leaning against the twisted posts that ill supported those roofs, watched the others work. Smoke rising lazily from a smokestack in the main building seemingly defined the soldiers' attitudes.

Nest Feather dropped to her knees to avoid being seen. *Only the five elders go forward from here.*

She Who Sits in Quiet turned to Nest Feather. "Wait here. Eat and drink sparingly of your cache and water. If we are cast away, or if you see we are in danger, save yourself. Forget us. Go back immediately to our band and tell our leaders."

Their closeness established during Nest Feather's na'íees, they exchanged concern for each other's safety by speaking only with their eyes.

Finally, as Hashké Bahnzin's mother and the three other women began down the hillside, She Who Sits in Quiet whispered, "Do as I say." She turned and joined the other women, one of them hoisting a small twig on which was tied a narrow scrap of material that passed for white.

Nest Feather stretched out on her stomach on the cold, pebbly ground, and through the stems of an ocotillo rising forty feet high in the gray winter sky, watched the women's careful descent down the steep hill, holding onto large boulders and smaller ones to steady their way.

As the women slowly approached the campgrounds, the hammering ceased, then the pinging. Several *innaa*, enemy Anglos, in blue uniforms congregated about the elderly women, who stood respectfully still. Another soldier, with one gold bar on his jacket sleeve, appeared from the main building and approached She Who Sits in Quiet.

Nest Feather held her breath and focused on her kinfolk. She thought of the gleaming eyes of that small brown mouse.

Another man, a Mexican dressed in soldier pants and a muslin shirt similar to that of her leader, walked toward her kinfolk. The wind whipping his black hair that fell over his shoulders, the Mexican spoke with the women before gesturing to Bar on Sleeve.

Nest Feather watched her People enter the main building with Bar on Sleeve and Long Black Hair. This interested the lazy soldiers, who conferred among themselves rather than continuing their work.

All that day and all the next day, Nest Feather kept her vigil. She huddled in depressions of the earth at night, covered by her own thin shawl and whatever brush she gathered from the plants nearby. Finally, on the morning of the third day, all five women came out of the main building. Long Black Hair walked with them to the edge of the campground. There he stayed while the women walked up the mountain to Nest Feather, who did not rise until the women hid her presence from Long Black Hair. None spoke as they returned along the same route taken before. More than a day later, the women neared their ranchería in the Santa Teresas.

Seeing their kinfolk return, the Black Rocks People ran from their gowahs, from their scraping of doeskins, from their making of arrows, and gathered excitedly around the women.

Hashké Bahnzin arrived. "We welcome back our brave warriors, for they *are* warriors who have weathered the conflicts and sufferings of our people. And they have advanced into the camp of the White Eyes, returning with powerful words. And to our smallest woman, our tribe salutes her vigilance."

The leader's mother said, "We asked the White Eyes about our boy taken from us near the Salt River. They knew nothing of him."

Hashké Bahnzin asked the question on all of the People's minds, "Were these men warlike to you?"

"These innaa treated us respectfully. Bar on Sleeve, the nant'án, was concerned for our bodies and was a generous host." She leaned forward to confidentially emphasize her further news. "The White Eyes feast at every meal."

The women spoke of the wondrous delicacies they ate in the Long Building.

And so much of it. Beef. Something orange called carrots. Beans. At their meals, Long Black Hair promised the women they would not become like the hated Bean Eaters. Reeking of ripe tepary beans, the pungence of the Papagos' belches and farts carried for miles on the desert winds.

Nest Feather studied Hashké Bahnzin's dark features as his gaze wandered over his People, clearly disturbed, murmuring of the White Eyes' gorging while they had so very little to eat. She knew of his deep concern. How could the People go forward without assistance?

TUCSON

Chile done, fire out so as not to scorch, masa for tortillas ready, and dark as night for more than an hour—¿Dónde está Raúl?

Firmly wrapped in her serape, Valeria stood outside her casa. Hombres returned home from the fields some time ago.

Boom!

Cannon shot. In the business center. All of Raúl's stories of violence, they are true. Indians!

She must find Raúl. Heart in her throat, Valeria trotted down the street.

Boom!

Hazy smoke rose from the city. Orange flames licked, creating an eerie glow.

¡Raúl—muerto al Zeckendorf's! She dashed through the streets.

Concerned and curious, people came out of their rooms to discover the cause of the hullabaloo and joined Valeria's sprint.

Quickly, up the Calle Real, only blocks away. *It is at Zeckendorf's! ¡Dios!*

Another boom of the cannon. The flames grew, and now she heard shouting.

A crowd gathered at the crossroads at Zeckendorf's and the Stevens House Hotel. Pushing between men wearing sidearms and women grasping their children, Valeria breathlessly emerged in front.

Mister Z pranced before a huge bonfire and shouted, first in German and then in heavily accented English, "The French capitulated! Hoorah! We Prussians have claimed Paris!"

Valeria frantically scanned the spectators' faces illumined by the bright, orange blaze.

"Napoleon the Third is vanquished! Hoorah!" Zeckendorf gestured for the crowd to join him in yelling, "Victory over the French!"

A man lit a handful of dried kindling and ran along another stacked pile of logs and brush, torching it. *¡Raúl!*

Retreating from the heat, Raúl leaned against Zeckendorf's store walls as the logs burst into flame.

Finally as another cannon roared, Valeria made her way through the people, past the bugler from Camp Lowell blasting high notes on his instrument, past some people singing, past people laughing. Everyone watched the licking flames grow higher and hotter.

Running to Raúl, Valeria clasped him to her breast, murmuring "mi amor" into his chest and covering his face and neck with kisses.

Raúl laughed but quickly grew irritated at such a display before other Zeckendorf employees. "Estoy bien. I am fine."

"Tu mano." She cradled his hand in hers.

"A little burn. Nothing more."

Mister Z withdrew from the bonfires, calling out to Raúl, "Many thanks!"

Valeria's large black eyes, gleaming in the bonfires' glow, had only focused on her husband, but when she heard the German speak behind her, she turned.

Mister Z chided Raúl, "Where have you been keeping this lovely lady? Far from cads like me, I hope." With a laugh and an open smile, he took Valeria's hand in his and kissed it.

Raúl spoke, "My wife, Valeria."

"The name suits. A beautiful name, a beautiful lady."

"Muchas gracias." Valeria blushed.

"Your husband's a good employee. Very smart with numbers. If there's anything I can do for you, let me know." Mister Z stepped away.

Raúl whispered to Valeria, "I need to finish up here. It's cold. Go back. I'll join you very soon."

"Bueno."

While Raúl tended the bonfires, Valeria noticed that Zeckendorf remained. Taking the man at his word, she neared the German and carefully pronounced her words in English, "Mister Zeckendorf, Raúl and I wish to celebrate our arrival in Tucson. You said we might ask your help." She smiled into Zeckendorf's rimless eyeglasses speckled with ashes.

TUCSON

Raúl admired how beautiful Valeria looked—her color up, her hair tumbling in curls down her back, her eyes sparkling. He saw the beginning of his wife's return to him. He also realized how daring Valeria had been as he scanned the recognizable faces of Tucson's leaders already gathered at Congress Hall.

Valeria knew it was doubt and reluctance that dampened Raúl's spirits. Resorting to her ready sauciness, she wiggled her shoulders, bare but for her shawl on this cold night, and rustled her skirt of many vibrant hues, full and ruffled below her hips, startling one matron and husband walking through the doorway. Throwing back her head, Valeria laughed. "Ay, muchacho, esta noche es por la gente prominente. Entremos."

As proudly as the truly prominent citizens they represented themselves to be that night, Valeria and Raúl entered. He presented their tickets—the ones Mister Z had purchased—at the reservation booth inside. Securing these for his newest clerk— who swept the floors, stacked the shelves, and sold the goods—and his comely wife constituted either Mister Z's generosity or his immense sense of humor. However, decked out as they were in his bolero jacket and her figure-clinging fiesta dress, both handsewn by Valeria, Raúl defied anyone to say that the Obregóns weren't the grandest looking couple in town.

They inched forward into the flow of people; it was all they could do with the logjam of two hundred prominent personages of Tucson, most of them still near the entrance. Spying a slender opening, Valeria pulled Raúl through, and they found themselves by a huge, ornately carved mahogany bar that stretched from one end of the room to the other. Most of the women continued on to the next room, leaving their husbands to order drinks. The few words Valeria could understand over the roar of voices in the cavernous room all pertained to the final deliberations on critical issues made by the legislature. She supposed many of these men lined up before the bar were legislators, who, having completed their assembly that afternoon, took advantage of the party by tossing back a few whiskeys before they returned home.

Fascinated by the four bartenders rapidly pouring two fingers of liquor in squat glasses and expensive burgundies in stemmed, crystal-cut wine glasses, Valeria and Raúl watched them pass the drinks to partygoers over the bar top, along which stood a phalanx of Tucson's best—Bill Oury, Jesús María Elías, Sam Hughes, Hiram Stevens, Ed Fish, Sidney DeLong, and the effervescent William Zeckendorf. Juan Elías, deep in conversation with a lovely señorita, leaned on the end of the bar.

That the Obregóns' pretense of importance was tested the moment upon entering tickled Valeria. Her vibrant laughter at its implausibility brought immediate attention from Tucson's leaders. One look at Raúl and she knew he was concerned they would be evicted because the men at the bar knew his true station in life. Valeria looked Raúl in the eye. "We are worthy to be at this celebration. You are active at the town meetings. And . . . you are the best-looking man here." Before Raúl could protest, she inserted her arm through his and led him to Mister Z.

To the strains of a waltz from Strauss played by several Camp Lowell and local musicians in the other room, Valeria said, "Buenos noches, Señor Zeckendorf. Happy to see you again, and thank you so very much." Catching the admiration of all the men at the bar, Valeria smiled proudly back at Raúl, who gripped the lapels of his ruffled bolero jacket; his swarthiness and broken nose offset by black hair and tight pants lent Raúl an intriguing and debonair appearance.

Having made their pleasantries, the Obregóns turned away and followed other newly arrived couples into the next room, where most of the tables and chairs had been removed to make room for dancing.

Watching the departing couple, Oury leaned over to Mister Z. "Was that your new clerk?"

"And his wife. Such chutzpah!" Zeckendorf guffawed. "I love it!"

Although Raúl and Valeria had never waltzed, they studied the few brave couples who took to the floor first. Ladies placed their left hand in the middle of the gentleman's right arm and their right hand in the man's left hand. Stepping backward, women glided and turned about the floor at the gentle insistence of their partner. Valeria knew she and Raúl could attempt this, given the slow one-two-three rhythm, the repetitive steps, and being seasoned dancers.

Smiling coquettishly at her husband, Valeria extended her hand, which Raúl claimed to lead her onto the dance floor. They laughed at their first awkward steps, but after a check to the left and the right as to what the other dancing couples did, they glided gracefully around the room to the admiring notice of many, including several ladies standing at the punch table.

In their dizzying waltz, which Valeria and Raúl now augmented with embellishments, they dipped and twirled past three women holding filled lemonade cups.

Valeria recognized Atanacia Hughes and Jesús María's pregnant wife, Teresa, but not the tall, thin Anglo woman. "We are being watched." Valeria inclined her head toward the women at the lemonade table.

On the next revolution, Raúl whispered, "It's Larcena Scott. The Anglo. She and her husband come into the store. Everyone makes a fuss over her."

"¿Por qué?"

"Many of her family were killed by Indians. She herself was stabbed many times and thrown off a cliff and pelted with stones."

"No."

"She crawled fourteen days without food. In winter. In the Santa Rita Mountains."

"Stop." Valeria released her hand from Raúl's grip and looked up at him. "You love terrible stories."

"It's true. They blame Eskiminzin." Raúl led Valeria toward the lemonade.

"Valeria," welcomed Atanacia. "¿Cómo está?"

Thrilled that Mrs. Hughes—the wife of a prominent leader, she had learned—recognized her, Valeria beamed. "Muy bien, gracias. Y usted?"

"Yo también." Hesitantly Atanacia touched Valeria's skirt, with its ruffles and flounces, which had enchanted everyone. "¿Hiciste esto?"

"Sí, señora. I make it myself."

"Muy bien hecha. Muy linda. La costura es muy fina."

Larcena chuckled. "I don't know what's been said, but that skirt is plain beautiful."

"Atanacia, tal vez a ella le gustaría ver su máquina de coser." In her low, lilting voice, Teresa's suggestion that the young woman might like to see Atanacia's sewing machine was difficult to hear over the band's playing of a fast gavotte.

"Por supuesto. Valeria, le invito a pasar por mi casa." Atanacia loved inviting people to her home; her favorite pastime was demonstrating her considerable sewing skills on her Singer.

Beaming brightly, Valeria laughed. "¿Cuándo?"

"Por la mañana."

Tomorrow. Of course. "De acuerdo."

Raúl gave a small bow to the ladies and pulled Valeria onto the dance floor. His lips close to her ear, he whispered, "Enhorabuena. Congratulations." He spun her away at arm's length. Her admired skirt floated out, and as he reeled her back tightly into his chest, her skirt twisted around her slim, shapely legs.

His face lowered an inch from hers. She recognized that devilish look. "Don't you dare."

"We are married."

"We are new here."

"You want to make an impression."

Laughing, Valeria took a step back. Raising her skirt several inches, she strutted around Raúl. *He smirks at me. I'll give him something to smirk about.* Raising her hands over her head, Valeria smartly clapped them. Raúl did the same. To the much faster beat for a jarabe only they heard, they danced.

We made a dent, a small dent, into the world of Tucson's elite citizens.

WEDNESDAY, FEBRUARY 15, 1871

Her insides twirled like the turning blades of the tall windmill in the Hugheses' back garden. More excited than nervous, Valeria approached the door of the rectangular adobe home and knocked. La criada answered and drew back to welcome the friend of the señora.

Atanacia, in another expensive dress, stood in a doorway at the end of the hall. "Bienvenida, Valeria."

"Gracias, Atanacia." Valeria crossed in front of the dining room, its doorway drapes open, allowing a glance in. *That room is larger than my entire casa.* She joined Atanacia in a small adjacent room dominated by a polished wooden desk over an iron base with open-weave sides and a footrest. Incorporated into an iron bar, which connected one side of the iron base to the other, were big letters spelling SINGER. Atop the wooden desk sat another mysterious black iron object, adorned with a small emblem embellished with little flowers, all painted in gold.

"Oh . . ."

Atanacia pointed to the black iron machine. "La máquina de coser."

"Es muy linda." Once Atanacia sat before the sewing machine, Valeria looked at the front, the handwheel on the right side, the needle that descended on the left and underneath, where Atanacia rested her feet on the treadle.

"¿Dónde la compró?" *Where did Atanacia buy this? Here in Tucson?*

"San Francisco. En nuestra luna de miel."

Atanacia rocked her feet, causing the needle to rapidly travel up and down a hole in the base of the machine. Valeria retreated a step, startled by the loud clacking sound. *An expensive honeymoon present. People in California must be used to its noise.*

"Permítame mostrársela." Demonstrating to Valeria how the machine worked, Atanacia placed two small pieces of material under the presser foot and rocked her feet. The spindle on top spun, feeding out thread to the needle that jabbed the cloth Atanacia guided through the machine until finished.

Clipping the thread well away from the machine, Atanacia held up her work and handed the sample to Valeria, who put her finest gloves on so that her hands—rough from sweeping the dirt floor and wringing a chicken's neck for dinner—wouldn't pull the thread or the material.

Valeria took in a little breath of anticipation and opened the flyleaf of sewn material squares. No stitches showed on the face. She turned the material over and studied the stitches on the back. *Perfect. Each stitch is the same length and holds the same tension within each stitch. Even stitches. This machine works very well.* "Funciona muy bien."

From a basket at the foot of the machine, Atanacia drew out a finished handkerchief, its edges rolled and sewn by the Singer sewing machine and, finally, embroidered by hand.

Valeria cradled the sample. *I've never held such fine work in my hands.* Atanacia's ripple of laughter embarrassed Valeria, but she turned the marvelous handkerchief this way and that, inspecting every stitch, every tuck. *Could I ever do anything so fine? My best work is our fiesta outfits. Oh, what endless possibilities la máquina could have. If only I could sew like Señora Hughes.* Valeria spoke with the speed of the Singer, "Enséñeme, por favor." *Teach me, please.*

Over the next half hour, Atanacia explained the parts of the sewing machine and how they worked and sat Valeria down in the chair to try the machine herself. "Pruébela."

Resting her feet on the treadle, Valeria accidentally pressed on it. The clacking noise disconcerted her again, but she laughed this time. Repeating what she had seen Atanacia do, she placed two squares under the presser and gently rocked her feet. Slowly, slowly the needle moved up and down to the end of the material. Clipping the thread, Valeria critically eyed her seam. *Perfect.*

Valeria jumped up, throwing her arms around Atanacia. *I'm a success!* Like small children once more, they jumped and hopped in circles, laughing and giggling, until Atanacia stopped.

"¿Quiere probarla otra vez?"

Of course I want to try again. "Sí." Valeria again sat before the sewing machine and grabbed more squares of cloth.

✦✦✦

That night in their casa as they ate, Valeria explained in great detail how the machine worked and how much she liked using it. She thrust her sewn samples under Raúl's nose. "I am a scientist. I experiment. I succeed. Ahora soy científica."

Raúl, flagged from a busy day, replied, "Es muy linda." A silence fell between them as he shoved food into his mouth. "No one was killed today."

Admiring her samples, Valeria offhandedly said, "Bueno."

MONDAY, MARCH 13, 1871

On a private ranch south of Camp Grant and adjacent to the west end of Arivaipa Creek, Nest Feather whacked at the strands of alfalfa with her small knife, one of three skinning knives she carried for preparation of cowhides or doeskins. The working rhythm she employed lasted as long as ten minutes before she needed a short break. Standing tall, Nest Feather placed her hands on the small of her back and leaned backward. Now she would inspect her knives for any imperfections.

She surveyed the blade, finding a little ding on the cutting edge, possibly made by striking a stone. From her skirt pocket, she withdrew a whetstone, dipped it in nearby Arivaipa Creek, and placed it rough side up on the ground. Nest Feather knelt and angled the knife's cutting edge against the whetstone. Holding the handle in one hand, and with the other hand, lightly pressing the blade down, she ran the edge upward over the whetstone ten times. Turning the blade over, she sharpened the other side, paying meticulous attention to the area where the ding had been. Finally she repeated the sharpening process using the fine side of the stone. As an experienced preparer of skins, Nest Feather could tell the sharpness of her blade without testing it with her finger or cutting through a stalk. Only a very sharp blade, honed after three or four passes, drew the bloody flesh away from the doeskin or cowhide without tearing the precious suede beneath.

Using her skirt, Nest Feather wiped the honed blade, which gleamed in the late afternoon sun, already dipping low in the sky and sending temperatures lower. *I am happy with the fine edge of the knife blade. Happy to be at work. Happy my People have returned to Arapa.*

A week after the Arivaipa women went to Camp Grant, they had returned for manta, coarse squares of heavy cloth for making clothing, and more importantly, to ask if Bar on Sleeve would speak with Hashké Bahnzin. Within another week's time, Bar on Sleeve and the Apache leader had agreed that his Arivaipa band could move from the Santa Teresas back to Arivaipa Canyon within sight of the camp. The Black Rocks People stood in lines every other day to receive their rations in the open parade ground. Soldiers, befuddled by their names, made markings in a book of the numbers in their families and distributed one pound of beef and one pound of either flour or corn per person. After a delay, Stoneman, the commander over all Bars On Sleeves, gave final approval of this arrangement; however, in exchange for rations received, they were required to harvest hay for the camp.

Hashké Bahnzin and his friend Charles McKinney, the owner of the property on which Nest Feather harvested, came toward her. McKinney called out, "Good afternoon!"

Not understanding what the White Eyes said, Nest Feather waited to greet the men in her native tongue. "The hay falls with grace."

McKinney smiled but shook his head good-naturedly. "This little girl cuts more and hauls more hay than anyone I've ever seen." He turned to Nest Feather. "Are you enjoying the work?"

The Apache leader winked at Nest Feather to indicate the White Eyes' good humor, but no one answered McKinney's dizzying fog of English, as they were interrupted by the sound of something rolling heavily up the main road. Cracks of a whip and an Anglo's foreign tongue loudly urging the oxen and mules concerned Nest Feather, although Indian warriors standing sentinel with rifles rushed forward to protect the leader, Nest Feather, and three other women working the hayfields. All gathered at the strange sounds.

Anglo outriders trotted up the hill. Nest Feather could see the anxiety in the White Eyes' faces at the sight of peaceful Indians gathered closely by the roadside. The outriders galloped back to the first of four high-sided cargo wagons coming into view. Its bullwhacker shouted something back to the other wagons, but none stopped.

McKinney stepped forward, waving his arms overhead, and shouted, "Hello, boys! About time we saw you come up that hill."

More outriders galloped forward, carefully keeping themselves between the Indians and the wagons, the beds piled high with bales, bundles, crates, and unknown goods under canvas.

Nest Feather particularly noticed a slender man seated on the bench next to the driver of the first wagon. In his mouth hung a smoking pipe much smaller and shorter than the nnee's ceremonial pipe. But it was his chin that fascinated her. It sprouted many dark hairs that covered his entire lower face. Even the outriders had hairy lips. *These innaa do not pluck out their hairs as do Apache men.*

Pipe Smoker stood, one hand to the bullwhacker's shoulder so as not to fall off. "McKinney! Are you all right?"

"Grand. Stop by sometime."

Nest Feather, never having seen a White Eyes closely until their return to Arapa, was intrigued by the innaa's strange looks.

After Pipe Smoker regained his seat and the four wagons and the riders passed by, continuing on to Camp Grant, most of the Apaches, Hashké Bahnzin, and McKinney departed with an incline of their heads—a friendly gesture.

One sentinel, his hair cropped to his shoulders, remained by Nest Feather. "They arrive from Tsee idzisgoláné."

His pronunciation of "Tsee idzisgoláné" sounds strange and rather juicy. She asked to make certain, "Rocks Which Have Many Dips?"

His broad smile revealed a missing upper front tooth. "Tucson," he said stiffly in the Anglo language.

Nest Feather focused on the warrior's right ear rather than the gaping hole in his teeth. "Is that far?" Some People hunted in that region, bringing back butchered meat and news of more and more innaa settling there. The Anglos' ranchería lay to the south along the banks of the Santa Cruz River.

"An easy two suns' ride for someone who knows the way. Like me." His black eyes twinkled with his boasting, his tongue resting behind where his tooth should have been.

"You have been?"

"Several times. With plans for more." He turned his head toward a chirping signal. A fellow sentinel beckoned him with a wave of his arm.

"I wish you good hunting," said Nest Feather, departing for the hayfield with some reluctance. This young warrior had singled her out for conversation. Only a few men of marrying age lived in her band. With two more bands of Apaches arriving for the safety of Camp Grant and in need of rations, perhaps more eligible young men would be among them.

Nest Feather was distracted by something on her arm—something light but stinging. A large mosquito drew blood from her arm. In the days since their arrival, the mosquitoes had become more and more annoying to her and the rest of the band, but particularly to the women cutting the hay. Hashké Bahnzin said that in time he would ask the nant'án of the camp about moving farther east along Arivaipa Creek, where fewer of these nuisances dwelled. *I would be so thankful if Sister, her husband, his first wife, and I could move deep into the canyon, beautiful and lush with plants and trees—the hair of the earth—where many birds chirp their beautiful songs heard by my ancestors long ago.*

✦ ✦ ✦

Other than the chill in the air and the increased winds through the canyons, Andrew Cargill thought the trip north from Tucson to Camp Grant had been uneventful, leaving him time to contemplate the vicious circle that put a few dollars in his pocket. *Everyone has worked for a military supplier at one time or another. It happens to be my time. Don't get too impatient. Lord & Williams is just fine. Until my ship comes in, I'll stay put for a while longer.*

Cargill's thoughts were interrupted when his train came over a small rise, revealing the unusual sight of Indians—Arivaipa Apaches, and women at that—harvesting winter alfalfa near the banks of the San Pedro River, the mosquito-infested stream that meandered close to Camp Grant.

With his teeth firmly clenching his pipe stem, he said, "Will you look at that?"

Indians working near the camp and not hiding in the surrounding mountains was out of the ordinary.

When the two outriders rode back and pointed at the Indians, he said, "Leave 'em be." But then he saw Charles McKinney standing with Eskiminzin among the Indians. Fearing McKinney had been taken prisoner, Cargill called out to his friend. But McKinney seemed his regular, affable self.

Cargill and his American outriders and drivers closely eyed the Arivaipa Apaches as they drove past. The women wore threadbare Anglo clothes in the forty- to fifty-degree weather.

Among them, a tiny girl, plain of face and no more than eight or nine, he guessed, held a knife. They locked eyes. Before the war, Cargill had seen that kind of slavery in his travels from New York City through the South to visit his mother's family in Hinds County. *I had hoped our Confederate loss ensured slavery had seen its last.*

Indians harvesting hay with small knives sent his mind racing—unexpected news, and not altogether good, at least for the retail suppliers of goods and the Anglos and Mexican ranchers in the Tucson area. One of his four cargo wagons was heavy with contracted hay from Tucson.

As the wagons clattered on, Cargill noticed some Apache men watching their women gather large stashes of cut stalks, lash them together with long burlap strips, and secure the bunch on their backs with a head strap. Lifting and lugging the heavy load, shoots falling on either side, the women walked toward Camp Grant, which Cargill knew to be the dirtiest, most ill-kept military establishment in the West. More than a few of its soldiers resorted to desertion or suicide, believing them suitable alternatives to continued military service at the malaria-prone U.S. Army post.

Taking a long draw from his pipe, Cargill blew out smoke and sucked on the pipe's mouthpiece, its sound harmonizing with the rattle of the cargo in the long bed of the tall-sided wagon. Butchered beef lay alongside ammunition, hay, and goods ordered by the camp's sutler.

Cargill's train rolled into the camp's open parade ground, where Indians held red tickets and stood in a line outside the sutler's store. In stark contrast some camp soldiers continued their routine: casual stirrings, smoking, and lounging about in front of a shed, from which appeared Joseph Felmer, the German blacksmith. Soot and sweat streamed down his face. "You fuckin' well took youse time. I'm low on ingot and high on homemade rotgut."

Lewd and funny Joe—one of a kind. Some other hard-swearing, hard-living men I've known—some now in high places—aren't worth the time of day. "Last wagon is all yours."

Cargill jumped down from the wagon when the train finally lurched to a stop before the adjutant's office. At the adjacent corral he saw Apache women dumping their hay before a private, who weighed it, made notes in a ledger, and gave each woman a red ticket stub. All sorts of comings and goings of Apaches in peace at a military facility, such as it was. *Never a more bizarre sight in all my born days.*

Cargill slapped his hat against his thigh, knocking off a fine layer of trail dust, stomped on the ground several times to get the circulation back in both legs after the long ride, and entered Lieutenant Royal E. Whitman's office.

The warmth of the potbelly stove immediately smothered Cargill, who opened his heavy jacket. Behind a desk sat a man of about thirty, squinting as he labored over a ledger, writing notes in the margins.

"Lieutenant, Andrew Cargill."

"Of course. How are you?" Whitman rose from his chair and shook Cargill's extended hand.

"Captain Stanwood away from the Post?"

"Yes, on a scout. He left me in charge in his stead. We need meat. I hope you brought plenty of carcasses." Whitman, being from Maine, disregarded pronouncing the letter *r*.

"What's happened here?" Cargill swept a gesture toward the door, indicating what he'd observed outside.

"Something fine. After talks, the Apaches came in. At first a hundred and fifty. Now we're up to three hundred in three and a half weeks."

"Interesting. Back out on the main road, I saw them harvesting what early hay they could find."

"For which they're paid tickets, swapped at the store for goods—manta mostly. For clothes. You saw how poorly clothed they are."

"We brought hay."

"You need not bring more."

Such a simple request. Such an impossibility. *This will not be welcome news to Lord & Williams.* A chuckle escaped Cargill's throat. "We have a contract."

"The Indians harvest hay under existing contract terms."

Out of habit Cargill drew his pipe from his coat pocket, sucked on it, and continued talking while balancing the pipe between his teeth. "Well, I guess that's something you'll have to take up with Dr. Lord and Mr. Williams themselves. Right now we need to unload, get these stores checked in, and receive payment. I'll go over the books early tomorrow morning."

Cargill and Whitman left the warmth of the small room and into the cold winds whipping around the adobe buildings where several soldiers accepted the goods that the bullwhackers and outriders unloaded while another soldier checked ledger entries for accuracy. Cargill's mind and attention wavered from business. He found himself constantly gazing at the Indians. *They joke among themselves. Look how thin they are. How wild they look.*

Whitman observed Cargill's distraction. "They came down from the Santa Teresas seeking food."

"This is all commendable, Lieutenant. However, I wasn't aware that the purpose of a military post was harboring Apaches." Cargill watched Whitman's visage glaze over and his chest puff out.

"They are peaceful. I wrote to Colonel Stoneman, apprising him of the situation. Per his reply and orders, the Apaches are welcome here to live and work. We shall continue as begun."

Given Whitman's defensive attitude, Cargill tamped down the warm tobacco in his pipe bowl and smiled into the weak afternoon sun. "Folks back home in the eastern states—with no Indian problems—particularly cater to the idea of extending charity to Apaches."

"I'm from Maine."

"How-some-ever, I'm merely alerting you that charity sometimes stops close to home. Folks in Tucson supply you with hay. You see, those suppliers might get a little bit upset."

"Cattle and beef contracts still stand."

Cargill chuckled, pipe bowl jostling. "Suppliers tend to appreciate earning money from the military just as they appreciate the protection the military is here to provide them."

"I saw the Apaches' need. They came in peace." Whitman defiantly watched the goods being offloaded.

Cargill realized that the lieutenant wanted—needed—some form of assurance. "When you believe you do the right thing, life is good."

Along the postal and supply routes, Cargill had come across too many instances of murder, depredations, and mutilations to believe fully the quick transformation of Apaches. And yet only good could come of it. Under President Grant's current peace policy, Indians were accepted as fellow human beings and afforded food and Christian guidance. However, most folks in Tucson only thought a good Indian was a dead Indian.

When the last of the goods were finally unloaded, Whitman squinted into the early-setting winter sun. "I must return to my office."

"It's late in a short day, Lieutenant. I hoped my teamsters and I could camp around by the corral."

"Of course."

Cargill eyed Whitman as he disappeared in his office. *He seems decent enough, but whether Whitman is naïve or something more I can't decide.*

At the blacksmith's shack where a new supply of iron ingots had been stacked, Cargill watched Felmer douse the anvil fire. Dark gray smoke and ashes rose up with a loud hiss. The strong, acrid smell sent Cargill into a fit of coughing. Felmer led him outside.

When his coughing was under control, Cargill pointed toward the Apaches streaming out of the post sutler's store with manta cloth squares. "Things seem a little different this trip."

Felmer laughed as he bolted and locked the blacksmith shack's wide door. In a thick German accent he said, "Yes, sir. A whole lot different. I'm told my wife's mother came in yesterday. By Apache belief, if I look at my mother-in-law, I'll go blind." Felmer's laughter rolled around his throat in a phlegmy gargle of sound. "From what I remember she looks like, any gott-damn man looking at her would go blind."

Cargill couldn't help but laugh. "You know these people."

"Well. Very well." Felmer pointed to the undulating hills, studded with forty-foot-tall saguaros. What might be mistaken for a number of small animals crested the far berms, descended into a dip between knolls, and were lost to sight. When the figures gained the top of a close hill and progressed toward Cargill and Felmer, the forms acquired their true appearance. More Apaches. At least fifty.

Deep lines around Felmer's eyes were black with soot from stoking his forge. "They come in every day. Eskiminzin's whole band is here. This is a different one. I know these hills. Expect more, lots more. You'll be hauling more beef."

Some Apaches arriving at the parade ground carried rifles.

"My Lord, they're armed." Cargill's sudden flare of nerves wasn't quelled by Felmer's amused squint; it only vexed Cargill more. He knew too well that identifying firearms constituted vital information in Arizona. "From here those look like needle guns. At McKinney's hayfield, the braves carried Springfields." Cargill grimaced. Needle guns used long bullets shaped like the Confederate submarine, the *H. L. Hunley*, and were equally as destructive.

"For certain. You're a smart man, Herr Andrew. Tell me how they got 'em." Felmer laughed again and slapped Cargill's back. "Goot to see you. I go now to my gowah, my squaw"—Felmer patted his stomach, protruding strangely with something stashed beneath his shirt—"and my fresh whiskey."

TUESDAY, MARCH 14, 1871

Cargill and his men all slept with one eye open. Bedding out in the open in Indian country was a dangerous proposition at any time, but having hundreds of Apaches within several hundred yards increased their unease. Not taking word of the Apaches' peace at face value, none of Cargill's men lessened their practiced vigilance. At first light, nervous and biting at the bit to get going south to Tucson, his men saddled their horses and hitched up the wagons. Cargill assured them that going over the books, his primary reason for accompanying the loads, would not take long. He banged on the door of the sutler's store.

Fred Austin opened it with a tin coffee mug in hand. "I thought you'd be ready early for the books."

Cargill accepted a mug of piping hot coffee with groggy thanks and leaned on the waist-high wooden counter to study Austin's ledger with a critical eye. *Neat. Thorough. All looks in order.* He transferred some information into his own ledger that he kept with him at all times. "Tell me about the hay."

"One day, not too long after Eskiminzin and his band came in, Whitman arrived at my door. He asked me to fire the Mexicans I had cutting hay on our contracted land."

"Whitman asked?"

"Yep. He wanted me to hire the Apaches instead."

"In exchange for tickets."

"Tickets for manta."

"Has he asked for any other accommodations?"

"Nope."

Cargill sipped his now tepid coffee. "I keep my hands clean. You do the same." Finding his pipe, he tamped down the tobacco and sucked on the mouthpiece. "Any recent Apache trouble?" Cargill tacitly referred to Camp Grant soldiers' history of retaliating for Anglo losses of men and property by raiding the rancherías of Arivaipa Apaches, most recently in September '69.

"Not here."

"Gentleman." A voice with a Maine accent.

At the store's entrance stood Lieutenant Whitman and Concepción Biella, the camp's interpreter and scout, whose black hair fell below his shoulders. Alongside them stood a barrel-chested, dark-skinned Apache.

"This is Eskiminzin, one of the leaders of the Arivaipa Apaches."

Cargill came around the counter. *Since Apaches have no words for "good morning," what does one say in greeting?* "I . . . welcome this meeting."

The interpreter grunted his words, listened to Hashké Bahnzin's response, and turned back to Cargill. "He says, 'Numbers on skins do not tell the entire tale.'"

Cargill, not anticipating that response, answered, "Tell him, 'Anglos read the numbers, hoping for a happy ending.'"

Hashké Bahnzin heard the interpreter's translation and sternly looked at Cargill; a wry grin broadened his lips, and he chuckled.

Whitman seemed satisfied with the encounter. "I wanted you both to meet at the beginning of this peaceful and long-lasting venture."

Despite the few words spoken between them, Cargill felt impressed by Eskiminzin's restraint, intellect, and wit, all contributing factors for this Pinal Indian's rapid assimilation into the Arivaipa band after his first marriage to an Arivaipa maiden and his subsequent rise to leader. However, that did not lessen Cargill's concerns about the Apaches' continued raiding and killing. *Tucson has seen so much of that. Will they believe one peaceful Apache leader? That same leader who is widely reviled as the most evil of the Apaches in the immediate vicinity?*

TUCSON

Bullets pinged off the rock, missing the whiskey bottle. Raúl hung his head.

"Do you know what you did wrong?" Juan walked up to him and without a thought, arm outstretched at shoulder height, lifted his pistol and pulled the trigger. The bottle exploded into splinters of glass.

"My trigger finger wasn't on the guard."

"Es muy importante. Look down the sight, your thumb cocks the hammer, and *then* move your forefinger onto the trigger. Accuracy, not always speed."

"My brother Mateo outshot everyone since he was nine. I hope he'd be proud I'm taking it up with you. But back then he mocked me for loving what studies I took."

"Shooting is your course now." Pacing, Juan returned to Raúl. "Do you like this horse better than the others at the livery?"

"Sí, stronger and faster. Pero, I am not a born rider like you."

Juan sat on a boulder and looked down from Sentinel Hill onto the village of Tucson. When his grandfather was a soldier at El Presidio, Spanish military sentinels watched for approaching Indians from this surveillance spot. "You don't need to be a born rider, just not a dead one." Juan opened his top shirt buttons and revealed a dark, irregular scar on his left shoulder near the collarbone. "Apache bullet entered my arm, coming out here. I was asleep at the few acres we had at the time, not far from Camp Grant. The Indians thought I was Jesús." He rebuttoned his shirt. "We practice for protection. For you. For your wife."

"Any word from the governor?"

Juan shook his head. "No, I think he went to California first to see Stoneman before going to Washington. It will be weeks, maybe a couple of months. Things keep getting worse."

"I've tried to think of new solutions."

"There are none. Subdue the Indian, put him on a reservation, or kill him before he kills you. There are no other solutions. Put that in your head and study it."

After a lull, Raúl stood. "I will keep thinking."

"You're good at that. Let's ride."

✦✦✦

A light breeze carrying the last of winter's chill whipped through the Hugheses' front door. Yet when Valeria walked inside with a dress over her arm, she immediately felt warm and comfortable because of the house's two-foot-thick adobe walls that moderated inside temperatures all year long.

La criada told Valeria to proceed to the sewing room. In passing the dining room, she noticed that its drapes were in disarray. With the sole exception of her first visit, the drapes had always been completely drawn. The base of one panel appeared kicked back, displaying some of the dining room's interior.

In only a quick passing glance, Valeria saw Atanacia and an Anglo man lean over the dining room table and strike a mallet on a metal die positioned on what she took to be a rifle.

Crates, some open and some closed, lined the floor. From the corner of her eye, she saw that Atanacia, holding up the gun for inspection, turned toward the partly opened drapes. Not wanting to snoop, Valeria walked on.

A short time later Atanacia bustled through the sewing room doorway, greeting Valeria with a kiss on the cheek and a burst of rapid Spanish, "How is your dress coming?" The waist of Atanacia's full skirt sat high over a bump.

In the mere second it took for Valeria to realize that fertile Atanacia was again with child, Valeria found the pluck to still her own jealousy that tossed her about like a windstorm. She accepted Atanacia's kiss and returned it on her hostess's dark cheek.

Valeria quickly unfolded the finished tailored dress of silk in a forest green and brown print; the full, gored skirt trailed slightly, and its overskirt gathered at the back with four sashes cascading down. Patiently she waited while Atanacia assessed the quality of sewing.

Atanacia's eyes danced. Her student had achieved perfection with every stitch. "Has dominado perfectamente todos las puntadas de coser. Enhorabuena."

Overcome with relief, Valeria laughed and hugged Atanacia, but feeling the bulge of her friend's stomach, Valeria pulled away.

Atanacia sat, leaning toward Valeria. "I've told several friends about you."

"¿Sí?"

"They need a reliable seamstress to alter some of their clothes. One friend has taken to eating too many chocolates." Atanacia grinned and shook her head. "They would pay well."

"Oh." *Never has the thought of sewing for money entered my head.* "Yes, yes, I could help them."

"My friends aren't satisfied with several other seamstresses. Too many delays, too many excuses. Bad work."

"I would be very prompt. I will work all day long."

Atanacia again smiled. "If the alteration requires it, and I'm not otherwise busy, I could let you use la máquina from time to time."

Valeria took Atanacia's hands in hers and kissed them. "You are so good and so good to me. Muchas, muchas gracias."

"I like to be of assistance. And, of course, if they are pleased, your name could circulate widely for more work."

Am I to believe I can earn money here? Raúl will be so proud of me. We could get better rooms. Her mind spinning as rapidly as a thread spool, Valeria relinquished the seat before the Singer to Atanacia and sat in one of the side chairs.

Often that afternoon spent sewing individual projects, Valeria found her eyes straying to Atanacia's stomach instead of her friend's animated round face. Valeria pondered how it felt to have a growing baby inside, pressing on your bladder, pressing its existence into every moment of your life. From what had been so brief for Valeria, she tried to recapture a few small details of fading memories.

Every time Atanacia turned from the sewing machine, Valeria had to deflect her gaze from the girth of Mrs. Hughes. She hoped it wasn't obvious. It probably was, betrayed by her flushed face, the heat of which consumed her. *Concentrate on the work. That's your purpose for coming.*

TUCSON

Raúl Obregón walked into what seemed a cockfight. A firestorm of simultaneous screaming, shouting, and name-calling enflamed the Tucsonenses, gesticulating with raised arms and fists. Raúl's ears filled with a madness of sound.

"More deaths! What is Stoneman going to do?"

"They dragged Trinidad out and butchered her in the woods."

"Poor Wooster newly settled."

"Tubac's deserted."

"Bill Cook killed at Crittenden!"

"Where's military protection?"

Fish and Tully, again unable to control the meeting, were joined down front by Bill Oury. In midair he snapped his quirt, unleashing the fury of its ten-inch, forked lash—its crack as loud as a pistol shot.

The courtroom stilled.

Raúl realized, having seen Oury several times, that like a rattler, you had to approach him with great care and keep some distance.

Tully reacted quickly. "Thank you, Bill. Now folks, let's settle down. We're all upset. What we need are ideas."

Next to Raúl rose a tall, thin man from New England, whose profile and presence Raúl thought could rival that of a stage actor. "Sidney DeLong here. Perhaps we might take another look at Mr. Oury's suggestion of using the talents of our townspeople."

"In what way, Sidney?" Interest aroused in Tully.

"I have come to believe that it is imperative that the military negotiate with us in regard to our public safety—not individually but as a whole. We need to form a force. A . . . committee. A committee of those who will stand up to the military, give them our opinions, and extend to them the use of our talents."

Whispers and murmurs of approval from Raúl and others hummed throughout the courtroom for DeLong, whose opinion mattered to them as he was an experienced Indian agent and new third partner of Tully & Ochoa, military suppliers.

"In that way we should, perchance, have a regular, conversant understanding of each other. One could only hope that it would be a better understanding."

"I'm in, Sid," called out one man, as others joined in.

"Me, too!"

"Good thinking."

Oury raised his voice over the crowd, "What's the first step?"

"Well, Bill, we need to act fast in this organization. I've word today that Colonel Stoneman will be at Sacaton in a few days' time."

SATURDAY, MARCH 25, 1871

Night having quickly fallen after their fast-paced ride from Tucson, Raúl accepted the reins from Juan while Oury, DeLong, and another man unknown to him tied their horses to the rail. The intensity on Oury's face alone made Raúl's stomach churn.

While the others bounded through the front door of the old Butterfield Station, Juan lingered to give instructions in a strained voice, "Wait outside and watch the horses. Only representatives from Tucson's Committee of Public Safety are to meet Stoneman."

"Claro." As Juan entered, Raúl caught a glimpse of the others waiting in a congested group inside the front door.

A man called out to Raúl before the door closed, "I'm DeWitt Thompson, station keeper for the Gila River Indian Agency. Sorry, but there's little room inside."

"Estoy bien, gracias." The door closed, and as he looked around, Raúl tethered his and Juan's horses to the rail. No one in sight now. *Mierda, I'm here. I'm taking a look.* He edged toward a front window from which the dim light of several lanterns shone brightly into the cold, dark night. Careful to remain undetected, he looked inside. A man in an army uniform, his back to the window, leaned over a large, unfolded piece of paper spread out before him. Taking him to be Colonel George Stoneman, Raúl chanced discovery by inching forward some more. *Un mapa, a map. This must be muy importante.*

Stoneman ran one of his long fingers along several areas on the map. Apparently satisfied with one landmark, he tapped his finger there thrice.

Raúl leaned closer, holding his breath so his exhalation would not be detected on the window pane. He could make out on the paper only three words: Los Angeles, California.

Disgusted that Stoneman wasted time on something personal rather than concentrate on military affairs, Raúl stepped away from the window and rolled a secret cigarette, the taste of which he would somehow mask from Valeria.

Inside, Juan and the others at first didn't mind being crammed uncomfortably at the station's entrance, and through the open doorway into the main room beyond, viewing Stoneman intently engaged over a document. It was encouraging that official business held Stoneman's rapt attention for such a lengthy time, but their ride had been long.

Juan studied the imperfections in the wall he leaned on until the Tucsonans broke their uneasy silence by speaking among themselves, their volume mounting as minutes passed. Juan asked Thompson to gain the colonel's attention.

The station keeper knocked on the doorjamb and addressed Stoneman by his brevet title received in the Rebellion rather than his official title, "General, the committee from Tucson is here."

Hearing the group announced, Raúl again neared the window. This time Stoneman raised his map, giving Raúl a better look at the plat. *San Rafael Hills. Residence and winery! Circles named . . . burgundy . . . and . . . orange grove. He wastes our time!* Raúl noted Stoneman's reluctance folding the map, which he inserted in his inside breast pocket before easing his chair out from the heavy wooden table. *This man is a giant. His legs are as long as most men are tall.* Stoneman sighed and beckoned with a flip of his hand.

Juan and the others advanced into the room; to Raúl they looked like impatient horses freed from the starting line. Names stated, the men surrounded Stoneman, who adjusted his sitting position onto his left butt cheek and crossed his long right leg over his left knee. He offered as an opening to the meeting, "I cast a glance at your 'memorial.'"

Juan looked hopefully at the others.

Anticipating good news, Raúl inhaled deeply from his cigarette, gazed up at the stars, and heard a man's voice say, "And?" *Oury's ready to quarrel. Not a good beginning.*

"And, if I remember correctly, it said the two hundred fifty names from Tubac and the Santa Cruz Valley who testified to their alleged losses were only half of what could be obtained, if necessary." Stoneman's languid tone only further irritated Oury.

"Is it necessary?"

Raúl blew a long stream of smoke through his lips and turned his attention back to the window.

Stoneman sighed. "Mr. Oury, is it possible that there are five hundred residents in the Santa Cruz Valley, as stated in the report?"

Understanding what Stoneman said, Juan flared hotly at the statement, his usual imperfect English now falling far short of even that. "This is truth. La verdad. We tell truth." He turned to the dumbstruck Oury. "You tell him."

Hearing Juan's voice, Raúl pressed his lips on the lit cigarette and stuck his nose right up to the window pane, crushing the rolled tobacco. *To hell with being discovered. Oury's mad and Juan's upset.*

"You doubt the veracity of our citizens?" Oury leaned forward.

Thompson jumped into the conversation, "I can add to the litany of losses. Two months ago, Apaches jumped my Pima Indians, took my mules, and torched my wagonload of hay. Not fifty yards from where you're sitting. I can show you the burned wreck."

Raúl wiped frost off the window. *Stoneman looks irritated with the station keeper.* "Mister Thompson . . ."

"So far I've lost two hundred seventy head of cattle. What more do you want to hear?" Thompson looked back beseechingly at the committee members.

"And from how many more people?" added Oury.

Is Stoneman uncomfortable? He keeps moving from one butt cheek to the other.

Stoneman looked down his nose. "Mr. Oury, what is in question is the number of legitimate residents within the Santa Cruz Valley, which is totally held in Spanish land grants. Those that are on the land not named on those grants are squatters."

"Squatters! My God, man. Most land grants were wiped away in '54 by the Gadsden Purchase. Few had papered titles. Most were abandoned because those residents fled from daily Indian raids."

To Raúl's delight, Oury stormed across the room toward Stoneman. *The viper's released. No, Juan. Don't grab Oury's jacket. Let him go . . . Damn, they stopped him.*

"Bill, not here," pleaded Thompson with a restraining hand on Oury's chest.

The colonel rose, separating himself from the members of the Public Safety Committee. Raúl gaped. Standing at full height, Stoneman towered almost a full foot over everyone in the room except for DeLong, who was a few inches shorter.

"If what you say is true, that there are five hundred men in the Santa Cruz Valley, you don't need help from the military. You are able to take care of yourselves."

Juan pushed forward to refute Stoneman's foolish assertion, to Raúl's misgiving. *Compadre, you're fighting in the wrong weight class.*

"We lose many peoples. My own brother killed. Lose oxen to Apaches. Y . . . y cattle . . . y caballos."

Oury interceded, "Colonel Stoneman, you were in the war. Don't you know what it's like losing hundreds of people over the last two years? We in Arizona Territory are fighting for our lives. We are fighting a war and we need military help."

Stoneman looked to the heavens. "I am constricted by my budget."

Had he been inside, Raúl would have joined Oury, Elías, and the rest of the committee in exchanging bewildered glances.

"Upon my appointment, there was an expenditure allowed of $130 per man in the territory. I'm now limited to $33."

Incredulous, DeLong asked, "How much money do you think a man's life is worth?"

"Let me set this forth, all over again." Stoneman paced around. "There are too many posts. Many require major building improvements. Some camps must be eliminated. I can't even build my own command headquarters in Prescott I'm so low on funds."

DeLong looked down his patrician nose. "Can't you appropriate an existing building?"

Stoneman cut DeLong a stern look, raised his chin, and looked down upon those gathered before him. "In my command there are only sufficient horses to mount one in five cavalrymen. The Third Cavalry from the East replaced the Eighth Cavalry, who were mounted on magnificent horses from California, well suited for mountain service. The Third Cavalry have come on broken-down horses totally unfit for the territory. There is no appropriation for remounts. I have a very tough job."

Raúl gave a start at the mention of horses. Engrossed in the conversation inside, he hadn't closely tended the committee's horses. Turning, he saw they were still safely tethered, yet a thought of Indians set his heart racing. Nothing stirred in the flats about him, nor the rock-rubble small hills in the near distance. Raúl went back to the window.

"Keeping a plow straight while holding a rifle and an eye to the horizon for Injuns ain't easy." Oury's low grousing was met with a hum of agreement from his group.

Stoneman had returned to his chair, where he again settled onto his right butt cheek before leaning forward, as if making an earnest confession. "I regret that I am so circumscribed by means for the work that is expected of me. My hands are tied. And I cannot exceed the mandated appropriation of $33 per man. I absolutely cannot reinforce the troops in the south of the territory."

"What we have now?" DeLong shot out his question to Stoneman.

"I don't anticipate withdrawing any troops. In fact, as soon as Captain Moore's company can be mounted on horses now used by C Company, First Cavalry, they'll be out scouting the valleys of Santa Cruz and Sonoita."

"¿Y Camp Crittenden?" asked Juan. Crittenden was close to the Elías family acreage south of Tucson. The camp's existence was imperative to the family.

"It should be occupied until after harvest."

Raúl shook his head, the same as Juan inside. He knew how mighty that blow would strike not only his friend but the entire region along the Mexican border.

"Only until then?" Oury unbuttoned his top jacket. "Colonel Stoneman, we've been hanging on by sheer grit."

Stoneman knitted his eyebrows. "The people in the East are not sympathetic to the Anglos in Arizona Territory. My vigorous prosecution of a winter campaign against the Apaches was met with sharp criticism. The East wants Sherman to order a modification of my plans to align with President Grant's policy of treating the Apaches with Christian persuasion, kindness, and domestication."

"Tell 'em to go to hell. Tell 'em ellos no saben lo que está pasando aquí." Elías couldn't stand quiet for long.

Oury translated for a confused Stoneman, "Juan says, 'The easterners don't know what goes on here.'"

Now that Raúl had learned so much in such a short time from Juan, he knew his friend spoke the truth.

"I'm loath to do that." Stoneman pushed off the table with his hands and rose to stroll through the station once again. "With no little reluctance would I press that point. I fear headquarters, in San Francisco and Washington, are already surfeited and wearied by the Indian question."

Like the mongrel terrier he was, Oury, along with Juan, followed the bony Stoneman around the room. "We need all-out war on the Apaches. We need help. I can't say that any plainer."

Stoneman sniffed the air. "Or more often. One-tenth of the entire army is now stationed in Arizona, a greater proportion than you have a right to expect." Stoneman stopped. He turned toward Oury and Juan and pointed his finger at them. "I caution you. The people of Tucson and its vicinity cannot expect anything more than has been done already. And if you continue your complaints of the lack of protection by the military, I will withdraw the troops entirely. That subject has been seriously contemplated and might yet be acted upon. And that, gentlemen, is my last word on the matter. Good evening."

From the table Stoneman swiped his hat—festooned with entwined silk braids—fitted it on his large head, and left the room.

Raúl stepped back from the window, immediately hearing horses trotting from around the station. Thinking the Apaches were swooping down on him, he jumped for the reins but was relieved to see that the horses coming about were ridden by the colonel's protective contingent of six U.S. Army officers, leading one unseated horse. Stoneman strode from the station and climbed on his horse, and the soldiers galloped away.

The Tucson men stomped out of the station in high temper, each taking his reins from Raúl.

"'Withdraw all troops?' How can that son of a bitch say that?" Oury snatched his horse's reins from Raúl's hand. In one swift motion he was in the saddle and kicking the sides of his horse. The stallion rebelled and snorted as it pulled wildly before Oury shortened the reins and corrected its course. Galloping off, Oury left his dust to settle over Raúl and the remaining members of the Public Safety Committee. They were not long in kicking their horses and loping after Oury, who drew in his horse to a more moderate canter.

As Raúl and Juan galloped up, Juan grabbed Oury's elbow and shouted, "We have to stay together."

"I know. There could be any number of savages out tonight that want to see me killed."

DeLong rode up on Oury's other side. "He means we have to think this over. Come up with a plan."

Oury bristled. "Right now I've only got murder in my heart. And those Injuns ain't my target."

"Calm down." DeLong extended his hand to caution Oury. "We have to think."

Raúl knew Juan's unspoken response to DeLong's plea, even better than Juan himself. *The time for thinking is over. The Elíases will be ready when Oury is, and that time will come sooner than later. Oury will come to them.*

Oury pulled the brim of his hat down lower. "What a waste of time. Eighty miles up and eighty miles back to town and two hours of blather from Stoneman in between."

His senses alive to the men's outrage, Raúl surmised that, as the meeting completely failed, there would be retaliation by the people in Tucson. And he aimed to be a part of it.

Instinctively the men scanned the horizon and the rocks and the cacti for any signs of movement, the moon casting a silver haze over the landscape—silver that prospectors could not mine.

TUCSON

Beside a pine coffin and a fine mahogany casket leaning against the wall, Raúl measured a farmer's height and width, recording them in a ledger for such purposes. "And how much do you weigh?"

"About two hundred, two ten maybe." The farmer gave Raúl a roll of bills.

Raúl counted and noted the payment in the ledger. "Thank you. The pine coffin will be ready in a week and held in the warehouse for you, when necessary."

"Cain't be too prepared. It's easier on the wife," the farmer mumbled as he ambled off, passing Mister Z personally assisting the Elías brothers as they tested the strengths of various ropes.

A horse's frightened shriek abruptly captured Raúl's attention. The next moment, a Mexican resembling a wild stallion—his wiry hair on end, his clothes covered in trail dust, and his spurs clattering—rushed into the store to look about. "¿Señores Elías?"

"This way," Raúl called to the caballero and led him down an aisle created by huge islands of crated goods.

"Señores."

At the recognizable voice of their herder, the Elías brothers turned, concern creasing their faces. Raúl and Mister Z listened to the Elíases' rapid conversation with their hired man.

"Apaches. Doce vacas y siete caballos." The caballero swayed nervously.

"¿Dónde, Pacquito?"

"Punta de Agua."

"¿Hoy?"

"Sí. Hace una hora."

"Cuántos Apaches?"

"Cuatro o cinco. Se fueron hacia el norte."

Enough heard: four or five Apaches headed north with twelve head of cattle and seven horses stolen from Juan's ranch. The brothers marched toward the front door, Pacquito trailing closely behind with Mister Z and Raúl.

Mister Z asked the question on everyone's minds, "Eskiminzin?"

"No sé," Pacquito said over his shoulder.

Emerging into the bright sunlight of a day that promised to reach the high eighties, the Elías brothers discovered a crowd of Mexicans and a few Anglos already forming in front of Zeckendorf's. The men jostled for prime positions to be seen, shouting out their eagerness to go with the Elíases after the stolen cattle. Juan and Jesús María pointed to eight Mexicans before them. "You, you. Get your mounts." Once selected, the men hurried away to various stables, where they collected their horses.

Jesús María turned to his brother. "Juan, I ride with Pacquito to Punta de Agua. The cattle will have scattered. Escoja a otro. Pick another. I'll not go. Yo no voy."

Gripped by the intensity of the Elíases, Raúl thought of his brother. *Mateo and his band stole cattle and horses, but none of them would hesitate to ride.* "Yo también. I'll go instead of Jesús."

Juan critically eyed Raúl. "Not this time. We ride quickly."

"¿La próxima vez? Will you take me next time?" As Raúl pressed his point, Jesús María tapped another Mexican, who ran down the street to the stable.

Now that the nine men selected for the trail were returning on horseback and circling their horses before Zeckendorf's store, Juan's thoughts focused on what lay before them on the pursuit. He plunged his boot into a stirrup and climbed onto his excited horse to the groan of leather. Juan reined away from the other anxious, fretful horses. "Sí, la próxima vez."

Excited, grateful, and his heart racing, Raúl backed up against the storefront where he watched the fantastic mayhem in the streets: ten horses pawing the ground, snorting, attempting to rear up; and ten men opening the cylinders of their Colt revolvers, checking the number of bullets left in the chambers, in their gun belts, and in their saddlebags.

A voice called out over the din, "I'm coming."

From around the corner of Zeckendorf's store rode Mister Z astride his favorite bay horse, his army cavalry hat atop his head, his saber sheathed in a scabbard at his side, ammunition belts crossing his torso. With a brush of his arm that dislocated the frameless eyeglasses on his nose, Zeckendorf drew his horse back on its hind legs and, grabbing his sword's grip, swiped the air with his saber. His steed's hooves pawing the air, Mister Z shouted, "Off to fight! We've the right! Ride well and give Injuns hell!"

Raúl was invigorated by his employer's transformation from charismatic merchant to poet and Indian fighter. *I want to grab a horse and join in the pursuit.*

When the bay's hooves came back to earth, Zeckendorf pointed his saber horizontally as if in a military charge, poised half out of the saddle over the horse's neck, and galloped out of town, down the street toward the open desert, with Juan and the nine other Mexicans in pursuit.

Through the dust cloud that billowed up, Raúl ran eastward for three blocks before drawing to a standstill. He could not keep up with charging horses. He would not be part of this pursuit, but he had their promise. *Next time. Next time, I, Raúl Obregón de Cardenas, will become an Indian fighter. Like Mister Z.*

✦✦✦

Their horses at a walk en route to Tucson the following day, Juan had suffered enough of Mister Z's morose, taciturn mood. Indicating by a slant of his head the Mexican rider ahead of them—the one with the Indian scalp still dripping blood down his leg—Juan said, "Mister Z, it was your scalp to take."

"Know it."

"You didn't."

"Nein."

"We knew what going over that gap meant." In his mind Juan could still see the fresh cattle and horse tracks four or so miles out of Tucson and how the tracks took off in the direction of the gap between the Santa Catarina and the Rincon Mountains: Cebadilla Pass.

"Ja."

"With a gun, it's easy to kill. From afar or close. Tú lo sabes. Solamente a different kind of hombre scalps."

"He was young. He'd lost a front tooth." Zeckendorf lifted his chin, accentuating his beard. "Would you, a faithful Catholic, have scalped that Indian?"

Juan leaned closer and patted Mister Z on the shoulder. "This Jew did not. I'm glad." They spurred their horses, joining the Mexican ahead.

Mister Z winked at Juan and pointed to the Indian scalp at the Mexican's side. "It's your prize, but I would appreciate its loan."

Among the first to see the returning posse herding the rescued cattle—what they'd retrieved—through the streets of Tucson, Raúl alerted the customers inside Zeckendorf's store. Quickly a crowd gathered outside; all gawked at the trophy scalp swinging from Mister Z's belt. Raúl beamed as Zeckendorf acknowledged the shouts of congratulations with his signature open smile and a wave.

And when Mister Z dismounted, he acknowledged Raúl before entering the store.

Raúl nearly exploded with immense pride. *What a great man. A hero. When the next time comes, I'll be in the scuffle and return as victoriously. La próxima vez.*

WEDNESDAY, APRIL 12, 1871

ARIVAIPA CANYON

Sister whispered in Nest Feather's ear, "Take your knives."

Two pairs of black eyes gleaming in conspiracy, Nest Feather and Sister scrambled over the swell of hills on the upper level along Arivaipa Canyon. Pushing, jogging, they hurried. Word had spread rapidly of the success of their warriors' last raid down in the valley—whether it was the San Pedro or the Santa Cruz or both, neither Nest Feather nor Sister knew. Brought back that morning were nine head of cattle and White Eyes' clothing.

Soon Nest Feather and Sister had sprinted three miles east from the ranchería, or about eight miles from Camp Grant. And yet they were not among the first. Many Apache women tussled with the men for cast-off clothing. Not even nearby bawling cattle disturbed the women from cackling, grabbing, pushing, shoving to snatch a blouse, a skirt, a petticoat, a man's shirt or pants, and other American or Mexican cast-offs.

Ow! Someone's elbow knocked Nest Feather's head. Pushing even harder, Nest Feather thrust her hands into the pile of clothing, bringing out two pieces. Sister and Nest Feather backed off, clutching their loot of a checkered blue blouse and a brown skirt. Onawa held both items up to herself—deciding between them—then threw the blouse to Nest Feather. "Gingham." Onawa strutted about with the skirt held up at her waist. Two spots on the front of the brown skirt showed great wear, where perhaps someone had knelt tending a garden. Both the skirt and shirt were slit and smudged with rusty-red clots. Dirt from farming, the warriors had said. Nest Feather and Sister overlooked the dark splotches quite unlike the soil in this region.

"Dressed in this 'gig-and-ham' blouse, I shall attract some young man ready to marry." Nest Feather pranced about.

Onawa laughed at her sister's dream.

An older warrior from the corral called to Nest Feather.

Knowing what was required, Nest Feather tightly folded her prize and stuffed it into the shirt she wore before presenting herself for work at the triangular corral, two sides of which were formed by the surrounding cliffs. Posts made of mesquite branches, pounded with large rocks into ground softened by rain, formed the critical third side, enforcing the cattle's containment. Smaller branches, whipped to the crisscrossed posts with rope and strips of cowhide, created a secure fence.

Nest Feather placed her whetstone, knives, and old rags under a small tree. As she honed the blades of her knives, her mouth watered for the taste of beef. The small rations distributed on ticket days at Camp Grant did not go far feeding the home gowah she shared with Sister's extended family. Behind Nest Feather the wails of two head of cattle rattled the air for a few seconds. Silence came quickly.

Nest Feather glanced behind her. Two steers had already been skinned, halved, and quartered.

Some men hacked off smaller portions and quickly departed for their gowahs with their rewards. The warrior who led the war party dumped the bloody skins before Nest Feather. Without a word he rested against a tree by another man while they waited for Nest Feather to flesh the hides. A third warrior stirred the cow brains cooking in water. They'd oil the hides with that paste after they took them back to the ranchería.

Nest Feather needed no instruction. How and why she had taken to this job and excelled over all the other wives and maidens in their band, Nest Feather had not been certain. The attraction had been immediate. Despite her small size and weight, she was strong. She could heave the heavy skins about without help, and the blood and remnants of flesh did not affect her at all. The feel of the blade—her stubby broad fingers around a knife's hilt wrapped with muslin rags and pressed into her small palm—made her smile. Nest Feather angled her blade on the flesh side of the hide for the first scraping. Flesh rolled along the length of the skin until Nest Feather sliced it away from the edge. She took even more care with the spongy area around the stomach, which stretched mightily. Some merely sliced it away, but Nest Feather worked her best with that difficult area, as skins were valuable in many ways—building gowahs, arrow quivers, breechcloths, celebration outfits, cradleboards, and moccasins.

She worked until the sun's rays faded, returning tired but with a "gig-and-ham" blouse.

WEDNESDAY, APRIL 12, 1871

TUCSON

Splaying a seam and running her fingers over the fine nips and tucks, Valeria extended the blouse toward the shop owner for examination. "As you see, the stitches in my alteration are very even and compare favorably with the original stitching of the untouched part of the blouse. I altered this for a great friend of Señora Atanacia Hughes." Casting a glance at the shop owner, Valeria saw a flicker of encouragement. Next she retrieved a short evening cape made of pink gossamer. Edged with ruffles, the see-through cape impressed those who beheld it.

"It's like a cloud." The shop owner hesitated to touch it.

Valeria threw it around herself and turned, letting the feather-weight cape billow. "I designed and made this for another friend of Mrs. Hughes. I'm delivering this to her this afternoon for an important evening party." Valeria draped the cape on a hanger and covered it with her pillowcase. "Finally another original work . . ." Valeria stood in the middle of the store for more room. "My fiesta skirt."

"Yessss, I've been looking at that." The shop owner watched how the skirt, in flashes of bright colors, twisted about Valeria's legs as she spun and how it fell and settled back in place when Valeria stilled.

Two Mexicanas, one middle-aged, the other young, and both carrying a bundle of folded clothing, appeared at the store's street entrance. The younger woman with light brown hair gasped at Valeria's outfit.

"Epiphania, you and María go on through to the back. I'll be there shortly." The shop owner returned her attention to Valeria. "I am impressed. Please give me your name and how to contact you."

"I'm Valeria Obregón. Perhaps, I could come back . . . a week from now? Maybe you would learn of your customers wanting alterations by then?"

"Yes. That would be fine."

Quickly Valeria gathered her samples, went out the door and, when no longer in sight of the shop owner, leaned against the building's wall. She was shaking. *It went well. Maybe I could be of help to this shop.* Catching her breath, she moved down Calle de la Alegría toward Calle Real, where her client awaited her gossamer cape.

"¡Señora! Por favor, espere." The light-haired Mexicana rushed up to Valeria. "I am Epiphania Rivera. Your skirt. It is beautiful. Is there any way . . . I know there isn't . . . but is there any way that I could borrow it? I want to impress my boyfriend, mi amor."

"My fiesta skirt?"

"Sí, por favor."

Valeria studied Epiphania's imploring demeanor. "I . . . I'm sorry. This skirt is very special to me."

"Ah, I am sure of that." Disappointed, she turned.

Didn't I make this skirt to impress Raúl? "Wait. When do you need a skirt?"

"This Saturday. Oh, I would be so grateful."

"You are Epiphania?"

"Epi."

This is not a wealthy client but someone who could be my sister. "I could make you something similar fairly quickly. I'll scrounge for material ends. Some of them might work."

"Oh, oh. ¡Muchas gracias! Andrew will be overwhelmed. But . . . but how can I pay you? I help María, mi tía, with rent."

"Don't tell your employer that I do this for you. It is between us."

THURSDAY, APRIL 13, 1871

Over the last two months of meeting after rancorous meeting on the Indian situation, Juan and Jesús María would return to South Main Street to sit at Jesús María's table and rehash what had been said over drinks.

Tonight, even before they appeared at another meeting, they sat at the table and sipped the fine whiskey bought at E. N. Fish's store. They mutely beheld the red-glinted, brown liquor as if drugged at the opium den.

Bitterness ate into Jesús María. Apaches had decimated their livestock and considerable lands in Tubac until the Elíases were forced to abandon them. After more than thirty years as wealthy landowners, they were reduced to a few acres here and there in Tucson. His heritage destroyed, the family wealth gone, one brother killed, and still the Indians continued the persistent raiding of their stock. No more. Jesús María would not let that happen. He could not.

Jesús María rose, snatched his glass from the table, and drank the fiery liquid in one gulp. He poured another shot, downed that in one gulp as well, and slammed his glass on the table.

Juan carefully studied his brother. "You have made a decision."

"Ahora o nunca. Now or never. We go. Vamos. Hasta el fin."

✦✦✦

Inside the courthouse, a handful of men—the movers and shakers of all the meetings—scrunched back in their seats, arms entwined over their chests. Raúl rested a booted foot on a chair in the row in front of him and watched the Elías brothers lounge in their seats.

The last pounding on the big drum outside faded away, and the older man who always carried the memorable banner touting a meeting about Injuns stuck his head inside the door, asking of no one in particular, "Shall we go 'round again?" The Pied Pipers of Tucson had no followers.

Juan answered, "No. They don't come tonight."

"Gettin' late." Oury pursed his lips as the man carrying the banner ducked back outside.

Jesús María and Juan glowered at Oury. Every town meeting was advertised as the "time for action," and none was ever taken. At least none by Anglos. The Anglos preached. Sharing a disgusted look, the Elías brothers rose and ambled to the door. Raúl joined them.

"Are we disbanding?" DeLong maintained correct posture in his chair.

Oury called after them, "¿A dónde van?"

"Dónde se encuentra la acción. ¡Mi cama!"

Juan and Raúl guffawed heartily at Jesús's rare admission that the only place he found action was in his bed.

"Necesitamos hablar." Oury advanced on them while DeLong and Bennett stood and appeared more interested.

"That is all you do. Talk. Habla y habla." Jesús paced.

Oury first eyed the brothers, then DeLong. "Tiene razón. It's time for action."

Immediate concern creased DeLong's forehead. He stood to confront Oury. "What exactly do you mean by that statement? We must be circumspect."

Waiting at the door with Juan and Raúl, Jesús María cried out, "¡Ay, caramba!" He opened the door, ready to burst outside.

"Wait!" Oury motioned the Elíases over to form a tight group with DeLong, thereby leaving Raúl alone at the doorway and out of hearing. "You heard Stoneman. We must act. Only we can be relied upon for protection." He lowered his voice, "I've heard that Captain Stanwood's taking forty soldiers in the next few days on a two-week scouting expedition along the Mexican border."

DeLong stared long and hard into the faces of Oury and the Elías brothers. "Whitman will be left in charge . . . half staffed. One of our wagon trains just came back from Grant." He turned his gaze to the court's hard-packed dirt floor. "But I still don't know that I like it."

Oury slapped his thigh. "Dammit! We've got to protect our own. Stoneman couldn't give a crap about us."

DeLong did not utter a sound.

Bill Oury said, "Let's plan."

Oury's pronouncement was as refreshing to the Elías brothers as the first rain of the season. Juan told Raúl to go home without them.

SATURDAY, APRIL 15, 1871

ARIVAIPA CANYON

In the outer reaches of Arivaipa Canyon, before the alluvial plain, Nest Feather spied a seven-month-old toddler crawling with increasing speed toward a jumping cholla. She swept him from the ground, her hands around the boy's waist, and hoisted him on her hip. "Cholla is no good. The needles hurt." She poked his tummy. When his laughter dissolved into unexpected tears, she bounced him up and down until a wide smile played across his chubby face.

Shouts of encouragement to those in a footrace from the last sycamore to a downed tree limb forty yards off brought Nest Feather's attention back to the other children of her band. One little girl touched the limb first and won over three small boys, who fell on the ground in exaggerated antics of extreme fatigue. Joining them were about fifteen of the band's dogs either licking the children's faces or sprawling on the ground.

Nest Feather loved babysitting the toddlers and small children but could only do so at the ranchería on the days Sister spelled her from cutting hay. On this rare day, Nest Feather sat upon a large flat rock and called for the six- and seven-year-olds to group around her. "Story time!"

The children plopped cross-legged before Nest Feather, who placed the toddler on the ground before her. "What story do you want to hear?"

"Changing Woman!"

"Child of the Water cutting off Owl Man Giant's head!"

"An enemy story!"

"Yes, yes. A Papago story. A story about the Rope under Their Feet People," the children all clamored. Lounging nearby, their dogs barked as if in agreement.

Shuffling from under the shadows of the largest sycamore tree in the canyon was the elder of their band. He, who had sung at her na'íees only three months before, seemed to have begun his life-ending physical descent.

Nest Feather stood and beckoned him forward, convinced that the loud laughter of the children had gotten through to his deafened ears; yet she was not convinced that he could see her or the large flat rock upon which to sit. Nest Feather placed a steady hand on his elbow and helped him ease down on the rock, next to where she sat before the children. She thanked the wise, venerable man for coming, and as parent surrogate for the afternoon, made certain that the children also thanked him for his presence. Pitched high and loud, their voices roused the elder. His eyes completely milky, he raised his head and smiled blankly, making Nest Feather thankful he had heard a few words.

She addressed her small charges: "A Papago story we shall hear." In a low, dramatic voice, she began, "Rope under Their Feet People have been our enemy for many, many moons. They live in the flat lands to the south, where they groove our earth. They grow beans. Tepary beans." Nest Feather made a grotesque face, bringing bright laughter from the children. "They eat these beans frequently. When not farming, Rope under Their Feet People hunt the nnee. They need slaves to work their lands."

The children gaped at each other.

"Their rope sandals silent, the Papagos creep into our rancherías. They tiptoe to each gowah before dawn when the nnee are still asleep. And when we wake and go outside, the Papagos pounce." Nest Feather's arms swooped out and over her head.

The children screamed. Some cried.

"We must be wary. We must be as watchful as the eagle. Will you do that?"

"Yes. Yes," the children whispered.

"There is one way to know if a Papago is outside your gowah. Do you know?"

The children's eyes enlarged; they shook their heads slowly.

Nest Feather leaned forward. "Remember I told you about the beans they eat? You know their presence because they stink." She rose and, turning her backside toward the children, wafted her hand underneath her bottom.

The children screamed with laughter, rolling over on the ground, which encouraged the dogs to scamper about. The elder laughed too.

Nest Feather faced them again, grimacing and holding her nose to renewed giggles.

TUESDAY, APRIL 18, 1871

SAN XAVIER DEL BAC, SOUTH OF TUCSON

Water almost reaching their horses' knees, Jesús María and Bill Oury sloshed across the northward-flowing Santa Cruz River above San Xavier del Bac. Even from that distance, one could see that the Franciscan mission's exterior required significant attention.

They guided their horses around the mission's adjacent, low east building, where visiting Catholic priests could room alongside a soap factory. Large, missing chunks of the layer of stucco over the red adobe bricks, particularly near the vigas along the roofline, told of significant water penetration.

Each dome-shaped, brush ki, supported by rickety poles, seemed ready to fall in on its resident Papagos, who came out of their homes to observe the unexpected horsemen. Even though Jesús María frequently visited Juan's Rancho Punta de Agua a hundred yards or so from the mission, he knew the Papago laborers believed him to be more of an interloper. They eyed him suspiciously as he and Oury tied their reins to a bent post in front of the perimeter stucco wall, where Juan waited for them.

The Elíases looked up at the bell towers of the mission's cathedral, the left one completely finished with dome and plaster, the right one never completed with either. The Desert People's legend asserted that a priest inspecting it during the final stages of construction fell to his death. Better left as is.

Some things cannot be left "as is." Juan caught Oury looking up at the towers as well, perhaps thinking the same thought. Unattended, the three went inside.

Oury and the brothers dropped to a bent knee and crossed themselves, observing proper respect to the statue of the crucified Lord. Standing, they beheld the remaining red and ocher paint on the highly decorated walls, which the church's dimness intensified. In greatest evidence was the long-ago theft of much ornamentation that destructively pitted the walls.

A solitary figure before the main altar at the front of the church rose from his knees and turned to face the visitors. Taller and broader of chest than either of the Elíases or Oury, the Papago waited patiently.

No matter how frequently Juan saw the man in ordinary clothing, he always sensed that he was summoned by a papal *visita*.

"Come, Children of God. You are welcome." His voice low and modulated, the Papago spoke with great solemnity in Spanish, as did his guests.

Jesús María, Juan, and Bill Oury progressed forward, and when they neared, they stopped a respectful distance from the Papago, who brought his hands up to indicate the murals streaked with water stains around him.

"Don Jesús, Don Juan, and Don Guillermo, you see around you the signs of too much water. An ironic problem. In two months we will pray to San Juan de Bautista for more rain to end the dry season. Perhaps we should pray instead for assistance in keeping artisans at their repairs."

"Chief Francisco, is that due to lack of money?" asked Oury.

Juan knowingly eyed the Papago leader. Francisco Galerita was a sage leader, one who dominated the Council of Nations with a firm and calculated hand. Nothing escaped his notice, and nothing occurred within the Papago Nation without his complete consent.

"You don't visit here as frequently as Don Jesús María and Don Juan, whose land touches ours. And yet you know the cause as well as I."

Juan supplied the answer in an attempt to further their visit at a more rapid pace. "The artisans fear for their lives working outside. Some must travel La Jornada del Muerto to reach the mission."

They followed Chief Francisco through a small doorway to an outdoor courtyard, where, squinting into the glare of the sun, they walked the length of a covered pathway around the square courtyard's four sides.

"The threat of death by the hands of the enemy is constant," asserted Chief Francisco.

"All of Arizona Territory is Apache country."

Juan had to stifle a laugh at Oury's stating the obvious.

Irritated at the meandering pace of things, Jesús María stopped walking. "And that, Chief Francisco, is the matter before us now. We need help from the Papagos." He heard his impatience affecting his own voice with a quaver.

"Tucson is in an uproar over the frequent raids and receiving no godda—" Oury glanced at Juan. "Receiving no help from the military. We had a meeting with Stoneman; he told us we had to protect ourselves."

Jesús María pressed the point, "Meetings are held almost nightly. We're determined to take Stoneman's advice. If our chase of the enemy leads us to Little Springs . . ." *When didn't marauders' tracks lead to Camp Grant?* "We need your help. The Papagos' help."

Chief Francisco ceased all movement. "Papagos war without end against the enemy."

"Will you help us?" Juan reiterated the question with more urgency.

"When?"

Jesús María pressured, "In ten suns, come with many People. Meet us at the foot of the Black Hill when the sun reaches its height."

"With this sunlight, messengers will travel to Coyote Sitting and Where the Mulberry Tree Stands." Chief Francisco gestured to the southwest. "The People in the villages there will respond."

"I need to know the number of People who will come with you in ten suns." Jesús María's face darkened with concern.

The saintly light that had twinkled in Francisco's eyes fled. "My People need assurance that our reward will be met."

Jesús María and Juan hesitated. They knew of Francisco's direct request. So did Oury. The taking of slaves for later resale was customary. It was the People's way with the enemy and with no others. As the seconds stretched out, Jesús María kept silent, reluctant to answer.

Oury said, "We don't come between the customs of the Papagos and the Apaches. We're saving the Mexicans and the Anglos."

Chief Francisco spread his thin lips in a straight line, which was to be taken as a smile. "I will send a messenger with the number of People."

As the Elías brothers and Oury rode away, Jesús María baited his friend. "You promised a very respectful number of Anglo fighters. Twenty? ¿Cuánto?"

"As I said. A respectful number." Oury quickened his horse's pace.

THURSDAY, APRIL 20, 1871

Juan and Bill Oury were announced by the maid. Sam Hughes looked up from his desk tucked in a spare bedroom, now used solely as his adjutant general's office. All three had been known to one another for some time now, sometimes as friends, sometimes as adversaries. Union, Confederate. Liberal, conservative. However, desperate times, such as these with out-of-control Indians, required all good men to come together, whatever their political beliefs. Each recognized the richness of that in the others.

Juan and Oury waited as Sam rounded his desk, as long as he was tall, strewn with official territorial documents.

"I thought you might need a walk," said Oury, who—despite his outsized persona—was only three or four inches taller than the Welshman.

Without hesitation Sam grabbed his bowler hat and rifle. "Ye come at the right time. Where to?"

"The river."

The trio crossed the few blocks of town without stopping to glad-hand Tucsonans, who always recognized Juan and Jesús María, the leaders of Mexicanos; Oury, a civic leader; and Hughes, the wealthiest of the Anglos.

Bill Oury and Juan eyed the surrounding land down at the deserted riverside of the Santa Cruz while Sam scuffed his foot through a clump of tall grass. The first of the snowmelt rushed down the river that would see additional swelling.

"When I first came to Tucson, only a little more than twelve years ago, there were beavers in the river. What fine hats they made." Hughes lowered his hat over his high forehead.

Juan strained to understand Hughes's accented English. If necessary he could rely upon Bill's translation later. However, the other men's animated faces spoke volumes in a universal language.

"Times change." Oury watched the water eddying below.

Hughes muttered, "They do."

"Did Sidney speak with you?"

"DeLong? Perhaps. About what?"

Juan smirked. *Hughes is stalling and wants to hear the words straight from Oury's mouth.*

Bill's face tightened with quick irritation. "You know about what, dammit."

"I've many details on my mind."

Onto Sam now, Oury grabbed Hughes's elbow, and the three walked farther up the river, away from Tucson. "We're on for the morning of the twenty-eighth."

"Short notice."

"First quarter moon both nights. Enough to see, but not too bright to be seen."

Juan interrupted, "La luna esta muy importante para nuestros éxitos."

"Important? La luna . . . Ah, the moon. Yes." Hughes walked on, but Oury restrained him.

"We need arms. Ammunition. Food and water."

"For how many?" Hughes looked down at his elbow that Oury had grasped.

Releasing his hold, Oury estimated, "Over a hundred, counting the Papagos."

"No. I'll not arm the Papagos. These are territorial stock. 'Twould be illegal."

Juan thought Hughes surely realized the absurdity of his statement.

"Not necessary." Oury smirked. "They'll do damage in close-in fighting with their war clubs."

"And how many braves will you encounter?"

"We estimate about a hundred and fifty."

"Overmatched?"

Oury stopped. "Not with A.T. stock."

Hughes asked, "Where is delivery?"

"Where the Rillito meets Pantano Wash."

A sound from across the Santa Cruz drew Juan's immediate attention. He drew his pistol from the holster and brought back the hammer to the cocked position. Oury did the same. Held waist-high, their Colts were pointed at a low bush. Hughes raised his rifle. When a coyote trotted out and ambled away, the three relaxed.

"I personally will not go." Hughes rested his rifle butt on the ground.

Juan gave Oury a knowing look. Both knew Sam was not a true fighting man. "Food? ¿Comida? You'll provide?"

"Yes. A wagonload."

Oury frowned at the flow of the Santa Cruz at his feet. "Those beavers had no account being in Arizona. I killed quite a few myself."

Juan did not doubt that for an instant.

THE ENSUING DAYS

"I will complete all these alterations within ten days." After thanking the owner, Valeria left the clothing shop on Calle de la Alegría and noticed Epi standing at the far street corner. Joining her, Valeria asked, "Did the skirt work?"

"I'm in love."

"Wonderful."

"Andrew loved the skirt. He saw how beautiful I could be. I am so grateful to you." Epi extended the folded skirt to Valeria, who shook her head and pressed the offered garment back.

"My gift to you. Be happy."

"Gracias desde el fondo de mi corazón. You received alteration orders?"

"Quite a few. I will be busy. And that is good for me."

"Then we see each other again."

Valeria waved. *People in love have no bottom to their hearts.*

◆◆◆

From the large front windows in Zeckendorf's, whenever business would allow it, Raúl could see Oury enter the saloons and retail establishments up and down Calle del Arroyo and part of the way up and down Calle Real. In the beginning Oury appeared energetic, his stride long and purposeful, but that slowed a great deal after entering and leaving several stores. Raúl expected Oury to reach Zeckendorf's soon and wasn't surprised when the experienced Indian fighter entered and asked where to find Mister Z. Raúl led Oury to a back corner of the vast store where Zeckendorf inspected goods in an open crate. Raúl took Oury's sweep of a hat as his curt dismissal, but a customer pinned Raúl in the next aisle, within hearing distance of Zeckendorf.

A bit weary, Oury came to the point. "Bill, you've been to the meetings. We're planning our own . . . party."

"Excellent. You must have a few already itching to go."

Oury hesitated. "Many are interested, really interested. But one said his wife wouldn't tolerate it. One or two begged off that they weren't spry enough. Now you don't have either problem."

"No. When is it?"

Finding support, a grin stretched across Oury's face. "April 28."

"The twenty-eighth . . . what day is that?"

"A Friday."

Immediately, Zeckendorf shook his head. "No, no. That won't work."

"Why not?"

"Friday Shabbat service."

"You can't miss one?"

"I don't want to. Sorry. But I can offer some provisions."

Raúl appeared behind Oury. "Excuse me, Vosburg's looking for his shipment."

Zeckendorf, Oury, and Raúl met briefly with the local gun merchant near the store's front.

When Vosburg was satisfied and left, Mister Z turned to Oury. "I have an idea. Why don't you postpone for a couple of days? I could go then."

Oury resumed his grin, although a grim one. "Nope. The conditions are right."

"Good luck." Zeckendorf returned to his brisk business.

From the entrance Raúl watched Oury leave, looking up the street and back down before heading south. *I now know what he's after.*

✦✦✦

Grinding gears making a hell of a racket, pulleys straining, milled flour spewing down a chute into waiting burlap sacks, and particles floating in the air made Juan, Jesús María, and Oury wonder how anyone could stand to work here daily. However, it all covered the sound of a conversation that was more of a shouting match between them and the Eagle Flour Mill owners: the Scotsman, William Fisher Scott, and Jimmie Lee, the tall, thin Irishman.

"Dear God in Heaven, no!" Fisher walked away, but Jimmie caught his arm.

Oury leaned closer, yelling in Fisher's ear, "We need Anglo participation."

Jimmie offered, "We protected our mine."

"And had to close it," Fisher reminded him. "No. Larcena and I are expecting a bairn come September. No."

Jesús María butted in, "Este es Eskiminzin."

"Don't you think I know that?" Fisher drew out each word to great lengths.

Jimmie waggled his finger at his partner. "You should seek retribution for what Larcena was put through. Don't you think she wants revenge?"

"No. No, she doesn't. She's happy. Revenge doesn't bring back her two brothers, or her father, or John Page."

"Fisher . . ."

"Jimmie. Don't you understand? I would love to see Eskiminzin rotting in hell. But Larcena's lost one husband to the bastard and she'll not lose another. I'll not go. I wish you a bonnie day full of success, but that's it." Fisher tramped to a far corner to supervise a worker.

Knowing his brother boiled inside witnessing this failure, Juan pulled Jesús María outside to calm down. But Jesús pointed his finger in Oury's face when the Anglo came out of the mill. "Los anglos sólo hablan y esperan a que otros actúen. I hold you to your promise of twenty Anglos." Jesús'd be damned if the Anglos continued to merely talk and wait while others did all the fighting.

✦✦✦

Raúl banged on Juan's front door and could hear Juan's mother's confused questions before the door jerked open. Seeing Raúl, Juan stood outside, well away from his house.

"I know you are gathering people to go on the raid."

"Raúl . . ."

"Do not refuse me. You said 'la próxima vez.' I am going. I'll do my part."

"Valeria . . ."

"Won't know until we return victorious." Raúl saw his future in Tucson wax and wane as Juan pondered. Quickly gathered in the Indian fighter's bear hug, Raúl knew he had won.

"Compadre."

THURSDAY, APRIL 27, 1871

The head strap cut deeply into Nest Feather's forehead; her neck strained with the weight of several agave stalks in the bulging sack on her back. Onawa and several other women similarly toted stalks while three men walked beside their horses that struggled to drag at ropes' ends several heavy agave hearts collected outside the canyon. Finally arriving at the ranchería and exhausted from their long day's work, they rested along Arivaipa Creek among the towering sycamore trees, their seeds spinning onto the moist soil by the sparkling creek.

When a handful of soldiers rode up, the Apaches rose, cutting their rest short. Lieutenant Whitman dismounted and greeted the elder singer, to whom he had spoken several times. News of the nant'án and Long Black Hair in their ranchería traveled quickly. Hashké Bahnzin appeared.

"Spring has come to these elevations. And considering the successful past two months here, I propose that there be a celebration this Saturday evening." Whitman listened as Long Black Hair then translated into Apache.

Internally Nest Feather jumped with excitement, but her face remained placid.

Hashké Bahnzin confirmed, "Two sleeps?"

"Yes."

"Camp leaders will consult on plans and spread the word as the sycamore spreads its seeds."

"Excellent." Whitman, Long Black Hair, and their escort trotted off toward Camp Grant.

When the soldiers could no longer be seen and Hashké Bahnzin left to seek the other leaders, Nest Feather and Onawa giggled and laughed. Women returning from the hayfield with armfuls of hay to bundle for sale the next day learned of the news and danced, the hay falling from their hold.

"No time for mescal," said one woman.

Onawa stepped forward. "Time enough for roasted stalks."

Nest Feather beamed. Her favorite sweet treat was the roasted agave stalk, its sugar extracted and hot and soft and delicious.

FRIDAY, APRIL 28, 1871

Entering Jesús María and Teresa's house, Juan found their children huddled around a small dining table, prattling more than munching on their breakfast of tortillas and soupy beans. *Dios, they're loud today.* "Tío Juan está aquí," he announced, tousling their heads and tickling their sides.

Jesús seemingly absent, Juan peered down the adjacent hall. The bedroom door opened.

Jesús came out with his stained sombrero in his hands, but Teresa—disheveled and pale, her pregnancy greatly in evidence in her thin nightgown—leaned against the doorjamb. "Vaya con Dios." She closed the door softly behind her.

That Jesús looked at the closed door and did not move gave Juan misgivings. Something amiss in the vast Elías family was constant as the sun, but never between Jesús and Teresa.

When Jesús came to the table, he ignored Juan and his children. He only cringed at the loud and abrasive chattering.

Jesús worries more than usual. Juan decided to remain silent, but he would watch his brother closely.

Jesús leaned over his youngest daughter and wiped bean juice dribbling from her soft mouth, her little cheeks full of breakfast and her feet kicking the table. Another of his younger children shrieked with delight. Unnerved, Jesús María fled toward the open front door. His cowboy boots thudding on the hard-packed earthen floor, he passed a tiny, odd niche that had been created by partially tearing through the thick adobe wall—their family altar. He stopped.

Juan took several steps but waited. Seemingly a restraining hand had reached out and pulled his brother back.

Jesús María looked at the ornamented silver cross, passed down from their father's father, a soldier at El Presidio, to their father, a judge. Two candles, slanting in their candlesticks, flickered. Obviously one or two of his younger children had lit them. Jesús María merely straightened the tapers and placed his sombrero to the right of their family altar.

Juan debated whether to overhear Jesús's prayer or give him proper privacy. Concern brought Juan nearer.

Jesús knelt. "Holy Lord God, Father, Dios. I am a poor man, rich with family. Our problems are many. I ride today with hatred in my heart. I ride today with purpose—to save our town, our livelihood, and my family's future. My Lord Father, all this depends upon whether we act. And yet my lands, my cattle, my family could be taken from me, no matter the outcome of what I ride to do. Despite my strength of will, my Lord Father, I . . . protect me and the others who ride. No one else helps us. We are totally alone."

He raised his hand to make the sign of the cross but stopped. "If it be your will that I do not . . . come back . . ."

These words are unacceptable. Juan opened his mouth to intervene, but Jesús María frowned and continued his prayer.

"If it be thy will, I pray you grant me a safe return to my beloved family. And I pray that you watch over my Teresa and the coming baby. I worry. This I pray in Jesus Christ's name." Jesús María crossed himself.

"Amen," stated Juan, who now knelt on one knee and began his own silent prayer before saying aloud, "Grant that I return, if it be thy will."

Jesús María whispered, "You are not going."

"Of course I am."

"I forbid it."

"Like hell."

"I am the eldest. You do what I say."

"You're not the only Indian fighter."

"Listen to me," Jesús María's whisper was now a coarse rasp. "If I don't come back, you must be father to my children."

"Then you stay."

"I was scout to Captain Tidball in '63. You were not. I must go."

"You don't know Cebadilla Pass. I was just on it."

"Not the entire way."

"I've killed Apaches."

"Not on their ranchería."

"On ours! Same thing."

"It is more. Much more."

"I want—"

"Be sensible. This is my plan. I am in charge. I must go."

Juan shook his head.

Jesús María's children called out to him, upset with the men's angry whispers.

"Todo está bien, mis niños." The brothers glared at each other. Not everything was well. Jesús María whispered, "You must stay."

Juan sneered. *Defiance of Jesús riles him like nothing else.* Immediately his forearm was bound in his brother's vise-like grip.

"Swear it. Before Dios, our maker. Swear it."

His mouth firmly set, accentuating the droop of his mustache, Juan grimaced. "I go." He listened to his own breathing, the in-and-out rushing of air through his distended nostrils. Juan expected a punch to the stomach any second, but as Jesús's intense eyes continued to rest on him, Juan knew that would not happen.

Jesús María countered, "Do one thing. Stay out of the fiercest fray. Stay back as much as possible. You must, if need be, act as father to my children."

Father to all? Soon to be ten children? Maybe one day far off, but now?

Jesús María further tightened his grip. "Swear it before God."

Wrestling out of his brother's grip, Juan spit out the words as if by rote. "I swear it. I swear to God that *if you die . . .*" Juan bit into every word with fiendish glee. "I will be father to your children."

They rose. Both fumed more with anger and hatred than brotherly love. More adversaries than kin.

"Amen."

"Amen."

Strapping on ammunition belts and holsters, the two went outside to the narrow street in front, where Jesús María rapidly saddled his favorite horse, untied the riata, and threw himself in the saddle.

Juan pointedly studied his brother's pistol, rifle, and load of ammunition. When he peered again into Jesús's face, Juan smiled. That wicked smile had enchanted many a señorita and ended many an argument between the brothers.

Smirking himself, Jesús María sighed. "Ay, muchacho."

They gave the horses their heads but only allowed the animals to walk through town. "Is Teresa all right?" Juan opened conversation, realizing he was always the first to yield between them.

"She had constant pains. All through the night I rubbed her lower back, but she felt no better."

"What about a doctor? Dr. Wilbur? Dr. Handy?"

"She wouldn't hear of it. She's not due for more than two months." He swallowed hard. "I kept thinking: can I leave now? Should I leave at all?"

"Does she know where we're going?"

"I told her that I must go into the mountains for a few days—that company attends."

"She knows."

For a few seconds Jesús mulled sadly. "You should have seen her eyes . . ."

✦✦✦

Valeria rolled up Raúl's second shirt and stuffed it in the saddlebag. "You don't use the satchel?"

"Too bulky on the supply wagon."

"This is such an honor. Master of a wagon train. Mister Zeckendorf must think highly of you. Where do you go?"

"Uh . . . south."

"Camp Crittenden?" Valeria received no response. "And don't worry about me here. I have another alteration to finish before you return home."

Raúl paused as he fumbled with the bag's buckle. *I never had a thought of what Valeria would do while I'm away.* Now his mind raced. Rushing into the main room, he knocked his shoulder on the wall. His holster slammed against his leg. Scared the pistol might go off, Raúl held his breath.

"I'm not used to seeing you with a holster." Valeria hugged him from behind, resting her head against his back. "Te amo."

"Yo también." *I must leave. Not another hug. No more words. I have to get out. Go. Leave.* Without turning, he hurried through the front door. "Adiós."

"Wait. Raúl . . ." Incredulous and frustrated at his abruptness, Valeria shook her head and stamped her foot. *No kiss goodbye.* She stepped outside to watch his departing figure turn the corner toward Zeckendorf's, where the wagon train would form.

Two men on horseback appeared from a side street and, at a slow gait, veered onto Valeria's street and headed to the desert. Valeria studied a middle-aged woman on foot, who followed the men until they reached the desert, where she stopped.

An unusual happening. Compelled by the circumstance, Valeria joined the woman. "Buenas días."

Distracted from her attentive watch, the woman failed to return Valeria's smile. "Is your man going too?"

"A wagon train."

"Oh, not into the mountains."

"I don't think so. To the south."

"I've seen at least a dozen go this morning. Muy malo. Not good. Pray for them." The woman grimaced as she turned back and left Valeria.

With mountains surrounding Tucson in every direction, Valeria puzzled over what the woman meant. *Maybe the riders are part of Raúl's train with natural dangers there.* Cast into a mood, Valeria went home, snatched her mantilla, closed the door, and headed to the church plaza, where she expected to see Apache Mansos displaying their fresh vegetables. No one was there. And she hadn't seen a wagon train forming in front of Mister Z's, though she did not know exactly where or how trains formed. At the church Valeria took the woman's suggestion—saying a quick prayer for her neighbors—before returning home to her sewing.

✦✦✦

As the Elías brothers slowly rode their horses past the tents that composed Camp Lowell, they noticed some of their Mexican recruits riding out individually or with one other out of town. Colonel Thomas Dunn, the camp's commandant, and two lieutenants watched from the camp's periphery with increasing interest at what looked like a parade of Tucsonenses riding out of town. The brothers tipped their hats to the colonel, who studied them carefully.

Juan whispered to Jesús, "Who thought of riding out alone or with only one other person?"

"Bill Oury."

Juan spit in the dirt. *Smart people ride with as many others as possible. This way is creating a lot of attention.*

Past the camp, the narrow streets of Tucson having played out and only the Sonoran Desert and the mountain ranges stretching before them, the Elíases spurred their horses, unleashing pent-up power, and sprinted across the flats.

✦✦✦

Raúl, a mile off in the desert and hearing others fast approaching, turned in the saddle. "Juan Elías rides like he was born in the saddle."

Joaquín Telles, riding alongside Raúl, didn't need to look. "All the Elíases do."

As the brothers joined them, Jesús María greeted Telles, "Amigo Joaquín. El sol brilla sobre nosotros hoy."

Telles laughed as he squinted into the sun shining brightly over them that day, just as the moon would shine that night. "Sí, y la luna brilla esta noche."

Jesús María noted Raúl's stiff posture in the saddle. "¿Su primera vez?"

"Sí. I've practiced riding and shooting with Juan." Raúl wiped away the sweat that trickled down from his scalp and along his sideburns, grown long to match Juan's.

"He's ready," Juan muttered to Jesús, whose fiery attitude needed no translation. *Raúl is already trouble. Someone will have to watch him when we get to the ranchería.*

To deceive any witnesses, the four rode in a northerly direction prior to correcting their course for the planned rendezvous site.

Except for his target practice with Juan, Raúl had never been away from the village of Tucson and never this far to the east, or so close to the Santa Catarina Mountains that he could admire their impressive beauty. He studied their sun-drenched foremost ridges, slanting to the north and cutting back on themselves at their tips. *They resemble arrowheads plunged into the earth's flesh.*

Disturbed at his unpleasant thought, Raúl squinted into the sun. *It approaches its apex in the sky and will again tomorrow and the day after, and I, Raúl, will see all of those sunrises and sunsets. I won't fail. I have prepared to protect our people. And Valeria.*

"¡Vámonos, compadres!" Jesús María kicked his horse into a gallop.

Eating dust, Raúl, Juan, and Telles gave their horses free rein to find their stride.

Near the meeting spot—the convergence of the Pantano Wash with the Rillito River—they slowed to a walk. At the dry riverbeds Raúl eyed about forty Tucson-enses digging into the grub dished out from a parked wagon. *Rice and beans by the smell of it.* Too hurried and excited to eat that morning and his stomach rebelling with a growl, Raúl tied his reins to a creosote bush and rushed to the wagon.

◆ ◆ ◆

Turning in his saddle, Jesús María spotted more Mexicans approaching from Tucson, grouped in ones and twos. With the compadres here and those coming, all Mexicanos were accounted for. Jesús María looked farther to the south and, with the help of his binoculars, focused on a dark mass in the distance. The Papagos. In the front Francisco Galerita carried himself regally astride a magnificent paint horse. Behind him a large contingent of Papago Indians—most of them on foot—advanced with strides that ate up distance. Francisco had promised one hundred warriors. Jesús María estimated that many Papagos easily. Soon they would arrive at the wagon.

Jesús María tied his horse to a low tree, its gnarled roots mired in the wash's banks, and joined Juan at a second wagon, its load already drawing the interest of a lot of the Tucsonenses, including Raúl, who was still spooning beans into his mouth. In the wagon bed lay open crates of guns and lots of them: Spencer and Sharps carbines all stamped with "A.T." on the barrels and plenty of ammunition.

"Are we getting those?" Raúl pointed his spoon dripping with juice at the cache. Selling all varieties of rifles and pistols at Zeckendorf's brought him an experienced appreciation of this load.

Juan nodded.

"Everyone?"

"Not the Papagos."

Satisfied that Sam Hughes had provided well, the Elías brothers accepted what was dished out at the chuck wagon.

The greasy smell of lard-laced beans sickened Jesús María, who merely ran his fork through the rice kernels, playing with them like his youngest daughter. Tossing his tin plate to the ground, Jesús María rubbed the back of his neck and ran his fingers through his shoulder-length hair, now showing gray. His arms propped on hiked-up knees, he looked down at the caliche soil, the sand between his feet. The bright sun bleached the desert landscape to a pale shade of yellow.

"You need a few minutes' sleep. No one will notice," Juan whispered.

"If only I could."

By the time they wiped their plates off with kerchiefs and packed them away in saddlebags, Raúl and the Tucsonenses gathered at the arrival of the Papago warriors and Francisco Galerita, his hand raised in peace. Seeing so many natives at once fascinated Raúl.

The Papago chief disengaged his foot from the stirrup and placed it in the cupped hands of one of his warriors to dismount. Planting his feet in the earth as firmly as the rocks of San Xavier's foundation, Galerita surveyed the numbers gathering about him. He gestured with his arm toward his complement of Indians. "We come, Don Jesús. Where is Don Guillermo?"

"Coming." Jesús María scanned the barren desert.

Oury had better come. And soon. Juan also looked to the west and the north for any more riders from Tucson. *Damned Anglos. The day of action has arrived. Wait . . . is that? Yes.* "Riders. They're coming now."

Jesús María grabbed his binoculars from around his saddle horn and raised them to his eyes, gritty and sore. A small adjustment to the glasses brought the riders into focus.

Bill Oury actively balanced over the pommel as if he were the one galloping rather than the horse. Behind him rode the citified Sidney DeLong; Jimmie Lee, the aggressive Irishman; the blacksmith, Charles Etchells; a Texan fairly new to Tucson and Lee's employee, David Foley; D. A. Bennett; and William F. Bailey, stonemason.

In disgust Jesús María thrust the binoculars at Juan, who looked through them. *Seven! Anglos paraded themselves at weekly and nightly meetings . . . and they mustered together seven? Bill Oury and only six other Anglos?*

Oury reined in his horse in a flurry of dust, as did the other six men. Once dismounted, Oury approached the gathering of men.

Seething—especially when he saw the big man wearing a snide smile—Jesús

María advanced toward him, closed his hand into a fist, and drove it into Oury's right eye.

The sound silenced everyone. Oury crumpled to the ground.

His entire body shaking, his hand red and hurting, Jesús María stood over Oury. "You're light in your number."

✦✦✦

The Mexicanos violently objected and spit out their fiery words over one another.

"¡Jesús!"

"¡Su puta madre!"

"¡Vete a la mierda!"

"¡Jesús María!"

"We don't go unless Jesús is leader!"

Aroused at the Papago and Anglo vote to name Oury leader, Raúl and his fellow Mexicanos wouldn't stomach the slight to Jesús María. Their heated bodies surged forward, shoving, pushing, arms raised, their shouted obscenities deafening. Raúl pressed ahead in the middle of his compadres. *My friends. Together in a common cause, a common complaint.* He belonged, like his brother Mateo belonged to his mob. Some Tucsonenses split from the group, heading for their horses.

Preventing a mutiny, Oury conceded leadership to Jesús María.

Oury demands watching. I must be careful. Raúl progressed through the lines for distribution of water and additional food to everyone, and ammunition and carbines only to the Anglos and Mexicanos. The weight and feel of the Sharps in his hands, his finger sliding easily onto the trigger in practice, grounded Raúl. *My future begins here.*

William Bailey stood next in line, also accepting a Sharps, even though strapped over his shoulder and hanging at his side was an army saber.

"Are you carrying that?" Raúl pointed to it.

"Sure as shootin'. I never used it in the Rebellion. Might find some use for it now."

Silence fell upon the group. Jesús María, standing on the now empty wagon bed, addressed them, "Now is the time. No noises. No talking. No fires. We must surprise. Last of all—if you see any Apache, kill it. Understood?" His gaze swept the congregation of men for any dissent. There was none. "Mount. Follow me." Jumping to the ground and securing his horse's reins, Jesús María put his foot in the stirrup and welcomed the groaning of the leather as he swung his leg over his horse and settled into the saddle.

Those on horse climbed into their saddles; the Papagos on foot shuffled forward.

Weakness in his legs, heaviness in his stomach, and fluttering in his heart stirred within Raúl when Jesús María grimly set them on their mission to kill with a strong, full arm gesture toward the small passageway between the Santa Catarina and Rincon Mountains. Astride his horse, Raúl gained composure.

Initially he had wanted to ride up front, near the lead, but Raúl now found himself comfortable amid the other Tucsonenses and stayed there, at the end of the group, enabling him to hear Oury curse aloud, "Ay, mierda."

Raúl watched as DeLong tore a sheet out of his daybook, upon which Oury scribbled a note. Addressing the driver who was stowing the last of his cook pans in the wagon, Oury said, "You know Hiram Stevens?"

Pivoting in the saddle, Raúl saw the driver tuck the note in his shirt, climb into the wagon, and slap the reins on his draft horses, taking off toward town.

At a walk, Raúl passed Oury and DeLong, the latter displaying nerves at the sight of the Papagos' mesquite-wood war clubs with spikes at their butt ends. At a trot, Raúl caught up with Juan. "¿Qué pasó?"

Juan glanced around to see who might hear, then leaned toward Raúl and said, "Oury forgot to close the main road." Spurring his horse, Juan quickly joined his brother at the lead while Oury and DeLong found their places among the handful of Anglos.

✦✦✦

The winding, narrow passageway carved through the rippling undulations of the mountain ranges—with its natural cutbacks, sharp turns, and dramatic rises—gave pause to the most seasoned riders. Once the elevation rose more than two hundred feet, Raúl ceased looking down to his right. He only looked straight ahead, his eyes glued to the horse rump in front of him, worrying whether he could dodge any low tree limbs protruding from the side of the mountain. As they climbed higher and as shadows deepened along the path under the highest peaks of the Santa Catarinas, Raúl sensed a chill in the air. The hairs on his arms stood up.

Still, they rode.

Happily, at about four in the afternoon, word from Jesús María came down the line to Raúl and the others that they were stopping for the night. Although still along the mountainous path, the land to the right sloped gently down to a stream, giving enough stretching room for both horses and men.

Unused to constant saddle time, Raúl stiffly swung his leg over the saddle, his feet heavily hitting the ground. Sandaled Papagos bringing up the rear quickly sought resting places.

One Papago horse—the rider still astride—slid awkwardly down the slope. Its heavy weight unbalanced and unwieldy, the horse fell forward over a large rock, trapping the Papago rider under him. Immediately the horse screamed in pain, its leg broken.

Every man stopped at the gut-wrenching sounds of the horse's shrieks of unbearable agony. Witnessing the accident in close proximity, Raúl and the Anglos stood riveted as Indians pulled the man out from under the screaming horse. Coming forward, a Papago, strongly muscled from daily farm labor, wielded his heavy mesquite war club and smashed the horse's head with one blow. In a coup de grâce, he thrust the club's spiked end into the horse's brain.

The shrieks immediately ceased.

Raúl sank weak-kneed to the ground. *Mi Dios, nuestro Padre, gracias por salvarme. Holy Lord* . . . Running a shaky hand over his forehead, he saw a few yards off that four white-faced Anglos—DeLong, Etchells, Bennett, and Foley— sat cross-legged, heads in their hands and looking down. As horse owners, all the men had seen equine accidents before; all had witnessed or personally shot horses for humane reasons. But never had they seen a war club used with such unbelievable power. Speechless, no one nearby talked, notwithstanding the restriction prohibiting them from doing so.

Once Raúl breathed steadily again, he took out a small piece of jerky. Eating seemed an abominable act, but necessity dictated. Munching, he again studied the four Anglos. The brawny blacksmith, Etchells, knelt before the other three Anglos and wrote something in the loose soil by the stream with his forefinger. After DeLong, Bennett, and Foley all nodded, Etchells wiped the evidence of his message from the dirt and resumed his resting spot.

Are they plotting something?

Juan and Jesús María wandered among the men to whisper, "We ride at ten. Get some sleep."

Raúl appreciated the reassuring look Juan gave him but wondered what was meant by the doubtful glance Jesús María cast his way.

At ten, when the first quarter moon shone high in the starry heavens, the riders led out, the Indians on foot following closely behind, continuing over the Cebadilla Pass. The parade of men tracked over the steep and treacherous path that snaked through the mountains. Saguaros, the tall sentinels of the desert that filled the slopes along the passageway at the beginning, had thinned out and altogether stopped at the higher elevations. Bare rocks and open-desert earth brightly reflected the moon's silver light, while the great abundance of low bushes and the oaks and mulberry trees—having taken over from palo verdes and ironwoods—ate up the light, creating deep black voids.

SATURDAY, APRIL 29, 1871

At five o'clock the next morning, Raúl brought himself upright with a start. His heart raced. He had fallen asleep in the saddle. As his horse plodded on he thought, "Caballo, I could kiss you."

Riding all through the night was a unique experience for the party of men, and it brought them teetering toward exhaustion at first light. Resting, the group stretched out farther along the trail than they'd anticipated and still had not reached the pass itself, which would take them eastward toward the Sierra Calitro Mountains.

After a silent meal taken next to a pockmarked, dark-skinned Mexican named Curro, and a full day's sleep that seemed like only minutes, a butt-sore Raúl climbed aboard his horse around five o'clock in the evening. Amid the Tucsonenses, Raúl joined the end of the procession when they set off again.

Finally the passage between mountain ranges was attained. The path opened after taking a few more twists and turns, and the contingent of weary travelers descended onto flatter land.

Juan, riding next to Jesús María in the lead, turned in the saddle and grimly looked back at Oury, Don Francisco, and the unflagging Papagos. *We should pick up the pace now. Very soon we pass a deep canyon. Past that, we ride through the low waters of the San Pedro and hug the foothills of the Sierra Calitro Mountains for the final push to Arivaipa and Camp Grant.*

The Papagos, either by prior knowledge or mere instinct, stoically and without mention quickened their pace, forcing the horses in front to move faster.

Juan wondered if they were gladly anticipating the battle.

♦♦♦

Biting into the warm, succulent strips from a roasted agave's stalk, Nest Feather closed her eyes. Its sweetness was so strong, she wanted to hold on to this moment as long as she could. All of the children had a small slice of roasted stalk, as did most of the women and men. A true celebration of spring and the renewal of the sacred earth.

Three bands of Arivaipa Apaches—Hashké Bahnzin's band and two others from the surrounding hills—crowded together near the narrow creek canyon, where the shadows formed early and stayed late. Soon it was dark and time for the dancing. Hashké Bahnzin sent an older couple up to the bluff as lookouts. They had celebrated much in their youth, so they didn't mind.

In the flats outside the canyon's west end, the rejoicing people created a large, fluid circle around a small fire. At the circle's center, medicine men from all bands began to dance, the first from Hashké Bahnzin's band. Nest Feather joined the circle dance. She dipped her left knee as she stepped to the side before bringing in her right foot. A simple, joyous movement repeated over and over as the singers chanted and drummed the steady rhythm of celebration, now led by the second Apache band. Flames darted up from the fire, brightening the People's faces already shining with broad grins. Some danced, others conversed, many laughed. Nest Feather, having stepped out of the circle, even noticed courting couples separating themselves from all others.

As the third Apache band's medicine man danced around the small fire, he seemed to falter. His steps ceased.

The singers' voices petered away and their drumming stopped. All the dancers in the outer circle halted.

Eyes looming large in the starlight, this medicine man warned, "A vision appears. G'ashdla'ácho o'áá stained red. Flee. We must flee death."

Men and women eyed one another. *What does he speak of?*

Hashké Bahnzin broke into the inner circle. Talking directly to the medicine man, but loud enough for all to hear, the leader assured, "We are safe in Big Sycamore Stands There in the shadow of the White Eyes' flagpole. We celebrate tonight."

The medicine man insisted, "Danger lurks. Tséjìné must leave." He turned to those around him. "Tséjìné, our lives depend upon leaving."

Ready to believe Hashké Bahnzin and intent on dancing, the Arivaipas refused to hear. The singers again came forward, beating their curled catclaw drum sticks loudly and steadily on their handheld water drums. Dancing circles quickly formed once more.

Hashké Bahnzin and the medicine man moved outside the circle, as did Nest Feather for a moment's rest. Voices raised above the drums and the celebrating Apaches, the medicine man repeated his warning, but Hashké Bahnzin shook his head. "We celebrate." Unheeded, the medicine man gathered his disappointed family and left the canyon.

Both a little amused and in disbelief, Nest Feather watched them go. Then she turned back to the circle of dance, catching sight of Sister and her husband moving together in the forward-and-backward dance that formed a part of Apache life.

Well before the others, Nest Feather returned to her gowah by the bright light of the stars above. The dancing had begun late at night; now it was only three hours before the sun stirred from his home to begin his daily travels. Excited and happy, Nest Feather was also disappointed. She had worn her gig-and-ham blouse but had not found a suitor that night.

SUNDAY, APRIL 30, 1871

ARIVAIPA CANYON

Around two a.m., Raúl looked up at the multitude of stars, brilliant and clear in a cloudless sky, and imprinted them in his memory. Yet la luna had moved lower in the sky. *A lover's moon. What moon isn't?* Raúl waggled the reins. *I should have embraced Valeria. I was so nervous, I lied. I had to leave. I should've kissed her as she wanted.*

Plodding along, time seemed interminable to Raúl. He had expected to see Camp Grant after moving through the pass several hours ago. Once more on open ground, Raúl looked behind to see the Papagos striding much closer to his horse. He goaded his horse with his boot heels, quickening his pace. Off to his right, a void appeared. *This must be the big canyon Juan spoke about.* Skirting it, Raúl peered into the eternal, impenetrable blackness. Quickly uttering a prayer, he shook his head to clear the thoughts running through his mind—thoughts as dark and deep as the canyon. *Let me conquer my fears as well as the enemy.*

Raúl followed the others, splashing across the shallow water flowing through the San Pedro River to the narrow belt of land between the thin ribbon of river and the rising, rippling foothills of the Sierra Calitro. A mounted Papago came alongside Raúl. The Indians, looking forward to the battle against their dreaded enemy, pressed the pace again. Raúl nudged his horse along; Joaquín Telles and Curro, as well as those before them, did the same.

Then all horses ahead stopped. Juan had ridden back along the line, motioning everyone to stop. He spoke quietly to Joaquín, who broke out of line and rode to the front with Juan.

In the moonlight Raúl glimpsed an animated but short meeting between the Elías brothers, Oury, and Jimmie Lee, before Joaquín, William Bailey, and a selected Papago set out together, going as fast as the land and darkness allowed.

Within fifteen minutes, Bailey galloped back to the Elías brothers. Shaking his head, Bailey pointed back from where he'd come. Oury slapped his leg with his riata; Jesús moved his sombrero farther back on his forehead.

Quickly Telles and the Papago with him returned to their spots in line. Raúl nudged Joaquín who said, "We're still about thirty miles out. Time's gettin' short. We can't be found in daylight where we are."

Jesús María's order of "double time" passed in whispers from man to man down the line.

✦✦✦

Sleepless, though tired, Nest Feather peeked outside her gowah. Nearby, warriors slept around a low-burning fire.

Creeping among them, figures advanced in the night, the stars and moon above beacons of light. Sharp knives hung from their belts, their bows slung over their backs. The figures tapped each sleeping Apache man on the shoulder.

Waking in starts, the Apaches quickly stood and silently followed the leader, who led them into the darkness of the winding, fertile canyon and beyond, where the wild deer romped freely and the White Eyes' cattle roamed within reach.

Concerned, Nest Feather watched from the gowah entrance, but the moon illumined the faces of their leader, Taccar, and another warrior. *Everything is fine.*

✦✦✦

The commandos' pace quickened; miles clocked off quickly.

About four o'clock in the morning, in an area where more and more dry washes threaded down from the Sierra Calitro foothills, the path forked. Clear passage between two cliffs lay to the east. The San Pedro River veered off to the west. DeLong, Etchells, Foley, and Bennett took the west-leading route, separating from the pack.

Passing by, Raúl spotted the Anglos' horses round a small hill. They were then lost to sight. *Was this what I saw them planning?*

His horse maintained a slow canter while Raúl's concerns over all that had transpired escalated: the unexpected halt, the sending of men out, the distance left, and the four Anglos disappearing. *Are we going through with this?* The gradual brightening of the dark charcoal at the horizon alarmed Raúl more. *We were to get there before dawn.*

Continuing, Raúl and the other men came to a plain, a widening between the foothills' cliffs. The land itself flowed like a river to the north, about two miles from the ranchería. And none too soon. It was approximately four twenty a.m.

Men in front of Raúl checked the bullets in the belts crossed over their chests. Others rested their hands on their rifles protected in saddle scabbards. *Almost there?* With a catch in his throat, Raúl turned toward Telles, Curro, and the other Tucsonenses; they seemed calm. A glance behind at the Papagos disturbed him. Their stolid natures had turned malevolent.

At not quite four thirty a.m., in the rapid change from deep charcoal to ash gray, Raúl made out the precipice of a cliff ahead.

We're at Arivaipa Canyon.

The still-bright first quarter moon hung unneeded, a wallflower at the sun's dance. Deep shadows in the canyon and along the fissured walls that doubled back upon themselves eased perceptibly with each passing moment. The grays of a new morning lightened.

The time is now.

Jesús María signaled a dismount. Raúl tied his reins to a bush while others ground tied their mounts, merely dropping the reins in front of the horse. Crowding around Jesús María, Raúl leaned forward to hear the orders. "Dos grupos. Uno—Papagos. Dos—Anglos y Mexicanos. La prima, Papagos." He motioned to Francisco Galerita. "Forward."

The Papagos did not move.

"No Don Guillermo." Francisco Galerita sat resolutely on his horse. Stunned, everyone looked around. Bill Oury was nowhere to be seen.

Scores of small rabbits hopped about, nibbling on wild grass sprigs. Quail, paired for life, sprinted across the divide, seeking low bushes on the other side.

The muffled sound of a horse's hooves came from behind the Indians. At a gallop, Oury rode up to the front. "Dropped my canteen."

It was a few minutes past four thirty, Sunday morning.

Creeping toward the edge of the cliff's south face, at the proposed point for their initial descent to the alluvial flats of Arivaipa Creek fifty feet below, Raúl and the Mexicans positioned themselves for their signal to move.

But at the cliff, two Apaches—an older man and an older woman—played cards. The woman threw down one card, which appeared to infuriate the man. She threw her head back in silent laughter, the moon casting a faint light on her high-cheeked face wrinkled with years of life in the Arizona sun. Gathering the discarded deck, the old warrior shuffled them by messing them around on the ground. These lookouts cast glances neither about themselves nor toward the canyon filled with their sleeping charges.

Passing by Raúl, two Papagos crept toward the engrossed gamblers. Standing behind the two card-playing Indians, the Papagos swung their war clubs down on one, then the other.

Without uttering a warning sound, the dead Apaches fell onto the ground atop the bluff, littered with discards.

Ninety-two Papagos, with the speed of raging waters in a flooded arroyo, streamed down the ravine's fissured walls at a point with the gentlest slope, only twenty yards from the widest expanse of Arivaipa Creek, and surged forward four miles, deep into the canyon.

Raúl looked at the quickly brightening sky, its gray changing to light cornflower blue. The moment of trial was at hand. The brotherhood he'd forged with these Tucsonenses only thirty-six hours ago surpassed any in his lifetime, including Valeria. Raúl felt the prod of a rifle barrel. It was Curro, who waved him on.

This is it.

Raúl found his feet, and following Juan's and Jesús María's motions to continue down the canyon, joined the others careening between loose soil and small ledges of granite down the cliff to the floor and into the heart of Arivaipa Canyon. Raúl's queasy stomach loosened. *Will I succeed? Don't let me fail. Make my brother proud.*

Off to the left, Raúl saw Bill Oury and Jimmie Lee racing up the north cliff, dodging the dense cacti and bushes. They placed their boxes of ammunition on the precipice where they had a clear view of the Apaches' domed wickiups below, then lay on the ground. Their A.T. stock rifles aimed at the fissured cliff walls on the opposite side of the canyon, they were ready.

Raúl, now running into the congested area of wickiups where Papagos positioned themselves outside many of the domed dwellings, heard the call of a roadrunner: the Papago signal of readiness.

At once, Papagos ripped off the gowah entrance covers. They manhandled Apache women, pulling them out of their homes. Some naked, some clothed, all kicking and fighting.

Already the cracking of skulls resounded. Screams filled the air.

Scores of dogs streamed out of the gowahs. They ran and circled. When they tried to bite the attackers, they too were bludgeoned with the war clubs.

At the first woman's scream, Raúl stopped, but the other Mexicans pushed him forward as they ran into the next, and the next, and the next wickiup where women and children woke to screams. Their last sight was Papagos and Mexicans breaking into their homes with guns and war clubs while the huge clubs smashed down upon their heads.

There are so many scrambling all over. Do I kill anyone? After a spurt of hot blood landed on Raúl, he knew that to be true—and liberating. *Be like Mateo and his banditos. ¡Ándale!* Seeing Curro running after an Apache youngster headed toward the depths of the canyon, Raúl tightened his grip on his Sharps and ran to join him, passing several Papagos dumping their dead victims in Arivaipa Creek and splaying their limbs in crude poses.

Raúl and Curro pursued the Apache youth past the far end of the wickiup cluster, where women and children fled their homes. Some tried climbing the crumbling earth wall before them with the help of two Apache men who, atop the cliffs, strapped ropes about their waists. In the remaining dark shadows quickly disappearing with the rising sun, a few women fleetest and surest of foot and one or two unencumbered with children attained the ravine's top, only to be gunned down from the opposite ledge by the Anglo sure shots. Lifeless, the Apaches tumbled on the rocks twenty feet below.

Nest Feather awoke to an empty gowah. Outside, screams and grunts brought her to her feet. Clothed but without moccasins, she ran from the gowah's darkness into what should have been the beauty of the sun brightening the skies over the mountains. Instead she found chaos.

Hundreds—it seemed—of violent strangers had invaded their canyon.

Nearby a Bean Eater, wielding a heavy club, brought it down on the head of Nest Feather's best friend. Blood and bits of the shattered skull exploded out, spraying Nest Feather, who spewed forth a scream of horror and terror she could not control. *The old nighttime story of Papagos bludgeoning our people outside their gowahs is true! Nightmares brought to life.*

Running a gauntlet between other Bean Eaters, Nest Feather fought for breath as she evaded shots from the cliff rim that splatted into the dirt inches from her feet. Mexicans shot the members of her clan point-blank, boring holes into their flesh, their blood spattering Nest Feather as she ran past. *This can't be! The unthinkable!* She waded into the shallows of her sacred Little Running Water, already fouled with blood that would stain her thoughts forever. *Which way to turn?*

Another sinister thought penetrated Nest Feather's fright.

Where is Sister?

In another of the deep turnings of the canyon, Raúl and Curro ran after a boy of fourteen clutching a bow and arrow. The boy sprinted to the east, rotating his head left and right, looking for a hiding place.

Raúl wheezed already; drops of sweat irritated his eyes. Holding his rifle in his left hand and shooting his pistol in his right as he ran, Raúl heard his bullet sing, ricocheting off a rock. The boy, untouched, rounded a fault in the ravine. Only steps behind, Raúl and Curro made the turn in time to see the boy taking cover behind a large boulder in front of a cave. Yelling and screaming, they pointed their rifles at the boy.

The young Apache bobbed up and down and side to side of the boulder, trying to make his bow and arrows appear as menacing as the enemies' guns. He shot an arrow, skimming past Raúl's cheek.

A flash of what could have happened flooded Raúl and enraged him. *Mateo shot a gun that close to my head once, boy. I charged him and got a broken nose for it.* He shot quickly, randomly, without aim, without any of the skill attained in practice sessions with Juan. Zinging into rocks or thudding into hillsides, his shots veered well off mark. His rage swelled. *I need to smell the blood of a dead Apache!*

Random sightings of the weaving boy frustrated both of them, yet it was because of Raúl's wanton wasting of bullets that Curro backed up. "Esto no es bueno."

As if awoken from a spell, Raúl fired a last shot at the boy, leaving him to his fate, and withdrew to the main arena of blood where easier prey could be sought.

Spurred by the sight of Hashké Bahnzin, nude and bloodied, clutching his small daughter to his breast and running into the depths of Arivaipa Canyon to the east, Nest Feather ran after him, but an arm wrapped around her waist and lifted her off her feet. She screamed, joining the constant wails of Arivaipa women. She kicked and bit the Papago's brown arm that held her fast. A distinctive howl cut through all sounds. *Sister!* Looking toward the canyon's west opening, Nest Feather witnessed hell.

Onawa, without clothes, held her toddler. Fear distorted her features. A Papago grabbed the howling boy, swung him over his head like a rag doll, and threw him to the ground. An Anglo, wielding his bloody army saber, ran by the dead baby and, in one slash of his saber, sliced the child's arm almost off before advancing on others.

The Papago shoved Onawa to the dirt and pinned her flat. She kicked and yowled, her screams one among many. He pulled her arms over her head. A passing Mexicano dropped his pants and raped her, thrusting deeply and savagely.

Howling at Sister's torture, Nest Feather brutally kicked the Papago, who effortlessly imprisoned her in his arms.

Raúl Obregón plunged himself into the Apache woman splayed out on the ground next to a dead baby.

Close to Raúl's ear, a pistol fired, blowing a hole in the Apache's breast. Blood seeped and pooled under her.

Woman's blood.

Splattered, Raúl drew out. He stood, peering at the victim's glazing black eyes and wiping her blood from his face. *Hey, Mateo, look at your bookish brother.*

Nest Feather wailed and stretched out her arms. "*Shi-deh!* Sister!" Unwittingly, Nest Feather gave opportunity to the Papago, who slung her around to his side like the sheaves of hay lying about the ranchería ready to bind for sale to Camp Grant. She kicked, soundly walloping her abductor, but he, vastly stronger, subdued her and ran for the bluff.

Raúl staggered back a step as someone grabbed the back of his shirt.

Releasing Raúl's collar, Jesús María still held his pistol at the ready. "We're here to kill." Rifle bullets from the cliff found their marks close by. "Go back to the horses. And stay there."

Turning and pushing forward through the continuing mayhem, Raúl could not locate the Papago who had been with him until he caught a glimpse of him ahead, running toward the bluff they had descended what seemed hours ago.

Within minutes, Raúl climbed the escarpment to stand a discreet distance from Oury and Lee, who had returned from the cliffs. Jimmie Lee looked directly at Raúl and gave him a conspiratorial wink, smiling grimly.

By that wink Raúl withered. *Lee's got me by the balls. He saw what I did. He'll hold it over me for life.* At the tethered horses Raúl discovered miserable Apache babies, their cries unnerving. *Children. I heard nothing about children.* Raúl approached a Mexicano who held a babe in arms, but stopped. Don Francisco lifted the small blanket around the baby, obviously to determine the sex; the Papago chief performed this small task with such rapacious intensity that it sickened Raúl; he turned away and waited for Juan. *He'll have answers.*

With all her might Nest Feather flailed her arms and legs but failed to escape or impede the Papago's rapid trot up to the south bluff's clifftop, where an older Anglo, speaking Spanish, met them and grabbed Nest Feather. The Papago joined the Indians' segregated group of enemy slayers. Now untouchable, these men would seclude themselves for sixteen days, eating and drinking only small amounts of food and water delivered by old women, until purified by ritual. Their duty done, their bodies fouled and contaminated by touching Apaches, enemy slayers withdrew completely from the warpath, until the next time.

Nest Feather gave the old Anglo as good as she gave the Papago, but the wiry man wrestled her toward a mighty horse where more than two dozen whimpering Arivaipa children clung to each other under the fierce stares of several Mexicans. Nest Feather pounded her captor's back until he threw her to the ground and bound her hands in front and her ankles together. From her gut came forth a roar, "I am Woman, not an animal!" Angling her head, her gaze lingered on the Apaches. Only then did she realize how many children there were.

Sobbing, all of the children wailed for Nest Feather, someone familiar. The two nearest her, only four and five years old, she had known since their days in the cradleboard and had served as nanny to them many times when their mother was busy with other tasks. Their cries cut the deepest. Wanting to comfort them, Nest Feather thrust her legs and arms forward over the rough ground and pulled herself on her side to reach them, despite knowing that the Spanish-speaking Anglo, a taller and thinner White Eyes, and a smaller, intense Mexicano of pale skin and graying hair—White Mexican—watched her every move. Reaching the two children, Nest Feather nestled heads with them until looking up into the face of an old Papago, eyeing her with a malicious gleam. *He must be their leader, the way he sits on his horse, the way that he orders the other Bean Eaters about.*

Nest Feather felt a sharp jab in her side. Again and again a Mexican prodded her with a stick as he might herd cattle. She rolled on the ground to join the rest of the captive children, wrestled into several groups by the Mexicans and untouched Papagos. Renewed wails from the children ruptured forth. Nest Feather tore at her ropes. *I must be free.* Neither gnawing the ropes nor working them against her skin released her from their bonds; they only chafed and scraped her body that oozed Apache blood.

Juan and a few other Mexicans ambled in, signaling the end of the fight.

Congratulations abounded that the slaughter took only half an hour, ending at around five a.m.

"I am glad to count you among the living." Juan clasped Raúl's shoulder.

Raúl waggled his thumb toward the children. "What happens to them?"

"Homes. They'll find homes."

Jesús María beckoned Juan with a wave. Raúl tagged along, joining the Elías brothers, Oury, Jimmie Lee, and several more Mexicanos in another descent into Arivaipa Canyon.

They walked through the carnage. Raúl looked down on one old man, an elder, lying dead, the body rested on the right side, revealing a gunshot wound to the left ribs. *What stories he probably told.*

Oury smiled at the hole the minié ball made. "We sent him to the happy hunting ground."

Raúl walked beside Juan as other Mexicanos searched the Arivaipas' domed shacks. Several children hiding in them were pulled out and taken. One or two still-pure Papagos forever silenced the remaining dogs that roamed among the dead. Raúl looked at his friend for a reaction, as he had seen Juan pet many an animal.

Betraying no emotion, Juan said, "I've never seen so many dogs. More than in Tucson, if that's possible."

Walking among the destroyed wickiups and the dead, they encountered the bodies of mainly women, a few children, one or two men, and the elder.

"Braves weren't overlooked," Jesús María answered everyone's nagging thoughts.

"That many braves could not have escaped us." Oury grabbed a pole propping up a sagging wickiup and yanked it loose. The home fell in a heap.

"Could they have been forewarned?" Lee's lilting Irish accent was a sharp contrast to the destruction they viewed.

"How?" Juan kicked the dirt.

Oury viewed the slaughter. "Still, the tally is good enough. Burn everything."
Raúl pulled a match from his pocket.

From the bluff top where she lay, Nest Feather could see the rising smoke.

Instantly she knew what was happening. The homes of her Arivaipa Apaches—made by Apache women with lean, leafy branches bent over and tethered together to form a dome and covered with deer skins—blazed within their sacred land of Arapa. But gowahs were easily replaced. The lives of her sister, their cousins, their clan members, members of their band whose corpses lay in odd positions on the hallowed ground could not.

Nest Feather became blinded by her tears, as deep within the canyon, flames licked and consumed the ranchería. In only moments the narrow ravine reeked with smoke.

Overhead, the morning sun had traveled well up into the sky. In spite of her bindings, Nest Feather struggled to her feet and instinctively raised her head to the east. Shocked, the other children watched. Some were swaddled; some wore clothing; some were shod in moccasins; others, like Nest Feather, were barefoot; the smallest were naked. Twelve-year-old Nest Feather realized that—being as small as a nine-year-old—only her petite form had saved her from death.

Seized again by several assailants dirtied and damp with gore and soot, Nest Feather fought back but ultimately was roped together with the four- and five-year-old brother and sister; the older children also were bound into groups of twos or threes. Babes in arms were taken on horseback.

Jesús María said to Oury in Spanish that exposed his weariness, "That girl can't walk hobbled."

Nest Feather steeled herself against the Anglo's approach. *Will he kill me? I would welcome that bullet.* Instead the Anglo unbound her ankles. *I still breathe—for now.*

Jesús María circled his arm overhead, giving the silent order to vamoose. As the assailants mounted their horses, saddle leather groaned—the only familiar sound of the morning.

Astride his horse, Raúl looked about the area: the green grass by the little creek, the Sierra Calitros beyond the rolling hills and vales of the desert, Camp Grant only five miles to the west. *I want these landmarks etched into memory. I am proud to have participated in this monumental achievement. Zeckendorf will be proud of me. Valeria will be proud. Our future children will revere me for this day.*

Falling into the steady pace set by the lead horses of Oury, Juan, and Jesús María, everyone moved out. At the rear, contaminated Papago enemy slayers, whether on foot or mounted, distanced themselves from all others by thirty to forty yards. Riding from the killing ground along the bluff that took them within plain eyesight of Camp Grant, Raúl scanned the parade ground, where not one soldier was in evidence.

Following the San Pedro River south, surrounded by men and horses, Nest Feather tottered on with the other children, smelling the sweat, blood, and fear on their bodies.

Two miles in, four horsemen waited—DeLong, Bennett, Etchells, and Foley. As the four Anglos joined the march behind Raúl, he noted how clean their clothes were. Raúl's own clothes were muddy, ripped, and bloody; only a smattering of trail dust spoiled theirs.

Juan and Jesús rode back to the four horsemen. Juan asked, "Any trouble?"

DeLong glared at the children but answered the Elías brothers, "None. Nothing. No one stirred from when we arrived at Camp Grant to when we left."

Jesús looked thoughtful. "¿Cualquier sonidos?" Sounds traveled.

"No." DeLong shook his head. And when the brothers moved off, he added, "Thank God."

At the start Nest Feather gave the children encouragement, but a Mexican silenced her in a gruff whisper. They stumbled on, progressing to the southwest. Some children found rides on horses, but not Nest Feather. Deeply bruised by stones on the path, her feet bled. Wincing with each step, she continued until a mesquite bosque, dark and ominous even in full daylight, came into view.

Jesús María called for a rest.

Nest Feather collapsed under a mesquite tree. Her feet, caked with blood and dust thrown up by the horses around her, throbbed. The two small children still clung to her, refusing to leave her side, thus separating themselves from the majority of the other children.

Raúl found shade near the outermost mesquites, while the stifled clanging of tin plates and long draughts of water from canteens brought welcomed routine to the day. Nearby, some of the Mexicans, still feeling exhilarated, regaled the four returned Anglos with stories of their victory between stuffing their mouths with what food they had in reserve. Juan gave a few morsels of food to the children before a nap was ordered.

Sleep failed Nest Feather. Gory visions rose up in the blackness: beautiful Shi-deh screaming, bullets flying, bashed heads bleeding. Awake, Nest Feather studied the sleeping men, the horses, and the long, treacherous mesquite bosque. Anything and anyone could be lurking in that crush of gnarly mesquite trees. Knotted roots grew out of the ground and formed loops. Limbs poked out in every direction. Weeds mounded in thick, thorny masses. There seemed no passage through the closely grown mesquites.

VENETIA HOBSON LEWIS

Raúl obliged Juan and stood lookout during the layover. Rubbing his temples to stay awake, he moseyed among the men and children. Then the face of the dead squaw appeared to him.

Black eyes staring. Dismayed, he stepped back. He shook his head. Turning about, Raúl looked for her. *Gone.* He stifled his nervous chuckle and looked to see if anyone witnessed his peculiar behavior. *No. Everyone's asleep.* He walked on.

Under a mesquite tree, Raúl noticed a petite, plain-faced girl against whom two very young children snuggled. *Soon my children will sleep thus.* Continuing on, the visage of vacant black eyes returned. Again he shook his head. It left him. *I rid myself of that forever.*

Silence returned. Only the nearby burbling San Pedro spoke to Nest Feather.

In an hour Raúl woke the men. Sounds returned. Some children cried out for their parents.

Juan took Curro and Raúl aside. "The way the children are bound hampers our advance. They need to walk separately, but tie their hands. And keep a close eye on them."

Raúl and Curro followed Juan's orders, receiving stoic looks from a few children, but not from the plain-faced girl, who glared at them. They doubled the knots of her ropes.

The Elías brothers pointed out the bosque's eastern edge, along which ran a gully, pooled with water from a recent rain. Years of fallen mesquite leaves shaped like fern blades carpeted a worn path leading back to the route the party had taken earlier. The men on their mounts and their tightly grouped abductees—now able to walk at a faster pace—took a wide path around the bosque, the horses' hooves making a soft, slushy sound as the leaves scattered under them.

Then there was another sound. Horses' ears flicked back and rotated to its source. Ahead of Raúl, Oury's stallion, eyes bugging out with increasing fright, fought its reins, twisting from side to side, snorting. The fractious horse sent Raúl's and the rest of the Anglos' and Mexicans' horses into a frenzy. Horse bumped against horse. Oury and others tightly squeezed their legs against the broad bellies of their horses but gained no control.

Lacking experience on a balking horse, Raúl fought frantically against his, pulling back on the reins, steering away from the other mounts. Someone's elbow knocked him off the saddle, and he landed with a thud. Turning over, he saw his horse's hooves churning midair directly over him. *Only moments to live.* Raúl scrambled away on hands and knees before the hooves came down near his head. Taking several seconds to gather his nerve, Raúl caught the loose reins and pulled his horse away from other recoiling steeds.

Nest Feather drew the Apache brother and sister closer to her on the edge of the path and away from the horses. The carpet of leaves before them moved without the slightest breeze. Several blades parted.

Out poked the heads of two brown mice. They ventured out. Then a dozen more mice scrambled out, circling and scurrying under the horses' thrashing hooves.

Nest Feather watched the tiny, whiskered animals create complete chaos among the mighty steeds above them. *Did not She Who Sits in Quiet mold my back, shoulders, arms, and hands to gain the strength to resist evil events when they come? Had not Changing Woman chosen the common brown mouse as my power?*

Several more horses reared on their back legs. A Mexican's fractious horse pushed Nest Feather and the children off the path. They toppled into the wet gully.

Nest Feather summoned her courage and, despite her shackling ropes, prodded and bumped the two children to the edge of the mesquite bosque. These children had traveled several miles in all directions beyond Arivaipa Canyon. No matter their age or if their hands were tied, they could survive.

"Hide," she fiercely whispered. "Hide until we leave. Then run back to Arapa. Go. Now."

Paralyzed, the little boy and girl stared until Nest Feather grimaced with her most foreboding visage. She scowled at the pair until they crawled over and under gnarled mesquite roots, disappearing into the bosque's depths. *If we all hid, the White Eyes would track us down and kill the three of us. I sacrifice myself for these children. They must live.* Turning, Nest Feather viewed the men's actions.

Having retreated from the horses' wild gyrations to the other side of the path, contaminated enemy slayers could not help Don Francisco, who barely clung to his saddle aboard the paint horse.

White Mexican jumped from his horse, ripped off his shirt, and threw it over the paint horse's eyes, subduing it. Most of the Mexicans and Anglos followed suit with their mounts.

Nauseated by the stench of the men's torn and bloodied shirts thrown about, bile rose in Nest Feather's throat. *My sister's blood. My nephew's blood.* She fell to the ground and retched. Wiping the spittle dangling from her mouth with her shoulder, she felt the worse for it.

Raúl tied his reins on a tree well away from the continuing bedlam of Don Francisco and other men subduing their horses. He walked by the plain-faced girl again. *The two little ones are missing. What cunning . . .* Wrenching her from the ground, Raúl shook Nest Feather violently.

Jesús María hurried over. "¿Qúe pasó?"

"Un niño y una niña with her. Gone."

VENETIA HOBSON LEWIS

Jesús María glared down at Nest Feather, whom Raúl retained in his grip. "¿Dónde están?"

She silently returned his scowl; the Mexican with a broken nose shook her again. When he stopped she gawked wide-eyed at White Mexican as if mystified. *From me, the palefaces get nothing.*

Juan rode up, pulled out his pistol, and aimed at Nest Feather. "No hay tiempo para esto. No time for this."

"¡No!" Don Francisco once again sat regally upon his steed. "Ella es mi recompensa."

Juan uncocked his revolver. *It's quicker to kill her, but Don Francisco gets his reward.* "Keep a close eye on her."

Raúl frowned. *¿Recompensa? What reward?*

Quickly the perpetrators mounted their quieted horses and set forth again.

Stoically controlled, although death had lured her to the edge, Nest Feather dared not look back into the depths of the mesquites but hoped the small boy and girl would soon leave the bosque and find their way back to Arapa. *Home.*

Throughout the daytime hours, the disparate band of captors and captives walked along the western ridges of the Sierra Calitros and into the foothills of the Santa Catarinas.

Nest Feather and the large group of children trudged lethargically in the middle of the Mexican horses, well in front of the Papagos, whose feet were as thick and strong as leather. But the children's feet were still tender. They limped in pain from stepping on sharp rocks and the cactus needles from the jumping cholla that littered the desert. When Raúl saw that their feet left a trail of blood, a halt was called at the entrance to Cebadilla Pass.

Too tired to move, the children waited while Mexicans and Anglos dismounted and led their horses behind large boulders and cedar bushes. Children sipped water from runoff areas in the canyon, but only after the horses and the men. Lookouts posted, most others took siestas.

Raúl sprawled on the dusty ground, instantly falling asleep. When he awoke he knew many hours had elapsed. He accepted little bits of food being distributed to everyone, and as he ate, the petite Apache girl, her hands tied in front of her, stood before him. Her face, streaked with tears, was smudged, grimy, dirty, and without expression.

All the while Broken Nose ate, Nest Feather's black eyes bored into him.

Raúl recognized her from the incident earlier in the day at the bosque. *She's clever. But she won't get past us now. And I sure as hell don't like being stared at.*

ON THE RETURN TO TUCSON

The party rode all night over the winding Cebadilla Pass, through the back side of the towering Santa Catarina Mountains, the eerie light of the waxing moon playing over the land.

With each step, Nest Feather winced as her painful feet hit the ground. Once, she dared look at the uneven granite cliffs and boulders, where the shadows of the moving men, their mounts, and the children wobbled in broken gaits.

Everything now had a familiarity about it to Raúl. He recognized certain odd shapes in the trees and the jutting of the granite into great cones and balancing rocks. But mainly he tried not to think. The apparition of the Apache woman stayed in his mind: her mouth wide open in a horrific scream, her fingernails clawing at him, her fearful black eyes, and then the bullet blasting close to his ear, the blood spewing out from her breast.

Raúl's half-digested dinner rose up in his throat. He cleared it, making a sound that instantly brought angry grimaces from the Mexicans around him. *All I want is the daylight, a bath, and Valeria.*

Night turned into day.

When the straggling band reached the Tanque Verde Wash in the Tucson area, a new burst of energy rejuvenated the men, but not the children. Dead on their feet, they moved forward nevertheless. Many huddled around the plain-faced girl as if she had magical powers.

Up ahead Raúl spied Jimmie Lee resting against a wagon, the oxen straining their reins to eat tufts of grama grass. Earlier, Lee had left the group, galloping ahead to summon more provisions and fresh clothes from Adjutant General Hughes.

Raúl and others laughed as a couple of Mexicanos grabbed armfuls of fresh shirts and pants from the high-sided wagon and threw them in the air above the heads of the others. Shirts rained down like candy from a smashed piñata, men catching the clothing as it fell.

Washing himself in the mountain runoff in Tanque Verde Creek where it flowed into the Rillito and tucking a fresh shirt into new pants brought normalcy, as well as a problem, to Raúl. *How can I explain the new clothes to Valeria? Were they part of the shipment I told her I delivered?* He glanced at the Papagos. They still remained a good distance away. Unwashed, without food, and, due to their beliefs, unable to touch anyone. *The one on the end, that's the Papago who held down that Apache I . . . He only looks at the ground. Good. I never want to see him again.*

"Give the children food and water," Jesús María said to no one in particular, knowing his word among the Mexicanos was law.

All the Apache children clamored, arms outstretched, for the removal of their ropes and food and water from two swarthy Mexicans who approached them. Nest Feather surged forward. *My ropes, too. Take them off.* All but Nest Feather were released from their ropes. Torn bites of chicken and tortillas were thrown at the children's feet, the Mexicans laughing and snorting as the captives scrambled in the dirt, devouring what leftovers they could grab.

Nest Feather wanted to kick the food away, but a great gnawing feeling in her gut stabbed her at the sight of it. She crawled on the ground, picking tortilla scraps from the dirt as fast as she was able, despite the ropes about her wrists. Like the other children, Nest Feather couldn't care where the food came from. They all crammed dirty bits of chicken and rice particles in their mouths. Then, their exhaustion too great to withstand, Nest Feather and the rest of the children curled up together on the ground.

Feeling drowsy, Raúl settled on a rock near Juan, but Oury and Jesús María cut everyone's rest short. All must immediately disperse in different directions, individually or in small groups, as they had left Tucson. Suspicions could not be aroused. Discovery of their convoy all together in one spot would be disastrous.

Raúl reluctantly stood, but seeing Francisco Galerita approach the children, he remained close to the Elías brothers.

Galerita surveyed the rewards that would come to him and his People. "They must be separated now."

Oury scowled at the sleeping Apache children. "Take the ones you want."

"Uno momento," Jesús María addressed his Anglo compatriot. "Amigos en Tucson requested twelve children for their homes."

"No, too many," Francisco held firm.

Juan stepped into the negotiations. "Diez."

"No."

The late morning's sun glinted off Jesús María's revolver. "Diez. Ten. And I choose."

Francisco's benign smile contradicted the determined look in his shaded eyes. "Do not look for more. The People will handle our share according to our tradition."

Raúl then realized why children were taken. Some time ago Juan informed him about the practices of the Papagos. Their share of the children would be treated like unassimilated enemies in Papago settlements until they were old enough to be sold as slaves in México. *This is dirty business, and I took part.*

Under Oury's stony stare, Jesús María agreed, "Sí, está bien." Turning on his heels, Jesús María walked among the children waking from their naps.

Nest Feather eyed White Mexican, who quickly chose three babes in arms and three boys and three girls, ranging in age from toddlers to seven-year-olds. Finally he stopped before Nest Feather. To him she presented her admittedly plain face, blatantly displaying as much hatred as she could.

"Ella."

Oury said, "She's trouble. Take another."

"Ella es muy inteligente. Take her."

Juan pointed to Raúl, who unceremoniously hauled the plain-faced Apache girl up by the arms. She screamed and cried and pummeled his back and his head. She kicked his thighs, but he held tight and dumped her like a sack of potatoes into the back of the high-sided wagon with the previously selected three boys and three girls.

A wail of howling rose up. Like calves for slaughter, Francisco's horse separated the rest of the Apache children, herding them toward the Papago camp.

Scrambling to the top of the wagon's side, Nest Feather stretched out her tied hands. *My Arivaipa children are being taken away. We must stay together.* Nest Feather bawled and yelled in Apache at the rejected children.

At Nest Feather's shouts, some children balked. They dodged horses as they tried to run to her. Tucsonenses ran after the children, grappled with them, and tossed them back into the middle of a circle formed by remaining pure Papagos, who closed ranks. Those children became prisoners.

Still fighting, Nest Feather hoisted her leg over the wagon's side, but Broken Nose shoved her back. Scrambling to her feet again, Nest Feather viewed the horrors before her: the Papago circle pushing forward, the children moving against their will amid a sea of horses, the shifting of their feet creating a little dust cloud. With grandeur, the Papago chief, astride the saddle of his steed, led the way with the contaminated enemy slayers well in the rear, all heading southwest toward San Xavier del Bac and other Papago settlements.

Juan and Jesús María entrusted the babes in arms to three Mexicanos, mounted on sturdy horses, for the ride into town before joining Raúl by the wagon to inspect the remaining children.

Before Juan gave the driver instructions to start off, he turned to Jesús. "I'll supervise the distribution of children at Jimmie Lee's house. Those requesting children arrive after dark. We leave."

VENETIA HOBSON LEWIS

"We can't find homes for the other children?" Raúl tilted his hat back on his head.

Juan did not look at his friend as he and Jesús María climbed into their saddles. "We are only concerned with these ten."

The crack of the wagon driver's whip over the yoke of oxen splintered the air. When the massive animals heaved forward, the wagon lurched, sending Nest Feather and the other children to the wagon's bed. They struggled to their feet, but with the wagon's progress so swift and bumpy over the tufts of grama grass, they were thrown down over and over again. Juan trotted next to the wagon, keeping an eye out for any child making an escape. The three Mexicanos with the babies in their arms brought up the rear.

A curt nod serving as his goodbye to the proud and self-absorbed Oury, Jesús María prodded his horse into a gallop.

Without orders, Raúl, the Anglos, and other Mexicanos climbed into their saddles and headed off toward Tucson, either individually or in pairs. Turning at the shout of his name, Raúl recognized Curro, who looked vicious even in new clothing.

"¿Una cerveza? Beer?"

"Sí. Una o dos." Raúl's laughter riding the breeze, he and Curro gave their horses free rein.

MONDAY, MAY 1, 1871

The tiny hand stitches blurred. Sighing, Valeria dropped the unfinished blouse in her lap. All day long she had worked. Now, by the fitful flicker of candlelight over the dark maroon satin, she must stop, afraid that she would ruin it, as tired as she was.

Pulling a lock of hair behind one ear, Valeria wondered when Raúl would return. Raúl's obvious excitement about the trip made him disregard many of her questions, so the details he'd given of the supply train were sketchy.

She rose from the chair and peered out of the front window at the darkness. A few stars twinkled. Then a face appeared. "¡Raúl!"

Valeria ran to the door, flung it open, and threw her arms around her husband's waist. He smelled of tobacco and cerveza. She pulled his head down to hers and salted his face with kisses, all the while pulling him inside. "Mi amor. I missed you."

Too much. Annoyed at Valeria's constant kisses, Raúl drew her arms away and put distance between them.

Candlelight played over his face, full of little cuts and a large bruise.

"You're hurt."

"I . . . a little tussle with a rope."

"Pobrecito. Come. Come sit and tell me." As he had overlooked her questions, Valeria now overlooked Raúl's reluctance. She couldn't stop her eager chatter. "Are you hurt elsewhere?" She drew his hand in hers and found other bruises there. She noticed his shirt—it was plaid. Raúl preferred solid colors. "A new shirt?"

"Sí. A . . . castoff from the wagon." He glanced toward the bedroom and edged closer to its doorway.

Valeria stepped back. He wore new denims. "Mister Zeckendorf is very generous."

"Yes. Uh . . . it was a good trip."

"Bueno." Valeria beamed; her husband had returned safely.

Now at the bedroom doorway, Raúl avoided looking at Valeria, who jockeyed about, moving wherever he glanced. "I'm tired."

"We'll talk later? I want to hear . . ."

"Later." He threw his bedroll on the bedroom floor, stripped, and tossed his clothes atop the bedroll before jumping under the bed covers and turning away.

Lonelier now than when he wasn't home, Valeria closed the front door.

✦✦✦

In a rapidly moving rig, Nest Feather sat rigidly between the strange man and woman to whom she had been handed, wondering who they were. She studied the seat and its rails, an upright board protecting their feet, and tried to plot an escape. Her thoughts were not sharp; her eyelids drooped, and her head bobbed. Through her thin clothing she felt the crush of the woman's satin dress on her right and the roughness of the man's worn denims on her left. The unknown language they rattled off, the same as spoken by most of her captors, was gibberish to her. With a gentle smile playing over the woman's face, she took off her shawl and covered Nest Feather's chest and legs, tucking it under. Nest Feather repulsed the woman's touch. The stranger seemed shocked. Again the couple chattered in the foreign tongue that was harsh to Nest Feather's ears. It did not ripple beautifully like the waters of Arivaipa Creek over rocks as did Arivaipa Apache.

"We wanted a girl. I am so happy."

"I hope this works out as planned, Paloma."

"The other little girls were already taken before we got there."

"It will work out." The man clucked his tongue to speed up the horse.

Unused to a carriage ride with its jolts and undulations and creaking noises, Nest Feather reached out for anything that would steady her, clutching what was available. It was the hand of Smiling Woman. Nest Feather looked up into the woman's black eyes and discovered they were not unlike the eyes of Sister, whom Nest Feather must now, even in her thoughts, refer to as She Who Is Gone.

It was only a short ride from the tall and lean Anglo's home, where Nest Feather had been given to the strange man and woman. They drove past businesses and homes, jammed together like stalks of corn, without end or beginning. The ride ended once the carriage circled a large, detached stucco house.

The home's size impressed Nest Feather. *This must be the gowah of the nant'án. The other small buildings are for his subordinates.*

Startled by Denim Pants's jump from the carriage, Nest Feather shrunk back from his proffered hand. The woman stepped from the carriage next, all the while holding onto Nest Feather's hand. Looking down from the bench seat, Nest Feather warily edged toward them. Neither the man's kind attention nor the woman's smile put Nest Feather at ease. On her own she stepped from the carriage.

Retrieving the shawl, they entered the large building.

Passing the first square room where a Mexican woman washed platters, they continued through a long, open space, encased with stucco walls and mesquite doors on either side, into a smaller stucco room.

More gibberish. Pointing to objects of unknown use.

The platter-washing Mexican lugged in a big metal barrel before returning with pails of steaming water.

Denim Pants disappeared before Platter Washer and Smiling Woman stripped Nest Feather of her clothing. Nest Feather grabbed for her gig-and-ham blouse, but Platter Washer, despite her weight, was quicker. Nest Feather fought the unknown women and their soapy cloth wandering all over her body, her hair, and her nails.

Screams and wailing and fighting back. Water sloshed.

Soaked women.

Cursing in gibberish.

Water on top of Nest Feather's head.

Fluffy, warm towel rubbed briskly on strange-smelling skin.

Ointment on feet.

Nest Feather ran her fingertips down her wiry hair, now bushing out, untamed and trailing down her back. Scowling, she looked up at Smiling Woman and Platter Washer standing over her. They considered her unruly mess of hair.

After Platter Washer left, Denim Pants reappeared. Nest Feather grimaced at the warm milk and bland oatmeal the woman tried to feed her. Unused to the taste of milk, Nest Feather pushed the bowl away as the man droned on, "We are the Escalantes—Paloma and Ignacio. I am a freighter. Born here in Tucson back when it was in Sonora, México. Esta es su recámara. Your bedroom." Nest Feather recognized softness in the worried but hopeful glance he gave the woman. "We hope you like it here."

The woman called for tortillas to be brought and smiled. "Su nombre es Ramira Hilaria. Ra-mi-ra." She pointed to Nest Feather's chest, saying, "Ramira," while exaggerating the trilling of the *r*'s. Pointing to herself, she said, "Paloma," and repeated each name several times. "I've always loved the name Ramira, and Hilaria was our daughter's name."

Nest Feather assumed something was expected of her. Some of the People in other Apache bands were known for their understanding and speaking of foreign tongues, but none near Nest Feather. At first she glared. Then, perhaps due to her extreme weariness, she tried to imitate the sound. "Err . . . rrrr. MMmmmmm irrr . . . rrrr." Her tongue would not ripple.

"Muy bueno. Para comenzar. Just a beginning."

In a moment Platter Washer returned with warm tortillas for Nest Feather, who tore into them hungrily.

While Nest Feather ate, Smiling Woman bustled about, pulling back the white bed coverlet, revealing more white cloths. She patted the bed and put her hands together under her tilted head.

When Nest Feather took a wobbly step forward, Denim Pants believed that the very tired child would collapse, so he picked Nest Feather up in his arms, to her surprise. She yelled, kicked her legs, and beat on him. Dropped in the middle of the bed, Nest Feather recoiled against the wall as far from Señor Escalante as she could get.

"She's afraid of men right now. Go outside, Ignacio." Returning, Paloma spoke slowly, softly, calmly of how much she and Ignacio had wanted a little girl—their own four-year-old daughter having died the previous year; how much they hoped their Apache child would love them; and how much Paloma looked forward to teaching her about their culture. Paloma whispered a little prayer for strength—for this girl and for herself. At last Paloma motioned how legs and body should slip under the coverlet.

Nest Feather's drooping eyelids widened. *Is this an attack?* She hesitated, then ducked her head under the covers to see if something lurked. *Nothing.* Dropping the coverlet, Nest Feather allowed her suspicions to fly away on a bat's wings into the night.

Señora Escalante closed the door.

Belly full, Nest Feather lay atop the bed, her head cushioned by the feather pillow. As sleep claimed her, the last image she remembered was Señora Escalante's smile.

TUESDAY, MAY 2, 1871,
AND ENSUING DAYS

Nest Feather, wrapped in a sheet, pushed uneaten beans around her plate, sopping up their juice with a tortilla, which she stuffed in her mouth. Yet with caution Nest Feather eyed every move of Platter Washer. *She moves about freely. I am fed, not shackled. Am I to be a slave here?*

A panicked Paloma Escalante rushed into the kitchen. "I peeked into Ramira's bedroom. She's not there. Her pillow's on the floor. The coverlet too. Where . . . ?" Finally noticing Ramira, Paloma placed a quaking hand on her upper chest, took a deep breath, and pulled out another table chair.

Will she beat me now? Lowering the rest of her tortilla onto the plate, Nest Feather regarded Smiling Woman. *Both hands must be free.*

Manuela, the cook and housekeeper, wiped her hands on a towel. "Es muy inteligente. Smart. She learns fast."

Nest Feather puzzled about Smiling Woman. *She sinks into the chair as if her bones are weak.*

"Thank God she's here. I thought she had escaped through the high window."

"Up with the sun, this one."

"I see." Paloma rose. "Manuela, please prepare beef for this evening. She should have a good dinner esta noche. I will be in the sitting room, if needed."

"Sí, Señora Escalante."

Nest Feather peeked around the door to see Señora Escalante collapse into a stuffed chair and hold her head. Returning to the kitchen, she gawked at Manuela coming back in from the outside porch. *Platter Washer holds the largest joint of beef I've ever seen.* Encircled with fatty beef, the joint was so heavy that the cutting board bounced under its weight.

Nest Feather watched Platter Washer slide a knife from a sheath atop the small table. Its blade dulled by use, the knife looked pitted to Nest Feather's experienced eye.

Manuela passed the knife only a couple of times against a rod of iron: first one edge to the front, then the other edge to the back. Eyeing the long blade, Manuela grunted and plunged the knife into the meat joint. She hacked away, trying to expose the bone.

Every time Platter Washer crudely pierced the meat with the dull knife, Nest Feather flinched. *I cannot watch the mutilation of fine beef that could feed my entire band.* She touched Manuela's arm, which stopped her from slashing. Placing her hand over Manuela's, Nest Feather took the knife from her and repositioned the sharpening rod on the table. She quickly and repeatedly, with great concentration, strength, and obvious practice, ran both edges of the knife over the rod. The bumps, scrapes, and dull edges of the knife smoothed down to a fine point. Nest Feather raised the knife and critically inspected the blade. Its luster had reappeared and now reflected the sun's rays shining through the kitchen window.

Aware of Manuela's keen interest, Nest Feather proceeded, despite one of the cook's shoulders hitching up, which Nest Feather took to be irritation.

As she had worked her smaller knife on a doeskin, separating the remaining flesh from the underside of the hide, Nest Feather took the joint of meat, laid it on the cutting block of wood, and insinuated the knife into the meat. It cut like butter. Nest Feather meticulously trimmed an area of fat away from the meat and laid it on the table. No meat appeared in the fat; it was clean, surgically separated. Nest Feather again pierced the meat with the knife, this time with the tip, and ran the blade along the bone, splaying it down to the joint. She rotated the joint and continued running the knife along the bone until it was clean, the meat hanging from the joint. After wiping the knife blade on the towel laid on the table, Nest Feather resharpened the blade with four quick strokes. Returning to the joint, Nest Feather cut the meat away, laying it in large chunks on the table. She laid aside the bone, bare of meat and sinew, free from any nicks or gouges.

She again looked at Manuela, who had backed up a step and seemed ill at ease.

Laying her hand on the first chunk of meat, Nest Feather sliced it into thin, even slices that she layered on the tabletop. Again she wiped the blade with the towel and resharpened the knife with four quick strokes. One each for the east, the south, the west, and the north.

Working with hides brought me such joy. It was my best and only talent in Arapa, the place of my ancestors. Arapa, where She Who Is Gone and many others were shot, slashed, raped, and bludgeoned. Even if I'd had hold of this knife when the Bean Eaters killed, the little mouse of my power would surely have been overtaken as I was, for there were too many killers on the hunt. And She Who Is Gone . . . her fearful eyes staring, staring, the life taken from them. Glassy.

With a hiccup of air, Nest Feather clutched the knife tighter. The last of her family was gone—never to be seen again. In the pit of her being, a groan grew and grew within until it ruptured, surging from her in a sorrowful wail. Grabbing the length of her hair to the right side of her tearful face, she sliced through her thick mane with the knife and threw the dead clump of hair on the floor.

She heard someone else screaming. It was Manuela, cringing against the wall.

Nest Feather's moan grew ferocious. She gathered the left side and back of her hair and slashed it off. Then she hacked off the hair in front, no length the same.

A scream without end spewed from Manuela.

Her long black hair on the floor in butchered clumps, Nest Feather held the knife in her hand. Vaguely she was aware of Manuela cowering on her knees, praying to God, and Señora Paloma rushing into the kitchen, stopping at the sight of them.

In a daze, Nest Feather, holding the blade erect in her small, firm hand, saw Paloma inch closer. In the background Manuela's whimpers were constant.

Smiling Woman spoke in a quivering voice, "El cuchillo. Put it down. On the table. Aquí."

Spent, Nest Feather did as she was told, only to have Paloma tightly grab her arm. Nest Feather looked up into the señora's face—into black eyes so much like those of She Who Is Gone. She wept. Pressing her head into Paloma's midriff, she was wracked with sobs. The warmth of the woman's arms encircled Nest Feather, and together they swayed while the señora said words Nest Feather didn't understand.

"This child suffers. What has this girl seen?"

✦✦✦

During the first week of her captivity, her hair trimmed to best—but minimal—results, Nest Feather wandered through the Escalante home with Señora Paloma at her side. She instructed Nest Feather on how to sit in strange Anglo clothing and walk in Anglo shoes that Manuela had purchased on behalf of the Escalantes, trying to forestall the guesses and rumors about a strange child in their home that were certain to fly around town with the speed of monsoon winds.

Home lessons went on unabated. Nest Feather explored room by room, scrutinizing every object. She also tried to improve her pronunciation of her new Spanish name, Ramira, which the señora exclusively called her. Holding up some item, Nest Feather listened to Paloma pronounce its name in Spanish and in English before the señora took the object and replaced it in its original spot.

Eventually Nest Feather was allowed to replace the piece, under the señora's strict observance, after repeating its Spanish and English names. Instruction continued the next day and into the third, when Nest Feather identified all objects to perfection.

However, the uniqueness of the home palled on Nest Feather. She had not been outside to glimpse the sun or the moon. Time after time she looked through the windows into the enclosed courtyard with its pots of vibrant flowers, the yucca and sage plants, and the windmill, only to be caught by Paloma. The windmill held a particular fascination for Nest Feather: its wooden blades spinning in the wind, rotating with the wind direction, creaking loudly.

One early morning, Nest Feather discovered that the door to the courtyard was left open. Nest Feather padded out barefoot and found Manuela by the pipe that rose from the ground and curved over the holding tank capturing water.

Cook plunged a wooden bucket into the tank and brought it out. "Windmill pulls up water from below ground. Taste." She held out the bucket.

Nest Feather dipped her hand in the liquid and tasted it. *Water.* Looking up, she contemplated the windmill. *This would help my People.*

Manuela laughed, until taking a good look at Nest Feather. "I think you're taller. Only days ago you came to my shoulder. Now you're up to my ears. You were underfed. I'll fatten you up, pobrecita."

Thereafter, as soon as the sky lightened every day, Nest Feather went to the courtyard, faced east, and raised her head and arms in reverence to the sun. Its molten rays climbing over the mountains to swim in the blue skies brightened her copper face. Her spirit warmed, Nest Feather continued her learning process, but her early daylight ritual did not go unnoticed by either of the Escalantes.

One morning, Nest Feather was joined by Paloma in the courtyard while Manuela made the beds.

"Do you like your Spanish name 'Ramira?'"

"No."

"Ignacio and I thought, because you look in the eastern sky for the rising sun, perhaps you would prefer the name 'Solana.' Sol, the sun."

Nest Feather's expression brightened. "Sí. Solana. Gracias, señora." She plucked a fallen creamy yucca bloom from the ground and unfolded its petals, saying her thanks quietly only to herself, "Ahee-ih-yeh."

Manuela called from the doorway, "Señora." Paloma went to her.

Nest Feather watched as Manuela held up a wadded and torn sheet. *The bloody sheet from my bed; the one I need to wear between my legs.*

Paloma's face darkened.

SUNDAY, MAY 28, 1871

Noon mass over, Valeria and Atanacia without husbands—Raúl never at church but at the cockfights, and Sam, as a Freemason, at home—emerged from the coolness of San Agustín Church along with others of the congregation into the unseasonal heat. Valeria accepted curt "hellos" from the leaders of the city, like Bill Oury, Estevan Ochoa, and Leopoldo Carrillo, knowing that they had grown to recognize her only because she now routinely attended services with Atanacia. "Good afternoon."

While Valeria and Atanacia spoke with the wives, Valeria was close enough to overhear the men behind her.

"You heard the word from Drum Barracks?" asked Ochoa.

Oury clapped his hands. "Didn't you hear those howls of joy? Stoneman replaced by General Crook. Our 'little governor' got it done."

"Hearing about it put me over the moon."

"Thank the Lord." Carrillo beamed.

Ochoa added, "¿Y Jesús? ¿Qué piensa?"

"No sé." Oury shrugged his shoulders. "I haven't seen him for several weeks."

A long, low note from a trumpet sounded; a solemn guitar accompanied.

Valeria was first to turn. "Whose funeral?" In only a moment, she realized how small the coffin was between the outstretched arms of Jesús María's eldest sons. *Oh, no. It's a baby. Terrible.* Her crucifix pressed to her mouth, Valeria realized her miscarried child never had a funeral. Her child, thrown away in the trash, had returned to ashes without a proper burial. Unashamed, tears flowed down her cheeks.

Father Francisco Jouvenceau walked beside the coffin. Jesús María and Teresa plodded behind with their younger children hanging onto their mother's skirts.

Behind them, Juan, clasping his own mother's hand over his forearm, hoisted most of her weight on his side and helped her move.

Watching one of their own grieving, the suddenness of change and finality anguished Valeria. A little light-headed, she took Atanacia's hand in hers; they and other congregants melted into lines on either side of the procession.

A hand on her swelling belly, Atanacia whispered in Valeria's ear, "Premature girl. María Felipa. So tiny. No chance."

"When was she born?"

"May 1."

In the increasing heat, Valeria watched perspiration trace down the faces of each Elías adult and child. Valeria remembered her neighbors in Texas who suffered a death in the family during the summer. What had happened in Texas must have similarly occurred at the Elías casa in the early hours that very warm morning. The life candle of the month-old infant had snuffed out on a day that only promised hotter temperatures.

Father Jouvenceau must have been hastily summoned to pray for the innocent child and her grieving parents. The entire family would have been gathered around the crib that had cradled so many babies, watching as their tiniest sister ceased to breathe, her thin chest stilling its minimal expansion until it settled forever. Tears would have flowed like water when the priest raised the crib sheet over the tiny departed baby. Father Jouvenceau would have muttered closely in Jesús María's ear, "Today. This afternoon."

Valeria stared at the tiny pine box. At Teresa's quick intake of air and her eyebrows compressing upward, Valeria knew the mother envisioned her tiny child resting inside in the dark, for she put a free arm around her other children holding onto her skirts as if to keep them from harm.

From behind, Abuela Elías spoke in a loud voice, disturbing the grandchildren and drawing Valeria's attention, "Necesito parar."

"Mamá," Juan moaned, begging her not to stop, looking ahead to only a couple more streets. "Unas calles más."

Valeria's heart went out to the strong man almost weeping, trying so hard to accommodate his frail, elderly mother.

"No." The mother's knees giving out, Juan caught her before she hit the ground.

Several men rushed from the church with a chair, and running to Juan, helped place his mother in it.

Watching Jesús María's family progress through the church plaza to reach the nearby National Cemetery, Valeria filled with a surging need to mourn. She broke through the congregation and joined the procession behind the trumpet and guitar players. Within moments Atanacia was at Valeria's side and many others followed behind—personal friends of the Elíases and even those who only recognized Jesús María on the street.

Abuela Elías, carried high in the church chair, advanced first through the large, arched gates before the rest of the procession entered the high-walled cemetery, where the remains of the dead were planted: those killed by gunshot wounds; yellow fever and cholera; those murdered at the hands of the indigenous native Indian tribes, if not fellow Tucsonans; and now a month-old baby.

After the short, music-filled burial service at the gravesite in the Catholic section, Valeria ran from the cemetery, searching Tucson's streets until she found Raúl at a cockfight.

Pulling him away, she tightened her grasp and told him of the Elíases' loss. His face crumpled into deep lines. She believed that he too thought of their lost child. "¿Estás bien?"

Raúl blew a long, drawn-out sigh.

Is he going to faint? Valeria found him a beer, which he drank in gulps. "Better?" No answer. She took the glass from him and placed her head on his chest. Heartbeats resounding in her ear, his soft lips met her neck for a moment. For a long time they held each other.

From the wake at the Elíases' small home, the mariachis' loud, vibrant music reverberated down the street. The Obregóns avoided the laughing neighborhood children darting about and went inside, where adults warded off thoughts of death with whiskey, rotgut, tortillas, and flan. Raúl and Valeria searched the home for the mourners, finding them in a small back room. Juan, Jesús, and Teresa's faces flushed from the comforts of much whiskey. Raúl murmured his condolences, but Valeria poised herself on the small settee next to Teresa and took the woman's cold hand between her two warm palms. "I'm so sorry." Thrown off balance when Teresa crumpled over her proffered hand, Valeria chilled with the numbing remembrance of her own loss of a child.

"It's my fault. I worried too much about Jesús on his raid."

"No, no. It was not your fault. Things happen . . . in the desert."

"Their medicine men conjured against our children."

"Who?"

"Apaches."

"I . . . I don't understand. ¿Por qué?"

As Teresa's heavy sobs intensified, Valeria knew this outburst would not subside for some time. She helped Teresa to her feet and accompanied her to the bedroom, away from prying neighbors, where the woman could rest.

Raúl poured himself a stiff drink and slumped in the vacated settee as Bill Oury appeared before the Elías brothers.

"I'm sorry for your loss, but I must speak."

What a . . . A little worse for wear, Raúl tried to stop Oury's insensitive comment by rising, but fell back.

Juan stiffened. "Not at this time."

"They make demands."

"¿Quién?" Exhausted by the day's events, Juan couldn't follow Oury's claim.

"Arivaipas. They want their children back."

Jesús got to his feet. "We want our child back." He walked away.

When Valeria returned to the back room, she found Raúl sprawled out in the deepest drunk she had ever seen him in. She pulled him up, and the two staggered the short distance to their home where she asked him, "What did Teresa mean about a raid?"

"Juan. Jesús. They're Indian fighters. You know that. I told you."

"Pero . . ."

Raúl collapsed on the bed, instantly falling asleep.

THURSDAY, JUNE 8, 1871

The Camp Grant affair . . . was murder, purely. . . . I will investigate the massacre of the Apaches at Camp Grant and be just to all concerned.

—*President Ulysses S. Grant*

CAMP GRANT AND ARIVAIPA CANYON

On the familiar route from Tucson to Camp Grant, the nighttime journey along the Cañada del Oro Wash, then along the Camp Grant Wash straight to the Post, Cargill searched for any signs of Apaches working in the hayfields, which had become a familiar sight during the months of March and April. Three to four weeks after the revelation in mid-May of the Tucsonenses' raid on the camp, the hayfields still lay empty of Apaches.

Only the creaking sounds of the heavily laden wagons broke the silence at the camp as Cargill's train rolled onto the parade ground. Eerily, no Indians were in sight. No one stood in line for rations. No one held tickets for manta exchange at the store. No smoke rose from the blacksmith shed, against which Felmer idly leaned. Cargill nodded to the German as a sign that they'd speak after he conducted business.

Goods unloaded and books reconciled, Cargill ambled toward Felmer. "Quite a change."

"Scheiße! You need to stretch your legs."

As they descended into the wide, flat land at the mouth of Arivaipa Creek, Cargill sensed a mournful, oppressive morbidity in the air that failed to stir, its oxygen sucked out by recent tragedy. For a long time neither Cargill nor Felmer spoke. Reaching the narrow, lush canyon, Felmer quietly recounted what he had learned from the Apaches.

"The dance—up on the shelf and down here—lasted well past midnight. Carse woke past four. It had begun. His ammunition was bad. The few braves who did not go on hunt climbed the cliffs." They continued walking, Felmer pointing along the way to stray fragments of bones overlooked in burial. Felmer stopped about a hundred yards into the canyon's interior. "About here, maybe a little farther in, was where Hashké Bahnzin was first seen after the Apaches dribbled back in. Gott." Felmer shook his head. "Naked. Ashy with dirt and filth. Having eaten nothing for a week or so. He stood here, where his gowah had been, his wives and children now slain. He wept." Shaking his head again he uttered, "Pitiful. Herzergreifend."

Standing in Arivaipa Canyon, under the inviting shade of the sycamores, listening to the enchanting babble of the stream, Cargill reflected upon the canyon's beauty and now its sorrow. "How many Apaches have returned?"

"Mere handfuls."

Having seen enough, Cargill wandered back, the tragedy and humidity sapping his energy.

Felmer caught up with him. "Did you hear that? Gunfire. To the south."

"McK . . ." Cargill stopped.

Indians on horses galloped toward them from over the hayfields at the foot of the south bank. Hashké Bahnzin and seven Apaches. The Indians' horses stirred the land, already dry and thirsty for the monsoon rains to come, sending behind them a dust cloud that dissipated in the still air and fell to earth.

The Indians reined in their horses before Cargill and Felmer. Hashké Bahnzin indelibly seared the German with his fiery visage filled with a hatred learned from those not of this land. In Apache he spat out, "I have killed an American."

"Lieber Gott! Why?"

"Revenge. I was going to take it out on you."

"Me?"

"God told me you were a friend and not to do it." Hashké Bahnzin drew his fractious horse in a tight circle, upsetting the other horses. "I then went down below, and with these hands and this lance . . ." He held it high. "I killed an American."

"Who? Who did you kill?"

"Charles McKinney, another friend."

Cargill understood the Apache's garbled pronunciation of McKinney's name. He bent over, his hands on his thighs. *Oh, Charles, you befriended Eskiminzin, and for what?*

The leader of the Arivaipa Apaches hissed, "The Anglos broke the promised peace. There can be no friendship between the Apache People and the White Eyes. Anyone can kill an enemy, but it takes a strong man to kill a friend." Hashké Bahnzin prodded his horse, piercing the air with a war cry, "We go to the mountains!"

Eight Apaches plowed forward on their excited horses.

Running to avoid being trampled, Cargill and Felmer labored with their news until they found Whitman at Camp Grant.

TUCSON

The señora, holding Nest Feather's hand, stood in the doorway of the Lord & Williams store. A child no longer, Nest Feather resisted the señora's guiding hand. She tried to shake it off, but the señora only tightened her grip.

"Stay right with me, Solana. Understand?"

Some words still held no meaning for her, but Nest Feather knew the word "understand." Pulled into the store, she froze. Crowded with caballeros and Anglos and a young Apache man quickly moving a long-handled broom across the dirt floor, this world seemed dim and noisy.

The camp's sutler store could fit into one corner. Talking, laughter, shouting, and dinging of bells filled her ears. This immense interior world smelled of leather saddles and holsters; boxes and crates were stacked to twice her height. Items she had never before seen rested beneath panes of glass: women's breechcloths with ruffled legs and hinged metal cases with small arrows that moved as they pointed to letters. White Eyes' blouses, without holes or blood, hung on wooden pegs.

"Who wore those?" Solana pointed at the blouses. Puzzled, Paloma gawked at her. "Qué?"

"Las blusas. Did an Anglo own?" *Why doesn't the señora answer? She looks stricken.*

"Ellas son nuevas. The blouses are new."

Nest Feather knew that the señora was disturbed, for she whispered "nuevas" to herself several times.

Nearby stood an Anglo man with a Mexican woman at his side. Mouths drawn down in unmasked hatred, they stared at Nest Feather, who felt as if pricked in the side with a knife, but not deep enough to kill. A glance up at the señora confirmed that she, too, suffered these wounds.

From another direction a kind voice said, "Hello, Paloma."

"Larcena, so good to see you," the señora's voice sounded relieved. "How are you feeling?"

"I'm not dizzy today."

Nest Feather stepped in front of Paloma, wanting a better view of the Anglo with a soft voice. She discovered a tall woman with hair the color of ripe wheat swept up on either side of her thin face. A slight protrusion at her waist told of a child to come.

"Why, who do we have here?" Larcena asked when the unknown little girl appeared from around Paloma's skirts. She leaned over to get a good look at the child, who took a step back.

Paloma kindly regarded Nest Feather. "This is Solana, the daughter of my cousin in Santa Fe. She stays with us for a while."

Believing she understood all of the señora's words, Nest Feather slipped her hand from Paloma's grasp. *Only White Eyes lie.* Nest Feather would not look at the señora but instead studied the Anglo woman, whose eyes, once round with surprise, narrowed while she studied the child's features with the swiftness of a hummingbird's wings. First she looked at the eyes, black as ravens; then the skin, the dusty brown of potato sacks; and last, the chopped-off hair that stuck out like wiry cholla needles that the ugly hat failed to hide. In turn Nest Feather studied the woman's light blue eyes, in which rested a glimmering light of understanding. When the woman straightened, she hugged the señora. Nest Feather knew the woman accepted the surface of the señora's dishonesty.

"Welcome, child," the Anglo woman raised her voice for the hatemongering couple to hear. "I have a little girl about your age. I'm happy that my friend has you for a daily companion. Unfortunately I must go now. I'm tired." Larcena passed the couple—who turned to greet her—and said to them without stopping, "Beautiful day."

Nest Feather drew closer to Paloma and allowed the señora to lead her, pulling her through the store toward a corner, where two men behind open iron bars counted coins and greenbacks and jotted down figures on parchment in black ink. While watching the señora hand these men a few greenbacks, which were duly noted on one of those ledgers, Nest Feather sensed the presence of someone at her side.

Turning about, ready to pounce, Nest Feather found the young man with the long-handled broom. His skin color was the same as hers; his eyes were as black as hers; the bridge of his nose was more hawklike than hers, but his nostrils flared as did hers. *A nnee in White Eyes' clothing!*

He whispered in the People's tongue, "You brighten this day as does the sun in its arc."

In the short time that Nest Feather had been away from Arapa, she had never seen an Apache or heard the voice of her People. Not as conversant as She Who Is Gone, Nest Feather groped for words, giving the señora time to turn from her completed business transaction to find the young clerk.

"Hola, Isidro."

The young man answered politely in Spanish and again in English.

Another of my People is as good at languages as I am. That pleased Nest Feather.

"Let's go, Solana." Paloma grinned at Isidro, who swept the dirt floor on adjacent areas, following them to the front entrance.

Nest Feather was not fooled. *Apaches have eyes at the back of their heads.*

Outside the store's entrance, Nest Feather held out the hand that the señora did not hold. "Esta no está hecho de manta. Qué es?" She held a blouse of scarlet hue, the brilliant color of many birds and nothing like the coarse cloth of manta.

As if struck, Paloma gasped, "Where did you get this?"

"Inside."

"It is not yours."

Nest Feather waved the blouse from side to side. "It was there. I wanted it."

"It belongs to the store, unless we purchase it." Paloma seized the child's hand and took the blouse away.

"You gave coins and paper. You bartered for la blusa."

"I paid our bill. This is not the way."

"It is People's way. We made fair exchange. Tickets for manta."

The señora shook her head. "No. No."

Nest Feather could not fathom the señora's distress. Paloma looked inside the store, then down at Nest Feather.

Isidro stepped outside. "May I help you, señora?"

"Sí, por favor. Could you ask Dr. Lord to come to me?"

Isidro disappeared and returned with Dr. Lord, who frowned down over his large, rotund stomach at Nest Feather. "Yes?" he asked.

"I'm so sorry, but without complete knowledge of how business is conducted on your premises, my cousin's child . . . uh . . . took this by accident. I would like to return it and apologize." Paloma swallowed several times.

Nest Feather glared up at Dr. Lord, who again fixed his attention on her. "That's a mighty fierce stare you've got, little lady."

"La blusa es muy bonita." *I stand my ground.* She glowered at Big Man with Big Paunch.

"And a little big for you."

"No." She wanted to say more but didn't have the words.

The señora intervened, "Could you put it on our account?"

"I could . . ." He hedged.

"Manta?" Nest Feather flicked her eyes toward Isidro, who lingered at the doorway, eagerly listening to the exchange.

Dr. Lord laughed until his stomach jiggled, enthralling Nest Feather for a moment. "Manta? No, missy, this is pure silk."

Paloma bit her lip. "May we return it, please?"

"Of course. We at Lord & Williams want to make all of our customers happy." Dr. Lord took the blouse and whispered something to Isidro, who disappeared into the store with the merchandise.

Nest Feather drew her mouth down. Blouse taken from her, she seethed but heard Dr. Lord mutter to the señora, "Perhaps it is not time to bring out your . . . cousin's child. I'd wait for a while. Just alerting you, ma'am." Big Man with Big Paunch looked down at Nest Feather. "Good day to you, little lady."

Only an instant passed before Nest Feather was grasped by Paloma. Dragged and pulled, Nest Feather wrestled under the woman's clutch as they rushed down the dirt street. Long strides broke into a jog, subsiding again for only a few steps. Nest Feather flew down the street, aware of dark-skinned vaqueros sitting atop their horses, grinning and laughing at them.

A pack of dogs separated and joined like a wave in the street in front of San Agustín Church where Paloma and Nest Feather arrived in a huff. Nest Feather gawked at the señora's stormy, working countenance thrust into her own face.

Paloma spat out her words, "The Escalantes do not steal. We are God-fearing and God-loving people who practice the Ten Commandments. This you will learn and practice. You will do as I do."

The señora pushed the church's oak door open, sunlight spreading down the middle dirt aisle like molten gold. They stepped inside and closed the door, returning the small church into semidarkness. Musty in the late spring's warmth, the church at once became suffocating to Nest Feather. Although Paloma bent one knee and dipped low, Nest Feather flared her nostrils and refused to move, instead looking off toward the seats where only a few people sat in quiet, moving beads along their chains.

Being inside a building still bothered Nest Feather. The walls of the Escalante home were painted white; Nest Feather pretended it was a cave of sunlight. Here, in this small building, darkness surrounded her, like in a gowah, but the odor wafting from the candles along the stucco wall displeased her. It was a sickening smell.

Under Paloma's close eye, Nest Feather strayed down the center aisle. The ribbons holding down her hat had untied, their ends straying down her chest like braids, but at least she could now swallow without chafing against the ribbons' knot. Women in black waddled in and out of a door on the right side. Nest Feather eyed the progress of one black duck who, like Paloma, bent her knee before a figure on the wall before toddling over to the bad-smelling candles.

Briefly and only once had Nest Feather seen such a figure. In the señora's room, hanging on the bedroom wall over their bed, was a small statue. But here, in this hot place, the statue was as large as Nest Feather. She skirted a round bowl and stood close, looking up at the likeness. *This man is beyond life. In several places warriors lanced him but did not expose the entrails. This is a sign of respect for this man.*

The longer she looked, the more the statue reminded Nest Feather of her Black Rocks People: thin muscles, no fat, mouth pressed together resolutely, stringy hair in long strands, barefooted. Carved in mesquite, the statue was dark like her skin. *He is not Apache. He has straggly hairs on his chin.*

From behind her the señora whispered, "This is Jesús. Jesus Christ, our Lord and Savior."

Nest Feather jumped. Her concentration on the statue had been so great that her always-alert Apache eyes and ears had been rendered useless.

"Jesús," she repeated. "Was he a leader?" The image of Hashké Bahnzin rose in Nest Feather's mind. *He looks nothing like this statue.*

"Much more. I shall tell you of him."

Along their walk home, Nest Feather listened to Paloma tell a few short stories about Christ.

Remaining silent the entire way, Nest Feather returned to her room, but not before overhearing the words whispered by Paloma, nestled in the arms of her husband: "I don't think I can do this."

MONDAY, JUNE 19, 1871

Raúl pushed the broom through Zeckendorf's front door and watched as forty or more horsemen, including Mister Z himself, trotted northwest down Calle Real, heading for the main road. Their destination, known by many, was Nine Mile Water Hole at the northernmost reaches of the mountains to the west. This morning General George Crook was to arrive.

Raúl coughed in the cloud of dust and dirt that billowed up, enveloping him until the final riders were gone. Turning back to the store, he brushed the gritty dust off his clothes and found that the grime had come through all of the openings: one door at the front, one on the side, and three large windows. *I'll have to sweep again!*

When finished, Raúl heard horses approaching at a walk. He saw through the window a weathered Indian astride a horse and a bearded white man with a pith helmet on his head, sitting on the most cantankerous-looking mule this side of Mesilla. Going outside, Raúl asked, "Could I be of help to you?"

The white man turned his mule toward Raúl. "You could, son. Where is the governor's home?"

A bout of nerves fluttered through Raúl upon deducing that this was General George Crook, the new and long-anticipated department commander known to subdue Indians. No military uniform for Crook: he wore a faded tan suit, a baggy white shirt with a wide sash of a tie, and cuffed leather gloves. "You're on the correct calle, uh, street. Stay on this road for the next six crossings. It is a large home on the corner of McCormick Street, close on."

"Thank you, sir." Crook nudged the mule with his stirrups.

Raúl added quickly as the men set off, "Quite a few men went out to meet you, General Crook."

The Indian, who looked part white, glanced back. "We never go the main roads."

"Archy," called Crook, "go to Camp Lowell. Let's get to work. Within thirty-six hours, I want to interview the scouts they've rounded up for me."

Raúl had to laugh. Mister Z and all the rest had galloped off to meet Crook before anyone else. He had stayed behind and grabbed the brass ring of being the first to see the great Crook on whose back rested so many hopes.

✦✦✦

Raúl happily related his encounter with General Crook to Valeria over dinner.

"I have some news too." Her voice was breathy from anticipation.

"Another alteration?"

"Yes, I got more work, but that is not my news." She had rehearsed the words in her head, but staring at Raúl, she rushed, blurting them out, "I saw a woman Epi recommended, and I'm fine. I'm . . . I'm ready." Valeria watched as Raúl grasped the true meaning of her words.

He beamed. "I'm ready too. More than ready." Flinging the chair back, Raúl gripped her hand and led her into the bedroom.

Later, when Raúl rolled off Valeria, sweat beaded on his back and down his armpits. He couldn't understand and knew that Valeria could not either. *It has never happened.* He caught her look of understanding and forgiveness. *I don't want her understanding, and I don't want her forgiveness, goddammit.*

When he had been atop Valeria and had looked in his wife's eyes, he saw *her* eyes, the black eyes of that Apache, the one who lay on the ground with a bullet in her breast.

The heat of battle, the heat of his body, and the violence around him had engorged Raúl with desire. With only a cursory glance at the woman, whose screams distorted the beauty of her face, he'd thrust. Again and again. He had needed to prove himself by taking that savage in conquest—and ever since, her eyes stared up at him in pain and in death, in his dreams and in his waking, and now in his bed with his wife.

There is no confessing to Valeria. As much as I love her, I do as I please, and my pleasure has always been my wife. The savage ruined that. The rape was now complete; he had been victimized by the image of her dying while he was still inside her. *The moment of my climax: the moment of her death. Her black eyes, full of hatred and fear, glazed over, unseeing for all eternity.*

God in Heaven, I want to forget. I returned a hero, but Valeria still doesn't know. Savages had to be subdued, and the only way was with the same force and cruelty they brandished on the Anglos and Mexicans.

Valeria laid a gentle hand on his arm. He jerked it away and turned on his side, away from her.

"Don't turn away." *He's been jumpy of late. What is the matter?* "¿Raúl?"

He kept his back turned to her. *Don't look to me for an answer. I can't bear my own silence. It hangs in the room like the stench of death.* "Nada."

"There must be something."

"No. Nothing."

Raúl doesn't complain about Zeckendorf's. He enjoys the cockfights. Could it be my work? "Is my making money upsetting you? I thought you would be grateful."

He threw back the sheet and bounded out of bed. "Why do you think everything has to do with you?"

Silenced, Valeria didn't know where to look to find the answer.

Raúl burst outside to the common privy in the back garden. Smug satisfaction played over his features as he urinated. *At least that still works.*

SATURDAY, JUNE 24, 1871

I am no advocate of Indian saintliness of character, but viewing the . . .
unprovoked butchery of well-behaved Indians [at Camp Grant], are
you not compelled to admit that the red man is quite as desirable a
neighbor as the majority of frontier palefaces?

—*Cincinnati Enquirer*

EL DÍA DE SAN JUAN BAUTISTA, TUCSON

Squawk! Squawk!

The rider gripped the reins of his horse and eyed his target—the head of a
terrified rooster buried up to its neck in the street. The horse pawed the dirt,
digging more furrows in the already gouged dirt street.

Raúl and Valeria, out for the full day of festivities, wormed their way through
clusters of families and bands of compadres crowding the street watching and
cheering the riders. Raúl bought them each a beer. The cool, tart liquid slid down
Valeria's throat. She laughed to be outside, in the brilliant sun with the most
handsome Mexicano at her side. Raúl kissed her cheek. Feeling happy, Valeria
giggled as she fluffed up the spring pink ruffles of gossamer she had sewn on her
white blouse. In a holiday spirit, she wanted to do everything, see everything.

Valeria gestured with her beer glass. "Mira." The vaquero at the end of the
street prepared for his run. Raúl grabbed Valeria's arm and pulled her through
the crowd of drunken cowboys standing in front of Foster's Saloon. She ventured
as far into the street as she dared.

"¡Ándale!" A sharp slap of the reins on its side, the horse lunged forward,
running at a full gallop toward the hapless rooster.

Valeria felt the rush of air as the horse passed. Taking two steps farther out in the
street, she cheered on the Mexicano, his left hand clutching his reins and his saddle
horn. With his right hand he leaned out and grabbed at the head of the rooster.
He missed. Struggling to right himself, he fell off his horse, landing in a pile of
horse shit. When the downed Mexicano got up, Valeria laughed the loudest of all.

Raúl yelled to another horseman trotting into place for his run, "¡Curro! Pull the gallo! Pull it!"

The pockmarked, dark-skinned Mexican flashed a toothy grin, and weaving a little in his saddle, leered at Valeria, who moved a step back. With a raucous laugh, Curro took his position at the top of the street.

"Who is that?" Valeria squirmed as if the man's attention had dirtied her.

Raúl gulped the last of his beer. "A compadre."

"How do you know him?"

Raúl drew Valeria in front of him and hugged her. "Watch."

Valeria narrowed her eyes as Curro galloped by, mounted on a large and excited chestnut gelding. Holding his reins and the saddle horn in his left hand, Curro leaned over. He grabbed the rooster by the neck, plucking it up from the dirt, and twirled the squawking gallo overhead, breaking its neck. Curro laughed as he flung the dead bird at George Foster standing in front of his saloon. "¡Fríe el pollo para mi comida!"

"Let's go." Valeria pulled at Raúl's hand. *That hombre can fry his own chicken for dinner.*

✦✦✦

The ringing sounds of wild caballeros outside on the streets of Tucson invaded Nest Feather's recámara, all the while she looked at a strange image reflected in the espejo. Before, only the waters of Arivaipa Creek had reflected her square face. This face looked similar, but clean and clear under linear eyebrows and chopped black hair, which had already grown out by two inches.

Somehow I look older. Does this face belong to Nest Feather, the daughter of Arapa? Do my eyes still see the skies and understand the seasons of the earth as they did in Arapa?

She drew in the smell of tacos cooking. *The señora and Manuela wear colorful blouses and skirts today, and the señor brought in cerveza. This must be a day of celebration. Will I be included? Not since Lord & Williams have I been outside. I've been scrubbing clothes and crockery under Manuela's stern eye.*

"Solana." Paloma appeared in the doorway.

Nest Feather saw the bonnet with trailing ribbons in the señora's hand. *Yes, I will be allowed out, but wearing the hat I would love to tie to a cactus.*

"I have another surprise." Paloma stepped aside to reveal Manuela holding a skirt of varying shades of blue and a white ruffled blouse. "For you."

Such beautiful clothes for me? Nest Feather's heart romped within her chest.

Her eyes darting from the señora to Manuela and back to the outfit, Nest Feather threw off what she wore to change clothes.

Tying the bonnet ribbons under Nest Feather's chin, Paloma said, "Es El Día de San Juan Bautista, Solana. We shall pray to him for rain."

Nest Feather drew out the new, full, ankle-length skirt and twirled, laughing.

"You are attractive. Once your hair is even longer, you will be even more so," Señora Paloma told her as they walked down the hall hand in hand.

I don't like holding hands with her. Nest Feather wriggled her hand out of the señora's grasp and held it behind her back.

"We begin at San Agustín's and proceed to the acequia. There will be lots of people. We shall take a short look, pray, and come back. Unnoticed."

A blast of summer heat enveloped them when Ignacio opened the grand front door.

✦✦✦

Street sounds clanged loudly in Nest Feather's ears. Strange odors hung in the humid air. A block away, closer to the church, women sold trinkets and spicy peppers, onions, and meat for barbacoa. Walking between the Escalantes, Nest Feather was hurried past the Apache Mansos selling produce and fry bread, but she looked back. The young man from Lord & Williams—the one who used the long broom—was among them, staring after her until the older woman kneeling on the ground by him demanded his attention.

Nest Feather and the Escalantes avoided men hawking wares and those drinking from whiskey bottles and stumbling in the streets. The Escalantes each took Nest Feather's hand, not letting go. This time Nest Feather didn't mind their protection. Trumpets and guitars blared, the music a strident cacophony to her ears, as they walked hand in hand through narrow streets toward the church plaza, where they joined a large group of the faithful before San Agustín Church.

Nest Feather stiffened. People crowded all around her, pushing her forward and into Señora Paloma, who patted her hand in understanding and clutched it tighter.

Father Francisco Jouvenceau made the sign of the cross to those gathered while his altar boys swayed incense burners.

At the vile smell, Nest Feather drew her mouth down; the señora noticed and placed her arm around the child.

Nest Feather stilled like the rest of the faithful and listened to the priest's words in Latin, Spanish, and finally in English with a faint French accent.

"Today we continue the tradition set by the great explorer Francisco Vázquez de Coronado, who, as legend tells us, stood at the banks of the Santa Cruz River on

June 24, the day of our patron saint, San Juan Bautista. His men and his horses had suffered greatly from a devastating drought. He turned to the only one who could help. Coronado turned to our Lord in prayer for precious rain. And the rains came."

Nest Feather watched two men carry a clay statue, painted in bright reds and greens and yellows, from the church. Directed by a redheaded man, they placed the statue high on a water tank in a wagon decorated with silver-gray boughs of purple sage plucked from the surrounding hills. Even the mule wore sprigs secured in its bridle. Charged with keeping the colorful statue upright on the cart, the churchmen sat on either side of it.

A Mexican band, playing a dirge-like hymn on their dented trumpets and guitars, proceeded down the street, followed by the wagon, Father Jouvenceau, and the faithful, with Nest Feather and the Escalantes at the rear. *I wish this hateful hat blocked out the terrible music.*

As the procession with the grim and somber visage of San Juan passed by, Valeria was enthralled to see Martin Touhey and Daphne the mule on their way to the acequia, the irrigation ditch off the Santa Cruz River where many in Tucson swam and bathed near the rocks where Apache Mansos beat their clothes clean. Valeria pulled Raúl into the faithful's march near its front.

Touhey halted Daphne at the water's edge, where the protectors of the statue placed the figure of San Juan Bautista on a temporary altar, before Touhey led Daphne and the cart under a small sycamore tree, away from the main group of the faithful, which grew by the minute.

Valeria and Raúl approached the water cart. She touched Touhey's sleeve.

The Irishman's face brightened with recognition. "Hello, missus."

Raúl shook the man's hand while Valeria devoted her attention to Daphne. "This is my husband, Raúl."

Touhey greeted him, "Top o' the mornin.'"

Along the procession, Nest Feather perceived the Escalantes' growing unease. They hurried Nest Feather through small openings between groups of the faithful and looked about the crowd and the houses built upon the adjacent small precipices. Not knowing what the señora wanted, Nest Feather minded her new Anglo shoes as they made their way to the front by the acequia, where she noticed a Mexican couple petting a mule and talking to the redheaded man who'd transported the statue. The woman wore a white blouse with pink ruffles down the arms and across the breast, and the Mexican man's nose had been noticeably broken.

Now at the front, Señora Paloma peered about. "Do you see him, Ignacio?"

"No."

Nest Feather looked at the strange faces all around her. Most were Mexicans, but some were White Eyes. At the fringe of the crowd stood Nnee with Broom, whom Señora Paloma had called Isidro. The young Apaches observed each other until Señor Escalante pointed to the altar and brought Nest Feather in front of him for a better view. Nest Feather lowered her head but watched Nnee with Broom in a sideward glance.

Father Jouvenceau stepped forward, making the sign of the cross over the hushed townspeople. "Let us pray."

Paloma whispered to her husband, "Mira." She pointed to the top of the hill. From a backyard overlooking the acequia, Bill Oury, Jesús María, Jesús María's family, and Juan watched the ceremony below.

At waterside Jouvenceau raised his voice for all to hear, "Blessed San Juan, we pray that you intercede with the Father for rain, blessed rain from the heavens above. Grant this monsoon season be one of great abundance. Fill our rivers, springs, and arroyos with life-sustaining water. San Juan Bautista, we ask your help in gaining this gift from God, as did Coronado more than three hundred years ago. In the name of the Father and of the Son and of the Holy Spirit. Amen." Father Jouvenceau repeated the sign of the cross.

Nest Feather remained silent, but the Escalantes and the rest of the faithful murmured, "Amen." The Escalantes, all three, received refreshing drops of holy water sprinkled by the priest walking among the faithful.

On tiptoe Valeria tried to see over everyone's head. She spotted Epiphania meandering away from the acequia. "Oh, I see Epi. Perhaps her boyfriend is near. Let's go see, Raúl." She pushed him toward the direction Epi had taken.

When the Escalantes became worried they still couldn't see the Elíases in Oury's backyard, Isidro arrived without notice. Nest Feather stoically eyed Nnee with Broom without disclosing the satisfaction his appearance brought her.

"Señor y Señora Escalante, please permit me to introduce your friend to my band. They are a little way up the acequia. My family and I shall take good care of her until I bring her back in a few minutes."

After Paloma and Ignacio exchanged worried looks, they realized it would give them the opportunity to find Jesús and speak to him alone. Ignacio said to his wife, "I'll accompany them and meet you up there."

Paloma told Isidro, "Watch her closely," before rushing off to find Jesús María.

Nest Feather chanced smiling at Isidro, although being without both the señor and the señora in this crowd seemed odd and upsetting, even dangerous. She had seen the long looks and heard the sideward sneers from others as they'd passed by.

With Señor Escalante and Isidro, Nest Feather approached the Apache Mansos, who formed a small circle around the rocks they used for washing clothes. The Apaches sat on some of the larger stones and rested their feet on smaller ones.

Turning to Isidro, Señor Escalante placed his hand on the young man's shoulder. "I entrust you with Solana for a few minutes. I will be up there." He pointed to the top of the hill.

Nest Feather as well as Isidro looked up toward Oury's backyard. There Señora Paloma spoke with Man Who Chose Me. A White Eyes joined them briefly before stepping away—the innaa who threw her to the ground and bound her. *The Escalantes know these evil ones?*

A storm brewing within her, Nest Feather turned to Isidro. Understanding passed between them.

Señor Escalante continued, "I'll wave to you, Isidro, when I'm coming back for Solana. We'll meet by the tree over there, at the edge of the crowd."

"Yes, sir," replied Isidro as Señor Escalante left.

Nest Feather and Isidro sat on the rocks to speak with his People. *My language.* Spanish and English had filled her life, her brain, and her mouth for almost two months. Nest Feather's Apache words treaded reluctantly from her lips until gliding, cavorting forth within minutes. Exuberantly she spoke the nnee's tongue. "Do Black Rocks People still maintain a ranchería in Arapa?"

Heads shook. "We've heard nothing of that band for several moons." Some women adjusted their feet on the small rocks which Nest Feather noticed moved easily when disturbed.

Too soon some movement atop the hill drew Nest Feather's attention. Looking up she saw Señor Escalante waving down at them.

Having seen the signal as well, Isidro stood and announced to his People that he and his friend must return.

Looking down at her feet, Nest Feather studied a palm-sized rock. Nudging it closer with her Anglo shoe, she picked up the stone.

The gathering of Apache Mansos left behind, Nest Feather and Isidro moved back through the crowd toward the designated meeting spot, again passing the young Mexican couple, who spoke with another Mexicana.

"Epi!" Valeria hugged her friend and introduced Raúl. "Is your Andrew here?"

"Somewhere. I've lost him. Maybe he went home. He hates crowds."

Nest Feather again saw the face of the man she would never forget. The man with the broken nose. *He is the most evil one of all.* Nest Feather allowed people to pass between her and Isidro. She had only moments before Isidro realized she was no longer following him. Turning back, she neared Pink Ruffles, whose friend had departed. Nest Feather stopped behind Broken Nose. She labored to keep her face placid. Her fingers ran over the sharp edge of the rock she held. *He didn't give Sister warning.* She raised the stone high.

Someone grabbed her arm. Isidro. As he loosened her fingers from the stone, it dropped on his moccasin, cutting it and his toe. Blood trickled onto the dry dirt, yet Isidro never let go of her.

Wrenching out of his grasp, Nest Feather tore off her bonnet and ran through the crowd, Isidro close behind. Down a street, any street she found, she ran toward the desert. *Free. I must be unbound.* Solana no more, Nest Feather ran where the wild creatures lived, where Arapa was within her mind's sight, where the winds tousled her hair without care, where she lived freely without the cage of a room with a door. *Doors shut people in or shut them out. There are no doors in Arapa. In Arapa there are only open, free canyons, the desert, the ocotillos, and saguaros. And the People. Here, I see my captors. They have left me alone so far, but I will never forget. Never forgive. Live with them around me? Imprisoned with them?*

At last captured by Isidro, Nest Feather was trapped within his Apache arms. She beat him on the back to let her go, and when he didn't, she clung to him as her wails, born in the pit of her belly, erupted, and her tears flowed bitterly. "He . . . he took Shi-deh . . . and . . ." Finally she stilled in his arms.

Isidro lowered his head to hers. "Solana, we need to return. Señor Escalante will be most angry with me."

"They speak names here. They like that. Why?"

He pondered carefully. "Among our People, we never use our given names, only nicknames. When among other than our People, would you accept 'Solana' as your nickname?"

She stared at him.

✦ ✦ ✦

That night Señor Escalante remained in Nest Feather's recámara while Paloma tucked her in bed, which was unusual, and when the señora perched on the bed's side, Nest Feather became suspicious.

"Solana, you and Isidro did not follow Ignacio's orders."

Nest Feather whispered, "I was at fault. I'm sorry."

"You won't do that again?"

"No."

"Good." Paloma caught Ignacio's approval and continued, "We spoke with a great man today. Don Jesús María Elías. We told him about educating you in languages and our religion. We want you . . . to remain here with us, not . . . Señor Elías suggested that we go to el cura Jouvenceau today and get special dispensation for you to be baptized. We took his advice. El cura Jouvenceau is willing to take you as a communicant, with baptism and communion and acceptance into the church."

"¿Sí?" *They always speak about the length of time before acceptance. Now it is immediate.*

"You love the sunrise. As a family we will go to early mass."

"You like noon mass."

"We can easily change. We'll go with you. You like the church."

"I like the man's figure. He is thin like most of my People."

The señora's voice came only in a whisper. "He will become your people. He is our Savior."

"My People are in the hills, in Arapa."

Ignacio stepped forward. "You like us?"

"Sí."

"We want you to remain here, where food and clothing are plentiful."

"¿Siempre? Always?"

Ignacio had tried.

Paloma took over again, "We want the best for you, and despite today, we think highly of Isidro. He is respected at his work and will prosper." She stood. "Your church schooling begins tomorrow."

WEDNESDAY, JULY 5, 1871

Atanacia was right. Satisfied customers tell their friends about my work and I get more commissions. I am so grateful to her.

Now regularly admitted into her customers' well-to-do homes on the northern end of Calle Real, Valeria walked confidently into the Etchellses' drawing room, where the lady of the house played with her seven-month-old daughter. A pang of emptiness hit Valeria. Not as strong as several months before, but a pang nevertheless.

The lady—a stunning Mexicana in her mid-thirties—looked up. "Buenas días. I am Soledad. Please have a seat." She gave her daughter a quick kiss on her fine hair and handed the child over to the servant, who left the room.

Valeria found that a business-like approach worked best with most of her clients. "I am pleased to meet you. First I want to assure you that I will do my best to please."

"Bueno. That is what I've heard from several friends."

"What do you want me to make for you?"

"Uno vestido, muy caro. A very expensive dress."

Usually customers want the most for the least amount. This is curious. "For the day or the evening?"

"Either."

The flippant answer surprised Valeria. "Do you have a style in mind?"

"No. I don't care. Make it as beautiful as possible."

"And expensive?"

"Sí."

"Please stand so I may measure you." With quick, light motions Valeria pulled the tape down Soledad's arms, around her chest, waist, and the length of her, all the while grappling for ideas. "Today you wear some ruffles. You like?" Taking Soledad's hum as an answer, they settled back in their chairs. "And flounces?" A nod from her new client. "I have seen lovely satin."

"Muy bueno. Very good. What about lace?" Soledad leaned forward to emphasize her interest.

"Lace, yes. At Zeckendorf's I have seen some beautiful lace. Intricate and delicate. And very expensive."

"Use a lot of it." Soledad settled back in her chair.

Troubled, Valeria clasped her hands together in her lap. Working her wedding band around her finger, she tried to broach a subject that had never come up so soon with her clients. "I try not to ask for a down payment before the dress is made . . . but . . ."

"Forgive me. Perdóname. Don't worry about money. We have accounts all over town. Just tell Mister Z that you work for me and to put the bill for the lace and other materials on our account. Simple."

"And my fee. I've had to raise it a little due to all the work lately . . ." Valeria looked down at the expensive rug below her feet, worried that her increased fee would dull Soledad's interest in giving her the assignment.

"Whatever your fee is, double it."

Valeria tittered. "Double?"

"Sí." Soledad seemed unconcerned.

"Muchas gracias. Uh, this dress will take some time. Do you have a specific date you need it?"

"No."

Again Valeria's mind filled with uneasy questions. "With your coloring, I believe a deep blue, a midnight blue, would be most attractive. It is a dignified color and lends confidence. In a satin, its sheen would be stunning."

"I like that idea."

"This will be a striking dress on you. Once Mr. Etchells sees you in it, he will never forget it."

Soledad leaned forward and spoke heatedly, "Bueno. He deserves everything he's getting. I want him never to forget."

Conscious of the blood visibly surging in the hollow of her neck, Valeria stuttered, "Uh . . . uh."

"My Charles did a very stupid thing. This dress is in reimbursement to me and our daughter for risking our future."

"If I may ask, what did he do?"

"He went on the raid. He did not participate in killing those terrible Apaches, but he rode on the trail with the others. That was stupid enough. He risked his life. Every time I wear this dress, he will remember that."

"When was this? Where was this raid you speak of?"

"The end of April. To the north. Camp Grant. Men do not know everything. A large group of men and not one was thinking."

"¿Mexicanos?"

"And Anglos. And others."

The servant stepped into the drawing room. "Señora, you wanted to be reminded of your luncheon."

Soledad rose. "I'm sorry, but I must leave."

Valeria, now on her feet, extended her hand. "Thank you for giving me this work."

"Of course. Make certain it is very expensive."

"Claro. It will be a large bill."

"Bueno. Charles will not be so stupid again."

Outside Valeria drifted down the calle perplexed, happy, upset, in a quandary, flirting with design ideas, but mainly surprised that her beautiful dress would be used for revenge. *Why haven't I thought of this before? Make him pay. But that wouldn't work on Raúl; I'd have to make my own dress.*

After sewing most of the afternoon, Valeria assembled dinner and waited for Raúl. That evening she took her Spanish Bible in hand, but the familiar verses failed to call to her. The day long and eventful, she only wished to be cradled in Raúl's arms.

Finally, in he rushed, uttering, "No one was killed today," and crossed into the bedroom, where he changed into his plaid shirt—now his favorite—that he wore away from home.

A voice from the open front door called to Raúl, startling Valeria, who wasn't expecting anyone. It was the pockmarked Mexicano.

Rushing to Raúl in the bedroom she asked, "Are you going somewhere?"

"Dog races."

"That man is here. I don't like him. He looks like your brother's amigos."

Raúl shrugged and called out to his friend, "Curro, come inside."

Now inside, the Mexican again yelled for Raúl.

"He is not to come into this house. Do you hear me, Raúl?" Valeria glared up into her husband's face.

He returned her fierce gaze as a silent reminder that she could not tell him what to do . . . *Black eyes filled with hate. Black eyes shining one moment, glazed in death the next.* Raúl shook his head to rid the image.

Valeria followed Raúl into the main room. "Stay. I prepared dinner."

"I'll take tamales for me and Curro." Raúl dug his bare hands into the dish of tamales.

She grabbed the clay platter from under his grasp. "You want to go to the dog races? Then *eat* like dogs." Valeria heaved the plate through the open door, barely missing Curro, who stood there, mouth open in surprise. The tamales she'd handmade the way Raúl liked flew off the plate and rolled into the dirt street among the platter's broken shards. A howl arose from stray dogs down the street. Charging to devour what they could, the fastest canines bared their teeth, snarling and growling the slower dogs away.

Raúl marched down the street, never looking back.

Curro followed. "Your wife's full of beans."

Much later, her knees sore from kneeling before God, her eyes red and stinging from sewing under a dim candle, Valeria blew it out and opened the door. She watched a barely perceptible lightening of the sky to the east ease the darkness into morn. *I am always at fault. My big mouth. That's why he stayed away all night. It hurts, this first time. It hurts.*

She slid down the doorjamb to the dirt floor. Hugging herself, she rested her forehead on her knees.

SATURDAY, JULY 22, 1871

A thrashing [is] the best method of conveying a syllogism to a savage. . . . It would not do to attack the Apaches with any very large command, but . . . trailing them up by practiced Indian runners, and then, when they were discovered, surrounding their squads. . . . I do not go to Arizona at all sanguine. I am not acquainted with the officers there, and in Indian fighting, men are better than numbers.

—*General George Crook*

EIGHT MILES PAST CIÉNEGA STATION

On the second day heading to Camp Bowie, Cargill scanned the Rincon Mountains east of Tucson. Around midday a few thunderclouds formed and swelled over the Rincon peaks.

Whether a full-blown monsoon storm would break or whether the clouds would dissipate, Cargill would learn firsthand as the afternoon wore on. His supply train of ten wagons, bringing up the rear in a long outfit that stretched at least a mile, rolled over the desert at the speed of a foot march owing to the presence of the Twenty-First Infantry, Company G, commanded by Lieutenant Edward R. Theller, and Company I, commanded by Captain Harry M. Smith.

Cargill knew these soldiers were eager to get to Bowie. Their previous assignment at Camp Pinal atop sheer cliffs and over deep canyons in the upper altitudes of the Pinal Mountains had made road workers of them, but the camp had shuttered overnight with the abrupt change of command from Stoneman to General Crook. The last detachment left that godforsaken place on the Fourth of July. After such a dangerous, backbreaking assignment, the infantry didn't mind a hundred-mile march from Tucson to Bowie in the heat of summer.

Last night around the campfire along the dry Pantano Wash at the foot of the Rincons, Cargill had struck up a conversation with the lieutenant's wife. The rare sight of an Anglo woman had given him pause to remember the niceties that a gentleman should observe in the presence of a lady. Rusty though some manners might be, he'd tried to make a fair accounting of himself. "How did you find Camp Pinal, Mrs. Theller?" asked Cargill.

"Over many mountainous and bumpy miles." Delia chuckled melodiously.

In her captivating face remains a glimmer of the coquette she must have been before marriage. She's enchanting. Cargill glanced at her husband who also enjoyed his wife's humor.

Delia stoked the campfire with a crooked twig. "You're a bookkeeper. Is that correct, Mr. Cargill?"

Sucking on his pipe, Cargill delayed his answer, "Hmm, yes. A respectable trade."

"And for what frivolous vocation would you trade it?"

Cargill laughed. "I like my job, although other careers are more lucrative."

"You must go to San Francisco. You could mint your own gold bullion coins."

"If only it could be that simple. No, someday my ship will come in."

"I haven't seen much water in Arizona, Mr. Cargill. Sight of the Pacific Ocean from the cliffs above San Francisco is quite beautiful. I loved it most as the fog came in."

Her voice last night was as soft and delicate as the California mist. Epi's voice is heavier, like a tortilla compared to a crêpe. Looking forward, Cargill caught a glimpse of the high-sided ambulance wagon pulled by horses ahead of the marching troops. This trip the wagon carried not the wounded, but some able-bodied soldiers and Delia Theller.

Once past the Rincon Mountains, as the Santa Rita Mountains to the south fell away, Cargill sat straighter on the wagon bench and peered at every creosote bush and every depression in the land for any movement. They were traveling along the Whetstone Mountains, where secreted among its undulations, circuitous canyons, and outstretched fingers of ridges, springs gurgled. Like all travelers, stagecoaches, and mail-riders, Cargill's supply train and the two hundred soldiers marching in front of him hugged the mountains for access to that water.

But it wasn't only the water that made this stretch of road to Camp Bowie notorious.

The Whetstones' undulations could hide any number of Indians. Cargill and every man in Tucson mourned the loss of Lieutenant Howard Cushing and three of his men only two months ago at the hands of Cochise and his band of nearly two hundred warriors within these mountains. And earlier in July, Eskiminzin led an unsuccessful raid upon a wagon train near Ciénega Station mail stop, about eight miles back.

Cargill looked back from his high seat on the first supply wagon to those that followed.

"Are yer chicks still there?" asked the bullwhacker.

Cargill, knowing his driver's attempt at humor cloaked deep unrest, kept his answer short, "Yep. It's a big train." Under the bench were spare cartridges. He checked the magazine of his Henry rifle. Full with sixteen bullets. He wasn't sheepish at all about his vigilance; being in charge meant Cargill was responsible for expensive armaments for Camp Bowie and extensive goods for the post sutler's store, which meant profits for Lord & Williams—maybe even a little extra for Cargill himself. *And couldn't I use a little extra now that I'm contemplating marriage? These Whetstones make me nervous. Can't the troops step livelier?* Cargill stood up on the wagon seat, holding onto the long-armed brake and the wagon's canvas top, and surveyed the land. All of his wagons still followed. To the north nothing moved. To the south in the Whetstones off to the right—"Holy . . ." Cargill's skin prickled.

Indians. From around one of the folds of earth, twoscore bare-breasted Indians, stripped for war, wearing only long breechcloths and headbands, cried their war whoops and streamed out on foot. Soft moccasins skimming over the desert, the Apaches ran straight toward the last three supply wagons.

Cargill shouted to his men, and all went into action. Those not driving grabbed their Henrys, cocked the levers and fired, cocked and fired, cocked and fired. His outriders' revolvers repulsed the Apaches on foot at close range.

But another fifty or so Apaches galloped out from behind a larger ridge to the east, their lean and lithe horses stretched as if never touching earth. Dust flying up from the horses' hooves swirled in the escalating winds of a building monsoon. Their arrows whizzed by the supply train, and their rifle shots exploded with near misses.

Bullwhackers instinctively loosened their grip on the reins. The yokes of oxen, lengthening their strides and moving faster, caught up to the soldiers, who knelt where they could and took aim.

Cargill's heart pumped wildly. *Surely the officers ahead will quickly respond.* Bursts of gunfire deafening him, Cargill aimed and shot at advancing Apaches, one falling wounded. Then he spied a lone Apache racing his horse toward his wagon. For a moment Cargill was stunned by the spectacle of the fierce-eyed Apache, whose long hair flew about like his horse's mane.

Almost to the wagon, the Apache brought his rifle up as did Cargill. Only a few yards were now between them. With only one shot left, Cargill fired. The Indian fell from his horse, which kept running.

Cargill pulled spare cartridges from under the seat and reloaded the magazine.

Captain Smith streaked into Cargill's view on his lathered horse. Behind Smith rumbled the ambulance driven by Lieutenant Theller, carrying five men and Mrs. Theller, who was partially crouched on the floor, her flying hair clearly visible. Smith pulled back his reins, his horse skidding in the desert. His officers at the ready, Smith drew his bayonet and yelled, "Charge!" The company's bugler sounded the attack, and the infantry rushed forward into a fierce melee with the Apaches.

Cargill looked back at the rest of his wagons and saw the determined faces of his men. Could they make the river two miles away? Captain Smith on his agitated steed appeared at Cargill's side, yelling, "Park! Round up and park!"

"No! We're on to the San Pedro."

"Park!"

"I'm in command of these wagons." Cargill motioned for his driver to quicken the pace.

All the supply wagons lurched and bumped over the desert, passing the infantry in assault, passing the ambulance where Delia Theller held a young private, bleeding profusely, in her arms.

Cargill looked back for a glimpse of the skirmish, which raged over the washes and the uneven terrains until the Apaches retired, melting into the Whetstone Mountains and leaving on the floor of the desert thirteen dead warriors and many others seriously wounded.

Hearing the bugle sound the cease-fire, Cargill yelled over the winds and the rumble of the wagon for his bullwhacker to stop. He stood up and waved his Henry rifle overhead, signaling the other wagons. The train slowed and finally came to a rest.

Cargill placed one foot on the wagon wheel's rim, the other on the hub, and jumped to the ground. His legs spongy, Cargill walked around in a circle. His second wagon pulled up next to him, then the third, and finally all of his wagons. He received the good news that all the men were fine, all the mules came through, and only three oxen were slightly wounded.

An army horse and rider galloped toward Cargill. Captain Smith jumped down from his horse before it stopped and stuck his contorted face into Cargill's. "Mr. Cargill, why the hell did you disobey my orders?"

"I am commander of my wagon train." Cargill's neck engorged with blood in an attempt to keep his temper.

"You drove with the Twenty-First United States Infantry. You obey my orders."

Cargill heard his own voice grow in volume as his containment failed. "No, sir. I left the military long ago. I follow protocol set by Lord & Williams and by myself. I did the right thing."

"You endangered not only yourself and your team, you endangered my troops."

Captain Smith pointed at the wagon train. "Had you parked as ordered, we could have fired on the enemy from within the protection of your wagons."

"Thereby killing all of my oxen and mules. And then, by God, how would I move my supplies?"

Captain Smith jabbed his forefinger at Cargill. "You and your men were damned lucky to survive. You took a great risk splitting the Indians—half going for the supplies and half for the infantry."

"I did the right thing."

"They could have caught us in the middle of a pronged attack."

"They moved into the mountains. My oxen and wagons couldn't protect the troops there."

Captain Smith again thrust his face forward, within inches of Cargill's. "Don't ever circumvent a military order."

"I did the right thing." Cargill's words sounded empty, even to himself.

Lieutenant Theller and his wife, having arrived in the middle of the argument, looked on. Cargill winced at the sight of Delia's dress smeared and soaked with blood.

Captain Smith whipped the cap off his head and threw it near his horse. "Number of wounded?" he demanded of Theller.

Unable to meet Delia's eyes that seemed to search for something in his own, Cargill turned from the woman, and walking to the far side of his supply wagon, leaned against it, his legs wanting to give out.

TUCSON

With increasing frequency, Valeria and Raúl ate in silence. Although some days he would describe in detail mortal accidents or revenge killings in town or, the worst for Valeria, the discovery of mutilated bodies along the highways or at the victims' homes.

One night she had heard enough. "¡Basta!" Valeria flung the word at Raúl, who smiled snidely.

He waited a day or two before announcing one evening, "No one was killed today."

Valeria thought a moment and decided to compliment Raúl, "Muy bien. Muchas gracias."

Moments later he changed into his plaid shirt and met Curro outside. Sometimes Raúl returned home; more and more frequently, he did not. When he did he continued his usual irritating pronouncement for the days without incident and spoke of nothing on the days there were murders.

Valeria suspected as much, for she heard through conversations with Epi and her neighbors of continued tragedies that beset the region. However, she also began to suspect that Raúl was disappointed when he had to report "No one was killed today." Each benign report aggravated Valeria more, and her irritation with him grew. The nights they retired together, he would grin at her before turning away on his side to fall asleep. Other nights he did not return from Mister Z's. *My bed is as cold as that of an old, repugnant widow.*

Once, when he was in their bed, Valeria rolled on her side and ran her fingers down Raúl's arms and across his stomach. He only endured it for so long before he withdrew her hand. Shaking his head, he turned away.

"Does your head hurt, mi amor?"

"No. Buenas noches." He fell asleep.

Another night, Valeria observed, "I haven't heard about Juan or town meetings for some time."

"The meetings are about the city incorporating and how to purchase property."

Valeria sat up. "How do you purchase property?"

"With money that we don't have." Raúl tried to find a more comfortable position in bed.

"We work. How much does it take?"

"In town, several hundred dollars for a small house."

"So much." Valeria lightly placed her hand on Raúl's arm. "But together, we could raise it. Don't you think?"

Raúl turned on his side, away from Valeria. "Renting is fine."

Valeria drew the sheet up to her chin but immediately threw it back and turned toward Raúl. "I know how to stockpile the money needed. Open our own store."

He drew the sheet over his head, but she pulled it from his grasp, revealing him. "You now know what the men here need and want. And I know what the women need and want. We could do this. Raúl, escucha. Listen to me."

"No. We aren't ready for that."

Perhaps he's right. We probably don't have enough money to start a retail store. Taking a different approach, she modulated her voice lower, "Raúl, we went to the dance with prominent citizens to advance ourselves. We need to keep trying. Go back to Juan. Forget about that Curro. He reminds me of your brother."

"I like Curro and the others. We have fun."

"What 'others'?"

"Leave me alone." He turned his back.

I don't know what to do.

One evening Valeria sat down at their small table after preparing a dinner of skirt steak she was lucky to have secured on a shopping trip with Epi, who'd spoken in raptures of Andrew—how attentive and amorous he was. *As Raúl of old had been.*

Raúl forked a bite of steak with a cut tomato wedge. Hungrily, he chewed. No compliment given for this rare meal.

Valeria forced a smile.

Finishing well before Valeria, Raúl looked up. "No one was killed today."

"No one was born today."

Raúl glowered at her, his face growing dark and ugly. Throwing his napkin down, he raked his chair back. It thudded on the dirt floor.

Her arms crossed over her head, Valeria cowered, cringing from the fist he shook in her face. *Will he strike me? Will he beat me?* Whimpering, she waited for the force of the first blow.

Moments ticked by.

Raúl focused on the wood wedding ring on Valeria's hand. Given with the greatest love.

Three paces to the door, Raúl threw it open and went out into the night.

After the door slammed shut, Valeria slowly lowered her arms from her head to her shoulders. *I've never been frightened of Raúl before.*

✦✦✦

Valeria flung open the cathedral door. It banged against the adobe wall. She ran inside, only reaching the back wooden chair before collapsing on the hard-packed dirt floor. Her hands clutched the top of the chair; her head rested against its back. There she stayed, sobbing, her weeping so loud that she disturbed a nun in prayerful vigil at the small altar on the side wall.

It took several moments before Valeria realized that a hand lightly touched her shoulder. She turned her head away, hiding from the gentle touch.

A soft voice in English said, "My child, what is the matter?"

"No sé." Valeria shook her head. Without effort, strong hands lifted Valeria to her feet and steered her to the front of the chairs where she and the woman both sat. Her sight blurred and her breathing labored, Valeria opened her mouth for air and wiped away tears and spittle with her shawl. Realizing she had forgotten her mantilla, Valeria quickly draped her shawl over her head. Once quiet again, she fumbled in her skirt pocket to find a handkerchief. The woman's soft hand offered a different handkerchief, which Valeria took. Dabbing at her nose she whispered, "Gracias."

"I think the word I should use is 'de nada.'"

Only then did Valeria look at the person sitting next to her—a Sister of St. Joseph of Carondelet. Her heavy black veil hung over her shoulders, making her bib collar appear whiter than it was. Clasped hands rested on her voluminous black skirt. Yet it was the kindness in the nun's hazel eyes, peering from under straight brows, that captured Valeria.

"You are Anglo," Valeria switched to her halting English in deference to the nun.

"Thank you so much for that. I am Sister Monica. And after a year here, I am still deficient in my Spanish. Maybe you could help me."

Valeria looked down at the wad of dirty cloth in her hand. She couldn't return a filthy handkerchief. "I shall, uh, lavar, wa . . . wash it."

"You've come here before."

"Sí, muchas veces."

"Many times, yes. In better times."

Valeria straightened her back, now aching and sore. "I am some . . . sometimes emotional. I am a big problema."

"Many people have big problems. That's why they come here. For solace. For prayer. For consultation. For forgiveness."

Valeria hesitated. *Many other Tucsonenses I've met have the same heartache, and they do not come running to the cathedral. They accept it. I cannot. Am I weak, or too sensitive? No, too much in love with my husband.* "Sor Monica, forgive me. But you would not understand."

"¿Qué es su nombre?"

The nun's poor attempt at Spanish brought a quivering smile to her lips. "Valeria."

"Valeria, forgive me, but don't underestimate me. I believe you have marital problems. I understand. For you see, I was once married."

Valeria raised her eyebrows, innocently exposing her naivete.

"Before I became a nun, of course. My husband and our small children succumbed to diphtheria five years ago. Through that, I found the Church. And its acceptance and comfort."

Valeria involuntarily clasped the nun's hands and leaned over to kiss them.

"Let me help you. Comfort you."

Valeria tried to still her trembling chin, to summon some kind of strength that she knew at that moment she did not have. "Raúl. I think he has another woman. He does not . . . wish to . . ." She knew the nun peered at her, even though Valeria turned her head the other way, the shame of his rejection so great.

"Sometimes there are other reasons. Is he ill?"

"No."

Sister Monica craned her neck to get a glimpse of Valeria's face. "Does he work regularly?"

"Sí, Mister Z's." Valeria momentarily cast her eyes at the nun.

"Ah. How long have you experienced this?"

"One month."

"Anything else unusual?"

Valeria shook her head, then said, "Three months ago he transported goods to a camp."

"Not Camp Lowell?"

"No, no. Away."

"When was this?"

"Raúl came back early May. He was away about cuarto días." Valeria sensed the nun's change of position on the chair and looked up.

Sister Monica's straight, fair brows creased as she confirmed, "Several months ago."

"And it is killing me. I want a bebé. I failed once. I want a family. I see so many with niños." The vision of Atanacia's growing stomach ballooned in Valeria's mind.

"Is it safe now for you?"

"Sí, but Raúl . . . what is the word?" Valeria lowered her head to hide her disappointment. *Can no one help me?* Tears welled up again, and her insides shaking, she could not find her breath. Angrily and louder than she meant to, Valeria said, "No, Raúl is hiding something."

"Valeria . . ."

"It can only be another woman. I'll . . ." She raised her trembling fists but covered her mouth to stifle her sounds of mourning, for it was undeniable to her. *I mourn the loss of my husband's love.* Cut off from him so suddenly, and with that security gone, she felt like a quail chick separated from its clutch. Sister's arm around her weighed Valeria down.

"Shush—sh-sh-sh. God is with us. Be still and listen."

Valeria wanted to wallow in her tears, rejoice in her sobs, and experience the shaking of her shoulders and the spasm of her diaphragm with each wail. But the small hand pressing on her back quieted her, and despite some resentment and disappointment, Valeria gradually stopped sobbing. She wiped her nose with Sister Monica's handkerchief and drew in the musty smell of old sacraments brought to Tucson from elsewhere and the smell of dust from the caliche soils. "I had nowhere else to go," whispered Valeria.

"God is with you always. And the Church is always here for you."

"Es la verdad."

"Try to understand Raúl. Your immediate thoughts may not be entirely accurate."

"Many times he does not come home. There is no other explicación." Valeria suffered the nun's probing scrutiny.

Sister Monica abruptly raised her cross to her lips and kissed it. It dropped back upon her chest and dangled twisted over the white collar. "You speak English well. Do you also read English?"

"No. I can read some Spanish. A few Bible verses."

"How do you occupy your time, Valeria?"

Brightening, she said, "Sewing. I am a scientist on Señora Hughes's sewing machine. And I also stitch by hand. I complete many alterations and new pieces of clothing I design."

"You must be very talented. I would like for you to do something. With each stitch taken, you must remember that God is with you. Give this situation up to the Lord, and he will work it out according to his plan. Believe that."

"I will. Thank you," whispered Valeria with renewed, profound faith. She lowered her head in prayer but watched Sister Monica cross the church to meet Mother Emmerentia at the nunnery's entrance. Their whispered words unintelligible to Valeria, she imagined that Sister Monica asked for guidance regarding one of their flock. The mother's square face radiated strength but hid any trace of empathy.

SUNDAY, OCTOBER 1, 1871

[We are told] that among the citizens of Tucson participating in the horrible death of these women and children were ". . . several of the most respected merchants." We know nothing about the "respectability" which [those men] . . . enjoy when at home, but we do know that in the eyes of civilization they are today regarded as among the most cowardly, cruel, and infamous butchers that the world holds.

—*Philadelphia Inquirer*

TUCSON

Valeria edged down the center aisle, following families with energetic children released from noon mass at San Agustín into the brilliant sunshine. Deep blue skies of autumn brought the craggy rocks of the Santa Catarinas in relief, as if Valeria, standing in the church plaza, could touch them. A welcome breeze stirred, breaking the heat that had lingered long into September.

Although she acknowledged the parents of several children running around the plaza, Valeria felt a little like a missing glove. Usually without Raúl, who frequented Sunday morning cockfights, today she was also without the companionship of Atanacia, who sent a note merely stating she couldn't attend church, no reason given. *A new mother again. Atanacia probably wants to cuddle with her baby boy.*

With a swift kiss on the cheek of Teresa Elías and a big hug accepted from Juan, Valeria turned for home but stopped at the sight of two men moving through the crowd with a great deal more purpose than a Sunday afternoon required. The unknown man in the lead strutted like he had business to attend; the second man was recognizable from his policing the streets—John Miller, deputy marshal. *My goodness, what business could they have here today?*

Juan whispered, "That looks like Willard Rowell in the lead. Teresa, I'll find Jesús."

Valeria read distress in the faces of the Elías brothers, who had also rounded up Bill Oury. They walked away, toward their homes, but Rowell and Miller's quickened steps brought them face-to-face. "Mr. William Sanders Oury, Mr. Juan Elías, and

Mr. Jesús María Elías, you are each under arrest for the murder of Apache women and children near Camp Grant on the morning of April 30, 1871. It is my duty as U.S. attorney general for the Arizona Territory to escort you to the city jail."

Rowell spoke in such a commanding manner that Valeria and many other people in the plaza stopped talking. Shocked, Valeria backed away from the confrontation. *Arrested? This can't be. It's unbelievable. Surely not Juan and Jesús.*

"Take them away," said Rowell to the deputy.

"Now?" Oury challenged.

Jesús María cried out, "¡Teresa!"

His wife screamed as she ran to him. Pulling at her husband's sleeve, she sank to her knees on the ground and wailed her guttural cries. The deputy pulled at Teresa, but she batted his hands away.

Enveloped by the family's terror, Valeria knelt beside Teresa and wrapped her arms about the woman, protecting her from the deputy, who turned away to prod the arrested men on.

Rowell in the lead and the deputy at the rear, Oury, Juan, and Jesús were led out of the church plaza to Calle de la Alegría and immediately north on Court Street.

"¡Jesús!" howled Teresa, who scrambled away from Valeria and tried to rise; all the while, her children bawled, "¡Papá! ¡Papá!"

Now standing, Valeria grabbed Jesús's sobbing wife by the arms and brought her to her feet. Thrusting her face into Teresa's, Valeria insisted, "Go with Jesús. Do you understand?" Haunted by Teresa's blank stare, again she ordered, "I'll see your children back home. Go to Jesús. Vaya con Dios."

Gathering the frightened Elías children around her, Valeria watched Teresa stumble out of the plaza to follow her husband and those arrested.

Emerging from a private courtyard—today's location for the cockfights—Raúl spotted a curious group of people, which included the Elías brothers and Bill Oury, marching up the street. As if thinking this parade would lead to food, dogs scampered ahead and among the men.

Raúl followed the group while other passersby and residents also took notice. They emerged from restaurants, saloons, and dwellings to look at the spectacle of a deputy marshal escorting some of Tucson's elite citizens up the street. Some tried joining the march but were repelled.

Raúl decided to overtake the group. Trotting along, he couldn't get Juan or Jesús's attention. They scowled; their boots pounded the dirt with every step; they were being paraded through town like caged animals from the Mexican touring circus that performed near their homes to adoring crowds. Oury's face flamed a deep red.

Raúl finally understood. *Deputy Marshal Miller and a man in a suit. ¡Ay! It can only be about the raid. Dios, am I next? Where did Curro go?*

Letting the crowd overtake him, Raúl trailed behind the curious townspeople past Calle de la India Triste, where in the whorehouses, loose women slept until later in the day. Crossing Calle del Arroyo, the crowd followed the group of men to the jail behind the courthouse in Court House Plaza.

Rowell stopped and eyed the followers. "Please disperse. We have business inside." The deputy opened the door to the jail, and Rowell ushered the accused inside a small room where Raúl could see Sidney DeLong, Charles Etchells, D. A. Bennett, and Jimmie Lee waiting.

The jail's front door closed, shutting off Raúl's view, but he lingered, as did many in the crowd. Sometime later Jimmie Lee came out and stopped to talk to David Foley. Raúl edged closer to them.

"What happened?" Foley asked of Lee.

"Paperwork today."

"What for?"

Lee's eyes blazed. "We're to stand trial in December."

"For what?"

"Murder."

"Whoa. For killing those damned Apaches? Murder?" Foley hitched his shoulders and squared his gun belt. "Well, hell, I'm not hangin' around town for the hangman's noose. This is the last you and Tucson see of me, boss." Foley melted into the crowd.

Raúl leaned against the jail's stucco wall. Breathing heavily, sweat pouring from his scalp and body, his shirt sticking to his chest, he tried to think. *I'm next. The deputy will haul me away and lock me up for murder. And Valeria has no idea what I've done.*

Raúl crossed the street and back onto Calle del Arroyo. *I need to speak with Zeckendorf or . . . someone.* He'd never told the truth to his boss about the three days he took off in late April, although Mister Z never mentioned it, as if he already knew. *How can I ask him now to help shield me from the law?* Raúl realized he had nowhere to go for counsel. *Not Juan—that would definitely put me at fault. Not the church. Valeria goes more and more. She could seek shelter from the church. I can't. And my gambling compadres? Except for maybe Curro, they'd hogtie me and throw me in jail for a reward. I have nowhere to hide.*

Raúl kept his head down and tried not to run as he headed home. From his location across the street, he saw Valeria inside sitting at the table, waiting for him. His dinner plate was likely already laid, his napkin folded, the fork and spoon placed properly for his use. Everything would be set except his arrival home.

Deciding what he craved was a whiskey, not food, Raúl went back uptown to Calle de la India Triste, his second home, a raunchy area fit for him. He had crawled down to the lowest level of existence. *This is where I belong. Not with Valeria.* He walked into the whorehouse he frequented and was shown upstairs.

Valeria pondered the day's earlier events as she played with her fork, moving it under the heavy ceramic plate before resting it on the plate's rim. Calming the Elías children at their home had proven only partially successful. Preparing lunch for them from what she found in their kitchen had helped the younger ones, but the older brothers realized the full import of the day when Teresa returned home and went directly to bed. Restive about the older children's assurance that they could organize the evening meal without mishap, Valeria knocked on Teresa's bedroom door, but there was no response. She spoke through the closed door, hoping that Teresa could hear, "I am not far away. I can come in a moment's notice." She waited a minute before going home to cook Raúl's dinner.

Now dark with twinkling stars peeking out through the intermittent clouds, Valeria came to the conclusion that Raúl would not return. *April 30. He was away on the wagon train to the south. Oh, Mr. Etchells! I hope he's all right. Soledad talked about an awful raid at Camp Grant to the north. And the older woman down the street. She said she saw a dozen men leave to go into the mountains. I took it to mean the Catarinas. Is that correct? Raúl might have heard or seen something later. I should ask him when he comes. But, of course, he doesn't answer my questions. Not any of my questions. Or he gives me poor answers. Like about his cuts and bruises. And the plaid shirt . . . and where he goes at night . . .*

Too tired to sew given the day's happenings, Valeria drank the beer she had bought for Raúl.

MONDAY, OCTOBER 2, 1871

The perpetrators of the Camp Grant massacre ought . . . to be punished
with the utmost severity.

—Pittsburgh Commercial

Andrew Cargill had always thought Judge John Titus, a distinguished man of
almost sixty, visualized himself as Justinian, dressed in a tunic and ready to cod-
ify any laws that might be found in the lawless lands of the West. Cargill's eyes
gleamed as Titus finished swearing in the sixteen members of the grand jury by
theatrically enunciating the words "so help you, God."

"I do," Cargill said along with the others, all fellow Tucsonans, several having
known each other for as many as ten or fifteen years. As they again sat in the
court's uncomfortable and worn spindle-backed chairs, Cargill entertained the
thought that these men, who always disagreed at town meetings, weren't likely
to find consensus in a legal case.

Judge Titus scanned the worn, tanned faces of those before him. "The sixteen of
you are to listen to the facts of an indictment as presented by an attorney. Should
you find there is probable cause—the lowest level of proof—that the facts presented
show a crime was committed and most probably the accused committed it, you
will take a vote. If at least nine of you agree, a simple majority, you will have found
that there is a 'true bill,' and the case will go forward to a trial by jury. Not you
folks, but others who form a trial jury." He paused to ascertain whether they were
actually listening to him. "If nine of you do not come to a decision, then there is
a 'no bill,' and the case will not go forward. Remember you do not decide guilt or
innocence, merely whether there is probable cause." He gathered his papers and
slid them into a worn leather briefcase. "While you deliberate your vote, the sixteen of you are sequestered. No one else in the room." Not seeing a raised hand or
hearing a question, the judge smoothed his heavy mustache and stood, causing the
jury members to rise again. "Now get to work." Titus closed the door behind him.

Cargill and the other jurors sat but called out hellos and howdys when James

E. McCaffry, district attorney for Arizona Territory as well as district attorney for Pima County, entered.

Cargill looked about the room. *I know for certain McCaffry's represented several here in minor misdemeanor cases. Not to mention sitting alongside me and the others in all the barrooms in town, raising a glass of beer or whiskey . . . and some rotgut.*

McCaffry asked, "Who is foreman?"

Cargill scanned the jurors in the room. All admired the dirt floor. After a pause Charles Hayden raised his hand. "I volunteer as foreman."

"And who is secretary?"

Cargill was amused that the jurors again failed to answer. *Go on. It couldn't be a lot of work.* He raised his hand. "I volunteer to be secretary. I have a legible hand." *And I'm sitting in the front row.*

"All right now, gentlemen. Let's begin." McCaffry presented the facts about a simple misdemeanor case, which several had seen transpire on the streets of Tucson.

After McCaffry stepped outside, the foreman asked for discussion. One juror blurted out, "I saw him do it." Others concurred.

The foreman said, "Let's take a vote." All hands rose. "Sixteen for, zero against."

Cargill dipped the point of a pen in an inkwell and wrote across a sheet of paper the name of the accused, the counts of law allegedly broken, and the vote count of the jurors. He scrawled his signature, set that document aside, and readied another sheet for the next finding of the grand jury. *No trouble to this.*

McCaffry briefly returned to learn the outcome of the requested indictment, took the signed document from Cargill, and left.

A man not known to most of the jurors entered the chamber. "Good morning, gentlemen. I'm C. W. C. Rowell, United States attorney general for Arizona Territory. The case I bring before you is one of first-degree murder."

All the jurors shifted in their seats. Murder was common in Tucson. Murder occurred daily. Which one would this be?

Cargill avoided eye contact with Rowell, and the attorney general did not look at him. Friends since they and Judge Titus had formed part of newly appointed Governor Safford's entourage two or three years ago, Rowell had recently asked Cargill for boarding house recommendations, needing temporary lodging for the three months the court was in session. Always in need of cash while he waited for his ship to come in, Cargill offered to share his rooms, which Rowell gladly accepted.

Clearing his throat, Rowell began, "On the morning of Sunday, the thirtieth of April of this year, a band of men from Tucson and the surrounding area attacked the ranchería of the Arivaipa Apaches located five miles to the east of Camp Grant."

Oh my golly. Cargill immediately heard murmurs among the jurors while chairs moved around. Nearly everyone in town had heard about the celebrated deaths of the Apaches, whom the military hadn't the gumption to either exterminate or adequately corral on a proper reservation. *That's what most people believe.* The murmurs quickly escalated into raucous accusations directed toward Rowell. Most of the men stood, yelling without pause and gesticulating at him, but the attorney general stood motionless.

"What the hell?"

"That was in defense."

"Apaches murder us!"

"They did Stoneman's job."

"Damnation! What a thing."

Cargill thought his friend appeared to be waiting for a firing squad to finish him off and was thankful that sidearms had been collected before entering the jury room. Despite the upheaval around him, Cargill remained seated and quiet. *I don't know how many, if any, of these men have seen the aftermath of the so-called massacre and the mass grave. I did. Heck, Whitman's not all bad. And seeing how hard the Arivaipa Apaches worked cutting hay . . . I don't know. I don't even know for certain who went. Of course, I could name a few likely ones. Only as a guess. But bringing murder charges against people with whom you socialize and know well . . . it's deeply disturbing.*

"Gentlemen, please. Please!" Rowell raised his voice over the jurors' continued shouting. "Mr. Foreman, please rap the gavel."

With a reluctant attitude, Hayden rapped for silence.

"Gentlemen," called out Rowell, "please be seated."

The jurors took their own sweet time returning to their chairs.

Order restored, Rowell began, "Let me state the facts."

One juror called out, "Everyone knows the facts. Defending ourselves against the savages because the military won't is no crime."

Rowell maintained composure. "That is to be determined. The Eastern Seaboard and the U.S. government are up in arms . . ."

The juror continued over Rowell, "I haven't seen them here, dying with the rest of us."

". . . over this incident. It is looked upon as outright murder."

Another juror shouted, "What do they call the deaths of scores of our neighbors over the last few years? Coincidence?"

Low, growling mutters among the grand jury members resurged.

Forsaking the gavel, Hayden banged his hand upon the desk before him. "Order. Order, please."

Keeping his head low, Cargill worried over his own actions. *Maybe renting part of my rooms to Willard wasn't such a great idea. He's giving each of us a good, stern look. He must be sizing up his options. From the angry faces around me, I'd say none of his options look good. He'll have to decide on the least offensive choice.*

"I would like to postpone for a few days any further presentation of this indictment to the grand jury." With one swipe of his hand, Rowell gathered his notes and left.

Rowell's sudden exit suited the grand jury just fine.

Charles Hayden rose. "I think we're done for the day. Remember we're not to discuss these indictments with anyone. And that means don't talk about it down at Foster's or Congress Hall."

✦✦✦

At a back table in Congress Hall, Rowell and Cargill hunched over whiskey and steaks.

"That didn't go well," Rowell admitted.

Under raised eyebrows, Cargill chuckled. "You're observant."

Rowell pushed his plate away. "I need more ammunition."

"Bad choice of words."

"They don't understand the complexity. This cannot be swept under the table. It must be addressed. President Grant calls it murder. The Quakers and other peaceful denominations of faith are calling for a full investigation and justice."

Cargill leaned forward and hoarsely whispered, "Willard, I firmly believe justice must be served. But I'm telling you, some members of your grand jury have seen mutilated bodies along the highways. It's difficult to fathom how human beings could inflict such . . . appalling acts upon another human. If the East could see a picture of one mutilation, perhaps . . ."

Rowell began heatedly and too loud, but he immediately dropped his volume, "These women and children were noncombatants, Andy." He looked around the saloon. Men at other tables and along the bar glanced his way, then turned back to their companions to whisper and shake their heads. Rowell bolted out of his chair and drank the rest of his whiskey in one gulp. "I need to think this over. I might be gone for part of a day, maybe two. I'll be back."

The needle plunged into the cotton. "God is with me." Advancing a quarter inch on the material's backside, the needle reappeared at the front. Valeria's fingertips grabbed the needle, pulled it through by the length of thread, and stuck it back into the material, taking another stitch. "He is with me." Never had she forgotten Sister Monica's suggested entreaty. *Every stitch is confirmation of his love for me.*

"Must you repeat that every stitch?" *Black queen on the red king. Nada. Nada. Four on the five. Nada.*

"Does it bother you?" *Raúl hates solitaire.*

He threw his remaining cards on the piles. After a sip of cerveza and a glance at Valeria, Raúl crossed his arms over his chest and leaned back in the chair.

Laying aside her work, Valeria admired her husband. *He is so handsome with the longer sideburns. Should I . . . ?* She went to Raúl and, standing behind the chair, slid her fingers over the heavy muscles of his shoulders before encircling him in her arms, her head against his neck. He stiffened. *He makes no move to touch me. He doesn't move at all; he's like the granite in the mountains.* Mere seconds seemed like minutes. *This is awkward and foolish.*

Straightening, she drew away.

"Do you remember when you were little you scraped your knee?"

Valeria remembered immediately. "Mi madre left me in the dirt." *Was my mother's abandonment of me significant to him as well? With him in this mood, I cannot ask.*

Raúl frowned at the ace of spades face-up on the table. Standing, he crossed to the door. "I'm going outside."

THURSDAY, OCTOBER 5, 1871

Rowell entered, tossing his hat and jacket on the adjacent chair to the surprise of Cargill, already at the table, eating dinner. "Where have you been?"

"Thinking." Rowell poured himself a drink. "I sequestered myself in a tent at Camp Lowell with my thoughts and law books."

The two men shared a silent dinner, after which Rowell rose. "Once upon a time, there was an attorney general of a faraway land. And he happened to leave a confidential telegram on the table of a good friend. And this good friend read it and acted upon the information in this wire, according to his conscience."

From his inside jacket pocket, Rowell took out a folded piece of paper, placed it on the table, and, with his forefinger on the paper, moved it closer to Cargill.

Cargill scoffed at the telegram's condition, which obviously had been unfolded and folded again many times. "How old is that?"

"Several weeks. It was forwarded to me from California before coming here. I'm tired. I'm going to bed. See you at grand jury tomorrow morning." Rowell closed the door to his bedroom.

Abashed at Rowell's strange behavior and story, Cargill feared to touch the wire. He contemplated it for a long while, decided he was being silly, and opened the paper. What he read dumbfounded him.

Moving back from the table, Cargill crossed his arms and covered his mouth with one hand before seeking his trusty pipe. *Tobacco always brings me clear thoughts. Ruminating on this requires the finest. What I have will have to do.* He packed the pipe with irritatingly clumsy fingers and lit up.

Staring out his window, Cargill thought about the wire well into the night. *I must come to a decision . . .*

TUCSON

In the jury room at the courthouse, Andrew Cargill, bearing deep circles under his eyes from lack of sleep, still debated with himself as Rowell wound up his presentation about the indictment before the grand jury.

"And those are the facts of what happened, who took part, and what they took away from the Arivaipa Apache ranchería that Sunday morning on April 30 last. I now leave you to your deliberations."

Looking at his desktop, chin resting in the palm of his hand, Cargill heard the door close, the stirrings of the others on the jury, and Charles Hayden speaking.

"All right, boys. Does anyone have questions?"

Someone blurted out, "Yes. Why in Sam Hill do we have to vote on this? This is outrageous."

As on the first day of grand jury, the men around Cargill groused and grumbled and swore a blue streak.

Do the right thing. Cargill raised his hand. "I'd like to speak."

"Go ahead, Andy." Hayden angled his chair to have a better look at Cargill.

"Uh . . . inadvertently, I . . . I read a confidential wire sent to Attorney General Rowell from the East Coast. And . . . uh . . . the telegram was from United States Attorney General Amos T. Akerman."

"This was not addressed to you?"

"No, Charlie. It wasn't. But I read it. And the gist of the matter is—if we do not indict the men who participated in that attack at Camp Grant, federal officials will place Arizona Territory under martial law."

"What?" Incredulous, Hayden turned to view the puzzled faces of other jurors.

Cargill hurriedly finished, "Then they'll try the attackers by court-martial under a much stricter interpretation of the circumstances. A small panel of military officers for a jury. No one from Arizona."

"My God," whispered several jurors.

Cargill pulled out his pipe. *Damn the court rules.* "I've wrestled with this all night."

Hayden frowned. "They would still be put on trial, even if we do not indict?"

"Yes."

Another juror offered softly, "They could be found innocent."

"It is possible." Cargill turned to view that juror. "But wouldn't their chances be better with trial jurors from Tucson?"

Everyone's focus drew to the floor, where the jurors' hopes to completely squash a trial had collapsed. Silence continued for some time before Hayden asked, "Questions?"

No response.

"A vote? All in favor of indictment?" One by one, sixteen hands went up.

✦✦✦

Nest Feather, the oldest of the ten children in the windowless church classroom, welcomed the rush of air caused by Mother Emmerentia's voluminous garments stirring the dead air as she paced among the chairs occupied by her catechumens, the youngest dangling their legs above the floor. Her mind straying, Nest Feather watched an ant crawl over her open Bible.

"As Christians, we should begin our day with the sign of the cross." The mother turned back to Nest Feather. "How do you begin your day, Solana?"

The mother's words in high, French-accented tones often sailed by without Nest Feather's understanding. "My day?"

"Yes, that's right."

"I raise my head and arms to the east." Her answer drew snickers from the other children.

Mother Emmerentia hushed them and frowned. "There is something else we do. We have spoken of it." No response forthcoming, Mother Superior turned to the other children. "Do we raise our arms skyward, class? Is that what we do?"

Piping voices proclaimed, "No!"

"No," Mother Emmerentia spoke as she wandered the classroom. "We are making progress, but we still have two more months of study on the catechism before you are presented to be baptized. And one day . . ."

Irritated that the Apache sacred morning ritual was scoffed at, given that the church knew Solana's heritage, Nest Feather raised her hand. *Recognition should be given by the White Eyes, no matter how small.* She kept her arm aloft despite knowing Mother Emmerentia had noticed it.

". . . when . . ."

Nest Feather stretched her arm to its full length.

"Yes, Solana." Mother Emmerentia folded her arms within her flowing sleeves.

"You taught us the words of Saint Francis of Assisi. Canti . . ."

"'Canticle of the Creatures.' Yes?" The nun raised her eyebrows.

Nest Feather continued, "The first creature to praise the Lord is 'especially Sir Brother Sun.' He is muy lindo and bears the same . . .'"

"'Bears a likeness of you, most high one.' Good, Solana."

"Then why do you not like that I raise my head and arms to the east where the sun rises?"

Mother Superior hesitated.

Mother Emmerentia does not like that I, an Apache, compare a saint's song to Apache faith and ritual.

Casting a glance at the open doorway of the classroom, where several mothers waited for their children, Mother Emmerentia finally said, "We have come to the close of our day. A good class, children. You are dismissed."

Both Ignacio and Paloma claimed Solana and asked for a word with Mother Superior. Smiling down at their child, Ignacio inquired, "How is Solana doing?"

Mother Emmerentia gazed at them steadily. "She has a very inquisitive mind."

✦✦✦

Valeria rested against her turquoise door, waiting for Raúl's return from work, something that he had done faithfully that week. No chill in the air gave a long, languid start to the evening. La Iglesia was turning pink with the setting sun's rays when Valeria noticed a man stop and dismount his horse at the end of the street. He ran his hand down the horse's flank and drew up its hoof. *That's Juan. Perhaps . . . yes, I must. I must ask him.*

"Hola, Juan." Valeria admired the care he took dislodging a stone from his horse's hoof. "Can he walk now?"

"No hay problema ahora. No problem now."

"Juan, I have a question." She hesitated, but he looked encouragingly at her as he stroked his horse. "Did Raúl go with you on that raid?" She witnessed the light fade from his eyes and wariness invade them.

"What did he tell you?"

"That he led a wagon train."

He inserted his foot in the stirrup and climbed onto the saddle, giving him a three- or four-foot advantage over Valeria's head. "A good wife believes what her husband says."

She peered up into an uninviting face. *He could have answered before getting in the saddle. He wants me to feel small and insignificant.* "I am a good wife."

"There's your answer." Juan squeezed the sides of his horse with his legs and set off toward his house.

Valeria watched him ride away. *I am the one being squeezed.*

MONDAY, OCTOBER 23, 1871

[Arizona] politics is largely a struggle between rival parts of the Territory to possess the posts and the control of the sutlerships. The capital town of Tucson, situated near the Mexican line on a bare, arid burning plain, is a town of traders and smugglers in great part, and although it is close to a century old, its existence would be doubtful if the army were withdrawn. . . . [Arizonans] will dare more for a dollar and less for patriotism and self-defense than any people in the Union.

—*Colonel George Stoneman*

TUCSON

With enough time left in the day to check in at work, Cargill walked the calles, aware that word of the indictments had spread throughout town, the news directly affecting more people in Tucson than fevers and consumption. Those receiving the news burned with outrage. Conspirators and gossipers fanned out and down all the narrow streets, relating the awful truth about Cargill that could send one hundred men to their deaths.

"It was him!" A man on the street pointed toward Cargill.

Another man asked, "Cargill sealed their fate?"

"Yes sirree, he did."

Cargill pondered how—or if—he should react. *When a person does the right thing and it turns bad, a man's gotta stand resolute. And alone.*

Once at Lord & Williams, Cargill tried to remain calm as every clerk and customer gawked at him. At first people fell silent; then, emboldened, they spoke his name loudly with blasphemous epithets that burned his ears and set his heart racing.

Abruptly Dr. Lord silenced the hecklers, "Enough." Letting a moment of silence fasten the mouths of those about him, Lord placed an avuncular hand on Cargill's shoulder. "Let's take a little walk out back, Andrew."

Cargill drew the worst expectations from the irregularity of the request. "Why, sure." A thin smile curdled on his lips. With leaden feet and a light stomach, Cargill followed Lord through the back warehouse.

Cargill listened to Lord chatter about anything to fill the time as they walked. "We sold our sutler's store to Fred Austin at Camp Grant. He's on his own book now. And I'm not sorry. I'm glad to see an end of business with that camp."

When they reached the open barn doors on the back street, they stopped.

"Fred's a good man." Offering up that compliment, Cargill wanted to feel the charity he expressed, but his empty gut and the acid taste in his mouth left him bereft of every emotion but dread.

Lord looked Cargill in the eye. "Andrew, this little business about your encouraging the grand jury to put these men on trial . . . is that true?"

"Well, yes, but . . ."

Lord pursed his lips, and looking down at the horse shit out in the street, he shook his head. "Son, did you have a thought in your head?"

"A crime was—"

"Rowell is playing his card two ways, Andy. He's looking to seize lucrative business opportunities . . ."

"That's not true . . ."

". . . all the while aspiring to be an important attorney. You were taken down the road."

"I don't think—"

"Well, I do think. And so does the rest of Tucson. This caused quite a stir in our store today. Some longstanding customers are threatening to move their accounts to Zeckendorf's or Tully & Ochoa." Dr. Lord's words hung in the air like the stench of a cheap cigar.

Trying to consider his employer's puffy, red face, Cargill focused on the dust on his boots or the flicking tails of the horses tied outside.

"We have to let you go, Andrew."

That brought Cargill's full alertness back to Dr. Lord. "I didn't seek the grand jury. I was chosen. I did my civic duty. Lord & Williams has benefited from my hard work."

"What you say is true, I do not deny it, but you cannot deny that your presence now constitutes a liability to our business."

Having seen the end of too many jobs and relationships over the last handful of years, Cargill kept his dignity intact by refraining from saying he needed employment to make ends meet. He squared his Stetson on his head. "I bid you good evening, sir."

Despite disappointments, Cargill was hungry. He entered the Shoo Fly Restaurant, where it immediately became apparent that the news of an impending murder trial for the men who rid the world of up to a hundred and fifty Apaches preceded him. Hat in hand, Cargill advanced toward a communal table with three empty seats.

Mr. Alling, the proprietor, barred Cargill's path. "Sorry, Andy. We're full up tonight."

"But . . ."

The flush of embarrassment reddened the man's cheeks. "No seats are available. Sorry."

Cargill caught the eye of several men at various tables. After the initial connection, they looked away and whispered to their tablemates, who ventured a quick glance before they too avoided Cargill's direct gaze.

That's the lay of the land. "Thank you kindly, Mr. Alling. Good evening."

Cargill donned his hat and pulled it low on his forehead. Scuffing his boot heels in the dirt street, he had no idea where he was headed, but soon discovered he stood in front of Foster's Saloon. Certain that his reception would be the same there, Cargill caught co-owner George Hand's attention at the bar. He exchanged cash for pails of beef stew and beer. George wished him good luck.

Cargill heard a woman's loud voice as he passed through Calle de la India Triste toward his rooms.

She called, "Donations! Donations for the school!" Sister Monica stopped a man from entering the saloon on the corner. "Pablo, do you really need that drink? What about your child's education? Would you contribute that quarter to the school instead?"

With a look back, Cargill witnessed the man throw his quarter in Sister Monica's pot and, with a longing look at the bar, walk away.

To the right of Cargill, a madam booted a drunk from her bordello, shouting, "You're too rough with my girls. Don't come back here!"

Sister Monica called to that man, "Mister Obregón, go home. Go home to your wife."

Unresponsive, Raúl kept walking.

Just another day and night in Tucson. Iniquity and business—one and the same. Once upstairs in his rooms, Cargill opened the pails and dished out the stew into two bowls over which he told Rowell about getting fired and being shunned throughout town. While contemplating his dinner bowl with disgust, Cargill ventured a bold question, "Are you going forward with this indictment, Willard?"

"Can't you see that I have to? Those men committed murder."

"*We* think so." Cargill stirred his stew.

"There are others who think that way."

"Enough to fill a jury box?"

Rowell suspended his spoon over his bowl. "Laws must be upheld."

"Sounds as if you're trying to convince yourself."

"People in the territory can't behave like savages." Rowell plopped his spoon back in the bowl without having eaten its contents.

"Not a particularly good turn of phrase, my friend."

"What I regret, Andrew, is that I've unintentionally put you in a bad situation. You were on the grand jury and . . ."

Swallowing the last of his meal, Cargill wiped his mouth with a worn napkin. "Accessible and ready to comply."

"I didn't foresee this . . . this . . . outcome for you."

Cargill pushed his bowl away. "Someday my ship will come in."

"Would you do me another favor?" Rowell stood and paced the small room.

Placing the whiskey bottle on the table with a thump, Cargill pulled out the cork. "Only if I can have a glass in my hand."

"That works. I need a clerk for the trial. Would you be my clerk?"

"Does it pay?" Cargill urgently asked.

"Yes."

"Good."

"You start now. First off, we have to list the defendants." Rowell placed several sheets of paper on the table next to the two small glasses that Cargill filled halfway with whiskey. "We know the Anglos and most of the Mexicans involved. Some of the soldiers can identify those they saw leaving town. A few of the implicated bragged a bit before they all decided to silence themselves. So . . . what we have left are the Papagos."

"I'll write." Cargill took a long gulp of whiskey and held a ready pencil. "You give me their names."

"We know the Papago chief's name. Write down 'Francisco Galerita.'"

"Done. Who are the others?"

Rowell deliberately put his whiskey down. "I don't know. We have to make them up."

Cargill took a moment to contemplate Willard's admission. A deep chuckle began in his throat. When the chuckle graduated into a full-throated laugh, Rowell couldn't contain his humor either. Laughing convulsively, Cargill laid his head on his bent arm on the table. Finally their laughter subsided. They took deep breaths. Pencil again in hand and refreshed whiskey in both glasses, Cargill looked expectantly at Rowell.

"The Papagos all seem to have taken Mexican last names. Let's come up with ten last names and go from there."

Cargill suggested a few before asking, "What about first names?"

"Let's put 'alias' in front of the names we make up."

"And that makes it legal?"

"Just write."

VENETIA HOBSON LEWIS

THURSDAY, NOVEMBER 2, 1871

Valeria dropped off alterations at the clothing store before rounding the corner where Epi waited. A few minutes with a friendly face brightened Valeria's days whenever she delivered her sewing.

Today Epi grasped Valeria's hands. "I'm to be married!" Like giggling children, they skipped in a circle.

"¡Enhorabuena! When?"

"By the end of the year."

"Why wait?"

"Andrew is involved in a big trial. He is the clerk for the prosecution."

"When can we meet him finally?"

"He's not even sure when he can see me. The big attorney is rooming with him." Epi scrunched up her shoulders.

"I must make you something. A blouse?"

"You have been so good to me . . ."

"A blouse." They neared the church, only a block away. "What trial is it?"

"About the massacre of Indian women at Camp Grant."

Mention of the raid jolted Valeria as if the Singer sewing machine's needle had plunged into the quick of her finger. "Yes, I've heard of it. Does Andrew know who was involved?"

"I asked. 'Too many to tell,' he said. Lots of Papagos, a few Anglos, a lot of our compadres."

Valeria spoke in a light tone so that her voice would not give her away, but she wanted to inquire before they reached the church, only a few yards off. "Oh? Is there a list of names somewhere to read?"

"Um, no."

"Did Andrew go?"

"Oh, no. The raid happened two weeks after you made me that skirt. I remember because . . ." Epi blushed. "I was with Andrew that Friday and all weekend. Looking out his window, I remember he thought it so quiet. So few men in town. No wagon trains, no bar fights. Quiet."

No wagon trains. Raúl left that Friday. Maybe Epi's Andrew did not see him. Raúl wouldn't go . . . Of course not. He didn't. I am . . . She twisted her wedding band of wood around her finger. *No doubts. None.*

At the church, Epi gave Valeria a quick hug. "Here already. I must be back at work."

Valeria watched her scamper back down Calle de la Alegría. *Not so long ago, my heart soared as hers.* Doubt drove her onto her knees in church.

Murmuring softly, Valeria cringed before her God. "My Lord, I am a hurtful, terrible person. My faults are many. The one most grievous is that . . . I . . ." She lowered her mantilla over her face and rocked back and forth. "That I don't believe my husband."

WEDNESDAY, DECEMBER 6, 1871

Valeria and Teresa Elías stood behind a photographer, who scurried among and about a large arrangement of men—nearly one hundred defendants, attorneys for both the prosecution and the defense, and Judge Titus. Due to the group's sheer size, Valeria and Teresa obliged the photographer and moved farther away as the few remaining defendants assembled before the courthouse.

Now positioned near the walls of a private yard at the entrance to Court House Plaza with other people waiting for gallery seats, Valeria squinted for a clearer view of the group being photographed. "Can you see any faces, Teresa?"

"No. I recognize Jesús by his socks."

The photographer rearranged the positions of a few men who stood behind other defendants sitting erectly in their spindle-legged chairs set out in the dirt. Then, running behind the camera box and ducking his head momentarily under a cloth that veiled the emulsion plate, the photographer confirmed the visibility of every face in the massive group of defendants, who must be seen and recognized in infamy.

Reemerging from under the cloth, the photographer took a step back, and with his fingers around the exposure cap, said, "Get ready. Don't move until I tell you to relax. And stare straight into the camera. Ready? On the count of three." Nervousness quivered in his voice. "One. Two. Three." He took off the cap, exposing the tintype.

Teresa whispered to Valeria during the twenty seconds it took to expose the emulsion plate within the camera, "Jesús is so disgusted with this whole affair, he doesn't want to live among any of these people anymore. He wants to move. Maybe to Los Reales."

"Got it!" The photographer grinned broadly. Grabbing the exposed plate from the large box camera atop a tripod, he ran under the propped-up side of a chuck wagon that had been fitted out as a mobile photographer's lab.

Defendants and attorneys rose stiffly from the uncomfortable stick chairs. No one spoke.

The congregation of men broke apart as they silently filed into the courthouse.

Valeria and Teresa moved toward the courthouse with other spectators, whose numbers kept increasing. Before entering, Valeria looked to the Santa Catarinas. Hazy clouds shrouded the higher elevations of La Iglesia while a thicker layer obliterated the lower foothills. *Not even the mountains can bear to look upon this trial as it begins.*

Lucky to obtain seats at the back, Valeria and Teresa found the multifaceted preparations for a day at court fascinating.

Oscar Buckalew, clerk of the district court, kept his eye on the doorknob to the judge's designated office located behind the bench.

Valeria assumed the thin young man assembling a pile of paper at the prosecutor's table was Epi's intended, Andrew Cargill, and the other man fidgeting with his pencil was the prosecuting attorney.

Teresa identified the men at the defense table, both known to the Elíases. James McCaffry and Grant Oury, brother to Bill Oury, conferred in whispers.

Almost comical was the contingent of newspaper reporters from Tucson, San Francisco, and other West Coast cities jockeying for seats with clear sightlines and within comfortable hearing distance to take down every word said at trial.

To one side in two long rows sat the American and Mexican jurors, all merchants and farmers and ranchers, groomed and shaved, wearing their best clean shirts and pants, and a jacket most of them saved only for Sundays. To Valeria, some of the jurors looked more likely to be guilty of some crime than the impossibly large number of defendants sitting in rows opposite the jurors. Those Papagos who were in court stood against the nearest wall, but a distinguished Papago, perhaps their chief, sat with the other defendants.

When the doorknob turned, Buckalew rose and loudly pronounced, "All rise."

A tremor of excitement thrilled Valeria as she and everyone in the courtroom rose. Abruptly, all talking, kidding, and joking ceased. The appearance of the white-haired and dour Judge John Titus sobered the expressions of every man and woman in the gallery.

Not until Titus assumed his position in a round-backed chair behind the bench did he glance to his right at the defendants. Some of them glared at him; some looked everywhere but at him.

"Be seated," announced Buckalew as Titus rapped his gavel on the desk.

The importance and the reality of the trial finally upon them anguished Valeria. *Good friends could be . . . punished. Raúl should be here. He . . . he . . . what? I still am uncertain.*

Titus cleared his throat before stating in clarion tones, "This is the case of the United States versus Sidney R. DeLong, et al. The defendants, numbering one hundred, are indicted for murder. All of the defendants but one, who is unintentionally absent . . ."

When nervous titters came from the gallery, Titus raised his prominent eyebrows—the hairs of which strayed wildly from a perfect arch. The chuckles subsided; the judge continued, "All of the defendants but one are present. Mr. C. W. C. Rowell, U.S. district attorney for the Arizona Territory, represents the United States. Messrs. James E. McCaffry and Granville S. Oury appear for the defendants. Mr. Rowell, please call your first witness."

Valeria noticed the rosary in Teresa's hands.

Rowell jumped to his feet, beginning the trial with his most important and highly anticipated witness. "I call Lieutenant Royal E. Whitman."

Teresa's worry beads began their slipping, circular journey.

Valeria saw a man in a front-row seat stand. His shoulders square, his uniform brushed of all dust, buttons polished, he walked with purpose to the witness stand, turned toward the gallery, and came to attention to swear his oath. Whitman sat, his back rigid.

Rowell began quickly, "Please state where you lived this past April, your rank, and your positions."

"I resided at Camp Grant in April last. I am a first lieutenant in the Third Regiment of United States Cavalry; nearly all my time is spent in command of the Post and quartermaster and commissary of the Post."

During a succession of questions and answers, Valeria learned about the assemblage of Apaches at the camp during February and March. Then Whitman spoke of the last weeks of April, "Between four and five hundred Indians were there between the twenty-fifth and thirtieth of April, comprising men, women, and children. For a long time I kept account in pencil. The proportion was a little more than one man to five of all others. I issued rations—one pound of corn or flour and one pound of meat to each individual. The last issue, before the thirtieth, was on the twenty-eighth of April."

Rowell circled his table. "Did the Apaches request anything else of you?"

"They asked, in addition to rations, for clothing. I told them I had no power to issue clothing but that I would provide them with work as far as practicable so that they could buy clothing. I made arrangements with them to furnish hay, under the existing contract. Delivering almost every day, they furnished the Post with three hundred thousand pounds of hay."

"Specifically, where were the Apaches camped?"

"They were living about five miles from Camp Grant, first by my authority and then by the authority of Captain Frank Stanwood, appointed by authority direct from the government."

Rowell neared the witness stand. "How did you learn of the events that took place on the thirtieth of April?"

"I received, on the morning of the thirtieth of April, a communication from the commanding officer of Camp Lowell, informing me that a party had left this place with the avowed intention of making trouble with the Indians at Camp Grant. I further state that I'd heard rumors previously but gave them no credit. I immediately dispatched the interpreters at the Post to inform the Indians and bring them in for protection. The interpreters returned in a very short time, reporting that the Indians' camp was deserted and burning—strewn with dead bodies."

"What time was that?"

Whitman jutted out his chin defensively. "I received the intelligence at seven thirty. I immediately formed a party of such men as could be spared at the Post, with a post surgeon, to go to the camp with wagons, bring in all the wounded that could be found, and further examine the state of the case."

Having taken a few steps away from the witness, Rowell turned back to view Whitman. "How many wounded were brought in?"

"On the thirtieth of April, none but dead bodies were found."

Valeria tightened her arms about her middle but found Teresa looking less interested, only drawing down the beads with minimal movement.

"I next sent dispatches containing information to the adjutant general of the department. Next morning I formed a party and went myself to the Indian camp." Whitman pulled at his tunic sleeves, which fit perfectly.

Rowell frowned. "What did you find?"

"I found the situation as had been reported. The camp was entirely deserted. I found dead bodies strewn indiscriminately over the ground, the remains of rations, etcetera. The dead bodies were very much scattered, and as it appeared, nearly all were killed by minié balls. Some of the bodies were easily recognized, but the exposure of one day in the sun had changed them very materially."

Valeria squirmed in her seat, the testimony already proving a test for her.

Whitman cleared his throat. "I saw about thirty or forty dead bodies—nearly all women and children. I found the body of one old man with whom I had talked more frequently than any other of the tribe. He was a particularly influential man. I saw the dead bodies of several women that I recognized.

"The dead bodies of the women were lying in different positions. Generally the bodies were found as they might have fallen when shot, some running. I'll state positively two were lying on their back entirely naked and shot through the breast, apparently with pistol balls, as the aperture was smaller than that of a gunshot wound."

Valeria cupped her hand over her mouth. *Raúl should hear these horrible details. He tells me so many. Why did he refuse to come with me this morning?*

Again jutting his jaw, Whitman declared, "My judgment was that these women had first been wounded and subsequently killed."

By the sounds of movement behind him, Cargill was acutely aware that great interest and perhaps sympathy had been generated within the courtroom by Whitman's testimony.

Rowell paced back and forth before Judge Titus when he pointedly asked of Whitman, "And what makes you determine that?"

"Because, in addition to pistol shots or gunshot wounds, their skulls had been broken or smashed."

Rowell continued, despite the small gasps from the gallery, "Do you personally know who committed these acts?"

The lieutenant shook his head. "I have no knowledge of the parties that did this killing."

"Did you personally observe anything out of the ordinary that morning?" Rowell pressed the pace of his questions to Whitman.

"I saw the dust of a body of men moving up the valley, in the direction of Canyon del Oro, about ten o'clock on the thirtieth of April, from the Post."

"In what direction were they moving?"

Although Whitman had mainly been directing his attention to the prosecuting attorney, he now looked directly at the gallery. "The men that made the dust seemed to be going toward Tucson."

Advancing closer to the witness stand again, Rowell seemed to demand an answer. "Could you determine the number in that body of men?"

"I should judge from the dust to be a large party."

"I have no further questions," Rowell quickly stated before returning to the prosecution table to sit.

Valeria believed Whitman to be a truthful person. *What could the defense possibly refute?*

McCaffry leaned on his bent fingers at the defendants' table and stood. "Lieutenant Whitman, why did these Apaches wish to live within the limits of Camp Grant?"

"As nearly as I have already stated, the stipulations were food, shelter, and obedience to order. They gave at that time no other reasons for coming in but hunger and a desire to live at peace." Whitman looked up at Judge Titus. "I wish that to be understood."

From behind tented fingers, Judge Titus uttered, "Lieutenant Whitman, please restrict your answer to the question."

Whitman made eye contact with Valeria and several other women in the gallery who were engrossed in his testimony. "They presented the appearance of suffering from want of food. They were understood to be prisoners."

McCaffry positioned himself in front of Valeria so that Whitman could no longer see her. "Would you tell the court how many rifles were turned in by the Apaches upon their arrival at Camp Grant?"

Whitman cleared his throat. "They were not requested to give up their arms, as they were very poorly supplied with arms."

McCaffry sternly knitted his eyebrows.

What an actor, thought Cargill. *He's treading the boards, forcing himself to remain straight-faced before those seated in the gallery, all the while knowing he scored a direct hit.*

Could that be true? Valeria heard the people around her mumble at such an incredulous admission, all except Teresa, who smiled.

McCaffry walked slowly past Rowell, allowing the buzz from the spectators to hum for two or three seconds. Cargill followed Rowell's lead and did not look up as McCaffry asked Whitman, "Please explain to the court the distribution of food to the Apaches."

"They were requested to present themselves for inspection, at first every day, then every two days, then every three. At the time of the killing, I was rationing them every fourth day, I think, but I am not sure. I can't state that it was not every fifth day."

"Did you keep a record of how many were rationed?"

"I have my ration record in writing. The books of the Post at the adjutant's office show the number rationed at all times. There is no further record."

McCaffry feigned confusion. "And how was hay supplied by the Apaches?"

"The hay was first delivered at my suggestion. Hay furnished by them was under the contract of Goldberg and Company, of this place. It was necessary to give them compensation for their labor." Whitman squared his shoulders again. "That hay was paid for, as received, by the post trader, F. L. Austin, under an arrangement between him and the contractors. Mr. Austin paid the Indians one cent a pound for the hay they brought in."

"Was that the original contract price?"

"The contract price for hay was $21, I think, in gold, per ton. The contract was for gold."

Again, a pretense of uncertainty colored McCaffry's question. "How were the Apaches paid?"

As if by rote Whitman said, "The Indians delivered the hay. It was weighed, and they were given tickets representing the number of pounds delivered. The Indians presented the hay tickets at the store. In return they received, for the most part, manta."

"To whom was the ration ticket issued?"

"In furnishing rations, the head of the family received the ticket for the whole family."

"Was there a set day for the issuance of these tickets?" McCaffry walked before the jury.

"When the Indians were all reported in, the count was made on a particular day and the tickets delivered. The hour was not set. After the count was made and the tickets delivered, I superintended the issue of the rations. The tickets were presented by the squaws, usually."

Crossing his arms over his chest, the defense attorney stood still. "When did the Indians first commence the delivery of hay?"

"I should say about the middle of March."

"And the tickets were delivered at that time to whom?"

Whitman readily answered, "The ration tickets were sometimes delivered to the men, sometimes to the women."

McCaffry audibly repeated Whitman's contradictory answer, "'Sometimes to the men, sometimes to the women,'" as he paced in front of the gallery and eyed several frowning men. "How many women were at Camp Grant?"

"I do not know how many women there were at their camp about the thirtieth of April."

"Were the Apaches in constant residence at Camp Grant?"

"The Indians were in and out of the Post, and I frequently went to their camp." The spindly chair had become uncomfortable for the lieutenant, who shifted his position.

"Were the Indians at Camp Grant depredating upon the whites?" McCaffry swiftly turned to eyeball Whitman.

Caught off-guard, Whitman hesitated before answering, "I heard such rumors, but I believed the rumors were untrue from my own observation."

"Were the Apaches always in good health?"

"There are at times wounded Indians at Camp Grant. I have no knowledge when they were wounded."

Deep in thought, McCaffry returned to the defense table. "Did you ever see the letters 'A.T.' on any arms at the Indians' disposal?"

"I never saw in the possession of an Indian on the Post arms marked with the Territorial brand."

Grant Oury whispered a question to McCaffry, who asked of Whitman, "Did you ever ask the Apaches to fight against other enemy tribes?"

The lieutenant sternly answered, "They positively declined to join any expedition that might be fitted out against hostile Indians. However, later they made the proposition to join a party against hostile Indians, provided that, in turn, they should be assisted in an expedition upon Sonora."

Valeria shook her head. *This is complicated and corrupt.*

"Exactly how large is Camp Grant?"

Thankful for an easy question from the defense attorney, Whitman replied, "One square mile."

"How many Indians were living there on the thirtieth of April?"

"On the thirtieth of April, no Indians were living at the Post. There were Indians living about five miles from the Post in a direction nearly east."

"Were the Indians in that area visible from Camp Grant?"

"They might have been seen with a glass."

McCaffry cupped his left hand over the defense table's edge. "How did you supervise the Indians' activities at the Post or their encampment?"

Wrinkling his forehead, Whitman answered, "No guard of soldiers was ever stationed over the Indians. There were no positive means of knowing whether the Indians were away from Camp Grant for one, two, or three days at a time. I gave passes for small parties to be absent for mescal over one ration day—say three or four men and fifteen or twenty women. They went ten to fifteen miles to the mountains east of San Pedro."

McCaffry leaned forward. "Did you place certain conditions on their residence there?"

"I frequently discussed with them the condition on which they were at peace. Their understanding when they first came in was that they were at peace only with Camp Grant and not with Arizona. I made them understand that the government had no enemies but breakers of law—that, if they were protected by the government, they should be at peace with all men within the boundaries of the United States."

"Thank you." McCaffry sat, poured a glass of water with a shaky hand, and took several quick sips.

During the momentary pause, Cargill looked at Judge Titus, who waited for Rowell's redirect. Since he offered no questions, the judge said, "Lieutenant Whitman, you may step down."

Rowell stood. "Your Honor, with the leave of the court, the prosecution wishes a nolle prosequi entered on the indictment against D. A. Bennett, who will give testimony on the part of the prosecution."

"So ordered."

Valeria whispered to Teresa, "What does that mean?"

"Turncoats tattle against friends in exchange for their guaranteed innocence."

Duly sworn, Bennett testified of the massacre party's outbound journey, "They continued to follow the trail to within twelve to fifteen miles of Camp Grant. I left the party there, and they went on."

"Did you see anyone else on the morning of the thirtieth?"

"I saw Mr. DeLong, Mr. Etchells, and Mr. Foley."

Rowell studied the dirt floor as he paced. "What were they doing?"

"They took the road leading to Camp Grant and arrived at Grant at daylight. We remained at the Post about two hours. We then started to return to Tucson."

"Did you—the DeLong party—meet up again with the other party? And, if so, what did you see?"

Bennett wet his lips. "We met the large party on the trail about nine or ten miles this side of Camp Grant. With the large party I saw those of the defendants seen the day before. I saw some Indian children with them that were not with them the day before. I heard some of them detailing the account of the fight with the Indians. They stated they had fought in Arivaipa Canyon. I heard several statements."

"What impression did you form based on these statements?"

At first, Bennett looked down at his lap, and then back up at Rowell. "My conclusion was that they had killed in the vicinity of one hundred and fifty Indians and taken some children."

So many dead. Valeria momentarily cupped her hand over one eye and looked down at her lap. *And children? They stole children. What happened to them? Teresa shows no sympathy, no surprise, but then, Jesús took part in this. Should I sit with someone else tomorrow?*

Cargill noticed a drop of sweat rolling down Rowell's cheek, which the prosecutor staunched with a ready handkerchief as he steadied his other hand on a chair at the prosecution table.

"Thank you, Mr. Bennett. The prosecution has no further questions of this witness." Rowell took his seat.

Judge Titus looked to McCaffry and Grant Oury. "Does the defense have any questions?"

McCaffry rose. "Not at this time, Your Honor."

A sharp rap of the gavel ended the first day of the trial.

Darkness overtook the late afternoon hours as Valeria hurried home. *No last look at La Iglesia today. Raúl will be hungry . . . Those Indians were hungry, too. The lieutenant seemed a good man—a man wanting to help. If I could have understood every English word . . . but I understood a great deal. Those women, needing and wanting so much, were flattened on the ground, naked, shot in the breast. Oh, those poor women. What did they feel in those last moments?*

At home Valeria went directly into the bedroom, taking a few minutes to rest. Her thoughts still revolved around the dead Indian women. She lay flat on the bed, her eyes coursing over every familiar knot and ax-hewn mark on the vigas overhead. *Not an unusual pose. I would be looking up at the ceiling like this, flat on my back . . . if Raúl and I still made love. Did those women have last thoughts about their husbands? Their children? Perhaps . . . no. Most likely no time existed for that. Gone, in an instant.*

✦✦✦

As she listened to Mother Emmerentia, Nest Feather decided that if Apaches had catechism school, it would be outside.

"Children, you have done well throughout your learning. All of you now will be presented for baptism. Many will come into the church together; however, some of you, due to family circumstances, will have a private baptism." Mother Emmerentia walked among her catechumens. "Your lives and your faith stretch out before you. 'Make straight in the desert a highway for our God.'"

"Our mountains are sacred. I will not make them low," Nest Feather whispered.

"Did you say something, Solana?" Mother Superior halted. "Would you please repeat it for the rest of us?"

Nest Feather spoke louder for everyone to hear, "Except for our sacred mountains, our desert is already flat." She accepted the children's derisive chuckles, but the nun's eyes, smoldering like a day-old fire and filled with displeasure and exasperation, took Nest Feather aback.

"You always take the literal meaning, Solana." Mother Emmerentia tapped her palm several times with the cross that hung from the waist of her skirt as she completed circling the small classroom. "Go with God."

Free of catechism school, the children ran from the room; Nest Feather waited for acknowledgment from Mother Emmerentia before saying, "Thank you."

THURSDAY, DECEMBER 7, 1871

Raúl chewed his tortilla as he spoke, "Business is brisk. I'm needed at Zeckendorf's."

"Everyone in town is at the courthouse." Valeria moved her chair away from the table and rose. "You're interested in town politics. You tell me of terrible killings. This is what the trial is about."

"I've heard it all."

"We should know how to protect ourselves. You're right."

"I'm not going."

Valeria took Raúl's plate before he ate the last bite of fried egg. "You don't want to go with me. You lie around the house the last two months. You say nothing to me. Do nothing with me. And you don't . . . touch me." After slipping the plate into a pail of soapy water, she turned to face him. "Is she better than me?"

"¿Quién?"

"The one you go to." She squinted.

Raúl held his head with both hands. "No."

"Go to the trial with me. Do one thing together. Do this one thing with me."

Without answering, Raúl left for work.

Valeria expected to remain only a few minutes at the trial, so instead of finding a seat, she stood close behind the last row in the gallery. Standing gave her a full view of all the seated defendants, even those trying to hide in the second row. Someone touched her arm. *Raúl.* Glad that he'd chosen to join her, Valeria nudged him and pointed to one of the defendants. "Curro." Raúl acknowledged with only a nod of his head, and she wondered if he had known or newly learned of Curro's indictment. *Could that possibly be the reason Raúl protested violently again this morning?*

Oscar Buckalew proclaimed, "All rise."

Valeria glimpsed a spot of vibrant color at the end of the second row as the gallery stood for the judge's entrance. *I know that blue.* Once the judge approached the bench and sat, the woman gathered her flounced skirt about her, taking a second longer to return to her seat. *It's Soledad.* Having identified the midnight blue satin, Valeria took special pride in how the expensive lace about Soledad's throat and at the end of the sleeves set off her client's fine features.

Sworn in as the day's first witness, Charles Etchells repeated much of the same story as Bennett the day before, only adding that the four men who had separated themselves from the main party "arrived at Camp Grant shortly after sunrise. We went to no quarters or building at Camp Grant. We remained at Grant an hour or two. We then went back on the road we had come."

Rowell said, "Let us go back to setting out from Pantano Wash. How did the party know which direction to take?"

Etchells hung his head. "The scouting party first struck the trail in the mountains, some twenty miles northeast from Tucson."

"Was this trail taken by choice?"

Still looking down, Etchells shook his head. "I was not aware that the party left Tucson with the intention of taking that trail."

"What was the intent of the party itself?"

"I know that the intention of the party in leaving was to kill Apache Indians, wherever they found them." Etchells chanced a glance at Rowell.

"Subsequently the party merely wandered over the land?"

Finally looking directly at the prosecutor, Etchells answered, "They intended to be guided entirely by indications. I saw Indian signs on this trail—horse tracks, also moccasin tracks. To the best of my judgment, the tracks were not over twenty-four hours old. The party discovered enough moccasin tracks to assure us it was an Indian trail."

Much the same as Bennett said yesterday. Is Soledad content? Valeria looked at her client, who made no discernible movement when Etchells was dismissed and awkwardly returned to his defendant's chair.

As James Lee took the oath as the next witness, Valeria recognized him as the owner of the flour mill. The tall, lean Irishman sat in the chair far too short for his long legs.

Rowell lost no time. "Mr. Lee, what happened after the party reached the Apache ranchería?"

Papers rustled and a frisson of excitement swept through the gallery as one of the perpetrators was about to give more explicit details of the murders. Valeria placed her hand on Raúl's arm and looked up at her husband's strangely ashen face.

Lee let out a long breath. "Leaving the San Pedro River, they followed an Indian trail to the ranchería, which was located partly in Arivaipa Canyon and partly on a bluff. On arriving at the ranchería, the party shot and killed what Indians they could."

Rowell took a position on the far corner of Judge Titus's bench, giving the gallery full view of Lee. "Who were members of that party?"

"Mr. William S. Oury was of that party. I did not see Juan Elías with that party."

The gallery buzzed with low conversation, giving Cargill a moment's rest from writing.

Lee continued over the nascent excitement, "There are parties indicted who were not there at all. A portion of them were those indicted." Jimmie Lee pointedly looked at Raúl.

Valeria followed the witness's direct line of sight back to her husband, standing next to her. Raúl moved his arm to disengage her hand, irritating Valeria. *What does Lee mean? Some of those indicted did not participate? A portion of them—the actual perpetrators—were indicted. Are there other killers not on trial? Some innocent men are on trial and some true murderers walk free. My mind spins. But why does he stare at Raúl? At the same time as the massacre, Raúl said he'd headed a wagon train. He had nothing to do with this bloodbath. And yet . . . I don't know.*

Without pause, Jimmie Lee continued his testimony, "After the attack, the party proceeded back to the San Pedro. Mr. DeLong was not of the party at the time of the attack . . ."

Valeria again gazed at Raúl. His face strangely white, his lips pressed together, he appeared distraught. She insinuated her fingers in his hand. It was ice-cold. He pulled it away.

No longer attentive to Lee's testimony, Valeria again tried reconciling those days Raúl had been away. *The last days of April. His vague answers. No cargo wagon trundled down Calle Real with goods from Zeckendorf's store. That's what Epi said. Raúl returned with bruises, cuts, and scrapes on his hands and face. His new shirt and pants . . . And he won't touch me at all.*

Their eyes met. Raúl canted his head away from Valeria, a wan simper playing fitfully on his lips.

He's embarrassed. About what?

Valeria eyed her husband again. The tips of his ears reddened.

Lee droned on, "On the occasion of the fight, I believe there were some prisoners taken—children. After getting together, the party came toward Tucson."

Raúl never spoke about Curro before or did things with Curro until after the wagon train. Curro's on trial. Raúl's reluctance to be intimate . . . Dios. That's how Raúl knows Curro. Raúl was part of the raid. He killed and . . . maybe . . .

Valeria gasped. She barged through the tightly packed people standing by her, disturbing listeners in the last row as she fled out the court's doors onto the street.

A cloud of dust from a passing horse simmered inches above the street. Dogs barked. Women shopped. Saloon music played.

The abrupt change from a stuffy, closed room to a busy street under a crisp blue sky on a chilly day disoriented Valeria even more than she already was.

Raúl was a second behind her. He yanked her arm and turned her around. She slapped his face. Hard. "¿Qué hiciste? What did you do?"

His hold on Valeria's arm now a vise, Raúl dragged her into a nearby alley, away from the main street. Slamming her back against the wall, he pinned her arms above her head.

This snarling man is not my husband. This is an animal inches above me. Valeria tried to kick his leg, but Raúl trapped her entire body against the wall with his. She buckled her chest, but her strength failed to budge him.

"Did you hold her like this?" Valeria moved her head from side to side, avoiding his sneer.

"¡Basta! ¡Basta!" Raúl kept her wrists pinned above her head with only one hand, and with his other hand he pulled on her chin, forcing her to look at him.

When Valeria turned her head, she spat in his face. Her saliva slid down his nose and his burning cheeks. *This is my last moment on earth. He will kill me.*

Flames smoldered in his eyes; they were glued upon her. In a whisper Raúl rasped, "I supported them. I . . ."

"Killed?" Valeria watched Raúl decide between continued deception and truth. Her back hurt and her scraped hands burned, but she dared not move.

After an agonizing moment, Raúl nodded his head.

"And . . . raped?"

Raúl scanned the street. A few men waited in line for any seats that might open up in court. By waiting they'd earned a prime spot for the entertainment provided by the Obregóns.

Valeria threw all of her weight on Raúl, unbalancing him. Snatching the opportunity, she ran from the alley. Out in the open and seeing that Raúl dared not follow her, Valeria's hurried footsteps fell into the regular path she always took in the late afternoon—toward San Agustín Church.

Inside the courthouse Jimmie Lee leaned forward in the witness seat. "It was the intention of the party to follow the trail wherever it went. I was one of the trailers myself. We traveled partly by day, partly by night. Part of the time it was moonlight, but we could follow the track without that. It was the custom of the party to stop and camp when we could not distinguish the trail easily."

Rowell paced. "What distinguishing tracks or imprints were found?"

"The site of a previous fight was pointed out. A raiding party of Indians had stolen cattle from San Xavier. They had been followed and one man had been killed, probably about ten days before, to the best of my knowledge. A company of cavalry horses had paused over the trail. We followed Indian signs to the ranchería."

Rowell glanced at Cargill still scribbling on his pile of papers. "Thank you, Mr. Lee. Unless the defense has questions . . . ?" Rowell noted a shake of McCaffry's head. "You may step down." Turning to the bench, he said, "By your leave, Judge Titus, the prosecution would like a nolle prosequi entered on the indictment against Mr. C. T. Etchells and Mr. James Lee, each having been sworn and having given their evidence on the part of the prosecution."

Titus leaned forward. "So ordered."

"At this time, the Government of the United States rests, Your Honor." Rowell sat.

Cargill laid down his pencil and massaged his cramped fingers. Hearing movement, he turned to see a woman in midnight blue satin stand up. Her dress rustling, Soledad garnered Charlie's and Rowell's attention as she left the courtroom. A man hustled to take her vacated seat.

While Cargill poured water for himself and Rowell, Judge Titus and the defendants tried to find more comfortable seating positions. Leaning against the wall, the Papago Indians remained unmoved. Some in the gallery stood for a moment as McCaffry consulted with Grant Oury. Cargill readied his pencil.

McCaffry rose. "The defense calls Mr. John T. Smith."

Duly sworn, Smith testified, "I have resided south of Tucson for the past year. Mr. Wooster lived one and a half miles north of my place."

"Mr. Smith, are you familiar with the occurrences of . . ." McCaffry gave Grant Oury a questioning glance.

Oury mouthed, "March."

". . . March last?" finished McCaffry.

Smith frowned. "Mr. Wooster was killed the twenty-first day of March."

"Would you please relate how you knew of his death?"

"Trinidad Wooster's brother informed me."

Without pause, McCaffry asked, "And what did you do immediately thereafter?"

"I took a lot of men up to Wooster's place with me." Smith sighed as he remembered that day. "I found the body of Mr. Wooster and subsequently that of his wife. We found his body in the corral back of his house. The body had been stripped. We found the body of his wife in the woods about three hundred yards from there. Her body was stripped and lanced in three places."

"Was there damage to the property?"

"Guns, ammunition, clothing—everything was taken from the place, and part of the shed over the stable was burnt." Smith shuddered. "No clothing was left whatever."

McCaffry approached the witness stand. "Can you describe any of the clothing that he used to wear?"

"I saw Mr. Wooster frequently, but I cannot describe his ordinary clothing. I did notice particularly a pair of moccasins that he wore. They are the sort of shoes commonly called tegua. They were very heavy of smoked, tanned skin."

"Would you say that you live in a safe, stable area?" McCaffry paced in front of the bench.

Smith shook his head. "The country where I have resided has been very dangerous during the last three years, particularly this last year. I am a farmer. It is not safe to be out on the farm without arms."

"Have there been other Indian attacks in that area, besides that on Mr. Wooster?"

A glance at the ceiling gave Smith the pluck to once again recount the losses near his home. "There have been six attacks by Indians during the last eighteen months. During those attacks, they—the Indians—have killed Messrs. Blanchard, Sanders, and Wooster and his wife, also a child of Mr. Kitchen's wife, and they have wounded Joseph King."

Standing still, McCaffry asked, "How many people currently live near you?"

"About three years ago there were some three or four hundred persons there. Now only about twenty-five, mostly transient. The town of Tubac is wholly depopulated. It's the most fertile portion of southern Arizona."

Looking over at Grant, McCaffry said, "At this time, I have no further questions of this witness."

Judge Titus took out his pocket watch, looked at the time, and snapped the lid shut. "We shall conclude at this point. Court is adjourned until tomorrow at ten o'clock sharp." He rapped his gavel on the bench and stood.

"All rise," intoned Buckalew.

Titus immediately left, prompting a complete emptying of the courtroom. It had been a long day.

Soon no one was left except Rowell, Cargill, and the lead defense attorney. Cargill noted that McCaffry seemed exhausted, licking his lips and running his hand shakily over his forehead. Cargill and Rowell gathered their scattered papers as McCaffry buttoned his suit jacket and hoisted his heavy, buckled messenger bag, full of notes and legal documents. He acknowledged Cargill and trudged outside.

Winter clouds—earlier threatening a cold rain—now hung low in the sky, impounding Tucsonans in town. Using the dreary evening as her friend, Valeria wandered outside the church for a moment's respite before being cloistered over-night with Sister Monica. Using the rough wooden support for the church bells to prop herself up, Valeria felt her heart beating as steady a rhythm as when the Singer máquina de coser sewed cloth, but all emotions had been totally ripped out of her. Internally she was a wasteland, like the Sonoran Desert. *Dios, you say that the truth will set you free. Raúl suffered with a different truth for months. Now it is passed to me. So heavy, I cannot breathe.*

A few people walked through the streets, but one man, carrying a messenger bag, cut through the church plaza from Court Street and continued down Mesilla Street without noticing Valeria. Recognizing the defense attorney, who appeared as exhausted as she, Valeria watched him enter Foster's Saloon on the next corner.

With a sigh, Valeria reentered the church.

FRIDAY, DECEMBER 8, 1871

DAY THREE OF THE TRIAL

Early to court as always, Cargill checked the points of his pencils and pens, straightened his stack of writing sheets, and greeted Grant Oury, who approached the defense table. Anticipation of another day at court mounted as each minute passed. Cargill scanned the courtroom to avoid counting the number of writing sheets again.

Grant organized his notes at his table, Titus passed through to his office, and Buckalew and the sheriff arrived. Soon Rowell appeared, dropping his valise next to the prosecution table. Cargill noted Grant's apparent unease when he rose from the defense table and turned toward the still-empty gallery.

"Quarter of ten. Doors are opening." Buckalew favored his wooden leg as he walked to the back door and admitted the waiting crowd.

Seeing Grant Oury scrutinize the faces of each person entering, Cargill turned and whispered to Rowell, "McCaffry's late."

Grant consulted his watch and motioned to an acquaintance in the front row. After exchanging a few words, the man left the courthouse with a purposeful stride.

Valeria acted upon Sister Monica's advice to take a friend and thought of Epi, who welcomed an excuse to leave work but was also sympathetic because several of her friends had suffered brutal injuries at the hands of their boyfriends or husbands. If Raúl appeared, Valeria must flee again to the church, so she tried her best to hide behind Epi, avoiding detection while they waited outside, chilled by intermittent winds that promised to bring in much colder temperatures.

Luckily Raúl was not seen, and they joined the growing number of women who flocked to the courthouse each day, the fascination for gory details enticing them. Hearing more of the tragedy during the trial became imperative to Valeria. *It's destroying Raúl. I must know more.*

As they found seats and took off their shawls, the garments unnecessary in the courtroom heated by the bodies of the many onlookers, Andrew Cargill again turned to view the defense table and the gallery beyond. He waved at Epi, who gushed to Valeria, "He looks so official."

Cargill answered Rowell's unspoken question, "That's my girl."

Preparations for the court's daily start now seemed routine to Valeria: the defendants filed in and sat, the Papagos stood against the adjacent wall, the jury members took their place, Judge Titus appeared, then the gallery rose.

Today Valeria sensed something amiss. Judge Titus looked sternly at Grant Oury after everyone was seated.

The assistant attorney for the defense said, "Your Honor, may I approach the bench?"

Titus nodded curtly. When Rowell joined them at the bench, the judge demanded of Grant Oury, "Where's Mr. McCaffry?"

"He has been delayed this morning by a pressing matter. I have sent a friend to hurry his presence in court. Until that time, I propose to conduct the questioning of our scheduled witnesses until Mr. McCaffry's arrival."

Titus raised his bushy eyebrows in a tacit question directed at Rowell, who said, "The United States accepts."

With that, Rowell and Grant Oury returned to their respective tables, and an unusually subdued William Zeckendorf, duly sworn, gave testimony about his trailing Juan's stolen cattle over part of the trail, by which he meant the Bridle Road—an Indian road. He mentioned that the Indian killed "had one of his front teeth gone, and noticing closely, he was a very young Indian. I thought the tooth was knocked out by a ball but saw it was not so, upon examination."

Valeria remembered Raúl's garrulous account of Mister Z's adventure with the bloody Indian scalp. The retelling in court upset her again.

Granville Oury called Joseph Felmer to the witness stand. The German blacksmith, tugging at shirt cuffs and jacket flaps of his newly bought suit, took the oath and sat down.

Cargill avoided looking directly at his friend, in case it distracted Felmer.

Grant Oury began the quiz of his witness with an easy question, "Where were you living on the thirtieth of April last?"

Felmer fingered his tight collar. "I was living about three miles above Camp Grant."

"How long have you lived there?"

"I have resided at Camp Grant for three years."

"Are you acquainted with the characteristics of any of the Indians who resided near Camp Grant?"

A door opened at the back of the courtroom, and everyone's head turned toward a pale James McCaffry treading carefully down the center aisle to the defense table.

Valeria identified McCaffry's infirmity without hesitation, given his destination last night and his appearance, similar to that of Raúl after a night out.

McCaffry laid his messenger bag on the floor and made eye contact with Grant Oury, who circled his index finger, motioning for Felmer to continue with his answer.

Cargill and Rowell, having shared drinks with McCaffry before, commiserated with his embarrassment but directed their attention to the witness.

After a moment's hesitation, Felmer continued, "I am well acquainted with the character of these Indians and I was personally acquainted with many of them."

McCaffry advanced to the bench when Felmer finished his answer. "My apologies to the court. My brief absence was unavoidable. I thank Mr. Oury for his assistance during my delay." McCaffry took a misstep, causing a momentary tottering.

This disconcerted Cargill and obviously ired Grant Oury, who retired to the defense table.

Resting his hand on the witness chair, McCaffry took a deep breath. "Previous to the attack in April last, were the Indians constantly present at their ranchería?"

"The Indians were in the habit of leaving the Indian camp near Camp Grant."

Rowell stood. "Objection. No personal knowledge."

Cargill always believed in Felmer's honesty. Having it questioned by another friend was unnerving to him.

Luckily McCaffry swung into an aggressive defense of his prime witness, and Felmer clarified his answer, "I personally knew some of the Indians who were absent."

"I'll allow it. Overruled." Judge Titus studied the blacksmith intently.

McCaffry moved in front of the prosecution table, blocking Rowell's clear view of the witness. "When did some of the Indians start leaving Camp Grant?"

"One party left there about the fifth or sixth of April last. They were absent about eight days. I know when they returned. Saw one Indian with his hair cut off—the Indian's sign of mourning." Felmer imitated a scissors' cut near his head. "I speak the Apache language. I talked with these Indians after they returned. I asked one where his brother was. He said, 'Don't say nothing about it—I have lost my brother.' I asked him how he came to lose him. He said he went on a campaign near Tucson or San Xavier to bring in some stock and that he was followed by the people here of Tucson, and 'they killed the brother of mine.'"

"Was this the only conversation you had with Indians about the brother who was killed?"

"I had other conversations at different times with the Indians. The Indian that was killed was left behind. He was the only one killed. They lost some of the stock with him but brought two horses into camp—one, I am sure."

"Mr. Felmer, did you personally know the felled Indian?"

"I was acquainted with the missing Indian. I had seen him frequently."

McCaffry walked toward the jurors before facing Felmer again. "Would you please describe the deceased Indian?"

"I should judge of eighteen or twenty years of age. His hair had been cropped sometime previous to that. He had one tooth out in front, an upper tooth. That was a distinguishing mark to me. I had known him at Camp Goodwin and had known his brother for the same length of time."

"Have you seen this Indian since that time?"

"Nein, I have not seen the missing Indian since." Felmer unfastened one of his jacket buttons.

"Have you conversed with other Indians at Camp Grant relative to other expeditions made by them?"

"One, a petty chief, Taccar, told me he had frequently been on expeditions: one at Tres Alamos; one at Sonoita; and at another attack, which they made on the Camp Grant road."

Advancing toward the witness stand, McCaffry pointedly asked, "Regarding the attack at Sonoita, what did the Indian tell you?"

"They stated how they killed Wooster at Sonoita . . ."

Gasps and murmurs erupted in the gallery all around Valeria and Epi, who were upset both at the testimony and at several visibly displeased men nearby, who prodded those seated around them. In hearing of so many Americans and Mexicanos killed, Valeria wavered as to her conviction. *Maybe Raúl defended me rightly. But what he did . . . I am confused.*

Judge Titus rapped his gavel. "Order."

Members of the gallery quieted while Cargill and correspondents from various newspapers furiously scribbled on their note tablets.

Finally McCaffry told Felmer to continue.

"They shot him in the door. They did not know the woman was inside but eventually found her and took her out in the mesquite and killed her there."

"Have you ever spoken with other chiefs there at Camp Grant?"

Felmer nodded. "I know an Indian at Camp Grant called Eskiminzin, a chief. I had a conversation with him previous to the last of April. He stated that he was with the party that killed Wooster."

Again the gallery convulsed with voices.

Judge Titus rapped louder, three times. "Order. Order in the court."

The prosecution's taking a barrage to the delight of the defendants. Cargill poured a glass of water for himself, but given Rowell's bristling, he set it before the prosecutor.

Without McCaffry's urging, Felmer continued, "I also talked with Carse, a chief. He was interested in all the business—I mean the killing. He told me he was accustomed to leading parties from Camp Grant, on stealing and murdering expeditions. He was never there at Camp Grant for more than two days at a time."

"For what applicable time period did that observation hold true?" McCaffry grimly studied the witness.

"This applies to the Indians who were at Camp Grant prior to the last of April, and at that time also."

"Did you converse with Eskiminzin at another time?"

Felmer fingered his tight collar. "I asked Eskiminzin whether he had killed Mr. McKinney. He said he had."

For a third time, the gallery stirred, commenting so loudly that Cargill turned about to see the commotion and caught the eye of Epi and the woman weeping next to her.

For a third time Judge Titus banged his gavel on the bench, this time saying, "Order! If there are any more outbursts, I will have spectators barred from this courtroom." Titus allowed everyone a minute to compose themselves before permitting McCaffry and Felmer to carry on.

"Mr. Felmer, what else did Eskiminzin say to you in this conversation?"

"He said, 'I was seeking revenge and was going to take it out on you, but God told me you were a friend and not to do it. I then went down below, and with these hands and this lance, I killed an American.'"

McCaffry stood by the witness stand when he asked, "To which 'American' did he refer?"

"I understood him to mean Mr. McKinney. He had been talking about Mr. McKinney just before."

"Did you ever speak to Eskiminzin or other chiefs about the killing in January last at Tres Alamos?"

Felmer responded that Carse, Eskiminzin, and Taccar had admitted to killing four Anglos and ambushing others at Tres Alamos, located along the San Pedro River, near the Indian Trail. No Indians were hurt.

"When did these three Apaches first arrive at Camp Grant?" McCaffry again walked toward the jurors.

"About the latter part of February last."

"In addition to your conversations, did you have occasion to interact with the Indians on a more personal level?"

Felmer smiled. "I had good opportunities of observing the Indians as to how they conducted themselves, because I lived close to them, and frequently some of them stayed with me at night."

While Felmer answered, Grant held out a small note to McCaffry, who read it.

McCaffry folded and pocketed the note. "Did you, at any time, witness any Indians with property stolen from Americans and Mexicans?"

"I saw property with the Indians that I recognized, namely arms, horses, mules, clothes, and saddles. The arms were improved needle guns, stamped 'A.T.' I saw three stamped guns . . ."

McCaffry interrupted, "Where were they stamped?"

"On the breach."

"What did you do then?"

"I called the attention of Lieutenant Calhoun, and I think, Mr. Austin, to the fact of these guns being in the possession of these Indians." Now long seated in the uncomfortable witness chair, Felmer squirmed.

"And when did you see these guns?"

"I saw the three stamped guns with the Indians between the first and fourteenth of last November."

"Did you see any other possessions in the hands of the Indians at Camp Grant?"

"A mare belonging to the mail-rider who was killed near Tucson. She had on a brand Mr. Contzen identified to me—one government horse branded 'U.S. K Troop, First Cavalry.' I saw a horse blanket matching the description of the one taken from the mail-rider who was killed. It was a dark-colored woolen blanket, with red and black stripes mixed. I never saw a similar blanket."

"I have no further questions." McCaffry strode behind the defense table and sat.

Rowell remained seated as he asked, "When did you first see all of the articles of possessions that you described?"

Felmer sighed. "These articles were all seen since the thirtieth of April last, excepting the arms."

The foreman of the jury stood. "May I ask a question of the witness?" When Judge Titus concurred, the juror asked Felmer, "Why did the Indians want to leave Camp Grant for these periods of time?"

"In conversation, the Indians said they did not like to stay at Camp Grant—to be bound down. They wanted to go to the mountains to hunt and make mescal."

"One more question, please," the foreman pleaded. "Did they leave at will? Or was there some . . . notice given?"

Felmer shook his head. "They would get leave of absence in numbers, from one to twenty—which was sometimes the whole tribe—to the number of fifty or sixty. Taccar used to take his entire tribe most every month."

Another juror rose when the foreman returned to his seat. "Did the Indians keep these goods?"

"It is customary for the Indians to sometimes trade the stolen property in their possession with each other. If it is good property, they do not dispose of it very often." Felmer leaned forward, his hands on his knees. "They generally keep it. They value most a good rifle, horses, mules, saddles, and blankets—rifles best. You could not buy a good rifle from them at any price."

The second juror also asked before sitting, "Did they take arms with them on these leaves?"

Felmer smiled. "The parties leaving the camp on leave are permitted to take their weapons with them. They have never been deprived of their arms at any time."

Back and forth, back and forth. Valeria admitted to herself the Indian depredations were more numerous and inconceivable than Raúl had informed her.

McCaffry rose again. "I have a few more questions for this witness, Your Honor. Mr. Felmer, have you any former experience with prisoners of war, how they are treated, and the restrictions placed upon them?"

"Ja. I have served in the U.S. Army from a private up to a first lieutenant. I have been familiar with the condition of prisoners of war for sixteen years."

"Were any of those prisoners of war allowed to retain their weapons?" McCaffry turned over a page of notes.

Felmer almost laughed. "Nein. It is always the practice of government to deprive prisoners of war of their arms."

"Where exactly was the ranchería located in Camp Grant?"

Shrugging his shoulders, Felmer took a moment to find words. "The ranchería was in no particular place. You cannot keep the Indians in any one place more than two or three days at a time. When it was attacked on the thirtieth of April, the ranchería was between four and five miles from the flagstaff at the Post."

A third juror raised his hand, received a nod of approval from Judge Titus, and stood momentarily to question Felmer. "Did the troops guard the Indians in any way?"

"Never knew of any troops guarding these Indians, with the exception of the three put in the guardhouse."

Laughter erupted spontaneously, breaking the built-up tensions in the courtroom. Until then Valeria had not realized that she had squeezed her hands red.

McCaffry allowed the laughter to extend to its fullest before he excused Felmer as witness.

The defense called a second lieutenant in the Twenty-First Infantry, U.S. Army, who testified that he helped investigate a murder victim, both shot by a gun and with arrows. However, in an unusual happenstance, all arrows, save one apparently overlooked, were removed from the body and the property. Experts told the lieutenant that the overlooked arrow belonged to the tribe of Indians at Camp Grant.

Having been on his feet for quite some time, McCaffry sat behind the defense table but called José María Yesques as a witness.

The appearance of Yesques stirred Valeria's interest as well as that of everyone else in the courtroom. Although a Mexicano, he dressed as an Apache, with long moccasins nearly reaching his knees and a band circling his forehead. "I have lived with the Apache Indians for nineteen years, six months, and some days. The Indians captured me at six years of age and killed my father. I have been a guide for the last two years, this year with General Crook."

"Are you familiar with the Indians at Camp Grant?"

José María nodded. "I've been at Camp Grant twice this year."

"Are you aware of any weapons that the Indians possess there?" McCaffry put his elbows on the defense table.

"They had five needle guns. They proposed selling one; I wouldn't buy it. They had one double-barreled shotgun. They also had guns commonly known as Mississippi yagers. Arrows, they have many."

"Would you describe any of these Indians as 'being at peace'?"

"Some of them can be at peace, but they want another commanding officer, as they think that the present commanding officer sold them." Yesques moved his hand in a negating gesture. "They think they are at peace here, but not with Sonora. Some said they were not at peace with any place."

Near the end of a very long day for McCaffry, his voice softened, "Did you have personal knowledge of these Indians raiding and attacking while away from Camp Grant?"

"Some went out for cattle, and the citizens caught up with them and killed one. I know the Indian that was killed well—his brother also. The Indian that was killed had a tooth out in front—I think, above. His brother told me of the killing."

"Was that the only raiding expedition in your knowledge?"

The fringe on Yesques's leather moccasins stirred with his slight leg movement. "Some of the Indians told me of attacking a train beyond the station at the Ciénega, and that they made a great mistake thinking there was no one but teamsters. But there were soldiers with wagons. In the fight, the Indians lost five of their number—among them two petty chiefs."

"When did this occur?" McCaffry turned over another page of notes.

"I think this occurred in July . . ."

Furiously writing, Cargill stopped at the mention of an attack in July at Ciénega

Station on teamsters with soldiers attached. *He couldn't be speaking of my fateful transport to Camp Bowie, but the similarity . . .* With a nudge from Rowell, Cargill returned to taking down testimony, but his remembrance of Delia Theller wafted on the winds of July.

It was late in the day when McCaffry asked one last question, "What were the dates of these conversations specifically about the raids?"

"In October I had the talk with the Indian with the tooth out. It was in June when . . ." A buzz of whispers rose from the gallery of people.

Grant Oury whispered to McCaffry, "Get him off the stand."

McCaffry jumped up from the defense table. "Thank you. You may step down."

That gaffe by the last witness caused Valeria to question the integrity of not only that witness but perhaps others. *Is every testimony entirely truthful?*

SATURDAY, DECEMBER 9, 1871

"I recall Mr. Joseph Felmer." McCaffry seemed to scowl.

Valeria watched the German blacksmith, in the same new and ill-fitting suit, make his lumbering way to the witness seat. Sitting by herself, she was as uncomfortable as he. Epi had helped her look out for Raúl again that morning, but she was required at work and left Valeria seated alone in the gallery.

When Felmer passed the prosecution table, he playfully grimaced, causing Cargill to chuckle.

Cutting the frivolities short, McCaffry said, "I remind you that you are still under oath, Mr. Felmer."

"Ja." Felmer sat.

"In your previous testimony, you stated that you were at Camp Grant on the thirtieth of April last. Is that correct?"

"Ja."

"Were there any Indians absent from Camp Grant on that specific date?"

"The biggest portion of the bucks—"

McCaffry broke into Felmer's testimony. "Please explain that term."

"Bucks, male Indians. They were absent from the ranchería on the thirtieth of April."

"How many males remained there?"

Felmer frowned in thought. "Twelve or fourteen of them were present."

"And how do you know this information?"

"I know from my own observation." Felmer pointedly looked at Rowell.

McCaffry rose from his chair. "Was anyone of your particular acquaintance there on the thirtieth of April last?"

"Carse."

"Did he comment to you about the attack staged on that date?"

"Carse told me his cartridges were not good and that if his cartridges had been good, and all the bucks there, they would have killed a good many of them, the whites."

McCaffry edged around his table and ambled about before the jurors. "When did the bulk of the male Indians return?"

"The absent Indians did not return until the ninth or twelfth of May." Felmer looked up at the defense attorney.

"In your previous testimony, you said that you had been in the U.S. Army. Is that correct?"

"Yes."

McCaffry eyed one interested juror in particular before asking, "Did you ever serve on scouting expeditions against Indians with the military?"

Felmer crossed his ankles. "Frequently. During the time I was in the United States service and since."

"What were the tactics used to attack and fight Indians on these expeditions?"

"The ordinary mode is to attack Indians at daybreak, if possible. Generally you trail them to the ranchería and wait for morning to take them by surprise."

After another glance at the same juror, McCaffry delivered his question, "In the fray of battle, is one able to determine the sex of the Indians?"

Felmer leaned forward in the witness chair. "You can't distinguish the females from the males—all look and dress alike."

"Do Apaches fight or flee from these attacks?"

"Sometimes they stand to make a fight. After the fight is over, they generally run to the mountains."

As McCaffry crossed to the defense table to sit, he said, "Thank you."

Rising from his seat, Rowell asked, "When were the last rations given out prior to the massacre on April 30?"

Felmer rubbed his chin thoughtfully. "Rations were probably issued two days prior to the thirtieth of April last."

"How many Indians were present at that distribution of food?"

Leaning his head slightly, Felmer answered, "A good many Indians, but most all females on that ration day."

"How many male Indians were there on that last ration day?"

"I should judge there were about twenty bucks. I had seen as many as one hundred bucks there previously on ration days."

Rowell approached Felmer and raised his voice, "Are you positive?"

Cargill looked up from his note-taking. *Joe's giving quite specific details.*

Felmer's neck reddened. "I am as positive about the last statement as I am about my previous statements, as to numbers."

Rowell studied Felmer for some seconds before saying, "Thank you. That is all."

While Rowell returned to his table, McCaffry rose. "A few last questions on redirect of this witness, Your Honor. At Camp Grant, were geographic limits placed on the Apaches?"

"There were no lines laid out as boundaries."

"At any time did the Indians give up their weapons?"

Felmer shook his head. "They were in possession of their arms at all times."

"Were the Indians known to visit the privately owned ranches near Camp Grant?"

"These Indians were frequently at the citizen ranches around the area, so much so as to be troublesome."

With a last look at Grant Oury, McCaffry said, "Thank you, Mr. Felmer. You may step down."

Cargill stifled a laugh as a wide smile of relief illuminated Felmer's face.

Valeria pressed her hands to her cheeks. *All of this happened not so far away, and I was only happily sewing.*

Gertrude McWard swore that she saw Mrs. Wooster's merino dress, red striped with black silk trimmings, at Camp Grant on the Apache wife of the interpreter, Concepción.

Next, with long black hair flowing down his back, Concepción Biella testified that at Camp Grant he swapped a jackass for a gray mare and saddle from an Indian whom he didn't know. Both the mare and the saddle were claimed, the mare by a Papago and the saddle by the justice's office.

McCaffry pointed to a well-worn saddle lying on top of the defense table next to Grant Oury, who stood so that the gallery and the witness could view it.

Many of the men in the gallery half rose to get a good look. Valeria dared stand to her full height to view the saddle.

"Is that the saddle you swapped for?"

"Yes, that's it," said Concepción.

Then Fritz Contzen, a contractor for the U.S. Mail, swore the oath in a heavy German accent. "I knew the saddle. That is the saddle I see in court. The man who rode the mail for me used it for six months, riding from here to Sasiba Flat. The last time in September. He was killed by Indians and the mail lost, about four miles from town, coming in."

"Thank you. You may step down." McCaffry stopped Grant Oury from moving the saddle. Physical evidence many times swayed a juror's mind more than oral testimony. "Defense now calls Samuel Hughes."

Valeria's interest was immediately piqued at the call for Hughes. She craned forward, eager to get a look at Atanacia's husband, who had been elusive whenever she took a sewing machine lesson at their home. She never expected the Welshman in his early forties to be so small and look so peculiarly distinctive—an open face, a hairline at the top of his head, and a closely cropped beard sans mustache. *Frankly it's difficult to envision him fathering so many children.*

His right hand held high, Hughes stood before Oscar Buckalew, who administered the oath as he had done each time, casting a glance at the written words he always held before him.

"I do." Hughes sat in the chair, making it look large.

McCaffry asked, "Mr. Hughes, would you please state your occupation and your duties."

"I am adjutant general of this territory. The duties of this office for the last eight months have been to receive the arms, mark them, and reissue them."

His duty is to mark guns. Valeria drew in a sharp breath. *Marked in his house. That was what I saw: the beginning of this killing. I stitched two pieces of material together with the Singer máquina de coser in the next room. Their children slept close by. How could they have brought such weapons into their home?*

McCaffry asked Hughes, "When did the marking of rifles begin?"

"I commenced marking the arms about the first of February last . . ."

I am wrapped in filth. Beginning her lessons shortly after the guns arrived in the Hughes home sullied Valeria's memories of the triumphs, small though they may be, of her sewing creations. *A "scientist" I called myself. What a fool I am. Everything, everything since coming to Tucson is dirty and ruined.* She caught a low moan in her kerchief before it distracted those around her in the gallery.

". . . I allude to Spencer and Sharps carbines and needle muskets," qualified Hughes.

"Specifically, where were the arms marked and with what designation?" McCaffry stood near the witness stand.

"The arms were marked 'A.T.' on the breech, on the left-hand side of the stock, and under the middle band, in the wood."

"To whom were they issued?"

Hughes's open-palmed gesture gave the impression there could be no other answer than the one he gave. "I have generally issued these arms to every person that was in need of them—generally reissuing the same arms to the persons that brought them in."

"Were any of these rifles not returned for reissue?"

Now contemplative, Hughes said, "Some of these arms were taken by the Indians from Mr. Wooster. Mr. Blanchard had some taken . . ."

Valeria whitened, appalled as Hughes ticked off almost a dozen losses of guns and their slain owners with disinterest.

". . . from Mr. Simpson when he was killed with Lieutenant Cushing. One from the Mexican mail carrier that was killed out by the mill. Numbers of others that I cannot recollect."

"Have you ever issued rifles to Apaches?"

Hughes emphatically answered McCaffry's question. "I have *never* issued any guns to the Apaches, and there is no other way for them to get them but from murdered citizens. I keep such track of the guns that I know where they all are except when captured by the Apaches."

"Thank you."

Cargill knew the cross-examination would be short, as Rowell did not rise from his seat behind the prosecution table to ask, "How many rifles do you estimate were taken by the Apaches?"

Hughes said, "I estimate about thirty-five or forty stands of arms have been taken by the Indians. All the rest of them are accounted for."

✦✦✦

Valeria pounded on the front door she had come through many times with pleasure and anticipation. Today she wanted to learn something far different than how to sew precisely with la máquina de coser.

Quickly la sirvienta opened the door to the Hughes casa. "Ah, la señora," said the maid as she backed away and permitted Valeria to enter.

"¿Por favor, dónde está la Señora Hughes?"

"Aquí, Valeria," Atanacia called from another room.

At the door to the main bedroom—a room Valeria had never entered—she found Atanacia lounging in a floral jacquard upholstered, high-backed chair as she cradled her three-month-old son at her breast, feeding him. She didn't look up at Valeria, but down lovingly at her child. His skin, much lighter than hers, reminded Valeria of how fortunate her friend was to have married a man who provided for his wife and children so elegantly and so well. *Today I do not envy them. Those luxuries come at a high cost that I would not pay, even if given the chance.*

"Atanacia, I have come from the trial." Valeria tried to make her Spanish flow freely and in the friendly manner they had shared.

"And did you find it interesting?"

"Very interesting." Valeria pressed her fingernails into her palms so that she would not shout at her friend, startling her and the baby.

"Sammie testifies today."

"I heard him."

Atanacia ran her finger over the baby's soft cheek. "What do you remember of what he said?"

"That he provided guns and marked them."

"Sí, es la verdad. One day I thought you had noticed the crates in my dining room. But when you didn't mention them, I supposed I was wrong."

Valeria looked away from the baby's innocent face. "I did see something. I am realizing that was what I saw."

"Crates with rifles. My husband complied with the men's wishes. As adjutant general he works for Arizona Territory in so many ways. I support him in everything that he does." Atanacia looked down at her baby. "Enough for now, mi hijo?"

Valeria watched Atanacia separate the child from her breast and place him in the bassinette before covering herself. *Other mothers ought to be suckling their babies, but they are dead. I should have had a baby at my own breast by now. Perhaps my neighbors are correct. I was lucky not to come to term.* "You allowed them to store the guns here?"

"I even stamped them with 'A.T.,' Arizona Territory. I was accurate. Like lining up stripes on materials. Mr. Bailey helped as well. And when the guns were returned, we cleaned them and returned them to the crates."

"Aquí, en su casa." Valeria couldn't understand her friend's actions. "¿En esta casa?"

"It had to be done. They were in the next room. You said you saw them."

Oh, Dios. If I had suspected more, I would have smashed those guns useless.

"Valeria, you look pale. Would you like some water?"

"No, gracias," Valeria denied herself what she needed. In her sight, the room undulated and spun. "I need air. Permiso . . ." She lifted the hem of her skirt and hurried from the bedroom, down the hall, and out the front door the sirvienta rushed to open, into the fresh, cool air of December. *I am finished with sewing lessons. And with the trial.*

✦✦✦

Standing on a chair in the Escalantes' kitchen, Nest Feather looked out the open door toward the Santa Catarina Mountains and was thankful for the brisk breeze coming in, for Manuela's oven overheated the room. Kneeling by the chair, Señora Paloma pinned up the hem of Nest Feather's white baptism shift, which had been Paloma's own.

"Not much needs to be taken up, you've grown so much, Solana," the señora muttered through the straight pins she held between her teeth. "Are you looking forward to the baptism?"

"Hmmm." Nest Feather watched the clouds over the Santa Catarinas. They formed and split apart, then formed again in different shapes and were now changing from a pale tangerine to a brilliant orange as the sun set. Too quickly darkness invaded. *The sun's journey has ended for the day. Tomorrow the sun will again begin his travels from the east. The beginning. Over these sacred mountains with many dips lies Arapa. And I am here.*

"It is now cold, Manuela. Shut the door, por favor." Paloma stood to see if the hem was even. "Turn around, Solana."

Balanced on the chair seat, Nest Feather turned, noticing all the pans, platters, and dishes on a shelf, and the señora's smile. *Jesus the man, the statue, does not smile. If he walked over our sacred mountains, which . . . ?*

"Solana, please change for dinner." The señora helped her down from the chair.

MONDAY, DECEMBER 11, 1871

Surprising even himself, Andrew Cargill arrived early at the courthouse, having slept most of Sunday, the court being closed on the Sabbath. He found the interior of the courtroom pleasant when absent of disturbing testimonies and people arguing about the Apache situation. Its packed dirt floor shone with the footsteps of galleries and jurors and faintly smelled of the sweating bodies of the guilty and the innocent.

As he laid out his pencils, paper, and water glasses in that precise order, Cargill heard the turning of a doorknob. Judge Titus's office door cracked open. Men's voices murmured indistinctly. When the door opened fully, Governor Safford exited.

Not expecting anyone in the courtroom more than two hours before the day's session, Cargill stood, stopping the politician in his tracks. *What's Safford's purpose here? And in the judge's chamber? What's happening?* As the governor's former aide, Cargill knew Safford calculated an innocuous statement.

"Andrew, I heard you landed this position as amanuensis."

"Thanks to Willard." Uneasy as to what further to say, Cargill ended the conversation by extending his hand. "Good morning to you, Governor."

"And to you." After their brief handshake, Safford briskly exited.

✦✦✦

In the witness seat, Dr. Durrant testified, "I was given an Apache captive, a boy of seven or eight, at Camp Lowell in 1869. I've kept him as my own child."

Grant Oury, alone again at the defense table, asked, "What is your relationship like with the boy?"

Cargill nudged Rowell, and with a slant of his head indicated James McCaffry, looking pale and pasty, walking down the aisle toward the defense table. *What a failing—McCaffry has twice demonstrated his weakness to the entire town, if not farther afield. And the sore feelings between the members of the defense are on obvious display.* Oury did not dignify McCaffry's appearance with even a sideways glance. McCaffry pulled out his chair, laid his briefcase on the table, its contents spilling out the ill-closed latch, and settled into the wood seat. He clasped his hands together between his knees and tightly pressed them together. Oury sniffed the air, McCaffry refusing to notice the slight. With his hand, Cargill shaded his face from spying further but kept writing down the testimony of Dr. Durrant.

"My affection for the Apache boy is returned entirely. He's very quick to learn. There would be no difficulty in making intelligent men of the Apaches." Dr. Durrant stepped down from the witness seat.

Cargill heard a fumbling of papers. Snatching a glance, he glimpsed McCaffry shuffling through the documents spilling out of his valise. Oury snatched a paper from his own neat file and pointed at the middle of the page. Himself now on the defensive, McCaffry rose with as much stateliness as he could muster. "Defense calls Leopoldo Carrillo."

When sworn in, Carrillo, a successful freighter in his early thirties, nestled into the small chair, his legs extending out enough distance to trip a person. Cargill noted that McCaffry widely avoided the witness's feet.

McCaffry stuffed his hands into his pockets. "Mr. Carrillo, are you aware of any Apache captives living within the homes of Arizona citizenry?"

Cargill and all in the courtroom but Titus stirred at this direct question. Sensitivities ran high on this subject. Many in town, including Cargill, knew that Carrillo had received two Apache children this past May. And seeing Jimmie Lee in court again, Cargill suspected questions along the same lines for him. Years ago Lee's sister had accepted and since kept two Apache captives in her home.

Carrillo entwined his fingers. "I have seen Apache captives in the hands of white men here in this territory, and I know how they are treated. The treatment is kind, generally so."

"Do these captives wish to be sent back?"

"They are contented and do not desire to return to the Apaches. All I have seen will cry if told they are to be sent back."

McCaffry took his hands out of his pockets and clasped them behind his back. "Do you know how many reside in Tucson?"

"I know of ten cases in this town. Many of them will even deny that they are Apaches."

"Thank you, Mr. Carrillo," said McCaffry as he sat at his table.

Rowell rose. "Are these captives from Camp Grant?"

"Some of these captive children are of those taken at Grant." Carrillo's eyes narrowed.

"Did money change hands to receive a child?"

Carrillo's penetrating gaze leveled on Rowell. "I do not know that these captives are articles of sale. Those that I know of have been obtained from their captors by exchange, not bargain and sale."

Rowell took a moment to form his next question. "Would you depict these children as slaves?"

"The citizens have obtained these captives more as an object of charity and have given them a Christian education, but they are not treated as slaves. They are permitted to leave and go where they choose, when of age, or when they come to an age of understanding."

"Thank you, Mr. Carrillo. No more questions." Rowell sat.

Cargill, sharpening his pencil with his penknife, sensed more than observed that Grant Oury stewed when McCaffry did not rise from the table to call the next witness. "Defense recalls Mr. James Lee."

The tall Irishman acknowledged that he was still under oath.

"Mr. Lee, are you aware of any Apache captives in Tucson?" McCaffry held steady his notes.

"I know of eight or ten captives, Apaches, taken five or six years ago. The Indian agent turned them over to the citizens, in connection with the United States marshal, and they have usually been treated like the rest of the family."

"Are these children regarded as slaves within the homes?"

Lee glared. "Some of them probably had to work harder than the others, but they've been well cared for and have received ordinary instruction."

"Thank you." McCaffry rested his notes on the defense table.

Rowell rose. "Your Honor, I would like to ask this witness several follow-up questions regarding his previous testimony."

Titus looked down at the prosecutor. "I'll allow that."

Circling his table, Rowell asked, "Mr. Lee, how did the various parties meet up on the Rillito River?"

"I left with the party from Tucson and was joined by the party of Indians on the river."

"By Indians, you refer to the Papagos?" Rowell briefly looked toward the Indian defendants standing along one wall.

Lee crossed one foot over the other at his ankles. "Correct."

"Were the Papago Indians armed with weapons other than their war clubs?"

"Yes. I saw some muskets, some needle guns. Generally all long arms and a few pistols. They had some knives also. I believe I saw two Indians with bows and arrows."

Rowell paused, then asked, "Did you know any of the leaders of the Papago Nation?"

"I know two or three chiefs of the Papagos in the vicinity of San Xavier. I know the chief that went in command of the Papagos to Grant on the thirtieth of April last."

"Thank you, Mr. Lee."

During the brief lull as Jimmie Lee left the witness chair and Rowell returned to sit at the prosecutor's table, Cargill massaged his stiff hands. As the silent seconds continued to tick by, Cargill grew bold and blatantly watched the defense attorneys. McCaffry studied his notes and consulted with Grant Oury for a few moments, prolonging the break in testimony.

An anticipatory hush fell over the gallery, the jurors, and the defendants. Was there anyone left in Arizona Territory who had not been called as witness?

Looking up at Judge Titus, McCaffry stood. "At this time, the defense rests, Your Honor."

Doubting this moment would ever arrive, Cargill wondered what might come next.

TUESDAY, DECEMBER 12, 1871

DAY SIX OF THE TRIAL

Andrew Cargill fidgeted with a pencil, dropped it, and picked it up in time to study the square back of C. W. C. Rowell, U.S. attorney and friend, standing directly in front of the jurors seated in two rows. He hoped that Rowell had the words and the empathy in his closing argument to give the jurors full understanding of this slaughter. Hand poised above his sheets of paper, Cargill began transcription when Rowell spoke.

"On April 30 last, the defendants seated and standing before you, men you may have known for some time, took it upon themselves to mete out injustice—not justice. Justice is in exercise in this courtroom today. Sidney DeLong and these defendants willingly plotted and committed the murders of scores of women, children, and two men of the Apache Nation. We may never know the exact count, but the life of even one snuffed out would place them on trial."

Rowell walked back and forth in front of the jurors, focusing on each man and making direct eye contact. "You have heard the testimony of three of the defendants, who *admitted* being members of that party that resulted in the loss of life. The attack was not predicated on any immediate danger; it was not predicated on any immediate threat; it was not predicated on any immediate change in military policy; it was not predicated on any immediately preceding loss of property or life.

"The proposal to attack had been discussed in many meetings, most of which were held in this very room." Sweeping his arm in a wide arc that encompassed the entire chamber, Rowell said, "Look around you." And indeed, most of the jurors did. "These walls heard the planning of these murders, and today they will hear true justice. These meetings to plot are evidence of the defendants' malice aforethought. They willfully met, willfully plotted, and willfully carried out their plot. You heard Mr. Bennett's sworn testimony of hearing stories from these defendants that they had killed and taken captives. You heard Mr. Etchells's sworn testimony: 'I know that the *intention of the party* in leaving *was to kill* Apache Indians, wherever they found them.'"

Rowell hesitated in front of one juror who looked particularly bored and leaned

220

toward him. "*Murder* is when a person kills a live being with *malice aforethought*." The juror sat up a bit straighter as the prosecutor continued.

"The women and children buried in Arivaipa Canyon or on that bluff cannot today stand here and identify their attackers. These women and children did not participate in any attacks upon Anglos or Mexicans. They were prisoners of war under the protection of the United States of America. These women and children, deprived of their very lives, deserve justice that only we can dispense. Do not deny them that as well."

He turned toward the accused—those seated and those lined up against the wall—and pointed. "These defendants committed murder. For that, they must be held accountable. Gentlemen of the jury, you must consider the facts and their sworn statements of complicity. I urge you to find the defendants guilty as charged."

Cargill stopped writing. Silence hung about the room like a mantle. *Damned if he didn't do it. Willard spoke from his heart. He deeply feels the loss of those Apaches and said what he believed. In the end that's all that he, or anyone, can do. But is it good enough?*

After Rowell carefully eased into his chair at the prosecutor's table, Cargill shook Rowell's icy, trembling hand and whispered, "That was mighty."

As the gallery squirmed in their seats before McCaffry addressed the jury, Cargill took a few moments to look at each of the jurors; some frowned and looked at their folded hands in their laps.

That held true for some of the defendants as well. *Juan and Jesús María look uncomfortable. And Bill Oury? Well, Bill always knows he's right and defies anyone to tell him otherwise.* From the corner of his eye, Cargill also noticed Teresa Elías and the wives of Jesús María's compadres sitting in the front row of the gallery, some wives attending the trial for the first time. Teresa's nimble fingers manipulated her rosary beads, over and over, pulling each one down to kiss the other. The other wives also worried their beads. *God must have a headache from hearing their constant supplications.*

A stirring at the defendants' table directed Cargill's attention there. James E. McCaffry, district attorney of Pima County and drinking companion, appeared to be back on form.

Pencil again poised in hand, Cargill assumed that every trial attorney made direct eye contact with each juror as McCaffry did and Rowell before him. *Did this influence the jurors to accept a trial attorney as a trusted and valuable friend?* Cargill studied the jurors' faces etched with lines from exposure to the sun, from the worries of feeding a family, and from the fear of losing their own lives and those of loved ones to depredations by wild Apaches. When McCaffry began his final argument, Cargill resumed writing.

"Gentlemen of the jury, Mr. Rowell most compassionately stated his case. But I assert to you that, in Arizona Territory, we are at war. We are at war with a nation that indiscriminately steals our property and our livelihood and takes our lives in the commission of it." Like Rowell, McCaffry paced the floor in front of the jury as he spoke.

"We are told that the Apaches at Camp Grant were 'prisoners of war.' I contend it is the reverse. The Americans, the Mexicans—all citizens of Tucson and of this territory are held hostage by the warring Apache Nation. Where else do farmers need to arm themselves against the enemy prior to sowing their fields? Where else must travelers arm themselves if they dare venture out? Where else do mail-riders lose their lives by arrows and bullets for delivering letters from home?

"In war, commanders plan ahead for both defensive and offensive battles. Reconnaissance may be obtained prior to planning or concurrently at the time of setting out. We have looked to the military to protect us. Despite some successes we are no safer. So far the military has utterly failed in its attempt. These defendants, these brave citizens"—without breaking eye contact with the jurors, McCaffry gestured in their direction—"risked their lives for yours that we may all be free to live in peace.

"The defense has amply gathered evidence, which you have heard, of the ongoing slaughter by the Apaches, who at Camp Grant were not even asked to give up their weapons." Here he adopted an incredulous tone. "Apaches who were not guarded, who left without leave and reason given—they are the enemy.

"Gentlemen of the jury, a charge of murder requires a condition of the murderer to be cold-blooded or reckless toward the life of the one murdered. These defendants are neither cold-blooded nor reckless but hold lives in Arizona Territory to such a high degree that they assisted in our defense.

"I urge you to find all of the defendants not guilty." As he delivered this line, McCaffry looked into the eyes of each man seated before him, and after a dramatic pause, he returned to his seat at the defense table.

Cargill deliberately placed a period on the page, finalizing the defense's argument. *How would I determine the guilt or innocence of these Tucsonans? How, Andrew?*

WEDNESDAY, DECEMBER 13, 1871

Raúl stood near the door. He hadn't attended the trial since the day he'd fought with Valeria. She hadn't been home since. At heart he couldn't abide where or what he was. The verdict would either set him free to live as he had been previously or imprison him forever, like the eyes of that Indian woman. They never stopped staring at him. Whether he had under him a paid whore or Valeria, that Apache stared at him—stared with surprised, frozen black eyes. He shook his head. *Still there.*

The first day he attended, Raúl had not seen any wives of the Mexicano defendants, but today all of them roosted in the front row of the gallery. Next to Teresa sat the very heavily pregnant Silveria Telles, Joaquín's wife. When they turned to view the full-to-overflowing courtroom, Raúl saw them transformed into ashen old women, their foreheads rippled with worry. Fright and concern glittered in their eyes, which were as round and black as their rosary beads.

Breathing shallowly, Raúl knew it was time. Oscar Buckalew, stationed at his clerk's desk, took out his pocket watch. Supporting their respective lead attorneys, Grant Oury and Cargill fidgeted with papers at their tables. A small rustling silenced the gallery. Certain that those standing next to him could hear the wild thumps of his heart, Raúl focused on the members of the jury appearing in the doorway opposite the judge's chamber. Looking as gloomy as a mine pit, they filed in and took their seats.

Next the defendants appeared in the doorway, Juan and Jesús María in the fore. Raúl watched Juan place his arm around his brother's shoulder, hug him, and say a few words. Jesús clasped his hand around the back of Juan's neck. They parted and walked through the door to take their seats as the accused.

Embarrassed by his sudden, unexpected, and maudlin reaction watching the brothers' goodbyes, Raúl stifled a snuffle. Juan and Jesús Elías would stand together, side by side, whether they rode into heaven or hell—the way brothers should.

The doorknob to the judge's chamber turned. Standing, Clerk Buckalew announced, "All rise."

A great sound rushed around Raúl as those seated rose. Then silence prevailed as Raúl and everyone in the courtroom peered at the chief justice of the Arizona Territorial Supreme Court, First District, the Honorable John Titus, as he entered with all of the dignity and pomp of his title and took the bench. "Please be seated."

Cargill whispered to an ashen-faced Rowell, "Here we go." Having taken notes throughout, Cargill intended to take down the instructions as well. Sharpened pencils lay at the ready before him.

Once everyone found seats or a place to stand, a stillness fell over the court-room, which weighed heavily on Raúl. He spotted Curro cringing in the back row of the accused.

No matter that Raúl was not legally charged with the crime by oversight, or by his riding out of Tucson on a street out of eyesight of the alert soldiers at Camp Lowell, or that, as a newcomer, he was still unknown to many in town, in his own mind Raúl believed his life was on the line. He pondered each word Judge Titus spoke.

Titus sipped his water and furrowed his bushy eyebrows. "Both the prosecution and the defense having presented their cases, I, as judge, now charge the jury with their instructions.

"Gentlemen of the jury: In this case ninety-nine or a hundred persons are indicted for murder. All are residents of Arizona and of this vicinity. All but one of the accused have been arraigned and have pleaded to the indictment. Three of them have been relieved of the charges contained in the indictment by nolle prosequi. The rest of them, ninety-six or ninety-seven, are on trial before you, and it is for you to say whether upon the evidence they are guilty or not guilty.

"The indictment alleges that the persons killed all belonged to the Apache Nation, who were in the custody of and quartered at the time near Camp Grant as prisoners of war under the protection of the United States, so far as to give this court jurisdiction of the case under laws of the United States. The killing is alleged and proved to have been on the thirtieth of April of the present year." The judge spoke directly to the jury, ignoring the accused and those gathered in the chamber.

"The indictment contains four counts. In the first three they are all charged as perpetrators. In the fourth and last count, the accused Sidney R. DeLong is charged with the actual commission of the homicide. All the others are charged as present aiding and abetting. If the allegations thus made in the indictment were proved, they would all be equally guilty.

"The indictment is under the law of the United States, whose definition of murder is derived from the common law and not from our code. 'Murder is when a person of sound memory and discretion unlawfully kills a reasonable creature in being, and in the peace of the commonwealth, with malice prepense or aforethought, either express or implied.'"

The judge waited a moment before continuing, allowing the jury time to consider the broad definition of murder. "In the present case we have then established two of the three elements which constitute murder." He held up one finger: "The homicide." Then a second finger joined the first: "And the perpetrators." Judge Titus again clutched his prepared instructions with both hands. "The third remaining element is the motive, and that is to be deduced from the definition of murder, as given.

"To constitute murder, the motive to the deed must be malice. Was this the mental or moral condition that led the perpetrators to perform the act described in the indictment and proved in the testimony laid before you in the present case?

"The person killed must be 'in the peace of the commonwealth.' One killed in actual battle in public or lawful war is not murdered, nor is he who does it a murderer. Killing a public enemy who is a noncombatant, doing or threatening no act of war, and is virtually at peace in or out of the country of the perpetrator, *might* be murder."

Cargill wondered if, because the Apache women were noncombatant, the jury would have to determine that it was, in fact, murder.

The judge continued with his focus solely on the members of the jury. "To kill one engaged in actual unlawful hostilities, or *in undoubted preparation* with others for active hostilities, would *not* be murder. In a country like this, the resident is not bound to wait until the assassin, savage or civilized, is by his hearth, or at his bedside, or at his door, or until the knife of the assassin is at his throat. He may anticipate his foe and quell or destroy him to secure his own personal safety. In a country like this, with few people and none or very little police, filled with murderous savages far more numerous than the orderly and peaceful, that, I charge you, is the law."

✦✦✦

In the rustic Catholic church, a refuge from a rare dark and wintery day in Tucson, Valeria knelt at her favorite spot near the center aisle in the middle row on the right side and prayed. At the front of the church, as if it were an uneventful day, she saw Father Jouvenceau praying on his knees before the altar; a few matrons also sought the comfort of prayer in the sanctuary; and one young Indian man, whom Valeria often had seen with the Apache Mansos selling their vegetables in the church plaza, sat on a front bench, turning frequently to look at the entrance.

But to Valeria this was no ordinary day. Head bowed, hands draped over the chair in front, her fingers moved each rosary bead in a steady rhythm. *My Lord Father, I must make a difficult decision. I am torn. First I think one way, then I think another. Help me find my bearings. Direct me, Dios, with a sign to steer me in your way. This I pray.* Valeria rapidly mumbled the Catholic ending to all prayers, crossed herself, and eased back onto the chair carefully so that her dark pink mantilla was not caught. Her valise, filled with all her belongings, resting beside her, Valeria continued her Hail Marys while incessantly rotating rosary beads.

Unexpectedly the sanctuary resonated with sounds of wagon wheels and dogs barking.

The street door had opened.

With the Escalantes on either side of Nest Feather, the three scurried down the center aisle toward the altar. They were late. Wrapped in Señora Escalante's brown serape, Nest Feather held up the long skirt of her soft white shift so that she would not trip. She noticed a pretty woman with a rose-colored mantilla covering her high forehead, running the worry beads through her long, graceful fingers with great speed. Perhaps her thoughts flew as fast as Nest Feather's own.

Despite Señora Paloma's urging, as she passed the woman with the rose mantilla, Nest Feather turned to view the Mexicana, who looked up with big, luminous eyes. *Pink Ruffles.* The woman smiled.

✦✦✦

As he wasn't an attorney, Cargill wondered if Titus quoted case law or whether the judge interpreted it according to his personal judgment; however, given Cargill's nascent and—thankfully—soon-to-be-terminated legal clerk career, he believed the tenor of these instructions seemed off-kilter for the prosecution.

Judge Titus cleared his throat before continuing his charge. "Another inquiry presented by this case is whether the defendants have violated any law of the United States, or whether that attack was not the exercise of a natural right to prevent or restrain the murder and spoliation to which the people of this territory have been and are now subjected by the Apache Nation.

"In a celebrated case of 1832 it was found, 'The Indian tribes are distinct, independent political communities, retaining the right of self-government, subject to the protecting power of the United States.' The Apache Indians have been at war with the Spaniards, Mexicans, and Americans for more than a century. The Papago Indians have been at war with the Apaches from time immemorial.

"By the barbarous codes of both nations, the slaughter of their enemies, of all ages and sexes, is justifiable, and such has been their practice. Having recognized and respected tribal organizations and codes, the United States has neither abrogated these codes nor prevented hostilities between these Indian tribes, for I submit that the evidence in the present case shows that the Papagos have been and are now subject to the predatory assaults of the Apaches. I charge you that

VENETIA HOBSON LEWIS

it *has not been and cannot be shown* that they are guilty of murder as charged in the present case at all."

Weary of the strain of listening to legal jargon, Raúl abruptly drew up. He couldn't have heard correctly. *The Papagos did not murder?*

+++

Valeria smiled at the girl, who merely stared stone-faced at her, as if smiles were not to be exchanged.

The woman beside the child seemed irritated at even the slightest delay. She took the girl by the arm and hurried her quickly down the aisle toward Father Jouvenceau, impressive in his canonical vestments, standing behind the baptismal font.

Valeria tried to tear her attention away from the girl but couldn't. *Look how erect the girl holds herself, how mature that makes her, despite her slight form. Being dark-skinned, she's possibly Mexican, but her eyes . . . they're almond shaped. She's an Indian. An Apache.*

+++

When Rowell slid his clasped hands under the table, Cargill let out a slow sigh. His hand was cramped and sweaty, damply indenting the sheaf of papers that he would've loved to throw in Titus's face.

Judge Titus droned on. "The application of these rules of law to the present case is clear. The government of the United States owes its Papago, Mexican, and American residents in Arizona protection from Apache spoliation and assault. If such spoliation and assault are persistently carried on and not prevented by the government, then the sufferers have a right to protect themselves and to employ force enough for the purpose. It is also to be added that if the Apache Nation or any part of it persists in assailing the residents of Arizona, then it forfeits the right of protection from the United States, whether that right is the general protection that a government owes all persons within its limits and jurisdiction or the special protection that is due to prisoners of war, as the Apaches killed on the thirtieth of April last are claimed to have been in the indictment."

+++

In catechism Nest Feather had learned that the red ribbons and bows for the celebration of Christmas, which adorned several tall candlesticks and relieved the starkness of the church's whitewashed walls, symbolized the berries of a bush from far away. *A living cactus from the desert should be used instead of mere cloth.*

Jitters plagued Nest Feather the closer she and the Escalantes came to Father Jouvenceau before the baptismal font.

The priest greeted the Escalantes and looked down at Nest Feather. "Is this the child who will be welcomed into the church?"

Ignacio Escalante stepped forward. "Sí. Solana Constancia Escalante de Huerte."

Nest Feather gaped up at the priest, who appeared critical, routinely bored, and ethereal all at once.

With pedagogic precision, Father Jouvenceau addressed Nest Feather. "As you are new to the faith, I will summarize quickly for you the various steps in this sacred rite upon which you are about to enter. First I will ask you a series of questions, child. You are aware of that?"

She bobbed her head.

"You must answer truthfully and with a pure heart."

The vestments make the priest powerful. Nest Feather turned to look at Señora Paloma, who seemed to bask in the religious aura of the priest.

Valeria watched Father Jouvenceau greet the couple and the new communicant, but she couldn't hear the words he spoke to the child, who looked at the woman, only an inch or two taller than she.

✦✦✦

Raúl shook his head. *Is this good or bad for us? The Apaches aren't to be considered prisoners of war. But if the Papagos can't be found guilty, are only the Mexicanos on trial?*

Cargill momentarily looked up from his page. Bewildered smirks cracked the faces of the Anglo defendants, while the Mexicanos and Papagos apparently hadn't yet realized the import of all of this droning verbiage.

Judge Titus turned over a page of his instructions from the dwindling stack before him. "Now gentlemen, what is the evidence before you on this branch of the case? Are the Apaches now in a state of hostility? Does or does not the evidence show that the clothing, arms, and other property of those murdered have been found in the possession of those Apaches on whom the assault was made? Does or does not the evidence show that an obvious trail or Indian road leads from places of murder and spoliation direct to this encampment? Have these Apaches admitted their participation in this murder and spoliation? If this is shown, is there any evidence that the United States government has stopped this or had done so on the thirtieth of April last?

"If you find the evidence proves these practices, you will accordingly find one of the following conclusions:

"First: that the attack was or was not a justifiable act of defensive or preventive hostilities, or second: that it does or does not cast such reasonable doubt on the motive as shall render you unable to say whether the defendants were actuated by murderous malice.

"Accordingly, as you find the affirmative or the negative of these conclusions, your verdict will be not guilty or guilty."

✦✦✦

Nest Feather listened carefully to the father's low, French-accented voice.

"After the questions, I will bless you in baptism with holy water from this font." The priest indicated the water-filled baptismal font next to him.

Nest Feather drew closer to the rough-edged stone bowl. *Like the ice-covered rock depressions high in the Santa Teresas.*

"Then the sacred chrism. With fragrant oil I will trace a cross upon your upper chest as you receive the Holy Spirit." For the child's preparation, the father turned toward a small table next to the font and picked up a tiny vial containing golden oil, momentarily opening its stopper. Sweet smells of olive oil and balsam freshened the air. Replacing the vial, the father again looked down at Nest Feather. "Finally you shall eat a small portion of bread, symbolizing his body broken for you. Your First Communion. Are you ready now to receive Christ?"

The moment of her baptism and acceptance into the Catholic Church upon her, Nest Feather felt her heart flutter, as if wild sparrows flew upon the winds of the morning within her body. She knew the words she must repeat. *If I say them, what will Yusn the Creator think? Little Running Water is still sacred to me, even after these seven months in the household of the Escalantes. From the day they spoke of God in the heavens, I listened intently. At first I knew they were mistaken. Apaches believe God is not harbored in a being; God is in everything in the world—the trees, the earth, the waters, the mountains, and especially the wind. And Arapa.*

The light touch of Señora Escalante fell upon Nest Feather's shoulders. She removed the serape, revealing Nest Feather's pure white shift.

Father Jouvenceau began the ritual. "You have completed five months of study in the Catholic doctrines. Do you confirm your intent to be one with the Catholic Church?"

After glancing at the señora, Nest Feather replied, "Sí."

"Do you acknowledge that Jesus Christ is your Lord and Savior?"

✦✦✦

Judge Titus began to rush. Like a horse smelling water, he sniffed the rapidly approaching end to his instructions. "Gentlemen, the immediate inquiry for you is: Were the defendants in the attack actuated by malice in the condition I have described? If upon all the evidence there remains a reasonable doubt in your minds of the guilt of the defendants, you must acquit them.

"The evidence is your province and yours alone. Does it show guilt upon the law, as thus declared to you, beyond a reasonable doubt, or does it not? You will now take the case under your sole consideration, say whether the defendants are guilty or not guilty, and the court will await your verdict."

His pencil fell from his grasp, and Cargill hadn't the strength or the will to lift it up again. Standing for the judge's recess to his office, Cargill realized how slumped over the written page he had been and pinned his shoulder blades together. When voices, no longer muffled, came from the gallery behind him as well as the clatter of knocked-together chairs, Cargill sank back into his seat. Rowell focused on the vacated judge's bench.

Escape tantamount to sanity, Raúl pushed his way through the men standing in front of the door and out into the street, where he could suck in fresh air.

✦ ✦ ✦

Nest Feather beheld the man's figure on the church's wall. *At night, I lie on the floor and mouth Apache words silently, so Señora Escalante can't hear. She doesn't like them. I find no word in Apache for Jesús, the Son of God. So I identify you as the east, the beginning direction. The first. The first, the east, the Son . . . You always seem so sad.*

Nest Feather peered into the deep, black holes that were his eyes. *According to the Catholics, this son changed from man to God, as Changing Woman returned from old age to youth with each girl's celebration of menses.*

This Christ is Changing Man.

As if from far away, the voice of Father Jouvenceau repeated the question, this time a little louder, "Do you acknowledge that Jesus Christ is your Lord and Savior?"

"No."

Nest Feather heard gasps from the Escalantes and looked up into the priest's eyes, dilated with surprise.

Stepping away from the baptismal font and Father Jouvenceau, Nest Feather faced the son, the east. *There is only one God, Yusn the Creator. I celebrate the renewal of my faith.*

As in her na'íees ceremony, Nest Feather ran around the priest, the Escalantes, up the aisle, and turned. Once, twice, faster, then faster. She relived the wind in her hair, the weight of her ceremonial dress of four doeskins, her longing to perfectly embody Changing Woman.

With each circle around the font and up and back along the aisle, Nest Feather's spirits rose. *My spirit flies. I pass through portals. I am without bonds. I celebrate life.*

Valeria stood as the Apache girl ran in lengthening circles. At first she was confused. *Is the girl's baptism over? This is strange. What is she doing?* But the look of ecstasy on the girl's face convinced Valeria that the Apache girl experienced rapture.

However, Valeria witnessed a totally different reaction from Father Jouvenceau and the mother, who, appalled and stricken, cried out, "What happened? Is she baptized?"

Nest Feather completed the third turn. She ran blindly back up the aisle for the fourth and last time. As she turned to face the altar, Changing Man beckoned her. Beside the Christ figure, a shimmering, golden light, like the one that had surrounded Changing Woman, appeared to Nest Feather. She focused on nothing else. She did not see Señora Escalante sobbing, being led by her husband to a front chair where he knelt before her, whispering her name, trying to ease her distress.

Finishing her run toward the golden aura near Christ's statue, Nest Feather halted, her head back, her chest heaving. Then a strong jerk on the arm spun Nest Feather around to see Señor Escalante's face filled with revulsion. As he pulled her arm, she staggered back into place before the priest.

Señora Escalante called out again to Father Jouvenceau, "Please! Tell me. Can she be saved?"

The priest scowled, turned on his heels, and, with his vestments flapping wildly behind him, strode out of the sanctuary.

Little frightened cries from the matrons and the abuelas down front shifted Valeria's attention from the unusual baptism. Disturbed from their prayers, the women abruptly rose from their chairs, one or two of which fell to the dirt floor. Many women shook their skirts.

A tiny creature darted through the chair rungs close to Valeria and her valise. Upon seeing it, Valeria gasped, "Oh."

It stopped. Propping itself on its back legs, it twitched its whiskers as its black eyes gazed up at Valeria.

"A mouse."

Then it was gone. Squeezing under the church's front door, it quickly disappeared outside.

✦✦✦

Cargill watched the jury make their way from the jury box to the door opposite the judge's bench. "It's still a difficult trial. They could take days to come to a decision."

Rowell eyed the departing men. "You think?"

Assembling all the sheets of papers on which he had written, Cargill surveyed the now empty courtroom for any lingerers who might overhear their conversation. "You can't say that Judge Titus's charge was overly stringent."

"Goddamn instructions."

"Willard, you gotta remember back when we first met Titus a few years ago. He was following Safford around Arizona City as a part of his entourage, licking his boots."

"We were all part of the entourage." Rowell threw a law book—a book he valued—into his valise. "Dammit, we got three of 'em to witness their guilt. Three. They confessed to the crime. We have the weight of the law behind us."

"Is that enough for the jury?" Cargill leaned back in his chair, wishing he could whip out his pipe and light up. *Damned if I don't.* He drew out the pipe from his inside pocket.

Flipping through a thick dossier of notes before him, Rowell finally laid his hand on top. "I appreciate your help."

"My pleasure. Well, of course, I would've rather been employed as an accountant . . ." Cargill chuckled, only to end in a cough.

"You need medicinal fluids."

"Yes sir, I do. 'Doctor' Charles O. Brown down at Congress Hall has a bottle that'll kill anything that I got. And me, too, if I overmedicate myself."

As they were about to rise from their chairs, voices came from behind the door to the jury room. The doorknob twisted.

Rowell and Cargill glanced anxiously at one another and at Oscar Buckalew, who limped toward the clerk's desk. "They're comin' back."

"Already?" Rowell's voice tripped along with his accelerating heart.

Returning his pipe to his pocket, Cargill muttered, "A leak, a smoke, and a vote."

✦✦✦

Her spell broken, Nest Feather—now a little frightened—stood at the front of the sanctuary, looking at the señora crying in the arms of her husband. Never had the Escalantes chastised her, and now she had caused them great distress.

Isidro appeared at her side. "Apache maiden, el señor y la señora want you to remain here in Tucson forever. So do I."

Nest Feather was puzzled by Isidro's statement. "¿Sí?"

"It is my desire to build a gowah—with you as wife. To stay with me forever. As my legal wife. Never to be taken from me by the White Eyes. Never taken from Rocks Which Have Many Dips."

"¿Aquí? Remain here?" Nest Feather's voice rushed out with the beginnings of distress. *Never to go back?* "What about Arapa? And the Black Rocks People?"

Isidro took a step closer to Nest Feather. "My People are here. We are the same."

"Our ancestral lands . . ."

"Always within reach. Over those mountains." Isidro took her hands in his.

"¡No!" Nest Feather pulled her hands away. "Arapa. I must go back to Arapa."

"What is there for you?"

"Little Running Water. The sycamores. Our sacred land."

"But who? Who remains?"

Not She Who Is Gone. Not He Who Is Gone. But others must have returned to Arivaipa Canyon. If not, perhaps they have moved to the Santa Teresas. "I will find the People. You could come with me." Nest Feather placed her hand on Isidro's forearm.

"Arapa is not as it was."

"But it can be."

"There are Anglos who have different thoughts. They are strong and in charge."

"We will fight them. You and I. Let's leave now. We can be there in dos días," insisted Nest Feather.

"I do not fight the Anglos. I do not fight the Mexicans. I don't want you fighting either." Isidro took her hand from his arm and clasped it. "I want you with me."

The blessings she granted others for a long, happy life in Arapa had come to naught. Living in the sacred ancestral grounds had turned against them. Would harboring the dream of Arapa in her heart be sufficient? Nest Feather hesitated.

Isidro pressed on, "Perhaps if you consult with the Escalantes . . ."

"I am no longer a child. I am Woman. I decide." She drew her hand away from his.

"If you go back, you will be on a reservation, never to leave. You will not be in Arapa. The White Eyes will not allow it. Be free, be free like the wind. Stay with me as wife."

Nest Feather remembered Señora Escalante whispering to her husband about someone taking her from them and the necessity of accelerating her baptism. The Escalantes had tried hard to give her a good life, and they now thought she had turned against them and their ways. She believed that Isidro wanted her as wife. *But are the extra grains of food enough to trade away my heritage?* "And our children? What about them?"

"They will be schooled in Apache ways, Apache Mansos' ways, and modern ways."

"But not on ancestral lands."

"Already the military settles on our lands and restricts us onto reservations."

Nest Feather peered into Isidro's soul through his black eyes. Apache eyes. With her fingers grouped together, she touched her forehead. "Arapa lodges here forever." She touched her chest below her sternum. "And here."

With great earnestness and in a hurried manner, Isidro said, "Let me talk with the Escalantes."

Knowing that she could not go back to find what had been taken from her by others, knowing that she must find a way for herself to live in safety, and knowing the kind hearts of these three people—the Escalantes and Isidro—Nest Feather nodded slowly. Most of all she knew that Changing Woman and Changing Man had led her here.

Nest Feather and Isidro stood before the Escalantes, who had been watching their serious conversation. Carefully referring to Nest Feather by her Spanish name, Isidro began his prepared speech for the granting of Solana's hand.

✦✦✦

Rowell checked his pocket watch. "It's not even been twenty minutes."

"Nineteen to be exact." Buckalew plodded down the center aisle and outside to alert the defense and the gallery of an imminent verdict.

Cargill wanted to ask Rowell if coming in quickly was good or bad for the prosecution, but the stern, analytical glare the prosecutor assumed as he once again studied the faces of the returning jurors precluded any more casual conversation; that, and the return of James McCaffry and Granville Oury to the defense table, where they fumbled with stacks of papers. McCaffry dropped some on the floor. When he leaned over to pick them up, Cargill noticed the highly visible sweat rings on McCaffry's formerly white shirt collar.

Cargill himself studied the jurors for the last time as they took their assigned seats. *The men look glum. Is that in deference to the doomed defendants, or are they merely avoiding expression so as not to broadcast their decision prior to its reading by the foreman? Such must be the constant mental calculations of a prosecutor or defense attorney. I wouldn't care for that vocation. Accepting people as they are, avoiding the few I don't like, works fine for me. Of course, adhering to that personal philosophy never has gotten me rich or gainfully employed for long stretches of time. Someday, someday soon, my ship will come in, for it is long overdue. Whether Tucson has sufficient water for that is another matter. I'll give it a year, maybe two ... then ...*

Bustling sounds of people returning filled the courtroom. Defendants' wives returned to their front-row seats, where rosary beads moved rapidly along their predestined route along the chains. Gallery members hurried back from a breath of fresh air outside, elbowing others to regain their previous seating in the courtroom. An undercurrent of apprehension sparked tension among them as they sat and made furtive conversation.

Standing by the outside door, Raúl inhaled deeply to steady his jangled nerves and quivering stomach; he smoothed back his ebony hair with an ice-cold hand.

Cargill felt a charge of adrenaline when the accused filed back in, creating an excited frisson of murmurs from the gallery. As they had throughout the entire trial, the Papago Indians stood in a group against one of the walls. Cargill examined the worried expressions that paled the defendants' faces, all except Juan Elías and Bill Oury. Juan assumed Jesús María's contemptuous look, while Oury leered at the gallery, telegraphing his imperious and scalding view of the proceedings.

Turning in his seat, Cargill looked back to see familiar faces: Teresa Elías and Silveria Telles sat next to each other, murmuring three Hail Marys as each small rosary bead descended; Señora Oury and her sister-in-law, the wife of the assistant defense attorney, held hands; William Zeckendorf wiped his glasses and placed them back on his nose; Soledad, again in her midnight blue satin, quietly observed Charles Etchells; and finally, Fisher Scott, Lee's business partner, waited stoically until he could hurry home with word of the trial's outcome to his wife, Larcena, who'd borne a son only six weeks prior.

Cargill ruminated on the import of recent events. *So many lives could be changed and cast asunder in a few moments' time due to the unprecedented murders of Arivaipa Apaches.*

At the turn of a doorknob, Clerk Buckalew announced, "Order in the court." When Judge Titus emerged from his small office, the clerk ordered, "All rise."

A rush of sound filled the chamber with the ritual of rising and again sitting. Silence returned, hanging heavily in the oppressive air.

Titus cleared his throat. "Has the jury reached a verdict?"

The foreman stood. "We have, Your Honor."

Cargill breathed shallowly. Every detail of the foreman's black lapels, his silver belt buckle shaped like a horseshoe, the drop of sweat appearing at the man's right temple and trailing down his weathered face, were etched into Cargill's memory as the foreman unfolded one sheet of paper. The foreman's right hand holding the paper trembled; he placed his left hand on the sheet to help.

"Defendants, please rise," Titus's voice rang full and true.

All of the defendants not already standing rose almost as one. McCaffry and Grant Oury also stood.

"Will the foreman please read the verdict?" Judge Titus leaned back in his chair and pressed his fingertips together.

"We find the defendants not guilty."

One brief moment passed before the gallery and defendants cheered and shouted. Curro howled and stomped up and down.

Raúl's skin was alive; his nerve endings prickled. Praising his Lord, he laughed and mightily pumped the hand of the man next to him before rushing outside, passing someone from the gallery who ran through the streets yelling, "Not guilty! They're not guilty!" Those on the street who heard the news immediately entered the nearest store or saloon to spread the verdict.

Some passersby remained near the courthouse, cheering, applauding, shouting their congratulations.

McCaffry shook Rowell's hand before leaving. Disappointed but not undone, Rowell tidied up legal details, requesting that a nolle prosequi be entered on behalf of the missing defendant, David Foley, who was somewhere in Texas.

A prosecutor's clerk no more, Cargill stood to view the mayhem in the gallery that the verdict had created: Jesús María had rushed to Teresa, who jumped up from her seat to be crushed in her husband's arms; Joaquín Telles knelt before his pregnant wife, Silveria, kissing her hands and face and lips while she blubbered, "Inocenta. That's what we'll name the baby. Inocenta."

✦✦✦

Valeria stood beside the stagecoach now loading passengers at the Overland Stage Station—the same station where, not quite one year ago, she and Raúl had arrived in the dusty village of Tucson. Only familiarity cleansed and tidied the low adobe buildings surrounding her. Her valise and small traveling case taken by the young man riding shotgun, Valeria turned her attention to the nearby streets from where shouts of "not guilty" grew louder and louder. The news didn't startle her. She expected such a verdict.

"¡Valeria!"

The sound of his voice pronouncing her name frightened her. Would her resolve be strong enough to carry forward with her plan? *His voice is so deep, so even. Never to hear it again shatters me.* Tossing her head, she stamped her foot in the dirt, raising a small disturbance of dust. *This damned dust. I will be free of it.*

"Valeria." Raúl touched her arm.

She turned and focused on his broken nose.

"I went to the nunnery. I begged them to tell me where you were."

She whispered, "It's a small town."

"Inocente. We've been found innocent."

"You weren't on trial."

Raúl took no heed of that and blustered ahead, "Not guilty. We're free. The jury came back in nineteen minutes."

"A jury of your peers. They kill, too."

The stagecoach driver called out, "All goin' to Yuma and California destinations, git aboard. We're leavin.'"

"Valeria," Raúl said, his voice now raised and insistent, "Valeria, don't go. Stay with me. I'll . . . be different. We'll have children."

"No quiero tener niños contigo. Quiero otra vida, lejos de aquí. No." She shook her head. "I don't want children with you. I want a different life far from here."

"I swear to you. I'll be the Raúl of old. Stay with me. I love you."

"I . . ." *So easily those words can slip from me.* "I cannot."

"You cannot?" *I have been found innocent. I am cleared from all guilt. I gave her my good name.* "I shall divorce you."

"Do whatever you have to do. The moment I step on that stage, 'Valeria Obregón' no longer exists."

"Last call," shouted the shotgun rider.

Valeria clutched the handle by the coach's door. She hesitated, but after hearing nothing more from Raúl, she lifted her long skirt, placed her small foot on the first step, and hauled herself up into the coach. Wedged between two large men on the back bench, Valeria looked neither to the left nor to the right, only straight ahead.

The shotgun rider slammed the coach door and climbed on the top seat alongside the driver. Raúl stepped back, away from the coach. With the release of the brake and an urging of the reins, the stage's four horses surged forward.

The coach passed Daphne the mule pulling the water cart as Martin Touhey broadcasted to anyone within earshot, "Water for sale. Fresh spring water!"

Taking an immediate turn west toward the Santa Cruz River, the creaking stage receded from sight.

Listening to the echoes of celebration coming from the streets of Tucson, Raúl turned and went back to work at Zeckendorf's.

BIOGRAPHICAL DETAILS OF HISTORICAL FIGURES AFTER 1871

ABDUCTED APACHE CHILDREN

In the spring of 1872 General O. O. Howard called a peace meeting between the Apaches, Anglos, and Mexicans. Six of the abducted children (four girls and two boys) homed in Tucson were returned to the Arivaipa Apaches. Presumably the majority of the other children were sold into slavery in México.

APACHE MANSOS

It is believed that the tame Apaches living around Tucson were completely assimilated into the Mexican population and culture within a handful of years after 1871.

ANDREW HAYS CARGILL

Cargill's ship never did come in, although his daughters confirmed he frequently repeated that phrase. He and Epiphania Rivera had a daughter, who was schooled and housed at Tucson's St. Joseph's Catholic School after Epiphania died in January 1876—the date provided in the diary of Tucson saloon keeper George O. Hand. Apparently Cargill and Epiphania parted long before that, as he married Caroline Van Kleeck in 1873 in New York. They had two daughters. Cargill's work varied from deputy U.S. marshal and postmaster at Castle Dome in Arizona to vice president of Castle Dome Mining and Smelting Co. to broker in Poughkeepsie, New York. A founding member of the Arizona Pioneers' Historical Society, Cargill died in Santa Cruz, California, in 1920 at the age of seventy-six.

JESÚS MARÍA ELÍAS

Elías moved his family to the rudimentary community of Los Reales on the banks of the Santa Cruz River near San Xavier del Bac. Elías again served as a member of the House of Representatives in the Eighth Arizona Territorial Legislature in 1875. For those in need of a scout, Jesús María continued to track Indians. He also ranched on his remaining land, which totaled eighty acres in Pima County— valued at $500 at the time of his death at the age of sixty-seven in January 1896.

Along with Jimmie Lee and several others, Juan formed a vigilante group that went after horse thieves. His group took advantage of horse thievery's status as a legitimate hanging offense. Juan married María Antonia Quiroz in 1875, and together they had two sons and a daughter. In 1892 he filed for compensation from the U.S. government for his losses due to Indian raids. The court beleaguered Juan about not being fluent in English, his lack of substantiating documents, and his participation in the Camp Grant Massacre. Requesting $21,650, he received only $1,680. Respected by all for his generosity to others and to the church, Juan died in Tucson in November 1896, within three weeks of his fifty-eighth birthday.

HASHKÉ BAHNZIN/ESKIMINZIN

In 1873 most of the Arivaipa Apaches relocated to the newly established San Carlos Reservation north of Arapa. Trouble followed. A power struggle among leaders left one man dead; Hashké Bahnzin fled. After capture he was imprisoned at the new Fort Grant near present-day Willcox, Arizona. Shackled and living under hard-labor conditions, he made adobe bricks. Returned to San Carlos in 1874 by the efforts of John Clum, Indian agent, Hashké Bahnzin took up farming and was often seen selling his crops in Tucson. In 1889 he and other Apaches were accused of aiding and abetting the Apache Kid, an escaped prisoner. Arrested again, Hashké Bahnzin was transferred to Fort Wingate, then to Fort Union in New Mexico, and, finally, to Mount Vernon, Alabama, a camp for hostile Apaches. After three years he returned to the San Carlos Reservation, again by Clum's efforts, where Hashké Bahnzin died of a stomach ailment in December 1895 at the approximate age of sixty-seven.

SAMUEL AND ATANACIA HUGHES

Years after the events of this novel, Atanacia attained fluency in English. Samuel became one of the richest men in Tucson through his many varied business activities. He and Atanacia had a total of fifteen children, most of whom survived childhood. As a devoted Catholic, Atanacia was buried in the Catholic cemetery. A spot next to her grave remains empty in reserve for Samuel, who, as a Freemason, was buried in the adjacent Protestant cemetery after his death in June 1917 at the age of eighty-seven. Atanacia was eighty-four at the time of her death in November 1934.

JAMES E. MCCAFFRY

McCaffry (also spelled McCaffrey) served as attorney general of the territory from 1871 through 1872 and also held the post as district attorney of Pima County for a few years. Subsequently he was appointed U.S. district attorney for the territory until the spring of 1875. According to George O. Hand's diary, from September 1875 through the year's end, McCaffry went on a drinking binge, complete with "jimjams" (alcoholic jitters or tremors). On the morning of January 4, 1876, Hand went to McCaffry's rooms and found the lawyer in a critical state due to alcohol. McCaffry died at noon. At his funeral the next day, members of the bar served as his pallbearers. McCaffry was only forty-three.

WILLIAM S. OURY

Oury was elected sheriff of Pima County in 1874. He proved inventive in his police procedures, solving one heinous double murder by noticing boot prints in blood at the crime scene. Apprehending suspicious characters, he asked to see the bottoms of their boots—one man's boots were covered in blood. Case solved. He continued ranching and serving Tucson in one official capacity or another. A founding member of the Arizona Historical Society, Oury died in Tucson in March 1887 at the age of seventy-one.

C. W. C. ROWELL

Converse Willard Chamberlin Rowell stayed in Arizona for approximately four more years after the trial, then moved to San Bernardino, California, around 1875. There he held several public offices, among them district attorney and city attorney. In May 1889 California governor Waterman appointed Rowell as a judge of the Superior Court in San Bernardino County. Rowell served for one term before returning to private law practice. On a business trip to Sacramento, he caught a cold that turned into pneumonia, and he died there in March 1893 at the age of sixty-five.

ANSON P. K. SAFFORD

Safford remained governor of Arizona Territory through 1877. He stands out, even today, as one of the most successful of Arizona's governors, stressing the need for education through public schools and promoting Arizona's wealth of resources. As the courts did not administer divorce cases at that time, Safford also has the dubious distinction of being the only governor who, in 1873, requested and received a divorce from his first wife through the Arizona Territorial Legislature. He moved to Florida in 1882, where he was actively involved in founding the small city of Tarpon Springs. He died in December 1891 at the age of sixty-one.

LARCENA PENNINGTON PAGE SCOTT

Larcena remained in Tucson and lived in the same house with her second husband, William Fisher Scott, for the rest of her life. By her first husband John Page, who was killed by Indians in 1861, she had a daughter. By Scott, she had a son and another daughter. To this day, Larcena is revered in Tucson as a symbol of perseverance and fortitude in the face of great personal suffering and loss. She died in 1913 at the age of seventy-six.

GEORGE STONEMAN

Immediately after being replaced by George Crook as commander of the Department of Arizona, Stoneman retired from the military due to medical reasons and requested his retirement be at his brevet general rank earned during the Civil War. Initially approving the request, President Ulysses S. Grant later rejected that rank after learning of Stoneman's medical reason—hemorrhoids. In California, Stoneman served only one term as California's governor at the express request of his political party. Afterward he and his wife bought acreage in the San Gabriel Mountains in what is now San Marino, California, and planted a vast number of wine grape vines. He died in Buffalo, New York, on September 5, 1894, at the age of seventy-two.

JOHN TITUS

Titus held the post of chief justice of the Arizona Territorial Supreme Court from April 1870 until his four-year term in office concluded. Thereafter he went into private practice in Tucson in a partnership with L. C. Hughes, Samuel Hughes's brother. At the age of sixty-four, Titus died of typhoid fever in October 1876.

WILLIAM ZECKENDORF

Zeckendorf traveled to New York City to find a wife, met Julia Frank, and the two married in October 1875. Their union produced two daughters and a son. Upon returning to Tucson after marriage, Zeckendorf continued with the retail business, forming and leaving several different partnerships with his brother Louis and his nephew Albert Steinfeld. As life and speculation were more interesting to Zeckendorf than retailing, he ultimately sold his establishment and, in 1891, relocated to New York, where Julia and their children had moved four years earlier. Zeckendorf lived there for the rest of his life and died in 1906 at the age of sixty-four.

AUTHOR'S NOTES

Many voices have been silenced—their stories left untold—for far too long. For the most part, white men wrote history and may not have given due respect to the roles played by women. I wished to give a voice to those women and Indians who suffered the most in the Camp Grant Massacre and to create a credible and truthful depiction of what living in Tucson was like one hundred and fifty years ago.

"Massacre" is the word used by the Anglos for this 1871 slaughter; to this day the Apaches believe it to be an act of genocide.

Nest Feather, Onawa, She Who Sits in Quiet, Isidro, the Escalante household, Curro, and Raúl and Valeria Obregón are fictional. However, they represent those in real life who did or might have suffered as a result of this tragedy.

The rest of the characters portrayed in this book were real people reenacting the events that they personally experienced as documented in personal memoirs, factual histories, the archives, and the Hayden Files. I thank the Arizona Historical Society, the Arizona State Museum, and each of their staffs for their excellent assistance during my research and for maintaining and safeguarding these precious primary documents.

What is said in Safford's speech before the legislature, the meeting with Stoneman at Sacaton, testimonies of individuals during the December 1871 trial, and Judge Titus's final instructions are their exact words. In Bennett and Etchells's testimonies, I changed their references to the four Anglos who split from the main party from "they" to "we," for they were in that group of four. Whitman referred to the Apaches living on the Camp Grant Reservation, however the reservation per se was not established until after the killing. Either "the Post" or "camp" was substituted. I corrected the number of defendants from "two" to "three" for whom nolle prosequis were entered. With one entered later for Foley, the figure rose to four. Due to its length, the trial of the perpetrators is severely edited but, I believe, with fairness. The attorneys' interrogation questions and their final arguments were not recorded—those I created.

As a novelist I added intimate scenes to flesh out what was factual, with care that nothing was said or done that went against what is known. Quotes from the newspapers of the time have been taken directly from those publications. My thanks go to Newspapers.com, the California Digital Newspaper Collection, and the Arizona Memory Project. In his diary George O. Hand entered "No one was killed today" when apropos. I employed that phrase in the novel for use by Raúl.

There are four instances where I altered history to better serve the novel:

Juan Elías did not go to the Sacaton meeting with Stoneman. The Committee of Public Safety was composed of approximately ninety-two Anglo men. As the reader mainly views the actions of the perpetrators through the Elías brothers, I needed Juan's presence at that meeting.

In the burial notice, no reason was given for the death of Jesús María Elías's one-month-old daughter. I chose premature birth, an unexpected event that Jesús María could not have anticipated before leaving on the raid and, at that time, would most probably prove fatal.

In reality Eskiminzin did not confess to Charles McKinney's murder until later that summer or autumn, when meeting with General Crook and Vincent Colyer.

I did not find the factual reason for James McCaffry's tardiness on two days of the December trial. It could simply have been his meeting with prospective defense witnesses. However, I employed the excuse that ultimately killed him—liquor.

Many sang high praises of Territorial Governor A. P. K. Safford. Andrew Cargill, his one-time aide and best man at Safford's first wedding, characterized the governor as "a rough specimen of the mining camp" and a philanderer. I used Cargill's assessment in portraying Safford.

Several names might confuse the modern reader:

Today the band of Apaches involved in the massacre is spelled "Aravaipa." The most ubiquitous spelling in the 1870s, used throughout the novel, was "Arivaipa."

The mountain range north of Tucson is currently known as the Santa Catalina Mountains. Early maps identified them as Sierra de Santa Catarina and then Santa Catarina, which was used during the 1870s and in the novel.

An 1859 army map indicates the name of the mountains east of the San Pedro River as Sierra Calitro. The name change to Galiuro Mountains occurred sometime during the twenty years following 1871.

Due to its length, many details of the perpetrators' journey from Tucson to Camp Grant and their return were deleted. Some details needed expansion:

> Having never found an explanation for how the Apache children were divided between the Tucsonans and the Papagos, I invented one.
>
> Sidney DeLong tried to send a message to someone or some entity to seek help or to deter the massacre. I chose to demonstrate what I believe were DeLong and three other Anglos' misgivings by inventing the terrible equine accident. Given the probability that the perpetrators assumed a mere skeletal troop presence, I believe these four surveilled Camp Grant to avoid active participation in the massacre.

As I reside within convenient distance of all of the areas involved in this story, my husband and I visited all of these sites at least once, if not several times. Specifically we drove over Redington Road and Pass (Cebadilla Pass)—even more difficult today, I believe, by car. We visited Aravaipa (Arivaipa) Canyon several times, once on the anniversary of the massacre at the approximate time of its happening. I recorded what we saw (rabbits, etc.), the time and temperature, the shadows, when the sky lightened, and how the full moon (on the morning of our visit) did not help visibility after a certain point.

I'm grateful to my husband, Mark, and my sister, Honey, for their constant support and for being my first readers. I thank these fine fellow authors: David R. Davis, my beta reader; and those who, since the earliest days, supported my novel's premise—Jan Cleere, Carolyn Niethammer, Susan Cummins Miller, Wynne Brown, and Sharon K. Miller. Many thanks also go to Sharon for being my independent editor.

I'm grateful to my two sensitivity readers for their invaluable input: Apache sensitivity reader Joe Saenz of the Chiricahua Apache Nation, owner of WolfHorse Outfitters; and Hispanic sensitivity reader Lucinda L. Abril.

My thanks go to J. Homer Thiel of Archaeology Southwest for sending me a copy of María Felipe's burial notice and for compiling the comprehensive list "Pioneer Families of the Tucson Presidio."

My thanks go to Stephanie Thomas for correcting the Spanish dialogue.

I thank Dr. Karl Jacoby, the Allan Nevins Professor of History and Ethnic Studies at Columbia University and author of *Shadows of Dawn*, a factual history of the Camp Grant Massacre, for answering a question about a witness's testimony in the 1871 trial.

Finally, many thanks to Clark Whitehorn, senior editor at the University of

Nebraska Press, and the entire UNP team for championing the stories of Valeria and Nest Feather.

Writing *Changing Woman*, I felt immersed in Tucson of 1871. The personalities were huge and colorful; the times were harsh, stressful, and dangerous; the land was, and still is, rugged and beautiful. I am privileged to live near Tucson, and I hope to tell more stories of the city, the territory, the state, and the West.

SELECTED BIBLIOGRAPHY

Arizona Citizen, 1871. Arizona Memory Project, Arizona State Library, Archives and Public Records. https://azmemory.azlibrary.gov/.

Basso, Keith H. "The Gift of Changing Woman." *Smithsonian Institution Bureau of American Ethnology Bulletin 196, Anthropological Papers, No. 76* (1966): 113–73.

Bray, Dorothy, ed. *Western Apache-English Dictionary: A Community-Generated Bilingual Dictionary*. Tempe AZ: Bilingual Press/Editorial Bilingüe, 1998.

Cargill, Andrew H. Papers. MS 134. Arizona Historical Society, Tucson.

Carmony, Neil B., ed. *Whiskey, Six-guns & Red-light Ladies: George Hand's Saloon Diary, Tucson, 1875–1878*. Silver City NM: High-Lonesome Books, 1994.

Catholic Church. *Catechism of the Catholic Church*. Citta del Vaticano: Libreria Editrice Vaticana, 1993. http://www.vatican.va/archive.

Cincinnati Enquirer. "An Eye-Witness' Narrative of the Massacre at Camp Grant." June 13, 1871. https://www.newspapers.com/image/30489434/.

Collins, Williams S., Melanie Sturgeon, and Robert M. Carriker. *The United States Military in Arizona, 1846–1945: A Component of the Arizona Historic Preservation Plan*. Tempe: Arizona State University Press, 1993.

Colwell-Chanthaphonh, Chip. *Massacre at Camp Grant: Forgetting and Remembering Apache History*. Tucson: University of Arizona Press, 2007.

———. "Western Apache Oral Histories and Traditions of the Camp Grant Massacre." *American Indian Quarterly* 27, nos. 3–4 (2003): 639–66.

Cosulich, Bernice. *Tucson: The Fabulous Story of Arizona's Ancient Walled Presidio 1692–1900's*. New York: Treasure Chest Publications, 1953.

Daily Alta California. "The Apache War." May 12, 1871. https://cdnc.ucr.edu/?a=d&d=DAC18710512.2.14&e=-------en--20--1--txt-txIN--------1.

———. "Arizona: Camp Grant Massacre, Trial of the Americans, Mexicans, and Friendly Papago Indians, Indicted for the Murder of Apaches on Reservation Near Camp Grant, April 30, 1871." February 3, 1872. https://cdnc.ucr.edu/?a=d&d=DAC18720203.2.48.1&e=-------en--20--1--txt-txIN--------1.

———. "Stoneman and Crook." May 20, 1871. https://cdnc.ucr.edu/?a=d&d=DAC18710520.2.37&e=-------en--20--1--txt-txIN--------1.

———. "The Trial of the Camp Grant Massacre Party." February 4, 1872. https://cdnc.ucr.edu/?a=d&d=DAC18720204.2.22&e=-------en--20--1--txt-txIN-------1.

DeLong, Sidney Randolph. *The History of Arizona from the Earliest Times Known to the People of Europe to 1903*. San Francisco: Whitaker & Ray Company, 1905.

———. Papers. MS 217, 1887–1915. Unpublished manuscript, handwritten and transcribed. Arizona Historical Society, Tucson.

Drachman, Sam Harrison. Papers. MS 0216, 1867–1934. Arizona Historical Society, Tucson.

Elías, Jesús María. Papers. MS 1475, Box 38. Arizona Historical Society, Tucson.

Elías, Juan. Jesús María Elías Papers. MS 1475, Box 38. Arizona Historical Society, Tucson.

Errett, Russell, and C. D. Brigham, eds. "Are We Civilized People?" *Pittsburgh Commercial*, July 29, 1871. https://www.newspapers.com/image/85675931/.

Etchells, Charles T. Papers. MS 1475, Box 39. Arizona Historical Society, Tucson.

Goodwin, Grenville. Papers. MS 17, Box 3. Arizona State Museum, Tucson.

———. "White Mountain Apache Religion." *American Anthropologist* 40, no. 1 (January–February 1938): 24–37.

Haley, James L. *Apaches: A History and Culture Portrait*. Norman: University of Oklahoma Press, 1997.

Hayden, Carl. Collection. MS 340. Arizona Historical Society, Tucson.

History of Arizona Territory Showing Its Resources and Advantages; with Illustrations Descriptive of Its Scenery, Residences, Farms, Mines, Mills, Hotels, Business Houses, Schools, Churches, &c. from Original Drawings. San Francisco: Wallace W. Elliott, 1884.

Hughes, Atanacia Santa Cruz. Hughes Family Papers. MS 1248, 1840, 1860–1914. Arizona Historical Society, Tucson.

Hughes, Samuel. Hughes Family Papers. MS 1248, 1840, 1860–1914. Arizona Historical Society, Tucson.

———. Papers. MS 366, 1872–1911. Arizona Historical Society, Tucson.

Jacoby, Karl. *Shadows at Dawn: An Apache Massacre and the Violence of History*. New York: Penguin Press, 2008.

Lee, James. Papers. MS 1475. Arizona Historical Society, Tucson.

Mails, Thomas E. *The People Called Apache*. New York: Prentice Hall, 1974.

McCaffry, James E. Papers. MS 0447. Arizona Historical Society, Tucson.

McGuire, Randall H. *Rancho Punta de Agua: Excavations at a Historic Ranch Near Tucson, Arizona*. Tucson: Arizona State Museum Contribution to Highway Salvage Archaeology in Arizona, No. 57, 1979.

New York Daily Herald. "Presidential Chitchat: The Camp Grant Affair a Wholesale Murder." June 8, 1871. https://www.newspapers.com/image/329680239/.

Opler, Morris Edward. "The Identity of the Apache Mansos." *American Anthropologist* 44, no. 4 (1942).

Oury, William S. Papers. MS 0786. Arizona Historical Society, Tucson.

Page, Larcena Ann Pennington. Papers. MS 1475, Box 98. Arizona Historical Society, Tucson.

Philadelphia Inquirer. "The Other Side of the Story of Camp Grant." July 24, 1871. https://www.newspapers.com/image/167861886/.

Record, Ian W. *Big Sycamore Stands Alone: The Western Apaches, Aravaipa, and the Struggle for Place.* Norman: University of Oklahoma Press, 2008.

Reynolds, Albert S. Papers. MS 0683, 1863–1941. Arizona Historical Society, Tucson.

———. Papers, c. 1926–c. 1936, re: L. Spofford and William Bailey (Bayley). Arizona Historical Society, Tucson.

Safford, A. P. K. Papers. MS 0704, Box 5, Folder 8. Arizona Historical Society, Tucson.

———. Speech presented to the Sixth Arizona Territorial Legislature on January 14, 1871. In *Journals of the Sixth Legislative Assembly of the Territory of Arizona: Session Begun on the Eleventh Day of January, and Ended on the Twentieth Day of February, A.D. 1871, at Tucson,* vol. 1, 39–57. Tucson: Office of the *Arizona Citizen,* 1871. http://bitly.ws/k3Ja.

Schellie, Don. *Vast Domain of Blood: The Shocking Story of the Camp Grant Massacre.* Los Angeles: Westernlore Press, 1968.

Scott, William Fisher. Papers. MS 720, Ledger, 1877–1908. Arizona Historical Society, Tucson.

Sonnichsen, C. L. *Tucson: The Life and Times of an American City.* Norman: University of Oklahoma Press, 1987.

Stockel, H. Henrietta. *Women of the Apache Nation: Voices of Truth.* Reno: University of Nevada Press, 1991.

Stoneman, George. Papers. MS 1475, Box 123. Arizona Historical Society, Tucson.

———. Report to his military superiors, October 31, 1870. *Arizona Citizen,* April 15, 1871. Arizona Memory Project, Arizona State Library, Archives and Public Records. https://azmemory.azlibrary.gov/.

Stratton, C. J. *Early Tucson: The History and Genealogy of Atanacia Santa Cruz Bojorquez Hughes.* CreateSpace Independent Publishing Platform, 2010.

Thiel, J. Homer. *Pioneer Families of the Presidio San Agustín del Tucson, 1775–1856.* https://pima.bibliocommons.com/v2/record/S91C1811959.

Townsend, George Alfred (Gath). "Arizona: Talk with General Stoneman." *Chicago Tribune,* June 12, 1871. https://www.newspapers.com/image/465741002/.

———. "Arizona: The Apache Question." *Chicago Tribune,* June 12, 1871. https://www.newspapers.com/image/465741002/.

———. "Arizona: Visit to General Crook." *Chicago Tribune,* June 12, 1871. https://www.newspapers.com/image/465741002/.

Turner, Jim. "Arizona's Spanish and Mexican Land Grants." *Humanities Now Blog,* AZ Humanities, November 4, 2014. https://azhumanities.org/arizonas-spanish-and-mexican-land-grants/.

Valkenburgh, Richard Van. "Apache Ghosts Guard the Aravaipa." *Desert Magazine,* April 1948.

Zeckendorf, William. Papers. MS 1475, Box 141. Arizona Historical Society, Tucson.

Printed in the USA
CPSIA information can be obtained
at www.ICGtesting.com
CBHW071217150224
4367CB00002B/88

9 781496 235138